About the author

Of Scots origin but mainly educated in England, A. A. Gilbertsen is the pseudonym of a former company director and consultant who spent many years advising businesses in the UK and several other European countries. In that capacity he dealt with some powerful characters whom – like Robert Maxwell – had reputations for taking very high risks.

As an investing underwriter, or 'name', at the world famous Lloyd's of London insurance market, he was often exposed to various large claims including those from the very secretive policies protecting victims of kidnap and ransom.

He and his Australian wife live in Buckinghamshire. Their three children are married to Italian, French and German spouses.

BLACK SEA SCORPIONS

Also by A.A. Gilbertsen

Pandora's Pension

A. A. Gilbertsen

BLACK SEA SCORPIONS

Vanguard Press

VANGUARD PAPERBACK

© Copyright 2018
A. A. Gilbertsen

A CIP catalogue record for this title is
available from the British Library.

ISBN 978 1 784653 68 2

Vanguard Press is an imprint of
Pegasus Elliot MacKenzie Publishers Ltd.
www.pegasuspublishers.com

First Published in 2018

Vanguard Press
Sheraton House Castle Park
Cambridge England

Printed & Bound in Great Britain

Dedication

To refugees from war and victims of terrorism. And, those who work to protect them and us.

Ch.1   Breakfast in Beirut.

Doctor Johnson was right. When a man knows he is about to die, it concentrates the mind wonderfully. Crouching behind the rubble of a low wall with fragments of hot metal and cold buildings flying around his head was exhilarating if less than comfortable. It certainly made Llewellyn Lancelot Lloyd's mind concentrate on a single point – the point of survival. Minutes earlier, his mind had been on the whereabouts of his companions and what he had been told was to be his 'primary objective.'

Not knowing if he would survive to see either his companions or the objective, his mind now throbbed to a repetitive tune. The rhythmic words voiced by The Bee Gees -"Staying alive... staying alive..." There was no dancing girl or engaging smile to ease the tension. Just splinters, dust, terrifying noise – and that annoying song in his head. How could he pursue any objective – primary or final – in that position? Saturday night had just become more feverish.

Lloyd's objective was the release and safe return of a hostage. This had been ordered by his employers – a large insurance syndicate – and their client. Now he realised that he might have reached the point of no return for himself or his charge. A tiny black and red beetle crawled up the wall before him, a few inches in front of his face. What chance of survival had he? What chance for either of them?

Searching for another beetle to comfort or copulate with it, the bright insect stepped smartly into an inviting crack in the brickwork. There were plenty of those to go round. Plenty of cracked bricks and disintegrating walls. One life's broken home, another life's shelter from the storm of gunfire and shattered masonry around them. No thoughts or wise words of

Doctor Johnson to console them. Survival was paramount but by no means guaranteed.

Another burst of gunfire and an exploding fragment of cement somewhere behind him brought more choking dust and tiny chips of stone to his face. A larger ragged scrap of something hard hit his ankle and lodged between skin and shoelaces. He bent down deeper below the wall, trying to extract the stone chip from his sock whilst keeping his body from the line of fire.

He imagined a fresh faced girl with a microphone, smiling as she interviewed him in London.

"And how did you enjoy your trip to Beirut, Mr Lloyd? Was the food to your liking?"

"I did have one memorable meal. A beautifully presented hot breakfast of brick dust and bullets."

He coughed and spat out some of the stone muesli from his recently dusted throat, splattering his shoes with some of the mucus spray. As he did so, he heard yet another round of small arms fire.

Sweat mingled with other smells. A warm dampness in the crutch of his pants told him that he had urinated involuntarily. Three more shots hummed like angry hornets above his head. Two passed over the sheltering wall, but the third struck it and ricocheted back into his upper left torso. The beetle fell from his shelter in the cracked bricks and scuttled off to find a safer home.

Lloyd felt a fresh spray of heavy fragments in his face and a sharp stabbing in his chest. Crumpled to a sitting position, his hand instinctively went to his shirt and another damp patch spreading around the point of pain. It was somewhere near to where he imagined his heart to be.

Before losing consciousness, a cry of shock and alarm flew from a very dusty mouth to his equally dusty companions. The shooting ceased, leaving an alarming silence for a few seconds. Then, another hand grabbed at his shoulder and jacket, revealing the wet stain now spreading over his shirt pocket.

A strong English voice tried to reassure him of continued life as he knew it.

"OK, old boy. We've got you now. Don't try to move while we assess the damage." The jacket was carefully peeled back and a brief inspection allowed Lloyd to see the remains of the bullet protruding from the notebook in his breast pocket. "Made a bit of a mess of your shirt I'm afraid but, stopped short of your ticker."

"What about the blood? Is there much of it?"

"Blood? Blood? This so called blood – it seems to be rather blue. Are you related to royalty, by any chance?"

A closer inspection revealed the source of the damp stain as the reservoir of a shattered fountain pen. The pen had been a birthday gift from a former girlfriend but now, the writing instrument was as fractured as the relationship. It had, however, served a possible life-saving task, literally stopping a bullet for its owner.

Some weeks earlier, in the world-famous insurance market – Lloyd's of London – he had received his marching orders. It was a standing joke for him to suggest that he was the proprietor of his employers' business, but in this situation he was its sole representative. The syndicate of underwriters who employed him as a loss adjuster – specialising in kidnap and ransom claims – had commissioned him to procure the return of the son of an Arab trader, Mr Hussein Bin Q'etta.

What the Arab traded in was not explained to Lloyd in detail. "Probably white slavery and black market anything," was proffered by one veteran underwriter. In reality his day-job was to control a wealthy trading company. In that role Hussein Bin Q'etta's preoccupation was the market price of 'West Texas Intermediate' – traded crude oil. He had contracted to sell more than a billion US dollars worth of it at fixed prices of up to seventy-five dollars per barrel.

As the market price was now well below that and still falling, his stance as a representative of OPEC was to continue to encourage excessive output by oil producers. That would ensure even lower market prices to destroy the competition coming from expensive shale oil and fracking in America It would also ensure a massive profit for his company.

Contact between Lloyd and the British Foreign and Commonwealth Office had been arranged with the assistant commercial attaché at the British Embassy in The Lebanon. Flights and hotels had been booked and further details were to be supplied on his arrival in Beirut. Once settled in a comfortable hotel, Lloyd had been met by a messenger with an invitation to an informal drinks party at the Embassy, where he would meet his host and temporary adviser. An hour later, the men were deep in conversation and Carlsberg.

John Sinclair Tarquin Elphinstone stood six feet three inches tall and weighed fifteen stone six pounds in his lightweight underclothing. Of athletic build and dapper conservative suiting, he could well be taken for an ex-serviceman – a retired infantry major or Royal Navy commander. In fact, his involvement in defence affairs was subject to The Official Secrets Act and not discussed by any outside of those in similar office.

At Welbeck College and at Sandhurst, the young JST Elphinstone had been nicknamed 'Stelph.' Coupled with the rest of his surname, that might have described his quiet approach to duties and a poker faced expression. He gave less disclosure of emotion than the average Easter Island statue. Among his colleagues and fellow members of The Naval and Military Club, the renowned 'In and Out' with its nick-name proudly displayed on adjoining front portals, his closer pals simply called him 'Jock.'

Without bearing any particular affinity to military personnel, Lloyd had always been comfortable in the company of fellow officers of the South Wales and Hong Kong police forces. Co-operating with an ex-officer of any service who knew the proverbial ropes and geography of one of the world's most dangerous regions would be a welcome task. Given the unassuming demeanour of the quiet diplomat in the Foreign and Commonwealth Office, co-operation with Jock Elphinstone would be quite acceptable.

Over a couple of cool lagers, a cool Jock Elphinstone had explained the latest situation regarding the kidnappers' unreasonable terms. An unrealistic amount of money in a variety of currencies was demanded by them to give them a good reason not to convert their young Arab hostage into a human donner kebab.

Surrendering to such demands in these circumstances usually resulted in the instant disappearance of money and hostage. The ransom had been ordered in small denomination notes. It would probably weigh more than the hostage. If handed over to the kidnappers, transport would require the aid of a fork-lift truck. Losing control of money and human life was not on the agenda. No. The demands were unreasonable and quite uncommercial, according to the assistant commercial attaché.

Lloyd had welcomed Elphinstone's straightforward appraisal. While he savoured his drink he waited for the most important part – a plan of action. The proposed solution came as a combination of incentive and deterrent – carrot and stick.

The carrot would be monetary. Just enough cash to see the kidnappers well rewarded without being distastefully wealthy. The stick would be more painful than their threats to the hostage. Without giving full harrowing details, Elphinstone hinted at unbridled violence offered by willing partners from one of many local armed factions.

The Lebanon was a veritable paramilitary Clapham junction, with several small armies of desperados, claiming Sunni, Shi-ite, Kurdish, Alawite and Orthodox Christian faiths. Having established the background of the kidnappers, their most hated and feared opposition had been selected as an alternative to accepting the rescue party's terms.

Although listed as a commercial authority, the assistant attaché might have appeared to be less than imposing in financial matters. He was certainly very commercial when faced with trade in human wellbeing though. Local intelligence supplied him with the probable number and strength of the kidnappers and their professed allegiance. From the information supplied, it appeared that they consisted of three young and inexperienced Sunni Palestinians, armed to the teeth with automatic weapons but not with excessive brainpower.

A sizeable sum was offered in exchange for safe custody and health of the hostage, who would have to be returned unharmed to a venue and friendly consort of the rescuers' choosing. Although it represented a fraction of the ransom demanded, this carrot would be more realistic than the novice gangsters' pie-in-the-sky aspirations and much less demanding in transport.

The alternative stick would be dreadful and certain elimination at the hands of their terrifying enemies, an armed group of Maronite Phalange fighters. As a precaution, two very aggressive members of that company had been retained to assist if and when necessary. None of this plan was officially approved by the Embassy or the local police or militia. Nor was it disapproved. If anybody questioned the proposal, it simply did not exist.

The attaché awaited a response from the Palestinians. He did not have to wait for long. As expected, a message from a mobile phone to a predetermined answering point repeated the threats and demands in full. With Lloyd's agreement a metaphorical white flag was raised. A vast fortune in paper money was promised in exchange for an unharmed hostage at an agreed venue.

Also with Lloyd's agreement, the supposed ransom would be accompanied by the two Phalange fighters, armed and eager to negotiate from the muzzles of their Kalashnikovs. Their financial reward in the event of complete success would be rather less than the smaller amount rejected by the kidnappers. Their satisfaction in eliminating the Palestinians would exceed that from the cash, several times over.

In such a tense situation, local knowledge was essential to give the rescue party any prospect of success and to give the hostage any chance of survival. The attaché's local knowledge of geography and logistics was excellent and that of the Phalange even more so. What was unknown to any of them was the Palestinians' grasp of the same or their ability to execute their threats.

Ch.2. A welcome from Burj-al-Barajneh.

Within a complex web of fact and gossip concerning rival ethnic groups in Beirut, the Phalange had some well established if biased sources of information. Tip-offs usually started at the point of any unusual activity in the Palestinian refugee camps in The Lebanon.

The notorious camp on the edge of Burj-al-Barajneh, housing between ten and twenty thousand refugees in squalid conditions, was a cesspit of discontented young men. With aspirations only of escape or an honourable death - two of those youths harboured wild hopes of untold fortune and enormous respect from their peers. Their plans were as secure as a sieve. There were many who would willingly inform on them for the price of a second-hand car or just the petrol to fuel it.

The two young Palestinians were usually accompanied by a third. Being less willing to risk his own life and limb, he acted as a go-between and general dogsbody rather than a soldier in the kidnappers' army of two. It was he however who had informed his seniors of the wealthy Arab's immature son, exploring the flesh-pots of Beirut in a search of sex and alcoholic adventure. It was he who had lured the teenage hostage to a deserted bomb site with promises of drink, drugs and the adolescent's dream of seventy-two virgins, without the usual premature martyrdom.

After a cocktail of cheap and mildly toxic narcotics, washed down with a few glasses of strong Lebanese wine, the hapless teenager had found himself as an unwitting part of human bondage, probably ending in martyrdom nearer to his worst nightmares than to the virgins of his wildest dreams.

Following an exchange of what they took to be negotiating offers, the quartet of kidnappers and hostage moved under cover of darkness to another bomb site. This was the agreed point of exchange for the promised fortune. The young hostage was parked with arms and legs bound to explosives, behind the broken wall of a derelict building and guarded only by the unarmed go-between.

Despite nagging reservations about their chances, the kidnapping duo and their little helper were unable to put aside the thoughts of the paper fortune awaiting them. The two principals then set up loaded guns and grenades to enforce collection in the event of dissent and waited for cash on delivery. Their ragged bodies squatted behind the remains of another wall overlooking what had once been a pretty town square... waiting and watching.

After waiting an hour and a half, darkness and tension delivered only tired eyes and frayed nerves. Twenty minutes later, another message arrived via their mobile phone. The mountain of cash was also waiting – waiting for them in the next street – or what remained of it. The hostage had to be presented there without harm or danger before the money could change hands.

A scurried scramble over the rubble confirmed that a large builders' sack was indeed standing in front of a pile of stones. There appeared to be some person or persons, waiting to receive the hostage. The return trip to their previous position was fraught with excitement and scraped knees.

Disconnecting the detonators from the explosives and wiring embracing the hostage took only a few minutes. When all but the final wires around the hostage's legs were cut, the helper was ordered to take the defused hostage to a corner of the street of a thousand ransoms. The armed desperadoes moved to where they could cover the area around the builders' sack and their pot of paper gold.

A call from them announced that whoever accompanied the ransom could walk to the hostage and take him away after the sack of money had been moved to their new location. The selected destination of the sack was close to the low wall sheltering Lloyd. Nearby, behind yet another pyramid of rubble was his new brother-in-arms, Mr Jock Elphinstone. At right angles to them, another pile of ruined buildings covered the two Phalangists and their arsenal of negotiating tools.

Once on the corner of the street, the hostage collapsed and his guard looked around helplessly. He called in panic to his gangmasters who answered with one burst of gunfire in the general direction of the prone hostage and another towards the builders' sack. Their wild shooting brought clouds of dust and stones and a devastating round of more accurate returned fire from the Phalangists.

Remarkably, none of the multiple rounds of ammunition struck any live target. Lacking any better plan, one of the Palestinians hurled a grenade towards the supposed source of danger. The exploding grenade brought only more rubble and dust to the scene. A thin veil of dust screened the main rescue party. Yet more firing delivered the larger scrap of brick to Lloyd's ankle and foot.

Two would-be slum-dog millionaires allowed greed to overcome caution. They both raised their heads a few inches above the protecting parapet. Three more shots rang out from a point a few yards to Lloyd's right. One of the three struck a wall and the ricochet struck Lloyd's chest. As he slumped to the sitting position with his hand clutched to what he feared to be a mortal wound, the gunfire stopped completely.

Elphinstone shouted something to the survivors and scurried to Lloyd's side. Hostage and his panic-stricken guard were manhandled to a more secure point where the remaining wire and explosives were removed from one and attached to the other. The builders' sack, its worthless shredded newspaper contents shaken but otherwise unstirred by the flying stone and metal fragments, was abandoned to its fate amongst the street urchins of Burj-al-Barajneh.

Having identified his wound as non life-threatening, a relieved Lloyd – relieved of his shattered fountain pen and brick fragments as well as prospects of imminent death – then relieved himself again. Opening his eyes and his bladder, he stood unsteadily urinating in a shaky dribble against the broken wall sheltering him. He crawled cautiously forward and peered over the parapet which should have protected the kidnappers. Of the final three shots that he had heard, one ink-stained bullet was still embedded in his pocket book and the others in the heads of two recently deceased Palestinians.

The remaining Palestinian, the go-between and erstwhile hostage guard, was shaking uncontrollably as he was approached by his late masters' executioners. In addition to their heavy automatic rifles and hand guns, one of them carried a glass jar containing some small dark creatures. He had a few questions to ask but fewer minutes to await the answers.

Unscrewing the lid of the glass jar, one Phalangist barked out his demands for information; names and places without time-wasting excuses or pleas for mercy. As the whimpering captive started to cry and scream denials, the top of the open jar was placed firmly against his face. Within seconds, his memory returned and information was freely discharged.

Dragging the collapsed youngster to a sheltering corner, the interrogator simply repeated the demands and switched on the recording application of his mobile phone. With the glass jar of writhing animals close at hand and closer to the victim's face, a stream of names, locations and their involvement in nefarious activities flowed out. The Phalangists then simply melted into the dust and dark corners of the ruined streets, taking their new-found informant and their negotiating devices, including the glass jar, with them.

Elphinstone and Lloyd also removed themselves and the former hostage from the scene. True to his nickname 'Stelph' effected their retreat quickly and quietly. Two hundred metres away from the killing field, a badly scratched Peugeot 504 estate car with driver at the ready swallowed the trio and sped towards a safe house in the northern suburbs of Beirut.

Safely returned to relative comfort, the young Bin Q'etta was stripped of his clothing and placed under a warm shower.

A clean body was fed with hot soup and examined by a Lebanese doctor. Before any form of de-briefing could take place, Lloyd transmitted his own brief message of success to an office in Switzerland. From there it would be forwarded to his employers in London and to an anxious Arab trader in Dubai.

Later that morning, the ex-hostage travelled by ambulance to Rafic Hariri International Airport and onward to Dubai. After ensuring their charge's safe reunion with his father, Lloyd was taken by Elphinstone to the Four Points Hotel in Saeb Salam Boulevard, not far from their safe house of that morning's activity.

Once firmly harboured in the bar, 'Cocky' Lloyd opened his account and his mouth to express gratitude and congratulations to his new friend Jock. Expressions served with welcoming refreshment and less welcome enquiries.

"What will happen to that young Palestinian survivor now? And what on earth was in that glass jar they were holding to his face? It certainly wasn't a bouquet of flowers."

"As to the first question, probably better not to ask. I certainly won't. Our Phalangist friends will employ him for as long as he's useful to them. They'll get what they can from him and probably dump him near another refugee camp. If he talks to anyone after that, it could cost him his life anyway. They – the Palestinians – don't appreciate informers any more than the other gangs do."

To Lloyd, satisfaction with the answer was like the curate's egg, only good in parts. He persisted.

"He certainly blabbed out a lot of something when they held that jar to his face. It reminded me of a scene in Orwell's book, '1984', when Winston Smith saw the rats coming at his face."

"Very close observation. But it wasn't rats in the jar. More likely scorpions. Nobody fancies being kissed on the lips by them. I certainly don't. Those guys who helped us – they rarely fail to get what they want out of their prisoners."

Lloyd shuddered at the thought but, instinctively hydrated his own dry lips with some of the Ksara Blanc-de-blancs in his early lunch-time glass. The cool wine washed his mouth but failed to quench his worrying thoughts. Not a devout moralist, he was nevertheless instinctively uncomfortable about anything less than fair play. His mind wriggled under the moral dilemma rising in it.

"Doesn't that – isn't that – just dragging us down to their level?"

The Elphinstone attitude remained unchanged – a model of stealth set in stone.

"Yes... it probably is. At least, I hope so. That's where we need to be if we're going to understand them and beat them before they beat us."

Not wishing to appear ungrateful for the invaluable efforts made by his guide and procurer of armed rescuers, Lloyd gave a sympathetic grunt of agreement. Not wishing to appear as thick as two short planks, he then tried to frame his next question in what he hoped would look like the wisdom of experience.

"Yes. I know what you mean." He didn't really but, it sounded right. "My biggest problem has always been to understand who's on whose side and what they really want out of life."

Elphinstone understood more of the attempted philosophy than Lloyd expected. He had often suffered the same sort of dilemma and search for a path to his own life, particularly when seeking to enter the mind-sets of enemies of the state, or women. Usually, the searches had ended in as much mystery as they had started. Often accompanied by some form of unsatisfactory activity and nearly always without a clear conclusion.

Before he could assemble his thoughts, another incident was raised by the puzzled Cocky Lloyd: the shooting of the Palestinian kidnappers.

"When the final shots were fired at those Palestinian tearaways, I counted three bullets almost at once. One ended up in my notebook and the other two in their heads. There were two Phalangists helping us, probably sharpshooters - but did the other bullet come from you?"

The assistant commercial attaché looked a little sheepish and offered a faint grin from a downturned face.

"Well... yes, actually. When one of the Phalangist shots hit the wall near you, I felt that I should offer some support."

"So, you actually shot one of the kidnappers? You must be a top shot. I won't say 'crack' but you know what I mean. Did you... were you... a sniper in the Army?"

"Only by default. By accident almost. When we were in basic training and had to show off our prowess with a gun, I was fairly certain that I would fail. I didn't have much self-confidence then. There was one fat-head in another squad who had boasted continuously that he was the best shot in Britain and would do anything to come first in the trials.

"We were told to shoot as quickly as possible as soon as an enemy target appeared. There were red targets for the enemy and blue ones for friends. Just before it was my squad's turn to fire, he moved the targets round to make us miss, or hit a friendly target and leave him as the best of the bunch.

"I didn't know about his little trick and just let fly at the first thing I saw coming up. I completely missed the target I was aiming at and shot the one next to it. As it happened, that was the red target that he had just moved and I was given my sniper's badge, or the equivalent. I didn't actually get a badge, not since I left the Boy Scouts. "

Lloyd didn't know whether to believe his bizarre show of modesty or not. Before he could think of anything to say, Elphinstone returned to the original question of identities and objectives.

"Wherever I've found myself working for our country's benefit, there's always been a mixture of parties with a mixture of interests. Nothing clear-cut. The only common denominator is that they all want something for themselves – something that they think will improve their own lives.

"Often, the best that I can do is to establish just what it is that they want and to try to get what we need in exchange. It usually boils down to money or the power to get more of something than they have already. Sometimes, there's the human side of power to grab at, but that's only a step towards more money or political influence."

"Today's little episode was rather sad, being just one young life for another – or another two in this case. But, behind the manhandling and fire-fights, there's a huge undercurrent of desperation and insecurity. The money side is just the scum on the surface."

Lloyd sometimes wished that he had never asked. Philosophy at this time of day, was more than flesh and red blood – or blue ink – could take. He grunted more sympathy and suggested that they spend the rest of the day in recovery mode. To repair, recover and re-assemble in the evening for the dinner that he owed to the assistant commercial attaché.

Only the faintest glimmer of interest flashed across Jock Elphinstone's impassive face. It was enough though. It had been a hard week and dinner with the insurance man would be the nearest that he was likely to get to relaxation with an Englishman – even a Welsh one.

Not wishing to invite further excitement for the day, the two men returned to the same hotel bar and to a relatively quiet table in the smart restaurant. A sundowner at sunset followed by a dinner at dinner-time – a perfect end to a successful if less than perfect day.

Ch.3. Tectonic forces.

High in the towering City of London, a senior insurance underwriter awaited the return and detailed report from his specialist loss adjuster. On the face of it, an untimely death of an insured peril and a huge claim from an agitated Arab trader had been avoided. However, there could still be collateral damage, as the military forces liked to describe mistakes and accidents. There might also be some related, if unspecified, claims.

There would undoubtedly be some large expenses but, 'large' would be a relative term and not applicable to such a potentially expensive loss. Anxious but no longer worried, he looked forward to reuniting with his colleague, who appeared to have adjusted the loss to a fraction of its potential.

The specialist loss adjuster sitting in a smart Beirut restaurant was aware of his remaining duties. They would fall into a 'tidying up' category and could wait until he was safe and sound in his syndicate's office near Number 1, Lime Street. In order to produce the best quality report, he argued that he should obtain top quality information regarding the culture of his current location. That would have to be completed in a couple of hours over dinner with the local expert beside him.

In theory, the assistant commercial attaché was mainly involved with commerce. In the Levantine region that involvement might be varied and interesting but it was obvious to Lloyd that security and military intelligence superseded trade and commerce. Lloyd's interest focused on the variety of ethnic and religious groups scrambling for power in such a small area. His conversation over dinner was directed at Elphinstone's personal attitudes as much as his grasp of demographic facts and figures.

Before he could arrive at any simplistic conclusion, Jock Elphinstone outlined a scene which resembled a mixture of geology and theology. It was not necessary to remind his companion of the long list of religious wars which had scarred the region for centuries.

"Perhaps," he ventured, "we should consider the position of The Lebanon and adjoining states, relative to the tectonic plates of land mass. These can produce earth movements even more powerful than religious fervour. As you know the inhabitants of each plate have characteristics quite different from those on others' plates. But for many of them, the other man's plate is always cleaner."

"This tectonic plate," he explained, staring at the dinner plates on which the two diners were now attacking a meal of grilled lamb and honeyed baklava, "is called the Arabian Plate. It's encompassed by fault lines running through Iran, Turkey, Syria and the coasts of the Eastern Mediterranean and the Red Sea. The north-western corner of it includes The Lebanon and parts of its neighbouring states, Syria, Israel, and Jordan. The Northern fault line continues westwards from Turkey through Greece and the Balkans, to Italy and those volcanic islands, like Stromboli and Sicily. Full of earthquakes and trouble.

"Although the Arabian Plate could be considered relatively small, compared to The Pacific or Eurasian plates, it is inhabited by most of the world's more belligerent tribal and religious groups. The volcanic activity along the geological fault lines seems to be mirrored in religious fault lines. There are continuous tribal and ethnic wars of some sort or other between the various groups – Muslim, Jewish, Christian – and several others including political and financial vested interests.

"As if those wars within the Arabian Plate were not enough, there's an even bigger picture of conflict between the Arabian Plate and the adjoining Eurasian and African plates. Never-ending wars between inhabitants of Africa, Asia and Europe. Despite millennia of failed invasions, each group is still attempting to occupy or influence the others. And the most

27

common point of conflict remains here – at this north-western corner of the Arabian Plate."

Lloyd was impressed but at a loss to even think about asking a question. His companion's knowledge of geology and demography was obviously deep and detailed. The volcanic activity between so many people in the region was getting hotter by the day. Dinner, on the other hand was getting cold and called for his imminent and undivided attention.

Elphinstone continued in diplomatic terms to explain his concerns in defence of his country's interests.

"With so many conflicting factions around here, a small incident like this one involving different groups could initiate a major war. Even a small commercial dispute between a Sunni and a Shi-ite might lead to a local gun-fight and then to an inter-tribal war. That's one reason why the rescue of this morning's hostage was so important. A small explosion here could lead to a local volcanic eruption or even an earthquake, metaphorically speaking. It had to be avoided if at all possible."

"And," he added sombrely, "there are bigger dangers of bigger bangs waiting to happen. We can't stop them all happening. We just have to keep an eye out for the sparks."

Between mouthfuls of food and wine, Lloyd's mind tried to digest the cocktail of fact and theory. The reference to bigger dangers and bigger bangs reminded him of 'Big dogs have big fleas, and little fleas to bite them.' He mentioned that old saying and then asked, "Who are the big dogs in all this, and who are the big fleas on their back?"

No longer quite so stony faced as before, Jock Elphinstone appeared moderately relaxed, relieved after sharing some of his enormous worries. Having exposed them to his fellow traveller, he even allowed a quiet smile to blossom, fading away again as he spoke.

"The big dogs – as you call them – are obviously Russia, the USA and Western Europe. When I say Western Europe, I mean the whole of the EU although I am primarily concerned with the United Kingdom. Unfortunately, the UK is not very big nowadays and the EU is the weakest dog in the kennels.

"More locally, the bigger fleas are Turkey, Iran, Israel, Saudi and Egypt. And the little fleas, which bite the hardest, are loose cannons here and in Iraq, Syria, Jordan, Libya and others all the way across North Africa, the Balkans and the Caucasus.

"This region is not only a cross-roads of tectonic plates and religious groups, it is the main entry point for weapons supply from the old Soviet bloc – north to south – and illegal immigration into Europe – east to west. And," he added darkly, "we're not just talking about Kalashnikovs. Although the AK47 has killed more people than any other weapon in the world, there are others even more destructive; physical and electronic, hardware and software."

Still slightly reeling from the fusillade of information and opinion – at least he hoped it was only opinion – Lloyd tried to concentrate on the priority facing Britain's guardian of political fumaroles and eruptions.

"So, what or who are you watching the closest just now?" He rolled a scrap of baklava around his mouth, enjoying the nuts and honey taste. The thought of honey made him imagine its collection. Even a honey bee, with hundreds of ommatidia in its compound eyes, couldn't focus on so many international interests as the assistant commercial attaché faced now.

"Good question. It's like trying to keep several plates – dinner, not tectonic – spinning on bamboo poles at the same time. There's a constant civil war going on somewhere or other near here. The so-called Arab Spring keeps springing up and knocking everything down. But now, the 'big dogs' as you call them, are getting bitten by some rather nasty fleas. And they are likely to get bigger teeth, like the big dogs."

By these mixed metaphors, Lloyd guessed that the 'big dogs' teeth' were weapons, stolen or procured from Russia or the US forces. Elphinstone didn't attempt to correct or confirm that assumption but continued to stare impassively at his coffee and Turkish delight. He had one more spark of information to ignite Lloyd's concerns.

"By the way, you might like to know that our friends of this morning extracted" – Lloyd gave an inward shudder at the thought of the extraction process – "a story of another hostage. A much bigger... uh... big dog's hostage. It might be subject to your employers' largesse. I'll send you any details if and when I get them."

Lloyd's focus suddenly sharpened at the hint of more direct involvement.

"Don't worry. If it's a claim on one of our syndicates, I'll get the case dumped on my lap as soon as I get back to London. If I may, I'll contact you at the embassy if it's something like this morning's work."

Lloyd expected a non-committal shrug or indifferent nod but Elphinstone seemed to be clearly interested in the latest rumour. He was even hinting at a possible role in resolving the reported hostage-taking, although it was possibly not concerned with British interests. Either the victim or the hostage-takers were involved with something that Elphinstone considered very important.

This was clearly much more than a commercial dispute.

Ch.4. A bell un-tolled.

Richard Rogers' unconventional architecture of the Lloyd's of London Insurance building is as much as most people outside of that industry know about it. With its 'inside out' design, it exposes the building's skeletal structure to the world, leaving enormous open spaces within the outer shell. This arrangement creates a three-dimensional open plan effect for the underwriters and brokers. With an array of central escalators they can view and move easily on a vertical plane as well as across the horizontal surface of their own trading floor.

As a specialist employee, the former detective inspector Lloyd spent more working time outside than inside those hallowed walls. He had a work-space rather than an office, with a shared desk and power point. On such a desk as that, his syndicate's clerk had deposited a modest file resembling a barrister's brief. It contained what he like to call, 'a minefield of information.'

High on the danger list of printed anti-personnel weapons was a recent marine insurance claim. Under normal circumstances, this would not have been part of Cocky Lloyd's specialist briefing. This particular claim related to a missing luxury yacht. It was registered as the 'Anna K', supposedly containing a missing luxury yacht-owner. The value of the vessel was substantial but it was dwarfed by the ransom claim from the pirates now holding its master. What distinguished the claim from others in Lloyd's experience was the location – or rather lack of location – of kidnappers or kidnapped.

On the ground floor of the vast open space, below the escalators and overhanging galleries inside the building, stands the famous Lutine Bell. It had been recovered from the former French ship 'La Lutine' or 'Elf.' The Lutine had been surrendered to the Royal Navy in 1793, only to sink some six years later carrying a fortune in gold. Having settled a million pound claim for the loss, the insurers no doubt felt entitled to retain the ship's bell and it was then employed to announce marine disasters and other significant events for the next two hundred years.

In the event of the reported loss of an insured ship at sea, the Lutine Bell would have been sounded for all to hear and check their exposure to a claim. Each time that they had heard the chimes portending some serious wreck or significant event, many of the underwriters and brokers had thought of John Donne and his sombre warning "never send to know for whom the bell tolls..." It was too early for them to enquire. A claim had been registered but the bell had not tolled. Not yet.

Last sightings of the hijacked floating palace had placed it in the Eastern Aegean Sea, somewhere amongst those Greek islands near the Turkish coast. Latest reports were already two days old so it might be in captivity anywhere between the Atlantic Ocean and the Black Sea or the Horn of Africa by now. The hostage might be somewhere else by now too – and in any condition.

Only one puzzling message was reported to offer a means of contact with the pirates. No one could say 'from whence cometh the message' either. It was anonymous – just a scribbled note on a scrap of paper. After staring at the papers and maps, researching all possible or probable locations and the routes which might have been taken by the missing boat, Lloyd tried to concentrate on the strange message that had been offered as a means of contact. It was simply recorded in the file as 'CKOP' followed by the mathematical character 'Pi' plus what looked like a reversed 'N' or the number ten or eleven and 'H.' If this was a clue, it was a clue to the clueless.

After multiplying various combinations of numbers, trying to calculate what he guessed might be the area of a circle on a map, his mind collapsed. If the 'Pi' and 'ten' or 'eleven' referred to an area, then there had to be some unit of distance such as kilometres or nautical miles. Perhaps the letters in the clue were map references and 'ten' was the value of the radius. Was that a geometrical 'r' to be squared and multiplied by 'Pi'? Lloyd needed much more than this to effect initial contact, even before thinking about negotiating with whoever and wherever. It was, he thought, simply too complicated.

Putting aside the mind-numbing puzzle of possible locations, Lloyd's thoughts returned to more familiar territory. His experience in crimes against the person, mainly with police in Britain and Hong Kong, told him of a regular link between criminal and victim. Investigation of the human victim – and to a lesser extent the missing vessel – should provide many more clues to the pirates' identities and modus operandi. He turned to the dossier describing the kidnap victim.

Information concerning the owners of the yacht brought an immediate contradiction. He or they were not the kidnap victim or subject to a ransom demand. The yacht was owned by a company registered in Gibraltar but it was leased to another company registered in Ukraine. *"This is not exactly going to simplify the investigation,"* he thought.

Concentrating on the background of the leaseholder, Lloyd found a short reference to its business. Although recorded as 'marine management' it also had a link to the mining industry. Extraction of resources below the sea was not unheard of but unless the 'mining' included drilling for oil, it was less than common. Like oil and water, marine management and mining did not seem to mix. It might be prospecting for 'rare earth minerals' or even rarer sea minerals.

Thoughts of minerals and trading in various commodities rang another bell. It was clearer and could be more helpful than the sad chimes from the Lutine Bell below. It rang in his memory, telling him to contact his old friend and onetime boss, Andrew Tulloch. Perhaps Andrew could offer some guidance to one or more of the clues in the mysterious disarray of facts before him. He would understand these things, he hoped.

Besides which, Tulloch owed him a serious lunch.

Ch.5. Helen of Troy.

Andrew Tulloch had been working in Zurich for over three years. Four years earlier he had engaged Lloyd to work with him in a remarkable financial search and rescue act to trace and recover millions stolen from their company's pension fund. That had resulted in partial success – what they later described as 'a pyrrhic defeat.'

Perhaps it had been a blessing, albeit in a very thick disguise. In employment terms it was a just a journey to the end of Jean-Paul Sartre's 'Road to freedom.' The only blessing for each was that the end of that road led them to recycle their experience in new careers.

Cocky Lloyd's combined police and corporate detective work made him ideally suited for his current post as a specialist loss adjuster. Recovering kidnapped human and tangible property resulted in large benefits for the recovered and for their insurers. Smaller benefits usually found their way to his pocket as a half-yearly bonus.

Andrew Tulloch had fallen on extremely well shod feet after rescuing much of the pension fund of his former company. In saving it, he had saved the reputations of the non-executive directors. They in turn expressed their relief by supporting his search for a new appointment. That had led to swift promotion and he soon found himself in charge of a Swiss-based company trading in commodities such as... oil and minerals.

After two years at the helm his new employer in Zurich purchased another firm based in London. Once a month, Tulloch would fly to the City Airport and taxi to an office in Leadenhall Street. A two day visit and local board meeting for Tulloch would occasionally coincide with Lloyd's office work in Lime Street, allowing their paths to cross once more over what they called their 'serious lunch' meetings.

'Serious lunches' for the former colleagues usually involved high quality eating and low quality talking. Discussions were inevitably lubricated – slurps of house wine if Tulloch was paying for it or whatever the waiter suggested if it was at Lloyd's expense. Time and cost inevitably hovered around the same level due to a ceiling applied by the two men, capping both. Today would be different.

Their meals were usually enjoyed as a dining duo but for once, Tulloch was not unaccompanied. And for once, his companion in arms was of the female persuasion, and very attractive.

Helen Tiarks was more than attractive. Her beauty had evoked comparison with the legendary lady whose face was said to have 'launched a thousand ships.' How any of the admirers could know what the original Helen of Troy really looked like was left to the imagination. That usually resulted in their conclusion that the Greek queen must have closely resembled Miss Tiarks.

Helen's attractions were not, however, limited to her appearance. Beneath the dark and shining hair buzzed a brain that had produced a first class honours degree in languages. Those – like the hymn book – were both ancient and modern. Classical Greek and Aramaic, as once spoken by Jesus and his followers, had been joined by modern Hebrew, as spoken daily in Israel; Farsi, as spoken in Iran, and Hazaragi as spoken by few in Britain but many in Northern Afghanistan.

After graduating and complementing her Masters' degree with a PhD, she had joined an international firm of lawyers and qualified as a solicitor. There she had specialised in advice to non-government and charity organisations with occasional forays into the cut-throat world of company mergers and acquisitions.

For some time Andrew Tulloch had enjoyed the company of another solicitor, a lady who had advised and supported him when he needed to extract himself from one employer and offer his services to another. Although Mary Deans was neither an expert in corporate takeover warfare nor available for lunch on that day she introduced her friend Andrew to a former class-mate who might act in both capacities. Mary sent her apologies for absence to Tulloch, along with the lovely, brainy Helen Tiarks.

In fact Helen's expertise in commercial mergers and acquisitions was limited to a year's experience working as assistant to a senior partner, acting for clients in predatorily or targeted – hunter or hunted – situations. Although she had helped to prepare and administer the law, that had been without her own 'hands on' involvement. Nevertheless, she gained the benefit of witnessing the high value poker games played out by the parties.

For the last three years, the demands of non-government organisations such as the International Red Cross and the United Nations High Commissioner for Refugees had occupied much of her professional career and social conscience. This was very much a labour of love rather than a step in the career ladder. With a surge in numbers of refugees, her social life had taken second place in a very busy diary. Her friend Mary Deans had suggested that a pleasant lunch in male company would be a refreshing break from other humanitarian relief so, as Tulloch explained, here she was.

"Yes," thought Lloyd, *"here she is."* His eyebrows lifted instinctively as his jaw dropped to balance them. The sight of such a stunning creature entering the restaurant with his friend, startled his senses into submission of his chair to the newcomers. A puzzled Tulloch accepted it after holding one of the other three chairs for his consort. The two men then attempted to take the same seat, bringing a moment of Mary's suggested refreshment to their female guest in a giggle of suppressed laughter.

Having provided the entertainment, Lloyd thought he should provide an introduction before the vision evaporated and the waiter materialised. Thoughts of business worries and kidnap tensions were left behind a relaxed round of 'hello' and 'nice to meet you' greetings. In fact, a 'very nice to meet you too' was the more emphatic response from Lloyd's lips. Having already met Helen in Mary Dean's company, Tulloch expected this reaction from his Welsh friend and enjoyed every smirk of it.

Several minutes of idle pleasantries turned to irritation at the lack of service from the restaurant staff. At last they ended their wait for the weary waiter when a morbid figure asked them twice if they would like a drink whilst waiting. Tulloch was tempted to point out that it was the figure standing before them who was supposed to do the waiting but simply advised him to bring their drinks with the first course before the time came for afternoon tea.

Before the atmosphere could lose its remaining humour, that was soon restored with an audible volcanic rumble from a fault line in the Tulloch tummy. A combination of indigestion and tension.

Meanwhile, tension in the Middle East increased as the cold and hungry refugees poured into Europe. The early editions of the evening newspapers reported clashes between police and asylum seekers in Calais; Chelsea increased their lead in the football league tables; and the market price of oil fell to under sixty dollars per barrel.

Ch.6. Undermined.

Meeting Tulloch for lunch had been prompted by Lloyd's need for information about the Ukrainian company who leased the missing yacht. That brought a smile of recognition from Tulloch and anecdotal description of an unwelcome approach to his company by one called 'RKM Group.' It had been often referred to as a 'corporate raider' but more often dubbed with less flattering epithets. The initial message from the bidding party had been curt and threatening. Tulloch knew that Lloyd would not absorb all of the details of the bid but hoped that the sparkling lady lawyer would.

After another round of drinks and giggles, Tulloch started to relate the tale of his clash with the RKM Group. Although his own company had traded very successfully it could not prevent approaches from others who claimed that they could run the business more profitably. He mentioned several bids that had been made over the previous year, usually offering payment of cash to his shareholders to be taken later from the reserves of their own company.

One such stalker, the RKM Group, had delivered an ultimatum. Either Tulloch would accept their offer and retire with a light 'golden handshake' or, a very hostile takeover battle would ensue. That would be fought with maximum acrimony and allegations of mismanagement, threatening dismissal without compensation: A 'take the money and take your leave' offer.

RKM's approach to him had been made through the Swiss branch of an investment bank acting for them. Tulloch had retained a British solicitor to act for his company. The meeting of the agents had been sharp and frosty. First to speak had been the British lawyer.

"Hello. My name's Nigel Quickstick and I represent my client Mr Andrew Tulloch and his company..." The personal details were abruptly cut by the banker who was accompanied by a straight-faced woman from his bank.

"Right, Shitstick. I'm George P Silverman. Let's get this meeting going. Show on the road, as you might say, hey?"

"It's Quickstick, Mr Silverman. Quick, as in fast, QUICK."

"OK Quickshit. All the same to me, eh? She", pointing to his female companion, "she'll take the record of this bull..." He stopped, looking round sheepishly at the embarrassed woman, "... this merger meeting."

Quickstick's neck was beginning to bulge and develop a purple tone.

"Well, if we're going to get an accurate record, we might as well get our own names straight, don't you think?"

"Sure... whatever. What do we – she – have to correct?"

"Let's start again with my name, which is Nigel. Nigel QUICKSTICK."

"Right. As in gear-change. No. That's Stick-shift. Did you invent that?"

"The name? Or the gear-change?"

"The gear-change."

"No. That was one of your chaps. Perhaps he was a relative?"

"Don't think so. What's his name anyway?"

"George P Dipstick."

All this time, Andrew Tulloch had been enjoying the verbal duel – insults at five paces – with suppressed laughter. For him, it was welcome relief from the abrasive attack. He was quite happy to see and hear the two intermediaries absorbing the bad-tempered exchange. Any bad blood would be spilled by them, and any adverse reaction blamed on them also.

An hour of vague threats followed from the banker parried by clear rejection by Quickstick. The meeting then broke up and left the sparring partners exactly where they were beforehand except for the large fee notes produced shortly afterwards. For Tulloch, the extravagant charges were almost worth the amusement and slap down that his lawyer had delivered to the attacker.

"Yes," he thought. *'Quickstick was a good name for him. He was certainly quick to give that stupid bull-shitter a lesson in how not to screw up a negotiation. Slapstick would be an even better name for that one. Not bad for a lawyer.'*

Tulloch was aware of his industry's problems: falling demand meant falling sales and falling prices. He was also aware that his own careful husbandry had developed an enviable reserve of cash: money that many weaker companies coveted. What he had needed then was support to defend against threats of corporate robbery with violence. He knew that he and his business were still vulnerable to takeover.

Mild sympathy, coupled with confidence in his friend's ability to handle commercial trouble, was expressed by Lloyd. In the absence of tea, a bottle of premier cru Chateau Palmer was directed to Tulloch's wine glass. It conveyed solidarity if not comprehension. A more thoughtful Helen declined the claret and sipped cold mineral water whilst considering the sketchy detail. She remained silent and listened without attempting to jump to any premature conclusion.

The picture of the RKM Group as outlined by Tulloch was certainly sketchy. Only the barest details without individuals' names or places to identify the characters in the plot.

"They said that they have big procurement resources and even bigger financial resources. That last bit didn't make sense. Nobody with plenty of money wants to buy expensive shares just to get more cash. Perhaps they have their own mines. Whatever they are mining, IF they are mining anything, it's unlikely to have avoided the slump in prices that we're seeing. Even gold, as the media love to say, is 'losing its shine.'

"I suspect that they were losing money and still have a lot of debt which they can't repay now. If interest rates go up, they'll be stuffed. Their only lifeline would be either to get some more loans at low interest rates or, to take over a company with plenty of cash and close it down after they've pocketed all the money. Or maybe they just want to get their money out of Ukraine and Russia and set-up in the West.

"If I knew for sure who they are and what their line of business is – apart from asset-stripping – then I might be able to help you more, Cocky. I've got a different problem now. To prevent someone like RKM from taking us over, I need to use some of our cash to get a stake in a decent company. That might make us too big to swallow."

The mention of swallowing prompted Tulloch to pause, pouring a mouthful of the mineral water into his glass from Helen's bottle on the table. The cool drink rehydrated a very dry mouth and slightly parched mind. In the brief silence around the table, the first to break the drought was a simple suggestion from the legal lady. She spoke softly and carefully.

"If you can let me have the correspondence from their agents, I might be able to find out something about them. Even if it's not conclusive, we might be able to draw up a clearer picture of who, where, what, etc., so that we can determine what we're up against."

With the offer of help from one so well qualified to deliver it, and who had been recommended by the reliable Mary Deans, Lloyd was immediately encouraged.

He had been slightly at sea in the financial conversation but hoping to sail in somehow. With the inclusion of the magic word 'We' in the final phase of her offer, he was inspired to invite La Belle Helene to discuss the matter, and any other matter he could think of, with him again. Perhaps even again and again, if he could persuade her to do so.

Thoughts of such a pleasant activity warmed him to reach out for the bottle of vintage Bordeaux and offer to refill Helen's glass. As that glass was virtually untouched by human

42

hand and the wine untouched by Hellenic lips, the offer was as empty as the glass was full. Helen however, was far too polite to point this out and far too busy thinking about the source of Lloyd's problem to worry about her drink.

She did not know much about marine management and even less about mining companies. The only mining businesses with which she was familiar were some very 'minor miners' operating in the poorest parts of the world. These were sometimes digging open holes in the ground in Africa and Asia, using primitive methods. In most cases it meant near slavery for employees wielding picks and shovels.

Such small operations could never try to take over a respectable company but they could have contact with others who might try to do so. Her contacts in Oxfam had administered to many unfortunates – victims of the harsh conditions or unscrupulous mining operators.

She told the two men that she would try to make enquiries with a friend in Oxfam before returning to her current work with the UNHCR and International Red Cross, all desperately trying to stem the tide of misery flowing through Syria and the Balkans. She realised that time was 'of the essence' as her next appointment was to be "next week in a refugee camp in Jordan – or perhaps in The Lebanon."

She confessed, "I'm not sure yet." But soon she would be sure – quite sure.

Ch. 7 Camp followers.

Jordan and The Lebanon have been a refuge to millions of displaced people for decades. For the various Palestinian, Syrian and other refugees sheltering there, the camps have become at best – like Oscar Wilde's definition of second marriage – 'a triumph of hope over experience.' Hope in the camps had often worn as thin as their malnourished bodies. In many cases experience had turned hope into desperation.

Zaatari camp lies a few miles south of the border with Syria. It houses, or tents, many of those who have fled from the multiple wars in that country. A similar situation occupies the Bekaa camp in The Lebanon between the Syrian capital of Damascus and the Lebanese capital of Beirut.

Non-governmental organisations – 'NGO's' – struggle to maintain life and health in these vast tented villages. In one such camp Helen paid a visit every two months or so to absorb information first hand from the residents and advise her client organisations as best as she could. 'Listen and learn – consider and consult,' was how she summed it up. Travel expenses and a small retainer fee would be paid by the clients but much of her work after that would be given freely as a pro bono vocation.

After the meeting with Lloyd and Tulloch in London – its mixture of amusement and talks of corporate raiders – allowing the meal to qualify as genuinely 'serious,' – Helen felt as though she had been on a short holiday. Returning to her chambers and its dusty legal arguments was something of a descent into drudgery. Visiting the Lebanese camp would be more exciting if not more rewarding in terms of food or pay.

Before embarking on the journey to Beirut, her telephone announced that Mr LL Lloyd – or 'Cocky' as he had introduced himself – would like to host a cosy little dinner for two. For the avoidance of doubt, as her legal documents liked to qualify, the diners would be 'him and her'. Without rejecting his approach, Miss Tiarks politely declined the invitation on the grounds of her inability to be in London and The Lebanon at the same time.

Mortification was expressed by Cocky and mild commiseration returned from Helen. The 'his and hers' dinner would have to wait until her return – "unless you happen to be in Beirut next week – ha, ha," she added. Mortified Lloyd became resurrected Cocky in a trice.

"As a matter of fact," he responded, although it was not strictly factual, "I just might be. I have some unfinished business to complete there."

The business he would prefer to complete was apparent to both parties. Helen knew exactly what he had in mind. She was a big girl now and her sharp brain had not been dulled by exposure to the misery in the refugee camps. There, she had witnessed countless births, deaths and marriages in some of the most poverty-stricken and wretched circumstances. Attempted seduction would not fool her.

"All human life is there," she had been told. Her mind had become accustomed to conversation and descriptions of which her mother would not approve. At least, her mother would protest disapproval, even if she was a party to it. In the dichotomy between possible pleasure and probable misery, she couldn't resist further enquiry.

"When will you be in Beirut then?" she asked in a non-committal manner, expecting an answer based on an assumption of her imminent departure. He hesitated before avoiding the baited trap.

"I don't have to be there on a specific date, as long as it's sometime before next month. I have to finish a report that's due in a couple of weeks from now. There's a guy I have to meet who could be gone from there by the end of this month and I need to get some more information before he goes."

With each party uncommitted to a date, the way was open for Helen to abandon his advances completely or arrange to meet when it suited her. Lloyd was not the sort of man that she usually met at work and she had not had much in the way of play for what seemed like a lifetime. It might be a chance for a move from the unending professional grind to a more social variety before all work made Jill a dull girl.

More clichés came to mind. Perhaps her new admirer might provide a change as good as a rest. Time was removing the chance for prevarication. Positive decisions had to be made at once. Her travelling bags were waiting in her bedroom to be packed and she needed to visit her bathroom quite urgently too.

"OK Mister Lloyd. I'll show you my timetable - by e-mail before I go. If you..." She nearly said, *'Show me yours,'* but stopped and added "...if you're going to be there when I am then we might be able to meet up for that dinner. Right now, I need to go to the loo."

The telephone handset was smartly restored to its rest and a pondering Helen strode smartly to the bathroom.

The next morning, a more perky Cocky Lloyd took the District Line train from Chiswick to Monument station, beside the old tower commemorating the Great Fire Of London. From there he walked up Gracechurch Street and through Leadenhall Market. Passing an array of poultry outside a butcher's shop he could imagine a scene from a Charles Dickens story. Thoughts of Ebeneezer Scrooge with the face of his parsimonious friend Tulloch brought a smile and a silent chuckle. The butcher saw the smile and hoped he had a new customer. A smiling Lloyd walked on.

His thoughts then returned to romantic liaisons with the legal advisor to the United Nations High Commissioner for Refugees and similar organisations. The warm ideas fell back down to cold earth as he remembered her destination and the scenes she would witness. By the time that he reached the metallic Lloyd's-of-London building in Lime Street, his friend

Andrew Tulloch was winging his way to Zurich and Helen was boarding an Airbus 320 of MEA at Heathrow airport en route to Beirut.

After a five hour flight, the UNHCR legal advisor was met with a small bus to take her to Bekaa camp in The Lebanon. By the time that the bus arrived there, half of the day and most of her energy had been spent travelling. There was just enough time, however, for a quick wash and snack before meeting the other representatives and some of the inmates of the camp.

UNHCR services at the camp included heavily subsidised health care for children and registered refugees under sixty-five years old. Those who had not registered with the UNHCR were expected to pay for their treatment. Many unregistered and unable to pay might possibly suffer and probably die. Some recent arrivals from Syria assembled to await registration before illness and disease overtook them.

These included a young Arabic woman who appeared to be in good health and strength with a gaggle of refugees in less favourable conditions. There was also a middle aged man who was not part of the same group but hovered close to them. He was eyed with what appeared to be either suspicion or downright fear by others in the group.

To complete the refugees' registration, the UNHCR representative took the woman's name as Aysa or Aysal, either of which she explained meant 'beautiful as the moon' in Farsi. Why she had a name in Farsi was not explained but she said that it was fairly common in Syria, and pronounced there as 'Aysil.'

The middle aged man was already registered. His name was 'Abdul-Nasir' - 'the servant of the protector.' From their reaction, the younger refugees seemed to need protection from the protector. Abdul, as he became known, had a reasonable command of English and Arabic. He too appeared to be fluent in Farsi but said his native tongue was Aramaic.

When registration was complete, the UNHCR representative offered to take Helen to the temporary office where she could discuss any individual refugee's status if they wished to be considered for asylum in the EU. Before bringing her attention to the legal and administrative process, Helen's curiosity overcame her fatigue and she made more enquiries about young Aysil and the older Abdul-Nasir.

Like the majority, the two recent arrivals had come from Syria. Neither had started from Damascus. Aysil had claimed that she had fled from somewhere near the border with Turkey but she was not Kurdish. In fact she was an Alawite, which is the religion of the ruling families in Damascus. As such, it would be unusual for her to be fleeing from Syria. She explained that her village had been over-run by Sunni insurgents and she had been lucky to escape with her life.

By the time that Helen's curiosity had been satisfied with the explanations from Aysil, her fellow traveller Abdul-Nasir had disappeared. As he was already registered with the UNHCR, his absence was not of great concern to them. What was of more concern to the rest of the recent arrivals was the fear of his return. Neither Aysil nor the UNHCR could explain the reason for their concern and the others in the group could not or would not say.

For the remainder of her first day in Bekaa, Helen interviewed a small number of the many refugees who, like Aysil, sought asylum in the European Union. Although exhausted by her dangerous travel through Syria and The Lebanon, Aysil was adamant that she would complete whatever was necessary to get access to the EU in general and Germany or Austria in particular.

After a tiring first day in Bekaa, a weary Miss Tiarks returned to her hotel in the Lebanese capital, where a message from home – or near her home – awaited. Mr LL Lloyd had rushed through his work in London and hoped to meet her in Beirut in two days time. He could hardly wait, the message said. She, on the other hand, couldn't just drop her important work so he would have to wait, whether he was in Lebanon or London.

He didn't have to wait for very long. Three days later, at the end of that working week, he boarded a BA flight to Beirut, hoping to combine the pursuit of pleasure with that of his next investigation. For those he had arranged two appointments. One with his former help and protector Jock Elphinstone and the other with his new romantic target Helen Tiarks.

At the British Embassy in Beirut he met the redoubtable 'Stelph' and arranged a friendly chat over a lunch, considerably more modest than the meal in London with Tulloch and Helen. Not such a serious lunch perhaps but nonetheless enjoyable and informative.

Their rescue of the Arab oil-trader's son from kidnap and probable death had been met by the boy's father with indifference to the rescuers' own health. He had also voiced his objection at the uninsured costs of the operation, including medical treatment for the rescued hostage. Despite the lack of thanks or appreciation from the father, the son was extremely grateful and even offered to pay for a new fountain pen to replace that shattered by a bullet in Lloyd's shirt pocket.

"To fight and not to count the cost" was Elphinstone's amused verdict. Lloyd had to agree. Cost counting was his pal Tulloch's province – not his. What he did want was to discover the whereabouts of the missing yacht, the 'Anna K', now the subject of an increasingly expensive insurance claim. That vessel was last seen travelling in the Western Aegean towards the Bosporus and might be tucked away in a Turkish or Lebanese harbour hideaway.

Disappointment came in two tranches; first, Elphinstone's regional intelligence network had no evidence to report of the vessel in local waters and secondly, Helen was obliged to return to Bekaa camp for the remainder of the weekend. A quiet and thoughtful 'Stelph' suggested solutions to both setbacks – accompanying Helen to Bekaa followed by a visit to the Aegean island where the yacht was last reported.

It took less than a few minutes after his return to the hotel for Lloyd to contact Helen and ask to accompany her to the refugee camp. Much to his delight she said she would be glad of his company and professed interest in her work. The journey was encouraging for him as she did all the talking and all he had to do was to look and sound interested.

By the time that they arrived in Bekaa he was actually quite interested. But by the time that he had seen and met some of the refugees in a state of despair, his interest turned to horror at the size and depth of the problem. Then he met Aysil.

He had been warned that she was quite different from the majority of struggling women in the camp. They were barely hanging on to hope and life, living one hour at a time and hoping for a miracle. Their drawn faces reflected mental and physical exhaustion coupled with a weak attempt to cling to their children and what was left of their lives. Most of their dreams of complete recovery had been abandoned long ago.

Aysil's attitude was more like that of the determined young men – economic refugees seeking a job as well as a better life. They sought one that would be not only better than the near-death situation they had just escaped from. It would be better in most aspects than any they had experienced before their lives were torn apart. They would not be satisfied with anything less than a comfortable home and a career or education in a wealthy country. Aysil's objectives seemed to be identical to theirs.

Helen and Aysil shared several similarities. Each was physically attractive and vivacious. They were also mentally proficient, possessing much more than just a strong command of the 'three Rs'. They both displayed the confidence of a very sound education and fluency in several languages. Being conscious of the refugees' precarious balance on the brink of disaster made them aware of how quickly people's lives could change – one way or another.

Some of the cockiness fell from Lloyd when he found himself in the company of what seemed to him to be two of The Three Graces. Apart from an 'O' level pass in English language, his linguistic skills were limited to a few phrases of

Cantonese and a working grasp of Welsh. Seeing the two impressive females and hearing their conversation switching from English to Aramaic or Farsi left him reflecting on the possibility of world-wide feminist supremacy.

Aysil was accompanied by another young woman. An Arab or Afghan refugee – he couldn't tell which – with a less confident bearing and nervous expression. She almost clung to Aysil's dress and constantly looked to her for either protection or inspiration. Lloyd wondered if she might be Aysil's younger sister or cousin, or just another lost soul looking for a saviour. Not entirely fluent but speaking more English than Lloyd could say in any Arabic language.

He was left with feelings of male inferiority, speechless during the multi-lingual conversations. Helen completed her discussions with Aysil and announced abruptly that they should return to the bus and to Beirut. She had spent more time than she could afford on one case and had to telephone her office in London before even thinking of what to wear to the promised dinner.

Still numb from the scenes of misery and the meeting of the two Wonder-women, an old Chinese command entered Lloyd's vacant mind. Announcements from the ancient Imperial throne usually ended with the order, 'tremble and obey!'

Cocky stopped wondering and meekly obeyed. He didn't tremble then but, he would later.

Ch. 8. From Aysil to the Aegean.

More than one telephone line between the hotel in Beirut to the City of London was occupied that evening before dinner. Whilst Helen reported to her office about discussions in Bekaa camp, Lloyd received a message from Lime Street containing some scanty information regarding the missing yacht. The underwriters had been told 'on the grapevine' that it might answer the description of a luxury vessel seen in the Eastern Aegean, near the coast of Turkey.

Lloyd's first thought was to look at a map of that area and try to guess where in that sea might be a likely haven for a runaway – or sail-away – yacht. One of the better-known islands nearer to coast was Lesvos or Lesbos – famous over the centuries for its association with the feminist poet Sappho – infamous more recently as the destination of 'people smugglers' shipping masses of refugees and asylum seekers.

His mind went back to another small Greek island and the characters that he had met there. A great deal of help then had been gratefully received from the island's customs officer-cum-ships' chandler Cyrus Constantiou. Diligent and observant, Cyrus had a natural habit of recording the movements of ships and aircraft in the region.

A quick scouring of internet websites revealed an address and telephone number for the chandlery. There was another address and contact details for the island's council. Cyrus had been elevated to high office in his harbour town. That could be useful if the missing yacht had ventured close to his island home. Lloyd wasted no time in dialling the telephone numbers for each location.

From the recorded Greek response to his calls, Lloyd guessed that Cyrus was unobtainable. Before recording a message in English, he decide to ask Helen if she could confirm the details of the Greek recorded messages. That could wait until they had sampled their well discussed dinner, possibly the first hurdle in his chase for her affections.

In the meantime, he thought he should try to contact 'Jock of the kidnapped hostage rescue' and arrange to meet him. Another call secured an appointment after breakfast at the Embassy. That would be more appetising than the brick-dust and bullets of their last early morning adventure. By then he had done all he could reasonably expect to do. Time now for dinner with the lovely Helen.

Dinner was not a disappointment for either of them. A meze of raw tabbouleh salad with hummus, sambusac patties and stuffed vine leaves was followed by tender grilled goat kebabs with rice. The Lebanese wine with the main courses gave way to arak and coffee with the traditional honeyed sweets. Lloyd's thoughts oscillated between the culinary delights before him and the feminine delights which he hoped might also be before him shortly.

Helen allowed herself to concentrate on accepting the more delicate offerings of food from the waiters and parrying the less delicate suggestions from an increasingly suggestive Lloyd. His suggestions became more indelicate with each glass of arak but softened as the hot coffee absorbed the alcohol and cooled his ardour.

Neither of them wished to spoil the epicurean pleasure with any embarrassment. The conversation moved gently away from the lightly amorous to more altruistic discussions. Lloyd broached on the subject of that afternoon's visit to Bekaa and its inhabitants. In particular, he brought up the subject of mysterious, serious Aysil and the contrast with her fellow campers.

Aysil had left an impression on his mind that was hard to erase. It was difficult to discuss that subject without detracting from his desire for affection from Helen but the immediate object of his attentions remained discrete and sensitive. She concentrated her observations of Aysil on the common problems facing refugees – pursuing their dreams of life in Europe or America.

Lloyd listened but didn't always hear. Aysil was becoming a mental stone in the shoe of his earlier romantic aspirations. Smiling attentively at Helen and trying to gaze in admiration without looking soppy was never easy at the best of meals. With the picture of Aysil continuing to prod its way into his mind, it was becoming harder with each mouthful. Emotions were becoming confused.

Confusion was eased with the arrival of more coffee and Arak at the table. As well as the welcome liquid digestifs, another figure arrived and was welcomed with an invitation to join them. Lloyd had mentioned earlier to Elphinstone that they would be dining in the hotel restaurant and suggested that he might like to drop in for a drink later. As any friendly diplomat would, he did.

The assistant commercial attaché had no intention of creating a crowd of three from the company of two. Being polite enough to have his own dinner before driving to the hotel he determined not to interfere with Lloyd's liaison with Miss Tiarks. However, he knew that social small-talk over coffee might supply a morsel of information. Small but possibly vital. Possibly vitl to others as well...

In terms of emotional atmosphere the next hour's conversation was a failure. After one extra coffee and drinks had been accepted, introductions were exchanged with mentions of homes and occupations. Then the three-way talk revolved around the ever increasing numbers of refugees and their sources.

Inevitably, the UNHCR and Helen's association with it was aired. Inevitably, one of the names that entered the conversation was that of the striking young Allawite woman with plans to travel on to Austria, Germany and beyond. Just how Aysil or any of her thousands of fellow-travellers intended to arrive at their goal was permutated from thousands of theories surrounding their plight.

Another name to feature amongst the residents of Bekaa camp was that of 'Abdul-Nasir', 'the servant of the protector.' More mature but less appreciated by the unprotected masses, his infrequent presence in the camp and more frequent rumours of his role with the refugees gave rise to suspicions of mastering a gang. Usually those involved with very illegal but lucrative travel activities.

During his visit to the refugee camp, Lloyd had observed Abdul talking earnestly to the mother of a very young girl. The woman bore the wounds of several months of displacement and worry but the child appeared to be as relaxed and cheerful as any with endless optimism for the future. She had particularly bright and searching brown eyes, reminding Lloyd of one of his cousin's children in South Wales. Somewhere, somehow he hoped that mother and child would find a safe home and happiness.

During the pondering and possible explanations, mainly between a well-informed Helen and ill-informed Lloyd, very little was contributed by Elphinstone. His attentions appeared to be directed to two areas: that morning's conversation with Aysil in Bekaa camp and the present conversation with the lady now seated next to him.

If he had wished to interrogate either or both of the diners – albeit in a very friendly manner – he could not have been more clinical, grilling his two companions gently but persistently. He was obviously trying to satisfy more than idle curiosity. When throwing verbal darts his timing was polished and his aim was deadly.

A seemingly inoffensive remark would be presented to no one in particular but would demand attention from any listener who could confirm or correct. Ensuing silence would only intensify the unspoken demand for an answer. With this system, natural or highly trained, Jock Elphinstone garnered the few scraps of information he regarded as vital.

His existing knowledge and experience would segregate most of the fact from fiction – opinion from gossip. The hard part was in piecing together any additions to a growing dossier of intelligence. Little pieces in an incomplete jigsaw of hard fact and assumptions. Too often the incomplete dossier would be seized by impatient military or political ambitions to justify their agenda – usually with a misleading conclusion.

Cocky was impressed by the fact that he couldn't avoid telling Jock what he needed to know. Whoever had taught the man from the Embassy to persuade people to provide answers that they sometimes didn't realise they had, must have been a Pavlovan genius. If Jock had not been trained formally then he himself was the genius. It was an object lesson in polite persuasion verging on painless mental torture.

Helen was even more impressed. Impressed by the grasp of complex political and military chaos in the region. Impressed by the soft but unyielding manner of gathering information and... most impressed by the tall articulate figure now seated beside her. Not pretty. No one would want or expect such a man to be pretty, but to her, rather magnetic.

Despite Jock's well-worn features, his bearing and incisive conversation quickly made him interesting to her. On hearing his name - 'Jock' - she had at first thought it was 'Jack.' Her mother had given birth to a boy, her younger brother, and christened him 'Jack.' Jack had never completely developed and had only lived for nine years before succumbing to one of several illnesses that his immune system couldn't withstand.

Jack had been dead for several years but never forgotten by his parents or by Helen. She thought of the young boy every other day and wondered how he might have become had he lived to maturity. She had hoped that he might have been someone handsome and clever and modest. Someone rather like the man sitting near her now. Someone like Jock.

His physicality was coupled with an obvious command of mental strength. Cocky was nice too, she accepted. Common sense in a wrapping of common sensibility. Perhaps not so appealing to her intellectual faculties as Jock but not bad for an ex-copper working in the boring old insurance business.

After months without close male companionship, having two nice men around her was very acceptable but sometimes disconcerting. A brief glimpse of the men's eyes, eyeing her face, her bust, legs or ankles, caused her to have the nearest thing to a hot flush that she had encountered. *"I could always blame it on the Arak,"* she decided.

After-dinner conversation faded to a halt. The party broke into its constituent bodies and said their good-nights as the man from the Embassy slipped into the warm evening air. The two visitors walked to the hotel elevator. Lloyd received a gentle hug, and two kisses on the cheeks were exchanged before each retired to their respective rooms and respectable beds.

Before leaving the hotel foyer to be received by his chauffeur, Elphinstone had spoken very quietly once more. To Helen, a soft goodbye and thanks. She was not quite sure why he was thanking her but she was more than happy to receive it from him. To Lloyd, another mutter of thanks and confirmation of their appointment at his office, "sometime between 10.30 and 10.31 a.m.," Jock suggested.

Like Helen, Lloyd was unsure of the reason for the thanks or the precise time proposed but quite certain that he would follow the suggestion. After all, his association with Jock had been one hundred percent beneficial to date. There was no reason to suspect any change of fortune from him now. Nor was there any reason to suspect anything sinister from the shadowy figure watching them from a doorway some ten metres from the hotel entrance.

Suddenly the figure evaporated into the darkness as the chauffeur emerged from the embassy car. Elphinstone appeared indifferent, possibly confident of his chauffeur's protection in an emergency. Lloyd was less confident. He retreated to the security of the hotel foyer. The shadow might have been the suspicious Abdul. On the other hand it might have been anybody. There were plenty of anybodies abroad in the streets of Beirut.

After five and a half hours sound sleep in his room and a reasonably hearty breakfast a reasonably Cocky Lloyd took a taxi to the British Embassy complex on Serail Hill. Morning coffee for the two men was taken in the same quiet atmosphere shared by the previous evening's after-dinner trio. Without prevarication, his companion from the Foreign Office gave Lloyd an insight into the concern facing him.

"You mentioned that your office told you to take a look into some marine activities around Lesvos, didn't you, Cocky?" There was no need for confirmation; he was not seeking an answer. "Our contacts in that area are up to their eyeballs in asylum seekers trying to make it to Germany or Austria the hard way. The Aegean is awash with people smugglers and drowning refugees, most of them taking the short crossing to Lesvos from Turkey. You'll know all about that from the daily news bulletins.

"I'm not going to suggest that you shouldn't go there to try to find your missing yacht. That's entirely your business and I'll help you if I can. If you do go, though, I'd like you to keep an eye out for one or two characters whose names came up in your nice girlfriend's conversation last evening.

"They're probably no different from the other refugees but if they have crossed into Greece I would be interested to know how they're coping and where they hope to get to. The girl who said she was Alawite – didn't you say her name was Aysil?"

Once again, there was no need to answer – even the nod of Lloyd's head was superfluous. "Sounds as though she has the strength and guts to make it to Europe but she might need some help from other – uh – other quarters.

"Then there was a chap who called himself Abdul or Nassir or Abdul-Nassir." Another unnecessary nod and grunt from Lloyd "We suspect that he might not be a genuine refugee and from what you two saw and heard at Bekaa, we might be right."

Lloyd was feeling slightly less cocky and rather more intrigued by the assistant commercial attaché's interest in such a tiny fragment of the refugee population.

"Why are you interested in what happens to them? If they arrive on Lesvos then they're not even in The Lebanon and in any case they're only two out of two million on the hoof from Syria or wherever."

A faint smile flickered across Elphinstone's face.

"Yes, that's very pertinent. About half of the refugees 'from Syria' are in fact from Iraq or Afghanistan 'or wherever' and I would like to know just where they started from, and why."

"Very pertinent", thought Lloyd. *"I'd better not try to be impertinent"*. He did want to be inquisitive though, on two fronts.

"What do you want me to do if I come across them whilst I'm looking for the bloody yacht and its master? And how can you help me to get it back to safety and its rightful owners?" Two simple questions, but he was fairly sure that the answers would not be so simple. He was wrong. The answers were as simple as they were unexpected.

"If you even hear that either of the two from Bekaa are on the island or you know where they are, just phone me with whatever details you have. Nothing more than that. But I don't have to tell you to keep it between you and me, do I? Someone somewhere appears to be listening in... sometimes."

"As for my side of the bargain, I'll do what we can do to help find your tub and getting it back to you, or make it safe for your clients."

Lloyd was taken aback by the firm tone and even firmer commitment. He was to act as a spy or spy-watcher and 'we' – by which Jock indicated that he meant the entire British Foreign Office and/or military intelligence – would try to get his client's yacht back.

The two individuals from the refugee camp were obviously much more important to his country's interests than mere asylum seekers.

Ch. 9. Chaos in Lesvos.

There was no easy way to get from Beirut to Lesvos. Public transport usually involved a 'Return to Go' on the travellers' Monopoly board – a flight to Athens followed by road and sea stages to the Greek island. Before the influx of refugees, most visitors to Sappho's old island were tourists using package holiday arrangements. With his office in Lime Street waiting for him to resume his duties there and report progress, Cocky Lloyd put the return section of his air ticket to work and flew straight back to Heathrow.

After briefing his colleagues with an outline of what he hoped to get from Cyrus the Greek customs officer and from the Beirut Embassy, he then took the next available flight to Athens and from there to Mytilene airport via Aegean Airlines. Accommodation would not be a problem, nor would local travel. The tourist trade had suffered badly from the invasion of refugees – there were hotels and taxis to spare.

The majority of unwelcome arrivals had much more dangerous travel arrangements. Packed and huddled in a tiny rubber dinghy or on an open life-raft, they embarked on the perilous journey from mainland beaches in Turkey. The cost to them was enormous: very large sums of money and a strong risk of loss of life. The journeys were bankrupting but to them the alternatives appeared to be more costly.

Thousands upon thousands of exhausted, soaking, sick and injured men, women and children, many too weary to cry, fought their way ashore on the Northern coast of the island. There they fell upon the unflagging mercy of local authorities and volunteers from organisations such as Medicins Sans Frontiers, the internationally renowned MSF.

With so many moving from mainland to island beach, and from island beach to their temporary rest before trying to get to the home and work of their dreams, Lloyd literally did not know where to start. Where to start looking for the individuals from the Lebanese camp or where to start looking for the missing yacht? There was no point in travelling further before taking advice and some sort of guidance.

His former occupation and advice came to mind, 'If you want to know the time, ask a policeman.' Time was limited. He had a watch and mobile phone to tell him the hours and minutes, but there were other matters that might be displayed or explained at a police station. As a former police officer in Wales and in Hong Kong, Lloyd was at ease in the main town's station.

With so many English speaking tourists over the past fifty years, translation was unnecessary. He was even offered a cup of tea. More importantly, he was offered a list of places to go and people to see, starting with the registration office and the main MSF point of arrival of refugees from the shores.

Missing yachts and missing persons would not always appear in the same lists of 'lost and found' but Lloyd was confident that he could search for both simultaneously. The chances of either being discovered were slim, he thought. Slimmer than a fashion model on the catwalk. That made him think again of Aysil and her appealing figure.

MSF were toiling magnificently to cater for the pitiful masses appearing daily on the shorelines. Insulating blankets and hot drinks plus medical examinations and, in keeping with their name, medicine. It was administered without questions about the patients' religion or politics – only about their physical condition. In the chaotic situation their first task was to get the new arrivals on to dry land. Out of the surf and into reasonable health.

Not all of those embarking from Turkey would ever see the sight of dry land or the light of day again. Whilst wandering along the road beside one of the beaches Lloyd's attention focussed on a small group of people including a policeman and a medic from MSF. They were examining a small body – recently extracted from the tide – still and lifeless.

Lloyd managed to get close enough to see the corpse in more detail, but then wished that he had not. It was a little girl of about five years, her face white and wrinkled by the salt water. As the medic turned the body to place it on a stretcher, Lloyd almost screamed as he saw the remains of two brown eyes in a pitiful little face. He couldn't tell whether it was the same child that he had seen in Bekaa but it was certainly the remains of one such as her.

Wiping wet streams from his cheeks he continued to approach other groups subject to help from MSF. Amongst the latest clutches of flotsam in their care, he had no sign of either Aysil or Abdul. Not that he would expect to find them immediately. Patience, time and questioning eventually reaped a few rewards. After two days of what seemed to be a hopeless task, he came across another rescue group.

Amongst them a harassed MSF official shouted directions to yet another clearing station where some of the previous weeks' inflow were wandering around in hope of transport to the Greek mainland. From there Lloyd was directed to a hard wooden bench on which a wet and wistful Aysil was seated, waiting and watching for her chance to move on. Lloyd could hardly believe his luck and even wondered if he was about to add Abdul and the yacht to his discoveries. He knew instinctively that he should deal with one slice of luck at a time.

Approaching deliberately without frightening her was a concern. He needn't have worried. Aysil eyed him with a mixture of fatalism and indifference as he stood near her bench and greeted her. He had hoped that she would recognise and remember him from the Lebanese camp. She should be pleased to see a friendly figure who might help to accelerate her journey from the island. His hopes were not dashed but not completely realised as she nodded a semblance of lukewarm recognition.

Having achieved what he would label 'a result' when reporting later to Elphinstone, he then attempted to generate some warmth into their meeting. That would depend upon his power to satisfy Aysil's immediate needs – help towards her targeted destination. In order to raise the temperature Lloyd knew he would have to give some form of promise, to get her on whatever transport was available. Unless he could arrange air travel for her, that would mean the docks and a ferry.

After her excruciating journey across the sea from Turkey, any form of sea transport smaller than the Queen Elizabeth would be viewed with concern if not absolute horror. Abdul and the missing yacht did not even enter into the discussion.

Ch. 10. Fellow travellers on the fault lines.

Although Abdul and the yacht had been carefully sidelined from his conversation with Aysil on the cold bench, Lloyd was determined to glean whatever he could from whoever he met. Starting with his promise of help towards mainland Europe, he tried to bring some level of confidence by driving back to the police station and asking for their influence to get a cabin or reserved seat on the ferry from Mytilene to Pireaus.

Having landed what he considered a great prize he was not going to abandon her or his chances of gleaning further information. He would ensure her security further by travelling with her. In that way, he calculated they would both be travelling hopefully which, as R L Stevenson remarked - was more important than arriving. At least it was at that stage.

Assurance was delivered by the duty officer. There were plenty of ferries with plenty of space aboard them. Having been registered as a refugee within the European Union, all that was required were the usual travel essentials – tickets, passports and money. Fortunately for Lloyd, money was now part of his stock in trade and the basic cost of the tickets could be stretched comfortably to add a cabin reservation plus meals for himself and one cold and worried Alawite woman.

Getting Aysil to accept his company on the eight hour journey might be more difficult but company was something that she considered immaterial. After the overloaded rubber dinghy journey from Turkey and the Spartan conditions of the refugee camp, the luxury of warm dry accommodation would overcome any personal objection. It was a little miracle come true although she suspected that there would be a price to pay. She just hoped that it would not be too expensive, or too painful.

Any fears that Aysil might have nourished over the sexual motives of her new-found saviour would soon be dispelled. Once the arrangements for the ferry had been confirmed, Lloyd returned to his other concerns. If he had physical desires for her body – and he certainly did harbour them – he placed them in the hold and directed his attention once more to gleaning any information about Abdul or the missing yacht.

Other than the dreadful sea-crossing from the Turkish coast, nautical vessels were as familiar to Aysil as the dark side of the moon – that beautiful moon featuring in her name. Before risking her life on the people smugglers' dinghy she had never seen a ship or boat of any consequence. Hens' teeth would be less rare than boats in her homeland's dusty villages. The mention of Abdul brought a much more positive response from her – positively hateful.

"That... man... he calls himself Abdul," she hissed. "He is related to devil. A cousin at least and a danger to us." Danger and discomfort during her earlier journeys had fermented a colourful development in her vocabulary. For some reason, Abdul was the yeast who had accelerated fermentation.

Lloyd was slightly taken aback by her viperous attack. *"What dastardly deed had Abdul perpetrated to engender such hate?"* he thought. Tales of sexual abuse, varying from aggravated rape to casual leering, were not uncommon among the refugees but he was not aware of Abdul having such a reputation. He couldn't imagine that someone who was not subject to official arrest or unofficial revenge could have travelled with his victims for so long without being detected.

The atmosphere between refugee and rescuer had risen slightly in temperature if not complete trust during the short journeys to the police station and the harbour. That level of trust was to rise further with the production of documents to board the good ship Nissos Mykonos and the attention given by Lloyd to her safety. Aysil appeared to thaw out a little and even seemed prepared to take him into her confidence.

"That man... he is not one of us." That sounded reasonable enough. Abdul didn't appear to be an Alawite or even a Syrian. He was more likely to be Kurdish or from another sect within Turkey. Possibly even a dissenting Iraqi Sunni. Aysil expanded her accusation. "He is not... refugee at all. He is illegal traveller and... how you say... bad bastard. He tries to look like refugee and takes money from us if we want to get to Europe. "

She looked as if she was about to break down and sob. A friendly arm looped around her shoulders without attempting to press further. Any expression of comfort or drying of tears was unwanted and unspoken. Lloyd knew that he should just support her and let her continue if and when she was ready to do so. He didn't have to wait for long.

"We... I had to pay someone like him – all I had – to get on a rubber boat. We all thought we would die in the sea. And..." Here she really did break down and sob, "some of them... some of us did die. A little girl who had been talking to me a few minutes... fall into the sea and her mother or sister fell in too... trying to get her back." Lloyd remained silent but maintained the gentle hold on her shoulders, thinking of the tiny body on the beach.

"We all shout to the boat-man to stop and get them back into the boat but he refuses. He just says he had to go on until we reached Lesvos or we be taken back to Turkey or Syria. We never saw the little girl or her mother again." Aysil then answered Lloyd's next unasked question. "We reported all this to the people who help us on the beach here. They said they would deal with it. But... nothing... "

There was still a two-hour wait before the ferry would leave harbour and the police station was only ten minutes drive away. His hired car could be returned to the agreed point in town within a few minutes from there too. Lloyd suggested a short drive and Aysil readily agreed. "What else can I do?" she asked.

At the police station again, Lloyd made a quick enquiry into the report of the sea smuggling incident. After that there was nothing more that he could do either except to return the car to the hire company and return himself and his charge to the ferry.

But vague worries remained whenever he thought of the shadowy figure outside the Beirut hotel and Aysil's description of the people-smugglers – and Abdul.

Ch.11. Smuggler's arrest.

The fate of Abdul the people-smuggler – Abdul the Bastard like the one in Aysil's account of the refugees' nightmare journey – remained unknown to the two passengers in a warm cabin on board the Nissos Mykonos. It would not be revealed to Lloyd until well after they had parted company in Piraeus. It was the preserve of the British Embassy in Beirut, where the assistant commercial attaché awaited further reports from his supplicant reporter. He also had a 'no news is bad news' report of his own to pass to Lloyd concerning the missing yacht, steadily enhancing its reputation as a 'Marie Celeste.'

Arriving at the ferry terminal in Piraeus after an uneventful eight hours from Lesvos, Lloyd and the Syrian felt relatively comfortable. Comfortable physically in their warm cabin on board and as comfortable mentally as two strangers can be after only a few hours together.

Those few hours had reaped dividends: understanding between them and a mutual dislike of the combatants in the Arab civil wars. The bulk of their dislike was reserved for the thieves and robbers taking advantage of the severely disadvantaged. And of those plundering the refugees, the people-smugglers in general and Abdul in particular took prime place in their hatred.

With Abdul and his like many miles behind them, Aysil might have been completely assured of freedom from their unwanted attention. She might also have been free from any money or resources for her onward journey. For some reason beyond Lloyd's understanding, her only concern appeared to be the urgency of her travel timetable. If her ultimate target had been to get to Germany or Austria, Lloyd expected that she would have told him of friends or family living and possibly working there, but no mention had been made of that.

In fact, when asked about contacts in the European Union she had quietly shut down her information board. Quietly but completely. What had remained open was the disquiet amounting to fear of any sign of her former people-smuggling travel agent – Abdul-Nasir. Why she should imagine that Abdul would be bothered to continue his own journey as far as the Greek capital or its main port was a question that Lloyd could not answer or even ask.

Exchanges of personal confidences had been modest but not unpleasant during the ferry trip. Having attended an established Methodist chapel in South Wales, Lloyd had never really understood the differences between various sects of other religions. He had taken the opportunity to broaden his understanding with a gentle enquiry of Aysil's concern.

Trying to take her mind off the past months of terror, he had broached the subject of her home, her family and religion.

"What sort of town did you leave behind you when you left Syria?" Before she could answer, he added, "Did the rest of your family get away from there too? Or..." He stopped, before he might re-open a deep wound. If he had opened anything, it was not the information bank. Aysil's responses were more involved with shrugs and blank stares than meaningful descriptions. She ignored the request about her home town in Syria.

"My family... my family... was all dead within a week of the invasion." She didn't describe the invaders either.

"Probably ISIL," thought Lloyd. *"But could have been other Sunni insurgents fighting Assad's troops."* That led him to another tack in his cross-questioning.

"I never really understand who's fighting who over there." He waved a hand vaguely towards the East. "There seems to be people from all sorts of places and all sorts of sects claiming to be Muslims but each claiming to be the only true Muslim. What sort were the invaders?"

"Just invaders. It didn't really matter what sort of invader they were. They just... invaded – and killed."

"Are you still involved with religion? I mean, do you still believe in God, after what has happened to you and your family?"

"I believe in a God and that God is still great – Allahu Akbar, as we say. But what God is can vary in peoples' minds. As Alawites, we followed a branch of Shia Islam – the Twelver school – and revere Ali ibn Abi Talib. Don't ask me what the other Islamists follow. It may be the same or similar at least but, that doesn't stop them killing us.

"When a war starts between people who have lived in peace for years, men forget their old friends from another way of thinking and try to justify killing them with whatever version of religion they think will sound right. Any excuse will do for them and the Holy Books will usually supply one, or more than one.

"I don't expect you to understand all of our thinking. Although I do expect that you know of similar fights and wars between people who claim to be from the same religion but a different – a better sect."

Lloyd nodded ruefully. *"Never mind Islamsts,"* he thought. *"We have enough in-fighting between the chapels back home in Port Talbot. Not to mention Northern Ireland."*

His nod was met with an unexpected rise in temperature between them. For a very brief instant she turned her head towards him and he thought he saw a tiny glimmer of something in her eyes. It was just a glance conveying acceptance of their situation. Agreement of something suddenly existed between them as if not with anyone else in the world. An unspoken message of mutual understanding. Nothing remotely sexual. It was stronger. It was several leagues above that.

The rest of the voyage was spent trying to get some rest and possibly some sleep. Too soon for Lloyd's liking, the ferry came to a gentle bump against the Piraeus dock-side and mainland Greece. Grabbing what little luggage he had and the pitiful roll of Aysil's sleeping bag and personal possessions, the two emerged from their cabin and walked along slowly with the crowd of disembarking passengers.

Once back on terra firma, Aysil resumed a more determined gait towards the road beyond the docks and a pedestrian bridge taking visitors to the Athens Metro line station. She was now travelling much more hopefully than she had been in the Lebanon refugee camp or Lesvos island. Lloyd walked briskly beside her, hoping that she would stop and give some more insight to her route into the Balkans and on to Austria. Some address or a venue for them to meet again soon.

Little was said by either and nothing was offered as a future meeting place. Arriving at the Metro station, Lloyd tried to elicit a favourable message from her but received nothing in return. He bought two tickets to central Athens and they boarded the little train together in silence. Just once during the short journey she looked again at him as he tried to meet her eyes with an intensive stare. He had hoped to give her a warm hug or possibly a kiss but that was the only message apart from a curt "goodbye" and a parting limp handshake.

She had not even told him where she would go next or whether she had money or other means of travel. Just "goodbye" and the memory of that last glance. He supposed that it was meant to tell him all she was prepared to let him know. Anyway, she was gone now and he had to find somewhere to stay or another destination.

He took a taxi to the Holiday Inn near to Athens Airport. From there he would fly to London on the next day.

She took a walk to Larissis main-line train station where she would board the train to Thessaloniki. Once there she would board a bus to Pristina in Kosovo. Two more steps in her long walk.

Before she arrived at the train station, her path diverted to take her to another building. An unassuming building in which an older man listened intently to her brief account in Farsi. He handed her some documents and an envelope containing several euros and some US dollars. Only then would she continue to the station and the train to Thessaloniki.

Once checked in at the Holiday Inn, Lloyd telephoned to the British Embassy in Beirut. He left a message with a receptionist to tell Elphinstone that he was returning to his office in Lime Street and would phone again from there to exchange reports. He then refreshed, showered and booked a flight back to Heathrow. The morning flight saw him safely back to Terminal 5. Then on to Chiswick and home.

Once back in his own bed he slept soundly apart from recurring thoughts about his graceful fellow-traveller. He was as certain as he could be that there had been the makings of a strong personal link – an understanding at least – between them. He was also certain that he would like to renew the link and strengthen the bond, if he knew if or where he could find her again.

Riding on the morning train between Chiswick and Monument, and walking through Leadenhall Market to Lime Street, brought more thoughts. More nagging worries about Aysil and her perilous journeys through Asia Minor and the Balkans. Then he remembered her fear and hatred of Abdul-Nasir. Abdul the hanger-on in Bekaa refugee camp. Abdul the people-smuggler. Abdul the Bastard.

Quickening his step into the Lloyds' building and his work station inside the concrete and steel beehive, he settled down to make an initial report on the missing yacht and any possibility of recovery. That didn't take long to complete. However, he would not submit it until he had contacted Elphinstone again and heard what news his contacts had procured. He would then tell him about Aysil, and about Abdul.

As a rule, telephone lines between London and Beirut are available without problems but today would be one of those exceptions to prove the rule. After three attempts and two cups of coffee, he finally connected with the British Embassy's commercial office and asked to speak with the renowned

'Stelph.' "Stelph – or Jock – or Mister Elphinstone," as the haughty receptionist replied, was unavailable but might respond to another message. No point in arguing. He left a simple message: "Please phone Lloyd."

Shortly after mid-day in London and tea-time in Beirut, his office telephone rang and the two men exchanged their latest. First to speak was Cocky, now less than completely cocky due to his doubts and worries about Aysil's future.

He related her nightmare crossing from Turkey to Lesvos; his meeting her there; the reports to the Greek police of Abdul's people-smuggling escapades; the ferry trip from Mytilene to Piraeus and on to Athens. He then went into considerable and harrowing detail of the drowned mother and child from the rubber dinghy and Aysil's absolute hatred of Abdul, which he now shared.

All this brought only the merest of grunts and "mmm"s from the Embassy office phone. Having exhausted his dramatic tales of woe, Lloyd sat back and offered only the meekest of summaries.

"Well, that's about it from me at this stage. What do you think we should do about Abdul? There's probably dozens of bastards like him but I would like to see him strung up if I could. And," he added, "any more news about what you keep calling 'MY' yacht?"

The Beirut response was short and to the phlegmatic point.

"Abdul, as you call him, has, I understand, been arrested. He was released without charge.

"I'm afraid I don't have any good news about your Flying Dutchman, or Marie Celeste. The last report we had was to say that it was somewhere near the Bosporus heading towards the Black Sea and a port. Probably Odessa or Novorossiysk."

"Novo-what? Where the f... flippin' 'ell's that then?"

"Novorossiysk is a very interesting place. It is to me, anyway. It's on the beam end of a couple of oil pipelines, one from Kashagen and the other from Baku in Azerbijan. It is also

Russia's second string naval base in the Black Sea. The first being Sevastopol, which is strictly speaking in Ukraine.

Now, what the... uh... flippin' 'ell your yacht is doing or going to do in Novorossiysk is hard to say, particularly as it's not there yet as far as we know. But one possibility is, that it has something to do with the fact that a lot of arms supplies to Assad's forces and others are shipped out from there to Latakia and Tartus in Syria. Food for thought, eh?"

Lloyd was, as he put it, "gobsmacked." What indeed was the yacht, and whoever sailed with her, doing or going to do in – where was it? – Novorossiysk? He was silent for a few seconds and then returned to the subject of the people-smugglers.

"What about Abdul then? Can we get him some other way? Didn't he give the police any ideas on how to get at the bastards smuggling those poor wretches and drowning half of them?"

Elphinstone could offer scant comfort. "Sorry old chap." *That always irked Lloyd, who thought of himself as neither old nor young* "the only piece of information that they gave me was that the main – or one of the main – smuggling gangsters is also from the Black Sea region. He gave them the same sort of password or clue that our Palestinian kidnapper friend gave to the Maronite Phalange fighters when they offered the glass jar of wriggly things to him.

"But", he added, "I think you said that you had already tried to crack that password or map reference or whatever it was, and drew a blank. I also tried to find out if there's any connection there with our rescued hostage or his dad, in case the kidnap was staged to get your insurance money, or just to get rid of his silly son."

"Well," said Lloyd, "if he did, he nearly succeeded. Nearly got rid of me too!" The two men chuckled although Lloyd gave an inward shiver to add to the merriment. He thought back to the glass jar and 'the wriggly things,' and shivered again.

Somewhere, he recalled, he had written down that map reference or password on a scrap of paper.

Ch. 12. The Asia miner defence.

Geneva's cobbled back streets always reminded Andrew Tulloch of his first appointment in the commodities trading business. This visit to his Swiss lawyers' office in the old city in the corner of Lac Leman was more relaxing although the reason for his journey from Zurich was still urgent.

Mr Quickstick's law firm had told him about another approach from the agents of the RKM Group, the thwarted bidder for Tulloch's company. The latest threat was aimed, not at his own business, but at a mining company based in Kazakhstan. They must have been as concerned as he had been in that situation.

On his last visit to London, Andrew's girlfriend Mary and her friend Helen had offered to look for information about the encircling sharks. He telephoned Mary from Zurich to ask if they had managed to discover anything. Being sensitive to her boyfriend's situation, she tried to adopt a very light-hearted tone.

"Oh hello, Andrew. Are you OK? I've been thinking of you every time I read about the fall in metals and oil prices and... "

"I hope you've been thinking of me more often than that, haven't you?"

That was replied by a short and almost silent giggle from which he could imaging a shy smile licking her face.

"Of course I have, you silly. But I am a bit worried about you... in case you're worrying too much."

He was pleased to hear and feel her affection but not hearing any firm news of the stalker was disappointing. An uncontrolled frown tightened his mouth as he tried to deny his concerns.

"Don't worry about me worrying. I just wanted to hear how you are and how you're getting on with the little enquiry I mentioned to you and Helen last month. You know. I asked if anyone knew anything about whoever the chairman of that company is. I don't know his name. I call him Ivan the Terrible – Ivan the Terrorist more likely. They're having a pop at another business now. Nigel Quickstick told me a few days ago."

It was Mary's turn to admit concern without letting her boyfriend feel her own disappointment.

"Yes of course I know what you mean. Anyway, I know that Helen has tried to look into it but I don't think she's had any more luck than I have. All we know so far about the company is what you already know – that it is registered in Ukraine. As far as we know the directors might be Russian or Ukrainian.

"I'll have another word with Helen this evening – she's just back from another trip to The Lebanon – I'll see what she knows about him. We're having a spot of dinner at her place – girls only – don't worry."

"Worried about me worrying again," thought Tulloch. *"That'll make me worry more, if anything."* He said his fond farewells as sincerely as he could and promised to phone again tomorrow or the next day. She said that she believed him and added a final "Don't worry too much." Just to ensure that he did, at least until he kept his promise to phone her again.

He was worried though. Perhaps it was just fear of the unknown. That was enough to make anyone worry if they knew what they didn't know. All that they had discovered up to that time, had been that the bid had come from a group of companies engaged in metals and oil trading. Most of those companies in the group had been purchased in the last two years to become subsidiaries of the stalker.

After he had repulsed the original takeover bid by RKM Group, Andrew realised that he had to shore up his company's defences urgently. He had examined two possibilities.

The first was to get a major financial institution, such as a Sovereign wealth fund, to invest a large stake in his own company and provide a blocking vote against any aggressor.

As a second line of defence, he might find a partner to set up a joint venture that could increase both partners' sales and protect each other against unwanted takeovers. A successful partnership would also offer greater attraction to bona fide investors.

He was all in favour of prosperity but wary of the words of Prospero in The Tempest: *"we are such stuff as dreams are made on "*, warning him against over-optimism. His dreams might lead to disappointment but without dreaming he would drown in pessimism. He would prefer to dream on. And... he had a possible partner in mind.

More Shakespearean lines ran through his head: "... *a tide in the affairs of men which taken at the flood leads on to fortune..."* That sounded much more promising than missing the boat or sinking *"... in shallows and in miseries."* His thoughts returned to reality and the aptly named Nigel Quickstick. *"Quick's the word and sharp's the action."*

"Not the time to vacillate," He needn't have worried about that. The short drive from Zurich to Geneva and to Nigel Quickstick's office was to discuss such a venture with a young Bulgarian – the head of the mining company now under attack in Kazakhstan. Vacillation did not describe the Bulgarian either. He was as impatient to proceed with the meeting as Tulloch was.

Any image of a Bulgarian businessman that lurked in Andrew Tulloch's head was soon erased when he met Vasil Antonov. The Bulgarian might easily have been mistaken for an Australian or Canadian executive who bought his suits in Savile Row or the better tailoring establishments in Hong Kong. Antonov's command of the English language was possibly better than many inhabitants of the English speaking nations, despite a subtle but distinct Eastern European accent overlaid with the mid-Atlantic twang of a Harvard Business School graduate.

The Bulgarian's objective in joining forces with Tulloch was to get a larger share of the Western European markets for his Kazakhstan company. With Tulloch's help it could result in selling more of the Kazakhstan miner's production to Tulloch's customers without increasing his own overheads.

The two men were of a similar age and had similar personal likes and dislikes. Most of all, they each had a strong liking for the rewards of their success and a strong dislike of threats against their livelihood. It only took a brief discussion to establish the compatibility of the two men and their businesses. It took an even briefer exchange of views concerning fast cars, football, beer and women – with a passing reference to finance and mining – before complete agreement would seem to be only a formality.

Despite the apparent fusion of minds concerning the finer points of life in the male domain and their businesses no mention of hard facts had been raised. It could take some time to put, as they frequently repeated, 'some meat on the bone'. And time was not on either man's side.

Tulloch and his colleagues had not wasted anytime trying to deny their company's exposure to takeover by RKM. The initial approach and meagre offer, which they had refused, was fairly common knowledge and brief details had been published in business media for all to see.

The two executives also agreed to mount a personal attack on their nemesis, RKM's chairman. Without identifying him this would be difficult. But if and when they could do so and discover any damaging personal information it would be reported in several channels of business media after careful leaks to them.

Combining such a personal attack at the same time as announcing agreement of a joint venture with Antonov's company should ensure defeat of the unwanted aggressor. The RKM Group would be tarnished by derogatory opinions of their chairman in the selected media. Unfortunately, neither Tulloch nor his assistants knew anything about him. Defamation of character required a character to defame and they didn't have one.

Each of the prospective partners then proposed to investigate and report to each other with suggestions of anything short of libel to detract from the aggressor's reputation. From the scant information in the public domain, his reputation might be similar to those of several villainous characters from past takeovers, including Tulloch's former boss, the late Patric Klevic.

Tulloch had always harboured doubts about the circumstances of Klevic's reported death. Despite getting the full story of the death and hasty burial of the powerful tycoon, they had only the words of Klevic's cousin and former partner to rely upon.

In terms of probability, a takeover bid by a dead fraudster was approximately zero. However, there were certain features of the manner and method of the aggressive approaches by RKM which made Tulloch frown and occasionally shudder.

The ghost of Patrick Klevic was walking over his grave.

Ch. 13. Two assassins in search of a character.

When Antonov returned to Geneva airport to catch his flight to Astana and to his villa on the outskirts of town, Tulloch remained in Quickstick's office for an hour to telephone Mary Deans again. She answered quickly when she saw the caller code on the little display screen in her handset.

"Hello. I wasn't expecting another call so soon. Not this year anyway." He sensed a silent laugh at the other end of the line. Something between a pleasant surprise and a little alarm bell had sounded in her mind. "Is something wrong? Or should I be flattered at this extra attention?"

He didn't return the laugh or even feel obliged to be on the same wavelength as she seemed to be. His mind was still buzzing with concerns of his meeting with Quickstick and Antonov.

"No. Nothing wrong. I just wanted to ask if you had talked to Helen yet."

"What do you mean? I told you that I would see her this evening, not at lunch-time."

"Oh! Yes, of course. I forgot the time difference as well as what you said about when you'd see her. If it's any consolation, I haven't had any lunch either and I won't have time for any before I get back to Zurich. I'll phone you again tomorrow if that's all right."

"Of course it's all right. Are you sure there's nothing wrong?"

"No. Just not concentrating. I had a good meeting with a very interesting bloke this morn... afternoon. His name's Antonov. Apart from getting on very well with him, I asked him if he could find anything about the guy from RKM I called Ivan the Terrorist – I must stop calling him that – from his contacts in Kazakhstan."

"Well, that sounds good. Now perhaps we might be getting somewhere."

"Yes but, I still would like you to push Helen to try finding out what she can."

"I'm doing that. Or at least I'm going to. THIS EVENING. Remember?"

"Yes – uh – that's what I meant. Must go now. It's getting dark here and I'm getting hungry. Bye-ee. Love you."

"Thank you. Glad you remembered that at least. Love you too. Bye now... Bye."

He replaced the telephone and stood still for a few seconds. Thinking about Antonov and 'Ivan.' The old questions 'who and what and where and when?' turned around in his mind. He then turned around as well, reaching for his coat and the car keys in its pocket.

After a brief word of thanks to his host, he left Quickstick's office and drove back to Zurich. An incident-free drive to his flat was followed by a welcoming hot dinner from the apartment block's service kitchen and the remains of a bottle of Chateauneuf du Pape. The food and drink seemed to settle his mind as well as the digestive juices rumbling around in his stomach in rhythm with the questions revolving in his head.

Another question then entered the mastermind. Had the discussions with his distant girlfriend turned into what he imagined to sound like the conversation of an old married couple? The thought didn't strike him as horrific but, perhaps he should be thinking of setting the record straight with Mary. Just in case she was getting ideas. The wrong ideas.

The thought of setting the record straight seemed to clear his own mind and allow it to think more clearly about the immediate and more urgent task ahead. He walked straight to the refrigerator and opened a large bottle of Grolsch lager.

For the next two weeks his mind was ninety-nine percent occupied with urgent business matters. Whether the affairs discussed with Antonov or those with Mary would materialise one way or the other, there was a business to run. Work to do and money to earn. The steady erosion of sales prices had to be balanced with reductions in costs if the business was not to flounder.

The remaining one percent of his time was shared between thoughts of Mary and of what she or Antonov could discover about his nemesis. Mary had indeed talked to Helen but, as Helen was unable to discover anything yet, their talking was not likely to interest him. Talking about clothes, cosmetics and men – and about men, cosmetics and clothes. It was not on his wish-list.

Mary agreed with Helen – at least she assumed that she had agreed – that she should set the record straight with Andrew, in case he had the wrong idea about their relationship. *"That last conversation – it sounded like that of an old married couple,"* she told herself. Perhaps she should set the record straight with him. Just in case he was getting ideas. The wrong ideas.

"Sorry... what were you saying?" she asked a slightly confused Helen. "I was miles away. Wondering about Andrew's takeover problems." The mention of Andrew made Helen regain her composure. She remembered that she had forgotten to pass on a small tit-bit of news.

"I forgot to mention. I'll be visiting the International Red Cross for a few days next week. I wondered if you'd like to come with me." It was Mary's turn to be confused.

"Well... thanks very much. But, I'm not sure that I need first aid yet."

"Oh. I meant to see Andrew, while we're there."

"Why? Does Andrew need first aid? He didn't say so when he phoned me at the weekend. Mind you, he might need it if he forgets to call me this evening." Helen smiled, not so much at the joke but, realising that she hadn't mentioned the venue. *"I thought everyone knew that the Red Cross headquarters is in Geneva"* she mused.

"No, silly. We'll be seeing them in Geneva and Andrew can drive over from Zurich. I know it's not next door to him but it's near enough for us to spend a day or two... " *she stopped before she said 'the night'* "together. What do you think? A good idea, isn't it?"

"Yes, it is a good idea," thought Mary. *"Then I can set the record straight. I'd better make sure I let him down gently."*

"I'm not sure. Let me check my diary and get back to you tomorrow." She knew there was nothing in her diary apart from a half-hour visit to her hairdresser and a note to call Tulloch if he forgot to phone her that evening, again. "Probably all right but I'd better check."

"In the meantime," continued Helen, "I must tell you about a real stunner that I met in Beirut, when I was there and had dinner with Andrew's pal, that what's-his-name Lloyd. You know, the chap he used to work with."

"Oh, Cocky." They both smirked. "Yes. Andrew said that he had met you again when you were in The Lebanon. I thought he was chasing you a little bit. Wasn't he?"

"Well... I suppose he was, and I wouldn't say that was entirely unwelcome. But the chap he introduced to me there was really... impressive, I must say. Works for the Embassy out there. Could even be of help to me with our work there... sometime." Helen's eyes dropped to the table legs and she hoped that she hadn't given the impression that she was blushing – again.

There was a brief and almost embarrassing silence, broken when Helen added quickly, "by the time we meet him in Geneva, I might have some background to that nasty piece of work that he asked me to try to check on."

"Meet who? This man you met from the Beirut Embassy?"

"No. You know what I mean. When we meet up with Andrew in Geneva."

"Oh... Right... With you." They both giggled again.

In Kazakhstan, Vasil Antonov had a similar priority to that driving Tulloch's schedule. His business was constantly trying to balance falling sales revenue with 'not-falling' costs. He was already sketching the outline of a deal for a joint venture with Tulloch's company. After jotting down a few ideas about products from his company and customers from Tulloch's, he started to think about possible problems.

Antonov instructed his marketing department to research any new competitors and the products which they would try to sell to the extra customers he hoped to get. After two days of market research and internet screening, a report was duly presented.

Most of the potential competition, the report read, would come from the international mining giants such as Rio Tinto and BHP and the former state-owned mining operations in Russia. There was one relatively new entry in the list which shouted its name to him however. On the cover of a shiny catalogue and company brochure was a photo of a huge mountain of copper ore with what appeared to be tiny toy earth-moving vehicles and the name in English of 'RKM Group.'

Looking into the brochure, with more uninteresting pictures of heaps of earth and equipment, he saw a list of the holding company's officers. The names of the chairman and operations directors were there for all to see. The chairman's name appeared as Mr Rustem Kazakov.

Vasil Antonov smiled to himself. 'Rustem Kazakov' was the name of a famous Olympic wrestler from the Crimea. It must be an adopted name for someone who wished to remain as anonymous as possible. This must be the infamous 'Ivan' – perhaps not Ivan the Terrible but – not Ivan the Soft and Gentle either.

Appropriately, he recalled that Rustem Kazakov had been a member of one of the persecuted ethnic minorities in Stalin's USSR. He was a Crimean Tartar. That might have been an influencing factor in the selection of a new name for the chairman of RKM Group. Many of the Tartars ousted from the Crimea before the war had filtered back after Stalin's demise.

Many more had remained in Ukraine and Siberia but this one had all the signs of a Crimean Russian.

One of the staff in Antonov's marketing department was also Russian, although not from the Crimea. His name was Georgi Petrov and he had no time for the latest wave of nationalism in Russia, which he was certain had been generated by Vladimir Putin and his ex-KGB colleagues to restore a new Soviet Union.

With friends in Georgia and in the Ukraine, Georgi was very wary of territorial claims and military advances by those claiming to act in Mother Russia's name. It all reminded him of the pre-war claims of German speaking Poles and Czechs in Danzig and the Sudetenland. When his boss Mr Antonov asked him to investigate Rustem Kazakov he was only too pleased to do so.

To begin his search, the anti-soviet Russian – well versed in exploring marketing opportunities – returned to the brochures that extolled the virtues of the RKM Group. They didn't offer much information about the Crimean Tartar with the Olympic wrestler's name but they did give an insight into the construction and history of his group of companies.

Georgi Petrov made a mental note to dig deeper into the chairman's personal history, with some personal phone and e-mail contacts to a former colleague in his old home outside Moscow. They had both been educated at the university there and had taken their first management posts in the mining industry in Norilsk, far up in the Siberian Arctic.

Norilsk was now labelled 'the world's most polluted city' but that had not been the only reason for Georgi Petrov's departure and his new appointment in Kazakhstan. The freezing weather had made Moscow feel like a balmy Riviera by comparison. Combined with the polluted location and grim history of the infamous Gulag, where tens of thousands of political prisoners died in appalling conditions, that was bad enough. The final deciding factor was another and more telling danger.

The frequency of industrial accidents had a life-threatening history similar to the Gulag prison and the city's level of pollution. Norilsk-Talknakh continues to be a dangerous mine to work in: according to the mining company, there were two point four accidents per thousand workers in 2005 and he didn't want to represent even part of the point four during his contract period.

He had not been alone in deciding to opt for a warmer and safer life. Two of his former university graduates had made similar decisions and had returned to Moscow. One of those had ironically been killed in a street accident near to Gorky Park but the other still lived and worked near to his alma mater. It was to him that Georgi Petrov now turned for information.

His old friend from university and the Norilsk-Talknakh mine was Dmitri Levin and he was very pleased to hear from him. Dmitri shared Petrov's dislike of the growth of what seemed to be totalitarian control of the government in Moscow. Several political opponents of the ruling parties had suffered arrest without trial – some without release due to death in custody. What might be labelled as a 'Soviet Spring' appeared now to be showing red shoots rather than green ones.

Dmitri had another reason for nursing a deep resentment at the threat of a new Stalinist regime; his father had been raised as a child in a state orphanage at a time when the numbers of orphans were growing faster than could be accounted for under normal circumstances. His grandparents had been arrested shortly before Stalin – former Georgian bank robber Joseph Jughashvili – had died. They had also spent time – enforced time – in Norilsk and were just two of the sixteen thousand who died there from hunger and maltreatment.

Despite the awful fate of his grandparents and the fear of a return to the protocol that led to it Dmitri Levin retained a supreme optimism for the future in general and his own in particular. He often recounted his father's joke concerning the time when the great Russian composer, Sergei Prokofiev, and the tyrannical Soviet leader had died almost simultaneously.

"Where else but in Russia could Peter and the Wolf die together?"

His careful and methodical work as a clerk in the Red Army intelligence service had brought promotion and a place at Moscow University, where he had met and befriended Georgi Petrov. After a greeting that was several degrees warmer than Norilsk could ever manage, even in a hot summer, Petrov's former colleague asked politely about personal health and the reason for the call.

Although he had a good job in a state-owned business in Moscow, Dmitri secretly envied his friend Georgi's apparent position of industrial power and wealth. Had he been aware of the falling sales and increasing costs in Kazakhstan then his envy might well have turned to relief in his own safe position. He had obtained that post partly due to his national service record in the Red Army and a good degree from university, but mainly due to his diligence and a remarkable memory.

"Hi, Georgi! Great to hear from you. How are things in Astana?"

"Oh, great, Dmitri. Although I would love to be back in Moscow and the University students' bar. Hard to find a good cafe here. The work's good though."

"Still going well, is it? The mine's doing well? I sometimes wonder if I shouldn't have applied for a job there too."

"Yes, yes. Well enough. It can always do a bit better, as we all know. But, under the circumstances it's doing very well. I'll tell you why I phoned you though, apart from catching up with things back home, I wondered if you could find out something about a guy who appears to be a big wheel in our industry but no-body here knows him."

"Oh. One of those, is he? The world-famous oligarth that nobody's heard of. There are plenty of those about, I'm sure. What's his name? Or probably his new name?" A snigger snorted down the telephone line.

"Well, don't laugh but, he's the boss of the RKM group and goes under the name of Rustem Kazakov."

"Who? The wrestler? I thought he died years ago."

"So did I but, either he's come back to life or this joker has taken his name to impress people, particularly if he comes from the Crimea. I suspect that he might be a Crimean Tartar who's spent some years in Ukraine, or Siberia.

"You used to work in army intelligence. If he served with the Red Army then perhaps you might have come across him at some time. What chances d'you think?"

"Army service? On whose side? No, not when I was there and unlikely that I'll find any trace of him but, I'll certainly try. Now, what are the chances of a nice cushy job for me in Astana?"

"A nice job? Probably at some time, maybe not right now. But cushy? No chance. We have to work our balls off here you know!"

The two friends laughed. They both understood the employment situation would be problematic unless the mining economy came out from the doldrums soon but there was always hope for the future. A little favour here and there could always move hope towards fulfilment.

In order to move it a little faster, Dmitri Levin was as good as his word. He knew that the Red Army records would not be open for his inspection but he knew a man who could do part of that for him. One more telephone call to his old army chum who had become a regular officer in the intelligence service and within a few days Dmitri Levin was in possession of a brief resume – the mysterious Rustem Kazakov. He spoke to Petrov later that day with the news.

"Hello, Georgi. I have a little bit of information about your Tartar from Crimea. His name really is Kazakov but, it's Bekir Kazakov, not Rustem. He obviously called himself that just to impress people. I was a bit lucky with the search. He has an army record from our wars in Chechnya. I believe that he even has a tattoo like the veterans of campaigns there. I bet he doesn't show it now though. It would scare the shit out of any businessman!

"That's all I can tell you now, Georgi but let me know if I can help further. And... let me know if you need a good man in your company in Astana." He laughed although they both knew that he was quite serious. A little help – a little hope.

"That's great, Dmitri. I'm sure my boss will be very impressed and he won't be allowed to forget where the information came from – be sure of that! Thanks again, my old friend. Poka!"

"Do svidaniya, Georgi! Good luck with your report."

Back in the Kazakhstan mining company's office, Vasil Antonov and Georgi Petrov pondered over the report of the strange chairman of the hostile RKM Group. Antonov had discovered some more details of that company. More than one investment bank had reported the rapid growth of the group.

That appeared to have been achieved by a succession of company acquisitions although none to date had been as large as the Kazak miner now under attack. And none as big as the combined Swiss-Kazak partnership proposed by Tulloch.

The recurring pattern of RKM's growth was of an aggressive takeover bid offering a small amount of cash and the issue of high valued shares. Most of the cash appeared to have been borrowed from unspecified sources and repaid from money taken from the reserves of the takeover victim.

"Lebensraum – Generalplan Ost," observed Antonov, wryly. "Hitler developed it into an art form. Take one country to feed the other then take another to feed them both. I didn't know it was still practised in business. That used to be called 'asset-stripping' – I suppose it still is." After a few hours working on more routine problems, he tried to contact his prospective new business partner. On the third attempt, he spoke to Tulloch, still at his desk in Zurich.

"Hello, Mister Tulloch – Andrew – it's Vasil Antonov. I have some news on your mystery man and his group of companies. His real name is Bekir Kazakov and he is an ex-

Red Army soldier who once served with their special forces. That's like your SAS, but in Chechnya.

He's a real life Tartar – yes, ha, ha – but not so very funny. We think he's one of those displaced Tartars who returned from Ukraine to the Crimea as a Russian. His modus operandi seems to be very much like Hitler's plan to take over the world. A sort of Lebensraum of companies, milking them of cash as he goes.

"What I haven't worked out is where he gets the initial cash to sweeten his takeover deals. Probably borrowed from Russian oligarths but they would want a pay-back to back him. Perhaps tens of millions of dollars or so in your case. Don't ask me how he raises that when he's already spent all of the cash he has just taken from his new victims." They both laughed but like Levin and Petrov they both knew how serious the matter was.

Antonov had one more tasty morsel. "He seems to be like all the other 'noveau riche.' He likes anything that shows off his loot. Serious displayer of serious 'bling' – gold watches and large expensive yachts, for instance. He has one – a yacht, not a watch – which he pretends to sail around the Med and the Black Sea. That must be worth a few millions at least."

Tulloch was stunned at the speed of Antonov's reply and his shrewd analysis of the aggressor.

"Yes, quite a few million I expect. I'll have to ask my old pal who works in the insurance industry. He'll know all about that."

True to his word, Tulloch told 'old pal' Cocky Lloyd, and Lloyd certainly did know 'all about that.'

Ch. 14. The Missing Link.

Lloyd was more than happy to make enquiries of the Crimean Tartar's company yacht. It sounded like one of several very expensive floating palaces which were insured with the syndicate who employed him. They were usually insured for over forty-five million dollars although costing less than thirty million. Yes, Cocky Lloyd knew 'all about that' all right. It could even be the missing yacht that he had been trying to trace.

He asked Tulloch for more details and Tulloch asked Antonov, who asked Petrov who, asked Levin. When the details came back along the information chain they ended on Lloyd's desk. They were more than similar to those in his 'missing vessels' file.

Similarity was not concrete proof. There were plenty of luxury motor yachts, the sea-going mixtures of cruise ship, penthouse and private casino, plying their way around the Mediterranean and adjacent seaways. There were plenty of those with Russian registered owners and plenty of owners with questionable sources of income and even more questionable personal histories.

Cocky didn't want to waste time trying to answer questions of income sources or personal histories. Not at this stage. His only immediate question concerned the precise identity of the vessel and its owner. If the identities matched those of the subject of his insurance claim then he was, as he put it, 'in business' and could continue his investigations as far as he wished.

After an hour of e-mails and phone calls to colleagues in Lloyd's of London, he had all of the files and details that he needed. The vessel that had been subject to a multi-million dollar claim for theft or shipwreck and possible piracy, with personal injury or death, was that leased to the RKM Group. The insurance claim or claims, amounting in total to nearly fifty million dollars, had been lodged by an executive of that company.

By itself, the value of the claim was not likely to trouble the underwriters unduly. It was insured on one of many policies written by them and largely re-insured with the huge re-insurance groups such as Munich-Re and Swiss-Re. The prospect of a false claim and fraud was of much more concern, not only to avoid the loss of profit but to alert the entire marine insurance market and international police forces.

As an investigator and former detective the prospect of unravelling an attempted fraud was doubly interesting. With the added interest provided by Elphinstone in The Lebanon he was delighted at this latest development. Only the fear of it being the product of a false trail disturbed his thoughts. It would not be the first time that a passing resemblance had turned investigation into a fool's errand.

More checks were made. The vessel, the owners, the dates and times of the yacht's last recorded sighting and most importantly, the names and location of the ship's registered home country and its crew. A quick reference to the official Lloyd's Register of Shipping confirmed that the missing yacht was registered in Cambodia. Although it seemed strange for a luxury yacht belonging to a large company in Eastern Europe to be registered in such a poor country in the Far East, he knew 'all about that' too.

Cambodia supplied the registration of over five hundred ships of various sizes, under a 'flag of convenience.' Of those registrations, more than half applied to vessels owned in China, Russia, Turkey and Syria. The Cambodian flag was especially convenient for owners of ships passing in the night or day through the sea-lanes linking the last three of those countries.

The pieces of the puzzle were beginning to stick together. They formed a picture which might be of interest to someone monitoring the movements of people and carriers in that part of the world. It was time to discuss progress with Jock

Elphinstone. Their verbal pact had been to barter news of the strange refugee Aysil and the objectionable people smuggler Abdul-Nasir, in exchange for similar information of the missing yacht.

As usual, Cocky Lloyd's attempt to reach the Assistant commercial attaché in Beirut by telephone brought only a recorded message from the attaché's assistant to apologise for her master's voice being absent for the day. In a dreary repetition Lloyd left his own message with his phone number and a time when he could be contacted on the following morning on a secure line.

The prospect of a long game of 'telephone tennis' loomed. To curtail that to less than one full set, 'cockylloyd@btinternet.com' then transmitted an urgent e-mail to request a return telephone call at a precise date and time when he would ensure being near his office phone. No further detail was added. At the appointed hour and minute, the phone on Lloyd's office desk top announced the return call as requested.

He reached out quickly to snatch the handset from its cradle but only succeeded in knocking the whole apparatus from his desk's mock leather surface into his waste-paper basket. A slightly worried voice crackled from the discarded letters and envelopes, calling for human contact.

"Hello. Hello - anyone there? Hello... oh, is Mister Lloyd there? Is that you Cocky? I thought I heard a shot. You're not under fire again, are you?" This was followed by a quiet chuckle and the assured Elphinstone tone. "Right, Cocky. Is it OK to talk now?" On receiving confirmation and an apology for the 'technical trouble' with the phone, he continued. "I believe you might have some news for me, or am I jumping the gun?"

"No, Jock. You're not jumping anything. And that noise wasn't a gun. Just my phone getting a bit jumpy. I thought I'd just ask you for the SP on what else I can do to track my reconnaissance targets and... and I have some interesting –

interesting to me anyway – information on the missing yacht. I hope that it'll tie up with yours and you can tell me what you want to know next about Aysil... and Abdul, of course. Not that I've found out much on them so far."

"All right. It's a bit disappointing that you haven't any more news of the refugee but I'm not completely surprised. She's probably in a huge queue at the border of Montenegro or Hungary by now. We'll catch up with her some time ... maybe. And Abdul too, I hope. Now, what did you want to tell me about your yacht?"

Lloyd thought about the significance of his findings, both from Andrew Tulloch in Zurich and from the Lloyd's Register of Shipping and his insurance claim files. *"What could a luxury yacht have to do with a foreign company's takeover bid"* and *"what possible motive would a Ukrainian company's chairman have to make a false claim?"* Before relating the information to Elphinstone he considered the common factors that might link Tulloch's predicament with the Crimean's claim.

"Well... it's possible that the so-called missing yacht may be safe and sound somewhere – and I'm hoping that you have some idea of where – and it also appears that the owner of the yacht is connected to a suspicious sounding takeover deal that's causing a lot of grief to someone I know. That's how I got to know about it.

"Under normal circumstances I'd say that my friend's story and my own findings were just coincidence. But I don't really believe in coincidence when it concerns things like this. The only common link that I can see between the owner making a false claim and the company trying to buy out my chum is the obvious one – money. But I would have thought that someone offering to buy out a big company would have plenty of that. Millions or billions. Wouldn't you?"

Elphinstone had not attempted to comment or interrupt with questions while Cocky was speaking. He waited for a few moments in silence until he was sure that Lloyd had finished his story.

"It depends on several possible factors. The claim may be quite genuine. The yacht might have been stolen just at the time when the owners were making their bid. It might be in the hands of pirates who are trying to squeeze lots of cash from the owners just at the time when they need it the most. The news of that wouldn't help their takeover bid.

"On the other hand it might be a scam in order to shore up their own bank account. They might not have as much money as they want the target company to believe – or their own bankers for that matter.

"I'm not an expert in company finances. You - or your colleagues in the City, you probably know more about that than I do. At least I hope you do." He actually emitted a soft chuckle at his admitted ignorance, which was not as deep as he had suggested.

In the Lime Street building, the loudest sound heard by Lloyd was that of his mind ticking over. Yes, it was all down to money – or the want of it. That brought back another quotation from Doctor Johnson, '... the root of all evil.' He remembered the other part of Andrew Tulloch's discovery.

"Oh, I nearly forgot. The chairman of the company who owns the yacht is a real-life Tartar. One of those exile families who came back to the Crimea from Ukraine after Stalin died. He's apparently an ex-serviceman from the Red Army and now claims to be a fully-fledged Russian. I don't know if you've ever heard of him. His adopted name is Rustem Kazakov but his first name is really Bekir – Bekir Kazakov. Doesn't mean anything to me though."

The voice from the British Embassy in Beirut remained quiet and pensive. However, Elphinstone was also hearing a loud ticking in his brain. Rather than blurting out his immediate reaction to the latest information, he held his thoughts in check.

97

"That's very interesting actually. Listen Cocky, I need to check up on a few things and call you back. Will you be in your office this afternoon – say three p.m. your time – that's still GMT isn't it?"

"Yes. That's right. GMT. I'll be here then and... well... look forward to hearing from you then. Bye for now. Uh... don't forget about where that yacht's got to."

"Cheerio, Cocky. Talk later." With that, the Embassy phone was silent. Lloyd's mind was still ticking though. He could see that money was the common 'root of all evil' in the big insurance claim for the yacht and its owner's finances. But what could a Russian takeover of a Swiss or Kazak company have to do with the British Embassy in The Lebanon?

Ch.15. Mind-numbing numbers.

Sitting in what passed for his office on one of the extended balcony floors within the Lloyd's of London building, Cocky tried to pass the time looking at more mundane matters gathering dust on his desk. There were several memos and routine publications with details of developments and recent cases.

None of these bore any resemblance to the confusing circumstances surrounding his searches for marine luxury and refugee poverty but they provided his brain with a suitable distraction. By focussing on matters that had no bearing on his current case, he was able to relax for a few minutes and as so often happened, his brain rewarded him for the break in concentration.

So often he had seen a tiny block enter his memory path and vanish as soon as he was concentrating on unrelated matters. With a clear path, the vital item locked in his memory cells suddenly and smoothly slipped into the desired slot. Often, watching quiz programmes on television, he had witnessed a similar situation. A simple answer sticking in the head of the contestant 'on the tip of the tongue' only to un-stick as soon as the next question was addressed.

Answers to his annoying questions slipped from the tip of his tongue and into his brain. *"What"* he had asked himself, *"is an Assistant Commercial Attaché doing in Beirut trying to track a refugee in Europe and a people-smuggler in the Aegean? And how and why is he trying to get news of a missing yacht?"*

Answers flowed freely. Elphinstone's rank and station in the Foreign Office was only a euphemism for what could be described as anything between a spy and an International Nosey Parker. He probably had gallons of information flowing into and through his Embassy office. Little pieces of the diplomatic and military jigsaw puzzle that a man of his professional intelligence could develop into a feasible picture.

Having arrived at the obvious 'what?' Lloyd then returned to the 'why?' piece of his puzzle. That was much more difficult to place. Perhaps the yacht has something to do with the people-smuggling business. But no. Refugees and asylum seekers travelled in miserable discomfort and danger. Not in the lap of luxury. Some person or persons were using the yacht for much more lucrative logistics.

Another question: If the yacht was so important, then why had it been removed and claimed as an insured loss?

Another answer: Perhaps the vessel was past its usefulness as marine transport and the owner now tried to convert it into liquid cash.

That would bring it back into the domain of Andrew Tulloch and his business nemesis. If the man he called, 'Ivan the terrorist' was as unscrupulous as suggested then he would be quite happy stealing the boat from his own company, claiming the insurance value and then, probably selling the boat to an unsuspecting buyer. The millions of dollars received from the insurance underwriters would be almost doubled.

On the corner of his desk, Lloyd kept a small electronic calculator. It served him well when he didn't have the time or inclination to use the computer system. With that in the palm of his hand, he totted up the potential plunder from such as a series of scams.

Adding the insured value of the yacht of about fifty million dollars to a 'fire-sale' value of thirty million less a 'guesstimate' cost of the operation at, say seven million dollars, then seventy-three million dollars of fraud proceeds might be available. Another thought slid quietly into the active grey cells. He put the calculator down and reached for the telephone again.

Andrew Tulloch was not in his office as he was visiting his prospective joint venture partners in Kazakhstan. Not to be dissuaded, Lloyd then made a local call to the office of Andrew's particular friend. Mary Deans was in her own office and available for anything involving Tulloch. Lloyd warmed to the friendly answering tone and came straight to the point.

"Hello, Mary. Yes, I'm fine but I can't find Andrew at his office. Is it all right if I ask you for some information about his... uh... business problem – you know what I'm talking about?"

"Yes, of course Cocky. At least I think I do. It's about that worrying takeover bid, is it?"

"That's it. Got it in one. Now, I know you might not be able to let me have details of the bid but, roughly how much did they announce that they would pay IN CASH, that's on top of the share swaps?"

While he was listening to Mary, Lloyd had picked up his little calculator again. Only the figures in Swiss francs had entered the machine. So far, he had a net figure of cash required by the bidding company totalling fifty to sixty million Swiss francs, slightly more in US dollars.

He thanked Mary and asked her to pass his best wishes to Andrew when she spoke to him - which would almost certainly be before he would. He put the telephone down and pondered on the similarity of the Russian's cash requirement in Swiss Francs and the possible US Dollar haul of the yacht pirates.

The phone rang again. It was Jock Elphinstone. Exactly on time. He had some more news. Some more mystery mixed with more pieces of the puzzle.

"Hello, Cocky. Still all right to talk? Good. As I told you earlier, your yacht's been seen in the Bosphorus, heading towards the Black Sea. Now we think it's arrived in the Crimea, in harbour in Sevastopol. Possibly going on to another Russian port after that. There seems to be a skeleton crew aboard with one passenger. Possibly the owner. Might even be your Russian Tartar.

"Whoever he is, he doesn't appear to be doing much work aboard. Our contacts saw him lounging on the deck with a glass in his hand and not much on his body in the way of clothing." The subtle change in tone suggested a stifled chuckle. He continued after the briefest of pauses.

"He may regret that, when the Black Sea sun bites him later. Oh, there's one other thing. He appears to be fond of tattoos. He has a few on his backside and one of those military swaggers on his scalp. His head's shaven and he has something unusual on it. Looks like a target in a sniper's view-finder and an animal of some sort, possibly a wriggly thing."

Lloyd was more than happy with the news. It was beginning to fit into his theory of the Tartar businessman and a fraudulent insurance claim. How he was going to deal with it now was of secondary importance. He realised that he had to get more definite evidence before accusing anyone of massive fraud. He also knew where to look and ask for the evidence.

"Well I must say you seem to have a fantastic source of information, Jock. And I'm very grateful for it. Can you tell me who gave you the news? Are they quite reliable? I don't want to accuse someone and find out it was just supposition." He could almost feel the cold shudder of refusal approaching.

"No, Cocky. I certainly can vouch for my sources but I certainly cannot and never will tell you who or where they are. I'm sure you realise... understand." An awkward silence ensued for just a few seconds. Lloyd knew he had tried to step over a red line and should offer some sort of friendly apology. Some assurance of confidentiality.

"Of course, Jock. Of course. Look, please don't think I would ever say anything that could compromise you, or your office. After all, I'm an ex-copper and I'm as keen as anybody to maintain security, especially if it's our security. But I do need to collect more hard facts before I can lay myself open to a slander case, or even just a client's complaint.

If you and your... uh..." *He was going to say 'excellent' but thought that wasn't enough* - "your wonderful gumshoes - that's what we call private eyes... "

Elphinstone sighed and almost snapped back. "Yes. I know what a 'gumshoe' is, thank you. And don't worry. Provided you can keep looking for our friends from the refugee camp – you know who I mean – then I'll try to find out enough for you to close your insurance enquiry, and possibly do your friend a big favour too."

Lloyd's relief was doubly clear. His apology had been accepted and absolved. Of a higher priority, his source of evidence, to save his reputation, was going from strength to strength. A final 'thank you,' was heartfelt and restored the dialogue to that of one between friends as well as co-operators. And he soon had another friend to thank.

Ch.16. Mighty atoms.

Lloyd's relief was bordering on joy. It increased further when he spoke to Mary Deans again some three days later. Tulloch was still in Kazakhstan but would be back in his regular day-job in a few days time. "And," she had added, "we're going over to Geneva to see him." Lloyd thought that he had missed something in the conversation.

"Just a minute, Mary. Hold on. Andrew lives in Zurich, not Geneva. And who's 'we'? Do I take it that I'm invited – IF I can make it whenever it is."

"Oh... sorry... I should have mentioned... I'll start again. You remember my friend Helen? You know, the one you met at the lunch with Andrew. Didn't you meet her again in Beirut? Helen Tiarks... "

A soft sigh escaped from Lloyd's phone. Mary felt it and returned to her point.

"Yes. Of course you do. Well, she has to go to Geneva and I'm going with her. Andrew can drive over from Zurich and we can all meet. You too if you like... if you can make it."

Lloyd held back from over-enthusiasm.

"Well, I don't know. Depends when it is and what I'm doing then. Of course, I would like to see... uh...." *Helen's name nearly slipped out but he caught it before it landed on his big feet...* "see Andrew again. Assuming I'm not in the way... or whatever." He was embarrassed at the prospect of an awkward meeting – the unrequited admirer and the unwelcoming admired.

Mary started to feel like a mother hen. Trying to assure the unassured, without making him feel like an orphan, without actually clucking while she comforted her big Welsh chicken.

"No. Of course you're not in the way. It'll be marvellous. We can all have a good gossip and get Andrew to buy us a slap-up meal. Helen will be delighted to see you again... I know." She put a little too much enthusiasm into her last crumb but Lloyd knew how to accept it as sincere.

He was fond of Mary and the last thing he wanted to do was to appear hurt or offended. He was also starting to think of what he might glean from a face-to-face meeting with Tulloch. An exchange of information on what was now a mutual target. Until they could meet and discuss it he felt slightly lost in a maze of fragmented information.

In the meantime he tried to concentrate on the contractual position of the yacht owners and their ever-increasing claim – now over seventy million dollars. The question of evidence arose in the investigator's mind. How to obtain possession of the vessel or proof of misuse and possible sale. He would have to refer once more to his friend in the Beirut Embassy, for Jock was obviously aware of much more than he had confided in Lloyd. Another telephone call, another polite reply to claim unavailability and take a message. This time, the returning call arrived within minutes. Elphinstone had something to tell.

"Hello, Cocky," - *a friendly tone with a suggestion of urgency* - "I've just received some interesting news. Your yacht..." - *I wish he wouldn't keep calling it 'MY' yacht* - "...has just moved again. It has sailed out from Sevastopol and may be heading towards Novorossiysk. We think that it might be involved with some activity which is less than... uh... internationally acceptable."

Lloyd pondered on the possible 'internationally unacceptable' nature of whatever activity involving 'his' yacht.

"Do you mean 'arms smuggling'? Or something like that?"

"Rather more 'something like that' than simple arms smuggling. Mind you, we can't be certain without searching the tub. And I don't think our Russian friends would invite us to do that unless we were throwing a party on it with unlimited vodka and women."

"Can't your ... uh... gumshoes find out what's on board?"

"There may not be anything untoward on board, not yet anyway. They are more likely to load any cargo when they get to Novorossiysk. If it's what we think it might be, then we could be in trouble."

Cocky was relieved to know that his telephone line was securely encrypted. To be doubly sure he checked the 'secured' button before continuing. Almost whispering.

"Are we talking about chemical weapons... sarin gas... or nuclear? They surely couldn't get high grade... uh... you-know-what from Russian supplies, could they? The Yanks would start world war three if that happened."

"Not from Russian supplies but, there are other less secure sources that they could tap. After that it would be simple to take the usual Russian supply route to Syria. Tartus or Latakia are the usual ports for that and they are no longer secure for Assad's forces alone. There are several factions who might take on the world if it meant martyrdom."

Lloyd gulped perceptively. The gulp could be heard a thousand miles away. It certainly was heard in the Embassy office in Beirut.

"Do you think they can get – 'it' from Chechnya or Azerbijan then? They seem to be stuffed with murdering bastards looking for a bigger fight. But they wouldn't get any help from the Russians in a high security port like what's its name."

"No. That is correct. But somewhere less secure has less use for such material now that it has agreed to stop upgrading uranium so that it can start selling huge supplies of oil."

"My god! You can't be..." He stopped before imitating John McEnroe on the Wimbledon tennis courts... "Won't the Israelis stop them, or at least tell the Yanks to stop them?"

"I'm sure they would if it involved official sources of that material. But officially there is no official source. This source is very, very unofficial. Someone – and we think we know who that someone is – has a tiny network of black market nuclear smugglers. Getting material that doesn't officially exist and moving it through to official transport and supply routes for an enormous amount of money.

"And", he added sombrely, "that money can be laundered through various commercial companies to build up a multi-billion dollar – or pound or Swiss francs – empire. You can see why we're rather concerned."

Lloyd's gulps grew louder and more frequent.

"There must be something you can do to stop them, can't you?"

"Not without months of accusations and denials to and from the Russians. They wouldn't admit that anything so dangerous was happening right under their noses. And we can't just send a gunboat to Crimea or Novorossiysk. Last time we tried that, it was about as successful as the charge of the blessed Light Brigade.

"But there is something which I think you and your friendly Swiss company boss can do." Without waiting to be asked, he continued. "Rather than trying to stop the supply – which might be on its way already – we want to stop the suppliers from being able to launder their dirty money.

"We can try to get them stopped by the Russians but while we're waiting for the Putin put-down I'd like your help to blow their chances of getting any more respectable businesses. It could take ages to do anything about the uranium smuggling but you might be able to tell the world that they are making a fraudulent claim at Lloyd's of London. Once that's out they won't be able to raise a smile, let alone a billion dollars."

Lloyd was relieved to hear Elphinstone's recognition of a security nightmare and how to wake up from it. He was amazed at his grasp of the commercial implications. *"But after all"*, he reflected, *"I suppose he is officially a COMMERCIAL attaché, isn't he?"*

He had one last question before other questions started to mount in his head.

"If you've known all this for some time, why didn't you let me in on the story and take action before now?"

The replies were succinct and to the point.

"We didn't and we couldn't. Even now, it's only my opinion and my suggestion." Then he added, "These things are not on full display in Technicolor or even black and white. All we have to go on are a few scrappy reports from our sources – the gumshoes if you like – and my own judgement and prognoses. Hunches, really.

"Anyway, see what you can do. And do let me know if you get any signs or sniffs of our other two... well... you know, the usual suspects."

In the heat of the conversation about uranium smuggling, Lloyd had almost forgotten the missing refugees. *"They couldn't be as important as the pirated ship in the Black Sea... could they?"*

Ch.17. Red Cross relief.

The telephone in Lloyd's Chiswick flat sounded a call to arms from Mary. She wasn't going to let him go now that she had persuaded Tulloch to meet them in Geneva.

"Hi, Cocky. Yes, I'm fine. So is Andrew – or so he says. Oh, and so is Helen, in case you're interested." The last offering was confirmation of what she knew but felt obliged to wrap in an aside.

"We – Helen and I – we're booked to fly to Geneva next Tuesday. We'll stay in the cheapo hotel next to the airport. Yes, it will be a bit noisy but we won't be there for more than a couple of nights. Can you get away for two days or so then?"

Lloyd confirmed. He didn't procrastinate. No 'perhaps' or 'I'll have to check my diary.' He knew that he could and would. He knew that meeting Tulloch was a priority and would have flown straight to Zurich and Tulloch's office if Mary's Geneva reunion had not been in the offing.

To put a seal on the attraction, Mary added, "Oh, I should mention, he'll be bringing a new friend. Or rather, a new business partner. Someone called Vassal or Vasel, a Bulgarian from Kazakhstan. That's quite an interesting mixture isn't it?"

Lloyd confirmed again. It certainly was an interesting mixture. Particularly interesting to himself. If Vasil Antonov's presence had not been on the agenda, Lloyd could almost have asked Tulloch to arrange it. In addition, the thought of meeting the lovely Helen somewhere more romantic than a refugee camp almost made him salivate.

The prospect of meeting an expert – at least he hoped that Vasil was an expert – in matters Bulgarian and metallurgical, set his investigative mind ticking. Without waiting for his office to book flights and hotel, he opened the lap-top on his bedside table and logged into 'Lastminute.com' and the flight reservations.

After all the activity of the past few days Lloyd was now facing a relatively dead weekend. It was resuscitated by a visit to watch London Welsh RFC playing against London Scottish at Richmond. The game was followed by a stimulating quart of London Pride bitter with another rugby fanatic who would happily celebrate or commiserate with supporters of either team. A friendly contest in a field of rugby clubs and breweries could be one of competing pleasures for a bachelor.

By Monday evening, memories of rugby and beer were left in the club-house. His thoughts had returned to marine developments in the Black Sea and refugee trails in the Balkans. Overnight, or over two nights, bags were packed with a thoughtful little gift for each of the ladies plus a thoughtful large bottle of Lagavulin whisky for each of the two men.

Mary Deans may have appeared to be more interested in women's fashion and romantic adventure than business organisation but she had arranged their short agenda with beautiful simplicity. Helen would spend much of the first day in discussion with officials in the International Red Cross - 'accompanied by her colleague', (Mary). After that, it would be every girl for herself in the glamorous shops and cafes of Geneva.

Arrangements for the men were equally simple. They could talk business, or sport if they had to, whilst she and Helen were busy. Then, when shopping and feet were exhausted, the men could take them to a first-class restaurant. Everything had been set in motion by the time that the two ladies and one gentleman met in the departure lounge.

The International Federation of Red Cross and Red Crescent Societies work in harmony in many troubled regions. Their address for visitors is located near the IKEA building on Rue de Pre-Bois which runs near the perimeter of Geneva Airport. Also near the airport's perimeter is one of the budget-priced IBIS Hotels.

Mary had done her homework. Minimum travel time and minimum hotel cost would strike an arrow in her boyfriend's heart and pocket, leaving room for convivial conversation and more shopping. By noon of their arrival all five of the happy band of brothers and sisters were safely checked into their hotel and out again to the nearest cafe.

Coffee, hot chocolate and apple-strudel muffins were the order of the day. One hour of recovery before the two legal experts taxied to their appointment with the Red Cross departments dealing with refugees in Jordan and The Lebanon. Tulloch hardly had time to introduce the ladies and Lloyd to the Bulgarian before the three men found themselves left to their own devices in the cafe.

Three more coffees were brought to the table as Tulloch revealed that Mary was not the only organisational expert. A conference room in the hotel had been reserved by him for conversation and refreshments. Time and expense were carefully contained once more.

For over an hour, Andrew Tulloch and Vasil Antonov described their proposed joint venture which they hoped would create a barrier to anyone trying to take over their companies. Much of it was still beyond Lloyd's comprehension but no longer beyond his interest for now he had a vital role to play.

Antonov explained in some detail, his own East-European background and Western higher education. This was more interesting to Lloyd, particularly the details of the Bulgarian's home country and ports on the Black Sea coast. After Antonov and Tulloch had covered their joint venture plans, Lloyd changed tack to discuss the background of the menacing RKM company and action that he might bring to expose it.

Broadcasting investigations into insurance fraud, as Elphinstone had suggested to Lloyd, were grasped by the two mining companies' chiefs as if they had been offered a couple of magic wands. Antonov was particularly impressed, not only at Lloyd's understanding of their predicament and his proposed solution, but at Tulloch's obvious good choice of friend.

"With friends like him," he chortled, pointing at Lloyd, "who fears enemies – or, is it enemas?"

Lloyd ignored it, assuming that something had been lost in the translation. He quickly moved on to the matter at hand.

"I can only give you a bare outline... he began.

"Are we still talking enemas?" muttered Tulloch. Cocky ignored him again.

"...an outline of what's been suggested. As usual, I can't do much but I'll try to spread the news of a possible crooked claim. I might need some help with that unless we have hard evidence to show that the boat's still in the hands of the owners. Perhaps you know a friendly newspaper or someone who can spring a leak to the media?"

The two mining executives looked at each other as if they were about to shrug their shoulders. Under normal circumstances an insurance fraud was not something that concerned them. Antonov added a feeling of helplessness with the expression of an innocent abroad.

"This is not the sort of business that we get involved in. Oh, I don't just mean getting involved with false insurance claims but getting involved with leaks to the media. Do we need to get the story to the press in my country? I mean, in Kazakhstan or, perhaps in Bulgaria or Russia?"

Tulloch had remained silent while the Bulgarian was fishing for ideas. He knew quite a lot about regular insurance – and about spreading information. Antonov's question of 'which country' had given him some more irregular ideas.

"Any bid for you or us after we've established the joint venture would have to be approved by the Swiss financial authorities as well as yours. If it went ahead it would be an acquisition of a Swiss company or its interests. They would not be too keen if they were aware, and knew that everyone else was aware, of any suggestion of fraud. Fortunately for us, they are very picky about foreign control of anything here. I can't even buy a house until I have been officially resident for ten years."

Success breeds success. Tulloch's reminder of the facts of Swiss company life gave a fresh lead to Vasil Antonov.

"Well, if the deal is rejected by the Swiss authorities, that should be an end to it. How long will that take though?" Tulloch smiled at Antonov's question. He sensed where the Bulgarian mind was leading to.

"Officially, quite a long time. What we can do is to make sure that the public knows that they're investigating possible reasons to block any bid and ensure that the Moscow Exchange knows that everyone else knows it too."

Cocky was also beginning to understand what was developing. Now it would be up to him to get enough evidence to announce that the insurance claim for the yacht involved possible piracy by a person or persons associated with the owners, RKM Group. There was no need to risk legal action against his employers or the Lloyds of London authorities by naming Chairman Bekir Kazakov as suspected mastermind – he could let the media do that.

He related all the official details he had of the yacht's possible location and its owners again. Slowly, and with frequent changes, a plan of action was constructed by the three men. Before they had time to look at their watches, a long-case clock in the hotel corridor struck six p.m. Before it could strike six-thirty the conference room door swung open to admit two women with shopping bags in their arms and smiles on their faces.

"Hello, boys! Enjoying yourselves, are you? While you've been talking about football and beer, we have been rushed off our feet." With that, Mary Deans and Helen Tiarks put their bulging shopping bags down on the floor and their shapely backsides on the most comfortable chairs in the room.

Tulloch was happy to accept the interruption as well as the joking sarcasm. He knew that Helen and Mary had been conducting some very serious discussions with the enormous

113

charities along the Rue de Pre-Bois. In a friendly way they had put pressure on them to ensure that more of the income from donations ended up in the hands and mouths of the hungry refugees in the camps and less in executives' pockets.

He was glad to have some respite from the past three hours of businessmen's talk and plans. He was always pleased to see Mary, never more so than now. Perhaps she was his lucky charm. She certainly possessed plenty of charm and he just might be lucky tonight. The thought warmed him to the task and her hand on his knee warmed him to the waist.

Ch.18. Lost and gained in translation.

Outside the hotel, the air temperature collapsed with the sunset. Andrew Tulloch always viewed dusk on Lac Leman with a mixture of nostalgia and remorse. Memories of meeting his and Cocky's former employer – another fraudster – flooded back. The sadness surrounding the tragic end to his mysterious female companion of that era had never left him but the presence of his current girlfriend brought a distinct improvement in temperature and well-being.

Mary and Helen were not going to let recreation be disturbed by nostalgia or business problems. Further discussion was limited to their immediate schedule of recovery – cocktails and baths followed by dressing and dinner. A quick step to the hotel bar would be followed by marching orders to reconvene promptly before a short trip to a restaurant recommended by Helen's Red Cross colleagues.

As usual, the notes on Mary's card were brief but distinct, with little or no room for divergence. The dinner party met, duly scrubbed up and ready for action, precisely at seven thirty p.m. as their taxi swept into the forecourt to collect them. Ten minutes later the maitre d'hotel of the Bistrot du Boeuf Rouge, near the South-West corner of Geneva's iconic lake and 'jet d'eau' fountain - conducted them to their table.

Mushroom-stuffed pork chop in mustard sauce and sautéed perch fillets (caught locally in Lake Geneva) were served with bottles of Swiss Pinot Gris. The wine was described by Antonov as 'rich and mellow – like a mature Chardonnay.' Despite the flamboyant description it was Helen's turn to be impressed – by an Eastern European's knowledge of Swiss, or any, wine. Tulloch dispelled any doubts on that subject, reminding them of Bulgaria's reputation for excellent vintages.

The three men were unusually quiet during the meal. Their contributions to the conversation were restricted to nods and grunts of approval or concurrence as the ladies chattered about shops and dresses and shoes without distraction or interruption. After an hour of one-sided conversation, Mary sensed that the social aspect of the 'friends reunited' had waned. It was time to restore equilibrium.

She turned to Vasil Antonov – a potential catalyst to broader discussion.

"Well, that's enough about our hard work this afternoon. Vasil – is that the correct pronunciation? Yes? I'm never sure. Do you visit Switzerland frequently? Or is this just a one-off trip?"

Antonov smiled. The old 'do you come here often?' starter question.

"Yes I do and – uh – no this isn't just a one-off." He thought he should continue after Mary's attempt to bring him into the conversation. "I spend a lot of time in different countries as well as in Kazakhstan and, since getting – uh – involved with Andrew's business I've been to Zurich, and Geneva, quite a few times."

A silent sigh of relief floated through Mary's mind. She appreciated the gentle diplomatic return of service. Antonov's reply had just enough information to spark a new thread into the small talk around the Bistrot table. She stroked another gentle volley to develop it.

"Andrew told me that your home is – or was – in Bulgaria. Do you go back there often too?" Before he could answer, she added, "I've never been to Bulgaria so I don't know anything about it. Is it very different from Kazakhstan, or from here?" By 'here' she meant Western Europe but, he understood and replied accordingly while the others continued multi-tasking; eating and listening.

"Yes. You're right. I was born there – in Bulgaria – and I do go back about once a month to see my mother and sister but, I've spent quite a lot of time in the United States and as I

116

said, I travel quite a lot in Europe as well as other places. Kazakhstan is quite different in many ways – very different country from Switzerland – but one company office is very much like another and most of my time there is either in the office or in the mining production plant."

It was now open for Cocky and Helen to bring their offerings to the table. Lloyd's mind still hung on the business of the afternoon but Helen's had drifted back to her last meeting with him and the striking Embassy official in Beirut. She sensed that direct questions about Elphinstone might not be appreciated by the man who had introduced them. She was not going to upset him now by sounding like a star-struck schoolgirl – or was she?

"How about you Cocky? Have you been back to your old home in Cardiff? Or was it Swansea? Or are you still flying back and forth to Beirut?" The last question was delivered with a higher tone and glazed smile that told everyone that she didn't give a monkey's about South Wales or Lloyd's old home but was probing for news of the star that had struck her in Beirut.

Lloyd didn't even pause to mention anywhere West of Chiswick. He still regarded Helen as something akin to the Mona Lisa – desirable but unavailable. He knew very well that she was smitten with thoughts of Jock Elphinstone. Those would continue to present a barrier to any chance of ever-closer union with her. However, he also knew that he had to respond positively or appear to be a poor loser. And the commercial attaché was still vital to resolve his commercial problem.

"Haven't been back to Beirut since I saw you there and introduced you to my friend Jock." He thought the best way to deal with the unwanted indirect enquiry was to confront it with a direct response. "I have been in touch with him a few times though and he's been a help to me with my work there. How about you? Have you seen him back there since then?"

Helen had indeed been back there, in spirit if not in the flesh, every day since that meeting in the Beirut hotel restaurant. Not just to warm herself with a mental picture of Jock Elphinstone but working long hours with the UNHCR and other NGO's on the unceasing pathos and chaos in the refugee camps.

"No. Not since then. I've been up to my eyes..." Lloyd's eyes momentarily stared right into those of Miss Tiarks and met a furtive return plea from them... "with the refugee problems. That's the main reason for my visit to the Red Cross and Crescent offices this afternoon. I told them that Mary was my colleague, which is true, and we had a positive response from them.

"It's the old question of getting more of the donations turned into the needs of the refugees instead of being spent on organisation and admin. And we have to get the food and other supplies there much faster and into the mouths of the needy. They know that already of course but we have to let them know that we know it and lots of other governments know it too."

Helen's detailed explanation of her visit to the Red Cross offices had the effect of calming any possible tension between them. The plea from her eyes to Lloyd's was received and sympathetically absorbed by him. He had his own emotional problem with the enduring picture of Aysil as she left him at the Athens railway station. He and Helen were two travellers on the same path, although they now had different destinations.

Of the five at the Bistrot table, only Vasil Antonov was unaware of Helen's attraction to Elphinstone. Yet even he could sense the rise and fall of emotion behind the brief question and answer session covering the encounters in Beirut. He was tempted to ask more questions about Elphinstone but he resisted the temptation and tried to change the subject.

He could also understand the stand-off between Mary and Andrew on the subject of long-term relationships. Having heard Tulloch protest several times that he would not allow Mary to get any fixed ideas about their future, he took the subtle approach to them both. Subtle as an avalanche.

"How about you, Mary? Are you going to – how do you say it – make an honourable man out of Andrew?" Mary was briefly, as she said later, 'gob-smacked, but not lost for words.'

"No fear! It would take more than my powers to make him honourable. Horrible perhaps - his idea of honour is receiving an MBE or OBE from the Queen!"

As the four Britons laughed at the protested escape from embarrassment, Antonov smiled without quite understanding.

"MBE? OBE? What exactly is that?"

Tulloch leapt in to divert quickly from the subject of 'long term relationship.'

"It's an official state award for services, Vasil. Like a medal. In this case, MBE stands for, "My Bloody Efforts" and OBE is for "Other Buggers' Efforts."

Vasil still didn't understand but, the light laughter from the others was enough to assure him that his own MBE or 'My Bloody Effort' had relieved them all from any awkward duelling and left the table open to further decisions about food and drink. Tulloch made the executive decision. Coffees and liqueurs were requested and delivered in short order.

After an hour of easy listening and easy talking, or even easier silence, the quintet reluctantly agreed. The witching hour approached and they should do likewise, towards their hotel and bedrooms. With only a short distance between there and the Bistrot it was both convenient and refreshing to ignore the taxis and walk back to the hotel.

The visiting guests' bedrooms were on the same floor and they took their leave simultaneously. Although they shared the same room, Tulloch said goodnight to Mary with a warm kiss and to maintain equality so did Helen and the other two men. The men then followed suit with lightweight embraces to Helen.

Lloyd's was returned by her with a firm kiss that was somewhat more than friendly and caught him off-guard. It said 'thank you' in silent lip language. As she turned to open her bedroom door, he caught another glance from her which he interpreted as confirming the thank you although he was not sure.

Then she was gone. Her door closed – softly but firmly shut.

Ch.19 Cracking the code.

Vasil was not so certain of closing the door for the evening though. "Should we... uh... take another small drink for the street... uh... the road?" The road in question was short and well-carpeted and led to the hotel bar with easy chairs encircling a small table. Three chairs were occupied and three glasses of Talisker single malt whisky delivered with a small bottle of Perrier water. If the road did not appreciate it, then the tired men certainly did.

Vasil relaxed further as the Scotch flirted with his taste buds and descended into his gullet. He started to offer 'good health' in a language that the others didn't speak but – they understood. Lloyd was also more relaxed. He had been hoping for an opportunity to ask Tulloch about the strange message that had been passed to him in Beirut regarding what he took to be the whereabouts of his target – the 'missing' yacht.

"Andrew, do you remember that odd message that I told you I had from someone in The Lebanon, about the missing yacht – the 'Anna K'? It surfaced again later and... well I'm fairly sure that it has something to do with where the yacht is going to. And if we know that, we should – we might anyway – be able to get some authority to catch it and see if there's anything unlawful about it. Apart from perhaps having your friend 'Ivan' in it."

Tulloch nodded. He understood what Lloyd was hoping to find but didn't see how he could help to find it. Exposing RKM would be only a means to his end game.

"Yes. Of course I remember you saying something about it but I'm afraid I still don't know what it meant. You said you thought it might be a map reference or something like that."

Lloyd nodded.

"Oh. I tried all sorts of combinations with numbers – the figure that looks like 'ten' or 'eleven' might be miles or fathoms for all I know. I even thought of asking a cryptologist or crossword puzzle expert but I'm not sure what I could ask them." Then, he thought he should explain his dilemma to Antonov.

"What I asked Andrew about, Vasil, was the meaning of a strange map reference or code that I have been given from two quite unrelated sources. It might, just might, be a clue to the yacht. Either where it's going or what it has on board." His voice tailed off lamely and he took another sip of the whisky.

Antonov looked blankly at his glass. If Lloyd and Tulloch didn't know what the so-called 'clue' or reference was, how on earth would he know? In any case he couldn't even try to offer any help if he hadn't seen it. The verbal description was meaningless.

"Well... uh... Cocky, if you can remember it, why not write it down and I'll see if it means anything to me. I find it always easier to understand anything when it's in black and white in front of me."

Lloyd took a cardboard beermat from the table and a ballpoint pen from his inside breast pocket. His hands were not exactly firm but he could just about point the pen-tip at a blank area on the little mat. *"Now... what was it...?"* he thought.

The moving fingers wrote across the beermat and having writ moved on. Vague memories of Omar Kayam crossed swords with his recall of the message. He tried to concentrate on the message. Starting with the initial letters 'CKOP' in capitals he then added the 'Pi' character, leaving a space from the capital letters. Then after another space the number 'eleven' followed by the final block capital letter 'H'.

"There you are, Vasil. Does that mean anything to you? Do you think it could be a computer password? I can't see that 'Pi' symbol being included unless someone's computer keyboard has Greek letters as well as English ones and the number could be ten or eleven. It's just scribbling to my untrained eye."

Vasil ignored Lloyd's use of 'English' to describe the letters on an American or Western European keyboard. His own computers could be controlled through several keyboards – an 'English' QWERTY keyboard; a German QWERTZU keyboard and a Russian / Bulgarian / Kazak / Greek / whatever – keyboard with Cyrillic characters on the keys. He looked again at Cocky's shaky writing on the beermat.

It had never ceased to annoy him that people in Western Europe and in other regions such as North America were blind to the possibility of the written word not being in their own script. The mysterious 'password' or 'map reference' was quite clear to him when he read it as the Cyrillic script letters that he and millions of Eastern Europeans read and wrote every day. The block capitals were, like the letter 'Pi', all Cyrillic and the 'number ten or eleven' was either Greek block capitals 'I' and 'O' or, a Russian 'reversed N' followed by the assumed 'H' that is a Cyrillic letter for the English 'N'.

In what Lloyd described as 'English' the word 'CKOP Pi 10 H' would read "SKOR P IO N" and, translation of that word from Russian to English was unnecessary even to his blinkered British friends. Despite that, Vasil Antonov felt obliged to state, what was often referred to as, 'the bleedin' obvious.'

"In our language – or in Russian and several other... uh... Eastern European languages it is simply 'skorpion.' You know, the little creepy thing like an insect with the poison sting in its tail."

Lloyd and Tulloch were lost for words but not lost for long. Tulloch didn't know what the significance of the so-called clue could be. He resorted to exercising his general knowledge just to show to the others that he could add something to the discussion.

"It's an arachnid, not an insect. We don't usually see them in England, except the human variety in the City. What's all that to do with your missing yacht, Cocky? Or, for that matter, what's it got to do with my – our – company problem?"

Lloyd was silent. Trying to think what significance an eight-legged arachnid could have to anything apart from another scorpion or its potential lunch. His conclusion arrived very quickly.

"Sorry... I don't know. There is an island called 'Scorpios' in the Aegean but I don't think that's where the yacht is, although it is owned by a Russian billionaire. "

"Well, if you don't know, I'm buggered if I do."

Having deciphered the initial mystery, Antonov volunteered to offer some more information. "*It might be useful or it might be a waste of valuable whisky drinking time",* he thought. He was prepared to take that risk and indulge in a little multi-tasking himself. Sipping some more scotch from his tumbler he threw into the conversation some of what might be called 'local knowledge.' Others might call it 'useless information' but at least it was information.

"It sounds like a cheap gangster title – a 'nick-name', do you call it? I can think of several men, and a few women, who might be called that. I've heard that it's quite common to see in tattoos too. Criminals in prison – those gangsters – sometimes have tattoos with 'skorpion' to boast about their involvement in crime."

Talk of garish body tattoos stimulated more interest in the minds of his fellow whisky sippers. Lloyd remembered similar situations in Chinese jails with Tong gang members covered in lurid illustrations to demonstrate their criminal allegiances. Tulloch thought only of the traditional sailor with an anchor and his mother's name or that of his favourite ship.

There was one other connection which neither of them really wanted to be the first to mention. Vasil saved them from any embarrassment.

"And," he joked cheerfully, "there's the 'sign of the skorpion' on the bums of guys with AIDS – to let the other prisoners know what happens if they try anything in the showers. That way they get to use the soap when it falls on the floor!"

They all laughed – Vasil at his own joke and the two Brits in relief at not having to admit that they knew it all along. Vasil was very pleased to have added to the laughter as well as to the information of tattoos on prisoners. Perhaps there were other applications of 'skorpion' tattoos in Eastern Europe. Perhaps there was one, or more, connection with the owner of the missing yacht.

"Perhaps not - who knows?" he asked himself. Then to answer his own question - *"who knows?"* He knew someone who might know. Georgi Petrov – his colleague and marketing manager in the office back in Astana.

Soon the whisky in the guests' glasses had been sipped to extinction and the hotel bar staff had closed the last open bottle. They wanted to close the bar as well and had no wish to let the guests continue with their nocturnal pub quiz.

The three guests moved slowly and uncertainly to their rooms. Once behind the closed door of his room, Antonov pressed a few buttons on his mobile cell-phone. He knew that Georgi would be awake by now. There were several hours' time difference between Geneva and Astana and the Petrov mind would be as alert as many and more so than most there. He pressed the 'send' button and waited. As predicted, Petrov's mind and voice replied quickly and clearly.

"Hi, Vasil. Haven't you gone to bed yet? I mean – your bed, of course."

"Yes. I should hope so. My bed indeed." They both laughed. Antonov was a well-heeled bachelor with a well-earned reputation for attracting well-endowed ladies in several locations. Georgi Petrov was married with two small children but liked to think of himself as playing the straight-laced part of an East-European 'Likely lads' double act with his boss.

"I'll tell you what I'd like you to find, Georgi. Any information or rumour about names or signs to do with 'skorpions.' You know. Things like crime gangs' symbols or signs or even just what they call 'nick-names' in the West. Do you know of anyone or any group who's called 'the skorpion' or something like that? You can forget the poofs in jail with skorpions tattooed on their arses. I'm thinking of something more sinister than that."

Petrov didn't answer immediately. He was aware of some choice nick-names of politicians and oligarths who might well be labelled as venomous. Some of those appeared to have eight arms when it came to taking other people's money – maybe more than eight. His hesitation was caused by a reluctance to divulge, even to his friend and boss, any of the classified information he had accumulated during his military service in Russia.

"Leave it with me, Vasil. You can wait until your breakfast time, can't you? I'll see what I can see and phone you back tomorrow. You understand, don't you?"

Vasil Antonov understood very well. Russian and Bulgarian military services had been close co-operators for decades. Often closer than Britain and the United States. He knew that even a friendly cell-phone conversation between Geneva and Astana could be monitored and reported to the latter-day KGBs and NKVDs in Moscow and elsewhere. As they could be and probably were being monitored in the UK's GCHQ in Cheltenham and the CIA's in Langley, Virginia.

Morning in Geneva brought a raw wet sky and a typical Swiss breakfast to the hotel guests, almost Calvinistic in its simplicity and plain quality. It also brought slight hangovers to the male members of the group. Calvin and other religious reformers may have considered it as divine retribution. Lloyd and Tulloch considered it as Antonov's responsibility for suggesting the late whisky-sipping contest.

Yet it was Antonov who supplied some relief to dulled minds and throbbing heads. Whilst they tried to blot out Mary and Helen's higher-pitched chatter from their tender eardrums his cell-phone sounded its own high-pitched version of

Jeremiah Clarke's trumpet voluntary. News from Astana flew in as soon as the Prince of Denmark's March walked out.

True to his word, Georgi Petrov had obtained some information which he added to that lurking in his memory since his days with Russian special services. Without compromising either his boss or his own delicate position, he mentioned a few characters. They might all qualify for the 'skorpion' epithet, "including but not limited to", he joked in the language of commercial lawyers, the Crimean Tartar and head of Tulloch's nemesis – the RKM Group.

One other subject that Petrov thought might be of interest, though not extracted from intelligence service files, was the practice by former Russian soldiers operating in Chechnya. The Chechens were, or were considered by the Russians to be, murdering terrorists. Very suitable candidates for the generic title of 'skorpion.'

Petrov reminded him that Russian military veterans such as Kazakov often shaved their heads and had a tattoo inscribed on the scalp showing a gun-sight view of concentric circles in which a small animal was targeted

"That," he added carefully, "might just be coincidence. Or might just not."

Ch. 20 Ships that pass in the night.

Little or none of this information meant much to Andrew Tulloch or his Bulgarian friend. Perhaps the man who was trying to steal their businesses was an ex-serviceman who had fought against Chechen fighters. So what? There must have been hundreds if not thousands in that position. And, knowing the nature of former soldiers, probably hundreds of them had shaved their heads and had the sniper's gun-sight and scorpion inscribed on their heads.

It meant much more to Cocky Lloyd though. Picking slowly through the collage of cheese and sliced meats on his plate, he mulled over the messages and rumours from Beirut. The cryptic memos from Elphinstone – the confession of the Palestinian kidnapper and the sighting of someone on board the yacht. As Georgi Petrov had suggested, "it might be coincidence – or might not." In Lloyd's experience, coincidences of that nature were uncommon. More 'not' than 'might.'

Before the little party could resume pursuits more fitting for a social weekend abroad, if Tulloch still considered Switzerland to qualify as 'abroad ', Lloyd made an excuse of wishing to 'clean his teeth.' The others could accept it or treat it as a euphemism for a visit to his bathroom for any other purpose. It made no difference. He stood up and walked from the table to murmurs of "don't forget to wipe your... toothbrush" and similar jibes. He ignored them and took his leave with a smile.

Once in his room another call to the British Embassy in The Lebanon flashed through the ether. The time in Beirut would be halfway to lunch and Jock Elphinstone was more than half-way through his morning mail. He accepted the call from Lloyd readily, politely instructing the secretary in his office to enjoy her cup of mint tea elsewhere without being distracted by his presence.

Behind a firmly closed office door he waited for the news that he hoped to hear. Two former occupants of the refugee camp in Bekaa had been conspicuously '*in absentia*' for too long and he was becoming as close to being worried as he would admit. For several minutes he had to listen to Cocky's description of the second-hand information relayed to him from Kazakhstan.

After what seemed like half an hour – actually seven and a half minutes – Lloyd had relayed all his news. Theories concerning venomous arachnids, often delivered with Lloyd's own counter-theories, featured frequently. When he paused for breath the assistant commercial attaché decided to save further expenditure of it.

Reports of Russian ex-servicemen and Chechen guerrillas were put to one side by the patient listener. Rather than commenting on the jumble of reports and conjecture, much of which was not entirely new to him, Elphinstone neatly re-arranged the topics of conversation into his own preferred order.

"Am I right in assuming that you'd like to have news of your 'Marie Celeste'? Yes. Of course you would. So would I in your position. I'm just as keen as you to keep up our exchanges of... uh... news." He almost said 'intelligence' but decided that it would sound too melodramatic. Too close to his actual occupation beneath the translucent veil of commerce.

"Our tame 'gumshoes' tell me that it sailed back to Sevastopol and spent one night there before moving on. We don't know where its next port will be but we have a good idea that it's moving south towards Istanbul or somewhere near Turkey. As soon as we can identify it in a relatively friendly port I'll let you know and you can let everyone know that your insurance claim – sorry – THEIR insurance claim, is a scam."

A sudden silence erupted at the other end of the line. It lasted a few seconds during which Cocky's ears were throbbing and his mind racing while he tried to think of how to spread the story without compromising his employers. Elphinstone seemed to be telepathic. He knew what Lloyd's difficulty would be.

"Hello, Cocky. Still there? Yes? OK I expect you might need some help arranging to... uh... spread the good news. Then someone can publish evidence of the vessel being safe and sound in the hands of the owners who are claiming a fortune for it at the same time.

"I can't say 'leave that to me' but I can say that Her Majesty's Foreign and Commonwealth Office might be asked by the press to comment on the condition of the yacht and its crew. At which time we will of course be reluctant to comment on unsubstantiated reports and the press will produce lots of substantiation to embarrass us. We just need to get the tub into port and get lots of incriminating photos taken by snooping news reporters. The rest will be up to you."

It was Jock's turn to take, what he described as, 'a breather.' Lloyd was no financial wizard but he could grasp the significance of such a blatant attempt to obtain millions by a fraudulent claim, especially after the news media had made a meal of the evidence and of the perpetrators. He also realised that the main targets of the fraudsters – insurance syndicates and re-insurers – would be only too glad to spread suggestions of serious money laundering.

Any attempt to takeover a respectable business using a laundry basket of stolen cash would indeed be as Brutus said, *'bound in shallows and in miseries'*. By the time that international press reports and a damming 'no comment' from the Foreign Office had been broadcast, no bank or institution would think of supporting it. No authority would give a second thought to the perpetrators, except to issue warrants for their arrest.

"That sounds great, Jock. Great. I can get some helpful contacts lined up in the City to leak the story as soon as you, or we, know where and how to get the evidence. Our people in the insurance industry will want to make an example of anyone trying to rip us off for millions and the Serious Fraud Office can try to get hold of anyone involved. Not much chance of that with a Russian or Ukrainian company but, it should stop them doing anything else outside of the old Soviet bloc."

Lloyd's thought then turned to his friends in the breakfast room below him. Neither of the other two men were unduly vindictive but they would leap at the opportunity to destroy the reputation of the people trying to steal their business. There would be no objection to requests for help in that direction. Even if they could not 'get their retaliation in first' then they would certainly get it in a close second.

'Smug' was not prominent in the Elphinstone vocabulary but he could sense that Lloyd's level of satisfaction was rising from 'cocky' to 'smug'. Before losing sight of his own agenda, the Foreign Office official brought Lloyd's attention down to the other side of their bargain.

"Now Cocky. As we seem to be well under way in recovering your yacht..." *"There he goes again",* thought Lloyd *"it's not MY yacht."* "Now... what about our missing persons? Any ideas on their whereabouts? You seem to be the last one to see the... uh... refugee girl – Aysil, wasn't it?" *"You know bloody well it was."* "And I haven't heard of sight nor sound of the other one. Abdul whatever you called him. Nothing since he was released by the police here. Has he gone back to smuggling people?"

Lloyd suddenly felt far from smug, or even cocky. He hadn't been able to find out anything since he parted from Aysil in Athens. He was embarrassed to admit it, even to himself. If it were at all possible he would be more than happy to find her and re-kindle her friendship or more – much more if possible... if at all possible.

"Sorry Jock. The last I saw of her was in Athens and I don't know how or where she went from there. She talked about going to Austria or Germany but I don't know how she was going to get there without more money. I had to pay for her to get to Athens from Lesvos in the first place. The standard route from there is via Thessaloniki and on to Macedonia if they can get through the border but again, I just can't say."

Elphinstone reverted to type. Neither surprised nor outwardly disappointed at the lack of news of Aysil's location. He already knew more than Lloyd and much more than he was prepared to divulge to him at this stage.

"Not to worry, Cocky. I understand. You can't be in two places at once. We do have some clues to her intended route. The last we heard was that she was well past there" – "*Does he mean Thessaloniki?*" – "and trying to get to Kosovo. We think she might go via Serbia but we don't know for certain. Do you know Kosovo? The capital is Pristina."

By now Lloyd was somewhat crestfallen. Not only had he failed to give very much information but it was obvious that Elphinstone, like Aysil, was way ahead of him.

"Yes, I've been to Kosovo. I stayed in Pristina but only for a few days. I do have a contact there though, if that's any help."

"I thought you might have some friendly face there. I may well ask you to try to find our girl, if she is there, as we think she is. It's very... quite... important to me. Would that be possible?" He knew very well that it would be not only possible but a welcome task for one who was depending on him to monitor and possibly trap the yacht and its suspected pirates.

"Would that be all right then? How soon can you get there and ask your... uh... friend to try to find the girl?" As Elphinstone expected, Lloyd jumped to attention and accepted.

"I can possibly reach him by phone from here today or tomorrow, if he's in his usual haunt. Then I should be able to go to Pristina from London on Monday or Tuesday, if that's all right." A firm but soft-spoken answering voice steered him to a more urgent path.

"That might be all right if she's not going anywhere soon. Might be better to get yourself to Pristina this weekend though, in case she's not planning a longer stopover than we expect. You can fly there directly from where you are now. Why not do that and avoid any slip-up?" Then, almost as an afterthought, he closed the case for the prosecution.

"While you're on your way to Kosovo, I'll see if I can arrange to collar your yacht..." "*Not 'your yacht' again,*" groaned Cocky – "and the... uh... merchants on board – when they reach their next port of call. How's that?"

In the words of a very confident American lawyer, Lloyd realised it was 'no contest.'

Ch. 21. Back to the Balkans.

In the Geneva hotel room Lloyd was pondering on Elphinstone's latest demand. He should have guessed that there would be some connection with the old trouble-spots of Europe. The routine direction of refugees from Asia Minor and trouble-makers from anywhere usually followed what 'Stelph' had once described as a tectonic fault line. And that faultline went right through the Balkans on its path between Turkey and Italy.

The geological fault line had witnessed millennia of earthquakes and volcanic eruptions – Sarajevo to Sicily. The human eruptions followed a similar path. Sarajevo had even been the flash-point of the Great War in 1914. What was it that the ever-prescient Otto Bismarck had said, so many years earlier?

"If another war breaks out, it will be in some silly bloody place like the Balkans." Sadly he was correct. The break-outs continued as frequently as the eruptions. Most people had ceased to count the numbers of both, and now the entire region was seething with desperate men, women and children struggling to reach more secure regions of Western Europe. Struggling to keep their lives moving on.

Somewhere amongst them was the girl that Lloyd had left behind him. Somewhere in the Balkans and possibly somewhere in Kosovo. It had been a few years since he had visited Pristina, and more than a year since he had talked to his friend Arian Bogdani. He still smiled at the translation of his first name that Bogdani had offered: 'God given.'

Had God given the name to Bogdani or given Bogdani to Kosovo? He had been a gift to Lloyd in the past and might repeat the donation now. A rummage in his 'carry-on' luggage unearthed a small lap-top computer. The rummage through the contact list was shorter and more productive. In amongst the e-mail addresses and names of people that he might never see again, was a telephone number for one 'ArianB/Kosovo.'

As so often happened to an urgent telephone call, the receiver was not answering. Lloyd was almost expecting that, hoping that there would be an answering machine or service to relay the message. His hopes were not dashed. Although the answering message recorded on the machine was slightly incoherent it was sufficient to suggest that his former contact in Pristina would get the request and possibly return the call to Lloyd's cell-phone.

Sure enough, within half an hour the little device in his pocket heralded an incoming call. To his relief it was in English – of a sort – from Arian Bogdani. After a few minutes of pleasantries to confirm each other's state of health the Kosovan suddenly asked if Cocky would be calling again in person rather than by telephone.

Lloyd was past the age of sudden surprises but, like the good boy scout of his youth - not too old to 'be prepared' for one. The question of a visit was unexpected but welcome after Bogdani had explained the reason for it.

He had remained in touch with Dmitri Petric, the former 'minder' and quarter-master sergeant to the notorious Patrick Klevic, of pension fund theft and arms smuggling infamy. His apparent death was still questioned by many.

From time to time, Petric had called from his old home in the West of Kosovo to exchange news or chat over old times with Bogdani. More recently the chat had included some interesting reminders of old times that would never be forgotten. Bogdani explained his reason for asking Lloyd.

"I tell why you might like to visit with me..." – he liked to use phrases that he had heard spoken in Hollywood films – "... in Pristina. I had a talk this week with Petric... Dmitri. You remember? No. You didn't have met with him didn't you? Anyway Petric talked me about someone else you never met but perhaps heard about. Vukasin Dragovic. Petric says he seen him, few days ago. He was not alone.

"No? Did I told you about Dragovic? He is Serbian friend of Klevic. OK. He WAS friend. Petric knew him better than me. He seen him sometimes when guns were brought to Kosovo for FARK. Some of them anyway. He was always around when money was taken. His first name – 'Vukasin' – would be 'Wolf' in English. I'm surprised he takes risks to come here but Petric says he does. I suppose he still deals in guns and... uh... things.

"I don't know why he comes but Dmitri says that he comes here anyway. Here to Pristina, not over there in West Kosovo. He comes here with a woman who Petric says is Muslim like most of us. That is a little bit strange because Dragovic is Serbian and not Muslim. Maybe he has her for pleasure and doesn't want to take a Muslim girl to Belgrade. Or maybe, perhaps, they have other business. "

Cocky took the information from someone he hadn't heard from in ages about someone he had never heard of at all and tried to assess its value. Clearly Arian Bogdani thought it important enough to ask if they were likely to meet soon. That was the only clear part of the conversation. He also remembered that the original reason for calling Bogdani in Kosovo had been to look out for any trace of Aysil. What was completely unclear was any obvious connection between her and the report of a Serbian gun-runner.

Yet another possible past connection was nagging his mind. If Klevic and his Serbian side-kick had dealt in smuggling armaments from Chechnya in the past, could they have dealt with the present-day smuggler posing as a mining company boss? Bekir the Tartar, or 'Ivan the Terrorist' as Tulloch had called him?

Such a coincidence would be *"rather more than coincidence,"* he thought. Then he remembered who had issued instructions to trace Aysil. The man with remarkable insight and interest in arms smuggling coupled with refugees' movements. Arms or people. It was all some form of smuggling. And somehow all connected.

The value of the phoney insurance claim – that was definitely Lloyd's own business. It outweighed any objections to a brief excursion to the Kosovan capital. Confirmation of his interest was delivered to Bogdani promptly and more clearly than the Kosovan's misty story of the Serbian and his lady companion.

Closing the call on his cell-phone, Lloyd immediately called flight enquiries at Geneva Airport to book a seat on the safest and most comfortable flight to Pristina that might be available that weekend. As he received a confirmed reservation subject to collecting a boarding pass at the check-in desk, he suddenly remembered where he was and why. He had left his fellow guests at the hotel breakfast table. They would have almost be eating supper by the time he rejoined them if he didn't get moving.

Running along the corridor, he by-passed the elevator and leapt down two flights of carpeted stairs, two or three steps at a time. Four figures leaving the dining room blocked his entrance.

"Hello, stranger! How are the worn-out gums and toothbrush? We thought you had gone back to bed, or gone back to London. Don't bother apologising. We've had a nice little chat about you behind your back. If you're really good, we'll tell you the least nasty bits while you get a taxi to take us out for a trip across the border to a French market and then to an expensive cafe for lunch."

The ironic greeting and gentle sarcasm was delivered by the ever cheerful Mary whilst the other three smiled and smirked. Apology for the time taken in his room was studiously ignored. Announcing his sudden departure and another apology for cutting short his weekend in Geneva was accepted but not without curiosity.

Explanation would have to be directed at the principal beneficiary of his action, his friend Andrew. "After all," he

137

reasoned, "I'm doing this largely for your benefit if it results in scotching the Tartar's chances of taking you over."

Andrew Tulloch was less convinced of Cocky's motives. He accepted that there was a slight chance of Lloyd's departure developing their mutual interests, but only a slight chance. Of what, where and when, he was most certainly uncertain. By the time that Lloyd would be flying to Pristina they would all be, figuratively at least, up in the air.

Flying to Pristina from Geneva was straightforward. The flight was short and without incident. It was without much comfort too, but that was to be expected on such a brief journey. It was just long enough for Cocky to gather his thoughts. Sifting through countless possibilities of finding either a connection, between Klevic's old associates and the Tartar, or of finding Aysil.

Of his latest objectives, finding Aysil loomed larger in his mind than anything else. For no apparent reason he annoyed himself by humming an old song from the 1960s, 'It's only a picture of you.' It irritated him to think of such sentimentality lurking in a hard-nosed ex-copper.

The mental picture of Aysil irritated him even more.

Ch.22. A gumshoe in Kosovo.

Having only hand baggage in the overhead locker, passenger LL Lloyd emerged quickly from the Airbus A320 and down the aluminium steps to the tarmac apron of Adem Jashari airport in Pristina. Through modest customs checks with a gesture of flashing his passport at the immigration desk, then out to the line of taxis plying their trade and playing their waiting game.

As an impatient German threw himself into the rear of the first taxi in the line and ordered immediate departure the second taxi in line edged forward. Lloyd entered it more smoothly with his hand-luggage and a light raincoat on the seat beside him. He handed a small sheet of the Geneva hotel notepaper to the driver with an address given to him by Bogdani.

Driving the fifteen kilometres of the E851 road into central Pristina took only a few minutes. The Hotel Sirius had been recommended as suitable for businessmen, possibly even for business-women, and had a couple of decent restaurants. The one on the top floor had views of the nearby Kosovo Assembly building and Mother Teresa Square. The Cathedral dedicated to one of the legendary figures of the Balkans stood out in the low-level skyline.

Apart from that, Lloyd considered it to be just one more city centre hotel. His frequent flyer brain sometimes woke up in a smart hotel bed, wondering which city had seen him getting into it. This one would do as a place to sleep and eat but perhaps not to meet those he hoped to see.

Of those to whom he had travelled so hopefully, Arian Bogdani would take first place in the list. He was there, standing in the hotel foyer, as Lloyd got out from the taxi and into the hotel.

"Hi, Arian. Nice to see you again. This looks like a nice place." He waved an arm, the rain-coat wrapped around its wrist, pointing vaguely at the walls and reception desk. Bogdani smiled and nodded. He realised that his visitor had stayed in countless hotels like this one and probably in more luxuriant surroundings.

"Hello, Mister Lloyd... "

"Cocky, please. Everyone calls me that. Except my mother, perhaps. Thanks for helping me again and thanks for the hotel booking. It really does look like a very good place."

"Well,... uh... Cocky. It should be OK But let me know if it isn't and I can get somewhere better... or more like your liking anyway." Bogdani chuckled and Lloyd followed suit. They both knew what he meant by 'like your liking' and the former Kosovan rebel suggested a key feature of that.

"They have best beer-bar in the top-floor restaurant. If you join me there after you checked in and left your suitcase..." he glanced at the compact carry-on case "... in your room and – how do you say – 'freshened down some'? Then we take a glass of beer and some small foods before we have dinners."

No matter how limited his host's command of the universal language of business was, Lloyd appreciated how much better it was than his command of any language other than his own English and Welsh. He was not even aware of which language was the *lingua franca* of Kosovo. He relaxed a little and warmed to the thought of a draught of beer after 'freshening down some.'

His room was only two floors above the reception area but the lift was waiting for him and his luggage. Five minutes in his room to dump his case, his raincoat, and the contents of his bladder, ended with hands and face washing in warm water. Then a swift exit upwards and onwards to the top-floor bar. Bogdani was waiting for him. Seated at a small coffee table on which sat two large glasses with condensation clinging to their exterior and cool amber liquid filling their interior.

"Here we are my friend. Gezuar!" Raising the damp glass to his lips, Bogdani slurped a generous mouthful of its contents. The new arrival did the same. They sat in silence for just about half a minute of drinking and wiping their lips. The cold beer washed away the last vestiges of dry mouths and over-heated brains. Two cool heads were definitely better than one, and cool heads would be required to find their quarry.

Looking around and behind their table, Lloyd was worried that their conversation might be overheard. He needn't have worried as the barman was fully engaged in conversation with his girlfriend on the other end of a very long phone call. He put the handset down and raised his eyebrows to ask if the guests wanted something from the bar. Bogdani's open palm waved away the offer and the barman resumed his telephonic love life.

"Now. Don't care yourself about him..." nodding towards the bar "... he won't hear us unless we shout. And I'm not wet enough..." pointing at the half-empty glass "... to start shouting. Let me tell you what I have found for you. Found for me too, of course. I'm still interesting in knowing what's going on with anything to do with... uh... what we found out... few years ago.

"I talked again to our old friend Petric. I was never sure that he was always telling the facts, all the facts anyway. He has told me about seeing, or someone seeing, Dragovic in Kosovo. I think he must be here in Pristina because it would be too dangerous for him near Albanian border, specially near anywhere like Bela Cerkva. You know?" Lloyd nodded with a half grimace. He did indeed know of the massacre during Kosovo's civil war. He pressed Bogdani further.

"Do you know when he might have come here? And was he alone or travelling with someone?"

"No. I don't know but probably two or three days ago. From what Petric said to me. And he was seen before that with the woman, maybe not a foreigner I think. She was in Muslim women's clothes anyway. Strange that a Serbian man should travel with a Muslim woman but not many would know that he was Serbian.

"The people who first told Petric would know because they remember who he was and who he had worked with. And of course, so do I remember. Can you tell me why you want to see him? Or do you want him to be caught or..." Lloyd tried to present a poker-faced expression.

"I haven't any plan to catch him or... anything else. Just to know what and where he is. I didn't know anything about him until you told me. But I want to find out what he is doing with that woman and where they are."

Bogdani stared at him as if he was expecting rather more explanation than that.

"Do you have some ... uh... business with the woman then? Some unfinished business..." He stopped his line of questioning and shrugged. "You don't tell me if you don't want to."

Cocky gave a half smile. He would certainly like to continue the unfinished business. Unfinished and largely unstarted. He still hoped to get closer to Aysil, if it really was Aysil with the Serbian man. But that would have to wait. Wait until they had ascertained the woman's identity and wait until they knew the reason for her and the Serbian to be travelling together in Kosovo. He outlined his immediate tasks to his host.

"I can't say much more than that until we're sure who, where and why they are here, Arian. If we can establish that then I may be able to work out what they're trying to do and what we should do about it. I'm not sure what your – or rather Petric's agenda is in all this either. But if our plans don't clash then we should be able to work together. Don't you think?"

Bogdani nodded. He did indeed think. He thought that Cocky had not told him everything – and he was correct. On the other hand he was mainly concerned with the possible damage that the Serb could do to him or his friends and the violence that the Kosovans might visit upon the Serbian wolf of Klevic's past arms deals, if they caught him.

"OK Cocky. I will try to contact Petric again and we might find out where they are. Pristina's not such a big place. They might be seen somewhere near here if they did travel here. He did say that Dragovic was in a car. If it is either registered in Serbia or hired here, I should be able to track it. Then we can concentrate the enquiries.

"Probably you'd like to unpack or change in your room. I will phone Petric and see you downstairs in reception room in... say... a half hour? I have a car in this hotel – in the parking park. We can go somewhere in it when I have some better ideas where somewhere is."

A more relaxed Lloyd laughed and nodded his thanks. He wanted to return to his bathroom and 'freshen down' some more before going out to what might be a wild goose chase. He also wanted to speak to Jock Elphinstone again before searching for Aysil and the Serbian gun-runner. His main worries were that Aysil might have already moved on and - how to explain 'wild goose chase' to Arian.

Before telephoning to Beirut, he completed his freshening process and looked at a tourist map of Pristina, displayed prominently on the wall of his room. He was looking for anywhere that a Serbian man and a Muslim woman would be likely to visit. He gave up after a minute or two scanning the travel agency 'places of interest' – *"interest to them"*- he thought. He had to get some more pointers from Elphinstone, and from Bogdani.

Without them he was lost. He felt like the radio comedy he listened to in his Chiswick flat, 'I'm sorry, I haven't a clue.' Fortunately both Elphinstone and Bogdani did. In fact between them they had quite a few clues. The usual delay getting his call transferred to the commercial attache's office irritated him less as it gave him time to think of what he was going to ask. As Elphinstone took the call so the main question came to mind.

"Hello Jock. I'm here in Kosovo and may be near to where Aysil might be going to or already gone to..." His voice trailed off. Elphinstone took over as expected. His authority was almost as irritating as the Embassy receptionist.

"That's a few 'maybes' and 'mights' Cocky. But I think I know where you're coming from, if not where you're going to. I can only give you a prognosis based on what I have been told. As far as I know, the Serbian man should or 'might' be hiring someone they hope can get her over the border towards Croatia. Possibly via Montenegro and Bosnia. After that he can go back to Serbia." Lloyd immediately responded.

"You said 'someone they hope can get her over the border.' Who are 'they' and where do you think 'they' might meet her, and him, in Pristina? Are 'they' more people-smugglers like Abdul?"

"Did I say 'they'? I meant 'she' but it doesn't matter just now. The main thing is that we – I – would expect her and the Serb to meet somewhere very public and easy to find without looking suspicious. Some obvious tourist attraction, if there is such a thing in Kosovo. Have you got a map there?"

"Yes. I'm looking at it now. There's a national assembly building and a Roman Catholic cathedral. And a big square about half a mile from here."

"The Catholic cathedral wouldn't be obvious for someone wearing Muslim refugee's clothes. Why do they have one there anyway?"

"It's dedicated to Mother Teresa apparently. She was born in Skopje – you know Skopje – where they had a terrible earthquake some years ago. It was part of Kosovo under the Ottomans – almost next door – it says here. Skopje's in Macedonia now. Why a Catholic icon's associated with the Muslims in Pristina I don't know but it seems to be important for the tourist trade. The big square's named after her too."

"A big square on the tourist track? That sounds perfect. You might have hit on it already, Cocky old chap."

"Yes, or as you just said, that's another one of a lot of 'mights.' But it sounds like the best we have to go on. My pal's waiting in reception. I'll ask him what he thinks and we'll try it. He's got a car but we could walk there in a few minutes if we catch sight of either of them.

"One last thing – you haven't told me what the Serbian looks like. Anything like Abdul, is he?"

"No, I haven't, have I? And he's definitely not like Abdul. I'm told he looks more like you Cocky. A bit shorter than me but otherwise could be about the same size and build as either of us. Darker hair and complexion though. Otherwise, nothing special. No scars or tattoos or green carnation in his button-hole, I'm afraid."

"Well. That's better than nothing. I'd better go now before the receptionist thinks my friend is trying to pickup someone down there."

"OK Good luck and... do let me know if and when you get any."

'Getting any' was not uppermost in his mind as yet but, Lloyd was not without hope for the near future, if he could find 'HER.' He sped down the stairs to a waiting Bogdani who ushered him through the front doors and round a corner to a small Volkswagen.

Despite years visiting and working in countries where cars drive on the right-hand side of the road, passenger Lloyd persisted in trying to get into the driver's left-hand seat. Bogdani was already sitting at the wheel and didn't appreciate a large Welshman trying to double the occupation of his seat.

"Sorry. Old habits..." he mumbled. Walking briskly round in front of the car he opened the passenger's door and climbed in. "Can we take a look around Mother Teresa Square and the cathedral? After that we should look around the station and any other public place where tourists are likely to be. Unless you know where the woman and the Serbian man are likely to meet with someone who can get them, or just her, over the border and on to somewhere inside the EU Schengen region."

Bogdani started the VW but before engaging the gears he turned to Lloyd.

"If they want to get into one of the Schengen countries, the most likely to accept them is Slovenia, and they would probably go there by travelling through Bosnia and Croatia. Hungary might do it but they are very defensive now and have wired up their borders to everyone. In order to get through the borders they would need papers – passports and visas – you know what I mean."

Lloyd did know exactly what he meant. What he could not fathom was why Aysil would want to travel as a refugee if someone could supply her with the means to travel on false papers to the EU. If she could do that then she might as well have done it from Syria or the Lebanon. There must be some other reason to require a meeting with someone in Serbia or Kosovo.

He would have to ask Jock to explain that later. Right now; the objective was to find HER and to find what he could about her next move. He tried to explain this to Bogdani whilst pretending that he knew more but couldn't divulge details. As he didn't have any to divulge to him he would not find that task impossible.

The two men in the VW drove around Mother Teresa Square twice, then drove around it in the opposite direction, as there was no sign of either Aysil or the Serbian reported by Petric. There were countless sallow-skinned men, some of whom could answer the description given by Elphinstone, but without Aysil or anyone like her.

They drove to the railway station and then back to the cathedral near the square of the same name. Several women wearing long dresses and headscarves were walking in and out of the station. Several men with the appearance of furtive hurried journeys on their minds scuttled through the main entrance but none would seem to be meeting a young Muslim woman accompanied by a Serbian man.

Both men in the VW car adopted an appearance similar to those seen in the station entrance. They glanced at each other and nodded in silent agreement. A mutual decision to return to the hotel bar. After refreshment and discussion, the search was resumed. In each man's mind was a picture of what they imagined to be their target.

From staring at the tourist map they also imagined the most likely venue for the quarries to meet. Each picture differed from the other. Bogdani could recognise the Serbian, Lloyd could recognise the Alawite refugee. But neither man had ever seen those recognisable to the other and neither could recognise the unknown third person.

Further trips in the VW resulted only in tired eyes and stiff bottoms. Other tourist attractions seemed to be unable to attract the combination of Aysil and one or two men unknown to Lloyd. The following day seemed to be heading for a similar defeat. After an unsuccessful morning and equally frustrating afternoon, Bogdani took pity on his guest and took even more pity on his sore rear end and dry mouth.

"Come on, Cocky. I think the sun has gone past the metre-leg. Don't you say that?" He deliberately misquoted the old metaphor, using the wrong measurement and limb to elicit some semblance of a smile on Lloyd's face. Before the smile could loosen Lloyd's tongue he continued with his proposal, which was passed unanimously.

"We could spend all night wandering round this town in the car and burning gasoline but I think that we will be better by sitting in a cafe and letting the town wander round us."

Once more there was no objection. Lloyd was as tired and disappointed as his chauffeur, or more so. A comfortable chair somewhere with refreshment to refresh was just what he would like to order. In a foreign city on a warm evening, a cosy cafe and cool drink would do nicely.

The VW's steering wheel seemed to know where and when to turn without instructions or movement from the driver. Within five minutes of the decision the car drew to a halt near a well-lit window of what looked to Lloyd like a Kosovan version of The City Barge pub in Chiswick. From the lively music and noise vibrating into the roadside the two men might have imagined several well-imbibed members of the chattering classes inside.

Being in a largely Muslim region, the chattering imbibers were usually fuelled with coffee and mint tea. But in the capital of an aspiring European city, the cafes were not completely teetotal – or coffee total. Coffee would be preceded by some welcomed glasses of beer and little snacks. The two men slumped gratefully into their chairs and sipped their drinks. Doing nothing in particular but doing it very easily.

After the first beer had found its way down Lloyd's gullet he felt it was, in Bogdani's words, time to 'freshen down'. A swift amble into a poorly equipped and poorly ventilated lavatory was sufficient for him to want to amble out again even more swiftly.

As he emerged through a ribbon curtain shielding the lavatory door, he saw Bogdani moving to hide what he could of his face from two men who had just entered the cafe. The newly arrived brace moved past Bogdani's table without looking down and sat about three metres from him. A waitress arrived to take their orders and in the discussion of drinks and food Bogdani rose while facing the other way from the waitress and her new customers.

He moved slowly towards the toilet door and Lloyd. Pretending to brush past his colleague, he whispered clearly enough for Lloyd to understand, "One of those men who just came to here is Dragovic. The other I know – he is just a taxi driver – but the first is definitely Dragovic. We should move out now but, can you pay the reckoning? If I go to the desk or the serving girl he might – he will see me."

For once, Cocky was very pleased to pay the bill. Finding one of the target characters without moving was a stroke of luck. Or maybe it was a stroke of Arian's good sense. Whatever the stroke was it was a good one. He settled the bill by holding out his hand to the waitress with some twenty euros in paper money.

The European currency was more welcome than any local variety, as it is so often in the less affluent Balkan states. She would take only enough to pay for the total charged. Her offer of change in Serbian dinars was gratefully refused. Lloyd then slipped as inconspicuously as he could, out through the rear exit then round to the front to rejoin Bogdani near the cafe window.

The two newly-arrived men inside the cafe ordered coffee and continued to talk earnestly but quietly. They were watched from the front door and window by the two who had just vacated their table. To avoid unwelcome attention, Lloyd and his Kosovan friend walked slowly apart and then crossed back past the window to observe the newcomers' progress.

After about fifteen minutes of criss-crossing like a pair of guardsmen outside Buckingham Palace, Bogdani signalled to Lloyd that something had stirred down in the forest of diners in the cafe. They parted once more and watched their two targets strolling out from the cafe and along the pavement towards a line of parked cars.

To their concern, one of the men then produced a car key with remote entry fob and the side-lights of a large Skoda blinked to signal release of the car's locks. Before opening the doors completely they continued to talk for a few moments then one signalled to his companion to get in. At that moment Bogdani and Lloyd followed suit. They entered the VW once more.

Bogdani started the VW engine. As the Skoda drew away from the kerb, he turned the wheel to follow it. Apart from the noise of the car, their journey was almost silent. They both knew what they hoped to see if their target stopped. After twenty minutes including a brief stop to buy some cigarettes, the Skoda drew up near the railway station. Bogdani stopped his VW some thirty metres past them, on the opposite side of the road.

For nearly half an hour watchers and watched remained in their vehicles. Two watching quietly with only the occasional whisper and the two in focus talking continuously and looking earnestly at the station exit. A small group of travellers emerged from the exit. One of the men in the Skoda pointed at a slim figure wearing a long dress and headscarf.

Lloyd followed the direction of his pointing arm and breathed a sigh of relief. His hopes of reunion with Aysil had not been washed away with the tide of travellers. He didn't wish to appear overexcited but grunted satisfaction to his driver.

"There! I thought they would lead us to her. That's her, with the beige headscarf. Oh 'beige' – that's light fawn – uh... light brown colour... "

"Which one?" asked a blank Bogdani. "There are three or four with brown headscarves. We usually call them 'hijab' and if you're interested, those long coats the women are wearing are often called 'jilbabs' by people here and in Bosnia. Probably the same name in Syria and places like that."

"Oh, sorry. The girl with the brown and green patterned... what d'you call 'em... 'Jill babs'? The patterned coat..." He broke off the description. "Anyway they're going off again. Have you got enough petrol to follow them?"

"It's diesel, and yes, we can follow them. Perhaps a hundred kilometres more. She's just arrived in Pristina so I don't suppose she has to go far from the city." He was right as usual. The Skoda drove only two kilometres along the main roads before turning into a small courtyard and stopping. The driver and his two passengers alighted and walked into the covered porch of an old house. Bogdani watched and wondered.

"Well. Here we are. Now what? They are inside, in the warm. And we are outside, in the not very warm." Indeed, the evening air was turning decidedly cool. A bat flew violently from a low-hanging tree, twisting and turning to catch insects pin-pointed by his in-flight sonar squeaks.

Cocky pondered on the question from Arian as the bat made one more ninety degree turn and disappeared into the dusk. Having traced Aysil and her guides, he was unsure of her – or his – next move. It might be natural for one who has just ended a rail journey to want to stop and 'freshen down', as Bogdani liked to say. Then she might be glad to have some food and a bed for the night.

"I don't want to lose her... them... now we have them in our sights. If you're tired of this stalking then you can leave me here and come back in the morning." His companion looked sympathetically at him. Lloyd, he assumed, was clearly deranged by the excitement in a foreign city.

"And what will you do if... when... they come out and drive away? They can't stay there forever."

"Uh... no... they won't do that, will they. I could phone you if they come out... How long would you be... getting here?"

"Too long. Anyway, we're actually quite near to your hotel. Maybe only three or four hundred metres away. We have driven round in a big circle since we left it this afternoon. I don't think they will be going to a disco or to the opera tonight. So we can just stay here for an hour or so and then get back to the hotel for some sleep. And then again -we get back here early tomorrow to watch them and follow them if they drive away. OK?"

In the absence of a better plan, a weary Lloyd agreed. It was as OK as anything. Probably better. One more hour waiting and watching. One more hour of nothing. The VW car was left in the quiet side street as the watchers stepped out in the dark to the light and comfort of the Hotel Sirius.

Sirius – the Dog Star. Being the brightest in the firmament, its reputation was reflected in the hotel foyer's neon signs as Lloyd and Bogdani entered. The light was not shining in the tired minds of the men as they headed for the nearest bar. Morning might shed a more intense illumination on their quarry and reveal news of where and when but evening was a temporary lost cause.

Lloyd's room was equipped with two generous single beds and they had no qualms about putting them both to good use. *'Any port in a storm,'* came to mind but he couldn't even start to explain it to Bogdani. His thoughts turned again to the missing yacht and its next destination. They remained there as the two men flopped onto their allotted spaces and quietly dropped off to sleep.

They dozed off without further discussion and without recognising another dark figure outside the hotel entrance muttering into a mobile phone.

Ch.23. Found and lost.

Rising as early as Lloyd considered to be respectable in polite circles, a brief stop in the dining room for coffee and croissants saw the start of the morning's watch. The faithful Volkswagen car was waiting a few hundred metres away and they still wouldn't be sure if Aysil and the two men remained in the old house or had driven to a place or places unknown.

Stepping out into the sunshine and on to the side road with the parked VW, they were just in time to see their three targets emerging, out of the house and into the Skoda. Once again the observation party followed in the VW as the Skoda returned to the station. At that juncture the Serbian got out and the Skoda continued its journey as far as a nearby service station.

The car was then refuelled and the driver walked off to pay at the cash desk. He then signalled his intention to visit the toilet, leaving Aysil and the Skoda unattended. Over his years as a policeman and an investigator, Lloyd had developed the knack of sensing when to grasp at an opportunity. Now was just such a time. He stepped quickly from the VW and ran over the forecourt to the Skoda and a startled Aysil.

After weeks of travelling in harrowing circumstances she was often uncertain of the difference between fantasy and reality. To see the man who had befriended her and helped her to get to Athens, now running to her side and talking quickly in English seemed more like a strange dream than an actual event. She stared at him while he repeated his assurances of help and friendship, assurances that went largely unheard and entirely ignored.

"What... who are you looking for... talking to me?" She wondered if she should wake up or carry on speaking to the unexpected apparition. "It's Mister L... Lod... or Loin... is it?" She stumbled over his half-forgotten name. Cocky didn't mind. 'Mister Loins' would do nicely for now. He tried to look relaxed and friendly. He just hoped that she could be as friendly as he would like her to be.

"Ah, Aysil, isn't it? I thought it was you. My friend here,"pointing to the car with Bogdani half in, half out, "just stopped for petrol – uh, diesel – and I saw you here too. Are you staying in Pristina? With a friend? I thought that you would have gone to Macedonia and perhaps on to Germany or somewhere like that." Enough questioning for now. Time to get some answers – any answer.

Aysil looked blankly at him and then at the car. By now Bogdani was standing by the driver's door, pretending to study the fuel prices. He kept moving to avoid recognition. He had a suspicion of the identity of Aysil's new-found companion and driver. Cocky broke the awkward silence.

"You do remember me, don't you? Lesvos... the ferry to Pireas… Athens..." She blinked and seemed to jerk back as if waking from hypnosis.

"Yes. Of course. I just didn't expect to see you here. Why are you here... in Kosovo?"

Before she could ask the obvious and demand to know if he had been following her, she paused. She realised that such a question would suggest that she had a reason – a just cause to be followed. That was not what she wanted at all. And she did have a good reason to be grateful for his help and comfort. "Y*es*", she reflected, *"comfort on the journey from the cold wet island to the safety of the warm Greek capital."* She managed to put a weak smile on a weakening face.

The smile thawed out the chilled atmosphere between them. Cocky smiled back and Arian Bogdani joined in the smiling. He was still smiling as the driver of the Skoda came back from the toilet. The two car drivers recognised each other. Bogdani called over to the Skoda.

"Hey! Josip. Filling up the car, or emptying down the bladder?" They both chuckled and Josip Broz the Skoda chauffeur waved his hand in greeting.

"Just following my natural instincts, Arian. You too, I see. Where are you off to now?"

Bogdani was not a creative thinker by nature but he created some thoughts now. He had calculated the Skoda's probable route and agenda while Broz had been answering nature's call. If Josip Broz was to ferry Aysil towards Austria or Slovenia, or anywhere within the Schengen visa area of the EU, then he would probably first drive due West. That way, he could get onto the M9 and E65 roads and avoid returning to Macedonia or Serbia, if she was still intending to get back into the EU. He answered Broz immediately.

"Oh I'm just been taking this gentleman to see some customers here in Pristina. We thought then perhaps to see the Kombetar National Park while he's here. Are you taking the lady there too? It should be very pretty."

Broz glanced at the lady. Perhaps she would like to see the national park sometime but today she had another appointment in mind. He answered for her.

"It's a good idea but we're not going that way, I'm afraid." He wouldn't say in which direction they would be going but in this way he had told Bogdani what he wanted to know. Before the two drivers could go their separate ways it was necessary to delay the erstwhile refugee.

"Pity. Maybe next time, Madame?" Aysil shrugged but kept smiling. "It's little late for us," looking at Lloyd, "to see the park today, anyway. But there's a wonderful cafe with pictures of the park, not far from here. Why don't we go there for lunch and our two passengers can see the park without travelling to it. And," he added thoughtfully "they can have a good talk. They don't seem to have seen each other for some time."

Another smile and shrug came from Aysil. Bogdani's clever circumlocution had arrived at the point where she could accept the proffered hand of friendship and try to discover what Lloyd's true agenda was. She turned to Broz and put the leading question to him like an experienced attorney in court.

"Will we have enough time to have lunch here before we go. It might be better for you to have a little food before driving, if you think it won't delay us too much." The Broz eyebrows returned the shrug.

"No. That's no problem. Probably better to eat before we go and not have to drive while we're both starving. I know the cafe, or I think I do, that Arian means. It is very nice, if you like somewhere quiet, not too noisy." Broz would have preferred to go quickly but he knew not to appear in too much of a hurry. "It's up to you of course but I wouldn't mind a little lunch. Wouldn't mind at all."

Lloyd kept quiet. Also not wanting to appear pushy. He desperately wanted to talk to Aysil and they could all see it. But appearances had to be maintained. Bogdani spoke for him.

"Good. So I'll go first and you can follow me, Josip. You probably know a quicker way but at least my way will get us there in one piece!" They all laughed although neither Lloyd nor Aysil knew what the joke was. Broz and Bogdani knew. The reason that Josip Broz was now driving the Skoda was that his previous motor had been involved in a total write-off when he had spun off the road and hit another car head-on. Bogdani turned the knife further. "No 'off-road' driving now!"

Broz opened the passenger door for Aysil and Lloyd jumped across the forecourt to join her in the Skoda's rear seats. Bogdani pretended to look hurt at losing his passenger while he smiled to himself at the success of his instant scheming. The two cars drove from the service station, one with two passengers, the other with none.

In ten minutes the cafe came in sight and in another five they were all seated at a large table with a red and white chequered cloth and four glasses on it. Lloyd sat as close to Aysil as he could justify and she didn't try to move away from him. In fact she even moved her backside closer to his and smiled an inviting little smile.

The two Kosovans kept their distance and discussed the menu. They ordered beer and plain water which was delivered with the customary bread and olives. Talking in the local dialect would signal the chance for their passengers to conduct a more private conversation in English. As soon as the drivers had stuffed some bread into their mouths and started their muffled exchanges, Aysil opened her enquiry.

"I was so surprised to see you. I didn't know you had business in Kosovo or anywhere near here. After I left you in Athens without really thanking you I thought I probably would never see you again." Lloyd smiled ruefully and swallowed the crumb of bread in his mouth.

"I didn't expect to see you again either. But I really wanted to." No point in wasting time beating around the bush. They might part again in a few minutes, then probably forever. He wanted to create more time and put less pressure on their discourse. The more time he could be with her today, the greater chance to continue what he was still hoping to be a close, very close friendship. "I was very sorry to see you walk away from me so quickly in Athens."

Then it hit him. That look. The same sad glance to tell him that she couldn't tell him more. He tried to return it but her eyes drooped and her mouth hardened. She took a small piece of her bread and chewed it thoughtfully. She was between the rock of exposing her plans and the very hard place of incriminating silence. Abrupt departure now would invite all sorts of enquiries and something said would give her plans away eventually.

Aysil tried to weigh up the alternatives. There was no alternative. She did not want to leave Cocky without finding out if he was trailing her and knew more than he had told her. She would have to stay with him for some time, alone and communicative. And she would have to tell some of the truth about her own feelings. Her immediate wish was to take him into ten percent of her confidence and for him to take her into one hundred percent of his.

The meal continued with as many warming vibrations as they could afford to radiate. Everyone agreed that the pictures of the National Park were quite stunning and that the food was quite disgusting. Despite the slightly artificial atmosphere and the mild indigestion it was acceptable and offered an opportunity for more discussion.

Before the bill could be placed on Lloyd's plate for inspection and settlement, Aysil complained of mild nausea and made a plea to stop for a while before further travel. She explained that her diet had been very frugal for months and the meal had created the need for a little rest to recuperate. They all knew what she wanted if not why she wanted it and they all concurred. Once again, Bogdani put the leading question.

"Would you like a doctor? Or if..." – at Aysil's wave of protest – "you just want a quiet rest, perhaps the hotel where Mr Lloyd is staying can offer a room for you to stay in, 'til you feel well enough to travel." Mr Lloyd was absolutely sure that the hotel would provide such a shelter and Aysil was certain that she would accept it.

The cafe bill was settled by Lloyd and the four victims of dyspepsia retired to take their respective automobiles to the Hotel Sirius. Broz drove with Aysil and Lloyd to the hotel in his Skoda. The Volkswagen and Bogdani just drove. Once there, Bogdani made his excuses to leave and Josip Broz informed the others that he had to get back to his old house which was 'only a few hundred metres away from the hotel.'

By now everyone knew where they were going and what they would do there. Bogdani stopped his car behind the Skoda. As he opened the VW door he turned to whisper to Lloyd. "I'll see you at eight for breakfast tomorrow. OK?" Cocky just nodded. Telepathy was a wonderful gift.

Driving to the hotel in Broz's Skoda had been uneventful. Neither of the three occupants wanted to say anything they might prefer neither of the others to know. On arrival Lloyd went straight to the reception desk and demanded his key. Time was flying from what remained of the day and he was prepared for Aysil to change her mind later about staying in his room if she insisted.

Opening the door of his room, he waved a hand at the two single beds and then at the bathroom door. "If you want to rest here then I can either leave you here or... "

"No. Stay with me, for now at least. Unless... "

"I'll stay, of course. I would like to. We can talk here if you want to." No 'or' this time. Staying and talking was mutually acceptable. An awkward silence returned but only for a second or two.

Aysil took a deeper breath. She knew what she had to do. It was what she wanted to do. She had to be sure of Lloyd's motives and reason for being so conveniently close to her in such a place. To extract more information she would start by offering a little to him. It would have to be truthful too. As someone ruefully observed later, it would be 'the truth, the half-truth and something like the truth.'

"You were surprised. I was too when we met again here, in Pristina. In case you wonder why I am travelling through Kosovo and not trying to go directly to Belgrade like the others, it is because I have a sister who was trying to get to Germany from Syria and she may be in Sarajevo, in Bosnia."

Lloyd nodded. "Yes, I know where Sarajevo is. I didn't know you had a sister. Why is she in Sarajevo?"

"She's not my real sister but close enough to be. Someone in Bekaa told me that she had been there – in Bekaa – and had said that one of her... one of the other girls... had asked her to go there as she – the other girl – had a cousin who could help her to get to Germany. I want to find them because she is my 'sister' traveller and maybe she and the other girl's cousin can help me to get there too."

Although this garbled explanation sounded almost plausible to Lloyd it did not explain who or what Josip Broz was and why he was driving a penniless refugee in a reasonably smart car. And of course it did not explain the earlier presence of the Serbian Wolf. He assumed that Aysil was unaware of his seeing Dragovic before her arrival and that it would remain in the un-told half of the truth.

"I had just enough money to get to Pristina from Skopje by train and I had been told that some men would drive people to Bosnia for a small amount of money. I have a little money to offer to that man, Josip, to drive me to Sarajevo. I hope to get some more there from my 'sister' or her friend and then go on to Zagreb or somewhere near to Slovenia and then somehow to Germany. I am still very grateful for you, getting me from Lesvos to Athens and that saved a lot of my money too. Thank you. It was very kind." Lloyd gulped.

"It was what I wanted to do, Aysil. I think you know that. It was what I wanted. The money is not important, not to me. What is important is, that I could help you then and that I have... uh... we say 'bumped into you' again." He wished he could demonstrate it literally rather than try to explain it.

As it happened, explanation was unnecessary. She moved towards him and they 'bumped into each other' with her arms linking around his neck. A tearful brief embrace was followed by her head resting on the part of his jacket between his chest and left shoulder. Neither had been in such a position for a long time and neither was going to disengage from it quickly.

"So, Mister Loin... how are you here now? What sort of business do you have here? Whatever it is, I am truly happy to see – to be with you here. "

The mental strain of hiding most of the truth added to the physical strain of travel. But now it was Lloyd's turn to unburden himself with a few half truths. He had been working on his story since they had met in the service station forecourt. He didn't really care too much whether it would hold water in Aysil's mind. He was just happy to have her so near to him and apparently pleased to be with him.

"It's Lloyd, Aysil. My name is Lloyd. Call me 'Cocky' as my friends do. It is easier to say than either of my real first names." She half snuggled against him but raised her eyes to interrogate his. This might be the moment of truth, the whole truth - to determine if and why she was being tracked. She was quite sure that it was not coincidence. It could just be that she had been hunted down for romantic reasons rather than the one reason she feared.

As she snuggled closer her soft hands ran over his jacket. If he was really a hired assassin she would soon find out but she preferred to establish if and where the assassin's bullets or other weapons were hidden before he applied them. All she felt was as she hoped. Only the lightweight wool suiting and firm pectoral and deltoid muscles beneath it. Her deeper breathing eased with her grip. Another soft embrace came as relief and reward to him for not trying to kill her.

As his lips were released from more pleasurable duties, Cocky – it would be 'Cocky' from now on – put them into information mode. He had been tempted, amongst other things, to say that his first name was 'Lancelot' which was almost true but he would then have to explain the whole story of King Arthur's knights. Better to stick to 'Cocky' and keep it short. Time was still passing.

"I'm in the insurance business, Aysil." *That was entirely true, at least.* "I have known Mr... uh... Arian Bogdani for many years... *"Three or four anyway,"*... and I asked him to help me to find some information concerning a big business problem and the company involved with it. Someone has told me that they might have some... uh... business connection in Kosovo or Serbia so I asked Arian if he could find out. There was no point going to Belgrade or anywhere else because I don't have any more details. In any case Arian lives here, not in Belgrade."

"There." he thought. *"That should sound reasonable, shouldn't it? I'll try to move on and hope she leaves it at that. I won't press her for more. Well... I'll press her but not for more information. Not yet."*

She was quite sure that he had not reached the fifty percent of truth mark. Not yet. But it was no less than her own level. She was confident of getting more without doing anything that she didn't want to do for the rest of her stay in the hotel. In the last twenty-four months of fear and danger she had not been able to relax or enjoy anything more comfortable than the room and furnishings now surrounding her. Nor had she felt so safe as now, in his very close company.

She would be absolutely justified in continuing it and taking as much pleasure from it as was available. It was essential to get as much information as she could and she was sure that she knew how to get it. At least she knew what she was going to do in order to try. They were still holding each other close while standing in the room. At some stage they would have to rearrange their positions.

Dusk was gathering outside the hotel windows. A pale gold light warmed the carpet and bedcovers in the room as they started to peel off their outer garments. At each stage of the disrobing exercise, as they looked for a coat hanger or chair to leave a garment, a furtive glance would reassure the other that they were to continue.

Within less than five minutes they were both naked and the deep breathing became deeper as they wrestled each other into one of the firm beds. Any thoughts of verbal interrogation were abandoned as their mouths engaged and their hands explored every available point. Cocky lived up to his name but still treated himself to another look into her eyes whenever light and bodily positions permitted. It warmed him as much as the hotel central heating and it spurred him on.

After an hour of all-in wrestling, all in bed, and occasional disengaging to get some air, Cocky rose from the bed to visit the bathroom. As he walked past the window he was puzzled to see the warm golden light still beaming from the same direction as it had been since dusk. He wondered how the romantic amber moon could remain there for so long until he realised that it was from the carpark security lighting.

No matter. It had added to the ambience, allowed him to see the look from her to his eyes. That was worth much more and even more beautiful than the moon. He returned to the bed and to his new love, for he was quite sure of it by now. Another half hour or so of clasping and kissing, followed by heaving and sighing, and they both slipped into the best slumbers that Lloyd could remember, or even imagine.

He had not set the bedside alarm clock in the hotel room. A bright Balkans daybreak brought him to waking life. His head tilted a few degrees to one side in order to see the clock display the time and tell Aysil. His head turned back to face the other way and found itself to be the only head on the pillow, or in the room.

The movement of head and body was more of a convulsion than a mere jerk. He hadn't just dreamed the night of beauty and passion that had just completed his life, had he? No. There was still a faint odour of Aysil's well travelled dusty clothing in the room and the washbasin in the bathroom was still wet. Had she just decided to leave him and flee? Or just decided to go down to have breakfast before they could leave together?

A hurried wash and brush-up and cladding before a rush down the stairs to the dining room and reception desk told him the worst. She was very much gone. He couldn't bring himself to say 'like a thief in the night' but that was roughly how he felt. Very roughly too. Why oh why should she want to go without so much as a 'cheerio and thanks for the bed' from his heart of hearts?

A sadder but not much wiser man walked the few hundred metres that Josip Broz had correctly stated as the distance from the hotel to the old house where Broz lived. Neither he nor the Skoda were there and nor, as Lloyd knew by now, was Aysil. After a few minutes of perplexed self-questioning, the Volkswagen with Bogdani at the wheel arrived to greet him.

"She's gone. I know. She has gone with Broz to try to get over the borders into Bosnia. Sarajevo, I suppose. Broz told me of her travel plots last night. While you were with her, Broz and me, we went to have a little drinks and he told me. By now they could be half ways to there. After Sarajevo... "

"I know. She's going to Zagreb and then to Slovenia - trying to get to Germany with her sister."

"There is no sister. She will try to get into Italy by going through Croatia near the coast, Rijeka, a little bit of Slovenia and then Trieste. She might be with another girl but not a real sister. Her sister might be alive somewhere but she's not in Sarajevo. And she's not going straight to Germany I think. Perhaps she will stay in Italy or Austria."

A very crestfallen and un-cocky Lloyd digested the news. Was it news or just opinion based on gossip? After the sudden parting of the ways in Athens, he told himself, he should have expected it to be repeated. But why? After all that he had done for her and the acts of passion verging on something between true love and true lust... was it only an act?

He decided reluctantly that it probably was just an act – to get information from him. In the exchanges of honesty during the passionate embraces he reflected that it was a good thing that she had revealed her plans to him – or some of them. A good thing that he had not told her all of his.

There were still several unanswered questions drifting through his muzzy mind. Why had she come to Kosovo to get help crossing the borders into the EU? And what was the true role of the Serbian Dragovic? Perhaps Elphinstone would tell him when he recounted his successes and failures to him.

Perhaps his friend Arian knew much more than he had told him already.

Ch. 24. The unacceptable face of love.

While one mysterious – by now almost sinister by association – refugee moved towards her goal in the German-speaking world, thousands more were moving relentlessly from horror to horror and on to other horrors. From the destruction of civil war to a crowded refugee camp, literally in a foreign field, or on to possible death by drowning and perpetual cold and hunger. Only the fear of staying drove them to leaving and facing the unknown elsewhere.

Of those fleeing from catastrophe, the majority were bound in sad little family bundles. Fathers clinging to wives and sons. Mothers clinging to daughters. Some were clinging to each other for no reason other than a shared objective and shared experiences. In every case the NGOs were trying to keep pace with the demands for succour, for a supply of help to keep going, and in every case the demand was exceeding supply.

As happened every month, Helen Tiarks was trying to help with whatever professional and compassionate assistance that she could deliver to her client organisation in Bekaa refugee camp. As usual, her help was limited but welcomed by the charitable groups. After scanning the registration records for the period since her previous visit she noticed that neither Aysil nor Abdul-Nasir had been in residence for some time.

Although that should not concern her under normal circumstances, the fact that she had met them both on her last visit but could not now, would eliminate two more opportunities to discover if any progress had been achieved. She mentioned their absence with a shallow enquiry to her guide.

"Any news of progress or travel situation for that girl Aysil? The Alawite girl who speaks such good English, and other languages. She was here last month but hoping to get permission to go to Germany or Austria. Mind you, aren't they all?" She laughed lightly but kept a fairly straight face. Not all were trying to get to Germany. But nearly all were hoping to get to somewhere even if they didn't know where that somewhere was.

For the great majority of human bundles their somewhere was constantly receding from their grasp but not from their dreams. For many who had been separated from part of their bundle, the dream was focused on the missing part – husband, son or daughter. For one separated part the dream was to be reunited with her heroine – her soul sister and love of her existence.

Sexual love between females was distinctly proscribed in the moral and legal codes of most of the regions from where the dispossessed originated, as it was for males. The love based on trust and common interest was accepted as it is in any society, albeit with suspicion in many cases.

Being extremely pretty – 'drop-dead gorgeous' had often been applied to her description – Helen had been subject to attempted seduction by hopeful suitors of both sexes on several occasions. Very few occupants of Bekaa camp had time or inclination to indulge in such pursuits, being preoccupied with staying alive and travelling hopefully. One exception existed to prove that rule.

Of all the tired and desperate women in Bekaa camp, refugees and medical staff, none was more desperate than Leila Safiya. Leila's name was Arabic meaning 'of the night' and indeed there was as one of the MSF doctors observed, 'something of the night about her.' Her second name, Safiya, was rarely mentioned but was 'pure' in origin if not in practice. Unlike the majority of female travellers there, she travelled alone.

A psychiatrist could have voiced many possible factors contributing to Leila's unsociable personality. Many matters that had left indelible scars on her memory and shaped her sexual preferences. She had claimed to be from Northern Iraq but was neither Kurd nor Sunni. Religion was not part of her driving force. That was escape from – and hatred of – her past.

As a young girl she had lived near her birthplace in Northern Afghanistan. Her family were Hazaras, ethnic descendants of tribes from Western China and treated as second or third class citizens by the majority Pashtun. As Twelver Shia Muslims they often associated themselves with Iranians or Syrian Alawites rather than Sunni Afghans or Chinese.

Although most of the Hazara tribesmen in that region were farmers of fruit or nuts, some of the young men had inevitably become involved in a very old occupation involving a less nutritious crop. The opium poppy fields were a major source of income for millions in Afghanistan and the trade in raw opium and refined heroin took much of the output through Leila's home region and on to Iran and the West.

When still a minor, Leila had been sexually assaulted by a middle-aged heroin smuggler from a Pastun-speaking area. He had regarded the attractive Hazara child as a lower caste chattel and tried to exercise what he thought to be his right to strip and rape her. The reward for his attempted 'droit du seigneur' was a thin bladed axe through his neck, wielded by Leila's brother Yousafi.

Whatever the rights or wrongs of the case, the two young Hazaras knew that they would face death from the other Pashtun smugglers who would apply another ancient common law, the law of Lec, or 'an eye for an eye' and a neck or two for a neck. The teenage killers fled from their home to Iran, together with the late Pashtun's stack of heroin. Death continued to accompany them.

Outside of China, Iran has the dubious distinction of carrying out the highest level of judicial capital punishment in the world. The majority of executions, although by no means all, are applied to drug smugglers and murderers. Leila and her brother Yousafi managed to qualify for both. They also were guilty of condemning another, less guilty but not entirely innocent girl to an undeserved death.

In a small town some two hundred kilometres south of Tehran, the smuggling siblings were befriended by another female teenager. She was quite mature for her age but possibly over-confident of her ability to flout the harsh local law. Leila was very impressed by her confidence and considered her as a role model and mentor. Admiration soon turned to adulation as Leila became as besotted with her new companion as she was with her brother.

Brother Yousafi took a similar stance with their new female friend. That turned not to adulation but to an intense and jealous passion. Together the two girls and the young man formed something between The Three Musketeers and a sexual ménage-a-trois. When another man appeared on their scene and forcibly demanded both girls' bodies and attention, Leila delivered the same service as brother Yousafi had given to the Pashtun smuggler in Afghanistan, this time using a sharp knife to the man's heart.

The victim's lifeless body was left to dry out in the bloodied street near to his place of work. That workplace was the local police station. While Leila was trying to get some bread from a market stall her brother and the subject of his jealous passion were promptly arrested and convicted. Despite the girl's innocence, she was sentenced to death by hanging, along with Yousafi.

The deceased policeman's colleagues ensured that the condemned teenagers would suffer the maximum pain and humiliation before as many of the townspeople as they could encourage to attend the public executions.

One of the policemen was the official town executioner who had boasted of his part in the public hanging of another hardened criminal some months earlier. That victim had been a thirteen year old girl who had been convicted of immoral behaviour. The merciless experienced hangman now placed nooses around the young felons' necks whilst announcing that another of his colleagues would operate the crane that would raise the ropes crushing the victims' breath and blood flows. Loud voices of approval sent cries of support in political and religious unison from the mob of ghoulish spectators to the revenging long arms of draconic law.

Leila watched in horror and uncontrolled tears as the two people closest to her were slowly hoisted into the air. Their bodies writhed in agony for several minutes before eventually stiffening in a hideous human puppet show. Other members of the smuggling party were less concerned. They were fully aware of the perils they faced daily and hardened to their companions' fate.

The policemen had been so intent on vengeance for their late colleague that they had omitted to seize the heroin carried by the young smugglers. Most of that was swiftly moved by Leila and other fellow-smugglers to a safer hiding place.

To try to wreak their own revenge, one bag of the noxious powder was left on the seat of the executioner's personal car. A survivor of the smuggling team then made an anonymous call to alert the legal officials to evidence of rife corruption amongst the local police. That exercise proved worthless as the proceeds of the bait were later divided between the same officials and the police but it delivered a small amount of satisfaction to the smugglers who had added some powdered chalk and rat-poison to the heroin.

Satisfaction was not anywhere near to Leila as she realised that she was alone and loveless. Her sole close companion now was the thought of death. Without Yousafi, her beloved brother and saviour from rape, and without her new-found female idol she had only her nightmares and a small amount of the smuggled heroin. She managed to continue her journey to the unofficial receiver of smuggled drugs in Northern Iraq during which she nurtured a longing for her lost loves and a complete hatred of men.

With the proceeds from her sale of heroin she continued through Iraq to join a straggle of refugees. They were fleeing from the horrors of civil war and invading fundamental Sunni terrorists – the self-styled Islamic State of Syria and Levant. Amongst the women and children in the stream of frightened people she met one more mature and more confident than the luckless condemned girl in Iran.

Leila's new object of adoration seemed to be totally in command of her own fate. Her ability to converse with people in different lands and different languages was very impressive. The comfort from her command of the situation gave Leila new hope for the future. In addition to a very powerful personality her appearance was also very striking. She told Leila that she was an Alawite refugee and her name was Aysil.

By the time that Leila and Aysil had reached the Lebanon and entered Bekaa refugee camp the two women were as close as friends could be, in fact even closer. Aysil had never mentioned a husband or male lover and Leila shuddered at the sight or thought of one. Women in the camp were generally preoccupied with their children or other relations and did not mix with the men. Leila had no intention of allowing herself or Aysil to do so either.

Without others to protect or consider, the two female friends grew closer and closer. They shared each other's food, and medicines, their hopes and fears, and eventually they shared their bed. Beds in the camp were in shorter supply than bodies to sleep in them. No one objected to the two female bodies sleeping and embracing together. It released another bed for another tired body.

Without warning or notice to her adoring lover, Aysil suddenly decided that she should move on. Moving on might be to another camp but Leila knew instinctively that Aysil's move would be into Turkey and a dangerous sea crossing to Greece. They had often talked of a safe haven where they could set up a home together and the favoured target was somewhere such as Sweden or Germany.

Both of those countries were far away and involved a great deal of work to obtain asylum and safety. Leila had no idea of how to obtain either but was certain that Aysil would do so for them both. Her confidence was strengthened as she saw Aysil talking earnestly with one of the officials from the NGOs. Her friendly approach to the attractive lady seemed to create a very positive atmosphere.

The positive atmosphere continued and when they parted, Aysil had been smiling. That suggested that she had obtained help and advice to take herself and Leila into the EU and security. A happy ever after conclusion to a far from happy beginning. Further meetings and discussions brought more smiles and optimism.

Leila's only concerns were at Aysil's strengthening friendship with the visiting lady advisor. Their warmth raised the level of Leila's apprehension. That was beginning to develop the jealousy that she and her brother had experienced in Iran. Then the attractive European lady returned to her homeland and Leila's worries subsided without disappearing altogether.

Apprehension turned to outright fear when Aysil suddenly announced that she had enough information to quit the camp and travel to Europe. No detail was offered. No suggestion of Leila being a travelling companion or any sort of companion. Only a look of compassion, or possibly a look of pity.

Possible reunion was all that was suggested in Aysil's look of compassion, rather than probable perpetual union. Suddenly Leila was alone again and threshing fears and conspiracy theories of her lover and the European seductress who had enticed her love away from her. Her fears developed and turned to hatred. She had witnessed the excruciating deaths of her previous lovers and now she was not about to surrender to a soft European rival.

Within two days, in which Leila failed to get the answer she longed for, Aysil was ready to depart. She might have gone earlier but for protracted negotiations with the traffickers of asylum seekers and refugees in Bekaa camp. Abdul Nasir and others had the reputation of taking the human cargoes from the camp but not necessarily delivering them to their destination.

Abdul had been one of several infrequent attendants to the normal camp routine. They would appear one day and be gone with a group of what could literally be called 'camp followers' during the next three days. Their objective was to take as many people as their associates in Turkey could squeeze into a flimsy rubber dinghy and as much money as they could squeeze from the passengers.

The attendants in the camp knew what was happening but did not have time to care about how or whether they could prevent it. If a dozen or more bodies vacated the camp and reduced the demand for medicine and food then it left more room for the incoming refuge seekers. Traffickers were human vultures but even vultures have their value in a field of death.

When Abdul disappeared, Aysil did likewise. Leila wept as she left but Aysil had promised that she would try to meet her if she could get to an address in Bosnia. Leila swore that she would live with her forever if Aysil had not joined another before that happy day. And 'another' would not be the accursed European bitch who had stolen her lover's affections. If that thief ever dared to show her face again in the camp then Leila would ensure that she would not get the chance to show it to Aysil or anyone.

Two weeks later saw another visit to the camp by representatives of The International Red Cross. They were accompanied by Helen Tiarks and Helen was observed, followed and confronted by Leila Safiya. There was no time for anyone who was aware of the tension between them to prevent a confrontation. No time to keep Helen from Leila or Leila from a heavy glass bottle that she smashed and slashed across Helen's face and arms.

In the commotion that followed, Leila was dragged from Helen by two male attendants and a dozen or more shards of glass were dragged from Helen's face and arms. In addition to the removal of glass, a large volume of blood and a few slivers of flesh and skin had left their rightful places in the former beauty's body.

The bloodied victim was rushed to the nearest medical tent where a tourniquet was applied to her torn arm with several smaller pieces of glass still embedded in her face and hand. She was given what dressing and antiseptic was available in the immediate aftermath and an ambulance took her to the American University Hospital in Makdissi Street, Beirut.

"With time," a young doctor in the emergency services department pronounced, "your arm and hand will be 'as good as new.' And we will save your face or as much as we can here and now." Knowing as he did that 'as much as we can' would never be as much as she had lost he added, "After that you will have to go back to the United States for cosmetics in your home town. They can perform miracles nowadays, don't worry. It just takes time."

Then as an afterthought to give further assurance he turned to the regular subject concerning his patients. "What medical insurance do you have? You don't need to answer now but some companies go the extra mile – or kilometre at least – to get the very best treatment. Don't you worry."

Behind her dressings and tight skin, Helen was not in a position to protest her British citizenship nor even to mumble her thanks for his well-intentioned platitudes. She just wished that he would get on with whatever he could do and let her think about her next action. That would probably be sleep, either induced by anaesthetic or by natural exhaustion. *"But please"* she said to herself *"please don't keep saying 'don't worry."*

When she woke from the actions that had induced sound sleep in the cool hospital bed, her entire body ached from the trauma to her limbs and face. The open wounds had been cleansed of glass fragments and dirt and expertly dressed. The wounded areas were largely frozen by the drugs applied with the dressings and most of the cuts were mercifully shallow.

Two deep cuts had been extensively stitched however. One long line of stitches in her arm would be uncomfortable for weeks but not socially life-threatening. The other cut was much more serious. It ran from her left cheek-bone - an inch below the eye - to her chin, passing half an inch to the side of her normally full but now tight and silent mouth. No longer likely to be referred to as 'the face that launched a thousand ships' unless someone with a warped sense of humour suggested that she had struck the bows of the ships with it.

Helen was not devoid of brains nor given to remorse for her fate. For much of her early life she had feared losing her looks but with maturity and concern for the less fortunate she had become much more philosophical. Now that it had happened it would just be a question of remedial treatment and, as the young doctor had said, of time.

Following an uncomfortable night with sporadic cat-nap periods of half-sleep, she declined food but accepted a cool drink. A second drink was offered and recommended to restore the fluid imbalance. That too was taken with thanks. Then, after the young doctor and a skilful nurse had checked her wounds and adjusted the dressings, she received a more welcome surprise.

"Miss Tiarks... Miss Tiarks. Can you take a visitor?" Tt was in fact more than one. The Red Cross visitor of the disastrous day in Bekaa was accompanied by a tall gentleman. An attaché from the British Embassy, offering what assistance the Embassy could provide. Helen gave an involuntary sigh of relief as she saw John Sinclair Tarquin Elphinstone standing next to her friend from the Red Cross.

Relief was tinged with apprehension. Fear of his reaction to her disfigurement. She needn't have worried. Jock Elphinstone was not given to vivid expressions of either horror or joy. He simply asked if he could help to get her out of The

Lebanon and into the duller but safer environments of London's Home Counties. He had already made enquiries about expert medical attention there. And he said all that without once saying 'don't worry.'

But worry she did, mainly about him.

Ch.25 The unkindest cut.

Some five days after the assault in Bekka camp and emergency treatment in Beirut, Helen was safely tucked away in the cosmetic ward of a private hospital near Guildford. Still sore and aching from Leila's blows and the emergency stitching but otherwise stable and eager to receive remedial treatment. Then she received another – a more disappointing if not devastating blow. The deep cut to her face could not be completely healed without a residual scar.

What had seemed to be a temporary setback was now regarded as a permanent crippling injury. The scar would not only be unsightly, for any woman, but could even affect the movement of her mouth and left cheek. Depending upon the degree of recovery, she was told, it might possibly give the impression of having suffered a stroke. She thought back to the young doctor in the American University Hospital in Beirut. "They can perform miracles nowadays, don't worry. It just takes time."

"But how much time? And what constitutes 'a miracle?" throbbed through her mind. *"In the meantime,"* she mused, *"Mary will probably – certainly – visit me and give me all the support I need. She can bring her boyfriend, or friends, I'm never sure how many or just who she has in tow at one time. They won't mind seeing me like this and after the plastic surgery I'll probably be as good as new... probably... possibly... "*

She broke down and sobbed softly into her pillow. The sound brought the shift nurse to her door. A cup of something hot and soothing was fed to her sore mouth with the use of a plastic straw and the support of the nurse's sympathetic arm. Then... sinking wearily back down on the pillow... sinking wearily back... to slumber.

When she woke again she half-expected to be told of another visitor. *"Either Mary and or Mary's boyfriend or friends... but he... they were still in Switzerland, weren't they? I don't suppose that Jack – or was it Jock? – Elphin-whatever will see me again. Not unless he gets transferred to darkest Surrey."*

"For the time being," she accepted, *"I'll just have to grin and bear it – only I can't grin with this scar tissue screwing up my face. Well, at least I can get on with some work if I can get hold of my lap-top and a phone. Actually, bother the lap-top. Just a phone would do for now. I wonder if Mary's too busy to answer."*

As so often happened Mary was far too busy to talk to her but that didn't stop her from doing so. She had been given all the gory details of the attempted murder by 'the jealous lesbian lunatic in the Lebanon' and was very concerned about her friend. Once Mary had been assured that Helen was out of immediate danger and back in Britain, she wanted to hear all about it from the horse's – or at least the victim's – painful mouth.

Recognising the telephone number on the little screen of her Apple iphone, Mary dropped the papers she was holding and pressed the 'answer' icon on the screen. She signalled to the three people standing by her desk to indicate a more pressing engagement would postpone their discussion. Her colleagues looked at each other and shrugged before sullenly walking from the room.

Mary almost screamed into her iphone. Then, remembering the three still standing by the open door, she modified the volume and subject of the conversation to an eighty-eight decibel, quasi-business meeting.

"Hello Miss Tiarks!" *"That should sound better than just 'hello Helen,"* she thought.' "How are we today?" Then turning to ensure that the recently evicted three had actually left the room, she crossed the floor to shut the door and open her heart.

"Can you talk without hurting? You poor lamb! I've been thinking of you ever since they told me of your dreadful attack, or rather that crazy cow's attack on you, you know what I mean, don't you? Look, or listen anyway, I know it's difficult for you to talk on the phone now but, can I come down to wherever you are to see you this evening? Not too soon, is it?"

Sunk deeply in her hospital bed and feeling slightly better already on hearing her chirpy friend's voice, Helen confirmed that this evening would be great. 'Now' would not be soon enough as far as she was concerned. She needed a shoulder to sob on and Mary had broad shoulders, for a girl or a man. *"Talking of which..."* she thought. *"Has she made a decision regarding her relationship or otherwise with Andrew?*

"Why should I worry? This is getting more like a 'Dear Diary' or Barbara Cartland situation. That won't help me. Unless Mary has a suggestion to supply me with a new face.... I wonder what Mister Elfstein or whats-his-name thought when he saw me after they removed the bandages... I wonder if he cares... probably doesn't give a sh... a monkey's." Helen adjusted her mind. There was no need to use bad language when only thinking – talking to herself. *"That won't impress anyone. No one here to impress or shock anyway."*

Helen drifted back into a soft slumber. Before she returned to full consciousness her mind oscillated between thoughts of her actual friendship with Mary and an imagined closer one with the impressive Embassy officer. He had already extended a friendly hand by arranging her return to London and to her present refuge, for she considered the hospital to be a refuge from curious and embarrassing eyes staring at her disfigurement. *"Yes, I'm a refugee too now, aren't I?"*

"How", she wondered, *"how would the other men at their recent weekend in Geneva look at her now?"* As Mary's possible partner, Andrew would be sympathetic but typically unemotional. Whereas Cocky Lloyd might be less so. After all, he might have been as close to her as Mary and Andrew but now he might be much more distant and unconcerned.

She couldn't even think about the Bulgarian. He was probably spoken for and living on the far side of the moon as far as she was concerned. Only worried about his precious mining company and the damned Russians trying to take it over. She couldn't even remember exactly what he looked like.

"That was a bit unfair," she thought. *"He was very nice and polite. Very keen to be a close friend to Andrew – that makes him a friend to Mary too."* Sleep overtook her again. A deeper sleep this time. Until she was half awake and disturbed by a shadowy figure beside her bed. Memories jumped before her – a dark picture of the crazed Afghan girl with the broken bottle and blood streaming from arms and face – 'My arms and MY face! Why did she have to do THAT?'

Helen opened an eye. Just one eye beneath a now perspiring brow and forehead. The Philippine nurse beside her bed dabbled a face-cloth into a small pan of cold water and padded her brow, carefully and tenderly avoiding the sore stitched areas of her cheeks and mouth. A dry towel was then applied, soft and gentle to the touch. The nurse's words were equally soft and gentle.

"Is that better now? Do you need any painkillers?" The nurse waved the towelled hand in the direction of an array of tablets on a tray beside her. "Just let me know if you do. They will help you to get more comfortable and sleep better too." Getting no more than a half shake of the head from the patient, she turned to leave with her mobile pharmacy but paused before walking away.

"Oh, I nearly forgot. You have a telephone message. A Mister... uh... Hellstone or something – I couldn't get his full name – called and asked if he could visit you. I told him 'not now' but said we would tell him when he could see you. I thought you would like to rest for a while before seeing visitors. Is he a relation? A... friend? Shall I call him back? He said he would be only a few days in London."

The reply from Helen was as confused as her dreaming. She definitely did want him to visit but did not want him to see her, not until she was sure that she looked better than when he had last seen her. Without screening face bandages that would not be a certainty and it might be a visual disaster. Besides which she wanted to see Mary before she saw anybody else other than the medical staff.

Help was at hand, both medical and emotional. The duty nurse and registrar applied some ointment to ease the pain in the stitched areas of her face. That enabled Helen's mouth to operate without giving the impression of a bad ventriloquist trying to say 'bottle of beer.' Another call from Mary confirmed that her friend would be with her within the hour.

Sure enough, Mary breezed into her friend's hospital room some forty-five minutes later. Apologising for not getting there earlier and dropping her handbag on the blankets covering Helen's bruised arm. A cry of pain was met with a gasp from the handbag dropper – an apology and combined giggles for both girls. A carefully restrained embrace and then, down to more serious business, chocolates and flowers. The flowers could have been watered with four eyefuls of female tears as Mary peered into the savaged and bruised surface of her once beautiful friend's face.

A more composed Miss Tiarks tried to take the pain from her bosom pal's bosom. A sore and stitched hand extended to wipe the tears from Mary's own face. This was not time for tears or recriminations. It was time for reflection and philosophy, or as much as they could reflect and philosophise.

"Now don't you start crying. You'll make me cry again and that hurts!" They both giggled again but Helen wanted to be absolutely serious. She had realised for some time that she had to make the best of a very bad situation and to get her friends to follow the same path.

"All my life I've been told how pretty..." She stopped before saying 'lovely'... "I am... I was. And it nearly always made me wish they could accept that I had a brain to get me through life. Sometimes I felt they were treating me like the dumb blondes in all those pathetic jokes. Now I'm a horrible mess." She waved Mary's protest aside. "Yes I know I am. I just have to... I nearly said 'to face up to it'. Now who's making pathetic jokes?"

The two friends giggled once more through their tears and hugged to soft squeals of pain from Helen and apologetic groans from Mary. Their friendship was never more needed and never more given. Although she had been trying to side-step the subject of her social life she was not sure how to say what she wanted to say without referring to it. A change of subject would provide an opening.

"I've just heard from our nice Mister... Elphinstone – yes that's it. You know he arranged to get me out from the Lebanon and back here for surgery? Well he apparently called – he phoned anyway – and asked if he could come to see me. I can't say I don't want to see HIM, but I don't think I want him to see ME. Not yet anyhow. Not until I know that I can – I nearly said 'face him' again – until I feel that he won't absolutely recoil when he sees what I look like."

"Of course he won't 'recoil.' I'm sure he's much too sensible to do that. And apart from the fact that he saw you in hospital in Beirut he's also seen some pretty awful sights out there. Much, much worse than a few cuts and bruises, I bet. You don't have to worry about that, my girl."

Mary was being honest as well as sensible but they both knew that her honesty was heavily enforced by a desire to comfort and cradle her friend's battered mind and body. She suddenly thought to return the recurring facial pun with one of her own to lighten up the conversation.

"Trouble is, you've got 'face' on the brain. Most people have, I suppose." More giggles. Slightly forced this time. *'Many a true word is spoken in jest'* – and they both knew it. Perhaps a stronger attempt at serious gossip and conjecture would be a better course to steer.

"You really do fancy him, don't you?" No beating about any thin bushes. Straight to the heart of the matter. "I'm sure he must fancy you too. With or without the bandages.

Seriously though, you know he's not the sort to be turned off by a few little scratches. They'll go soon enough anyway. You must see him as soon as you feel up to it and get him, not exactly hooked but at least to know that you care about, well... what he cares about you."

"For a lawyer," Helen thought, *"Mary makes a strong case. I wonder if I could make as strong a case for myself?"* She nodded gratefully for such a *"strong knot of human bondage"* came to mind but went out again as something pinched from a Somerset Maughan picture of pathos. Pathos was not to be on the menu if she were to return to her previous sprit.

After another hour of light chatter and frequent laughter she felt as though she was one of the luckier girls on the planet. Survival from the frenzied assault was lucky by itself and to have survived and be supported by friends like Mary – and Mary would ensure that many others followed suit – that must be the best of luck.

That night's sleep and rest was also the best, or at least the best since her entry to hospital. The following morning was as good and she quickly ensured that the gentle Philippine nurse would return Jock Elphinstone's call with an invitation to visit whenever he thought it suitable and convenient. The nurse returned to tell Helen to expect a visit that very day.

She added that he had been warned of the serious damage to the patient's arms and face but advised of the damage being reduced to negligible proportions in the near future. *"As a nurse,"* Helen reflected, *"she makes a good advertising manager. Let's hope she's proved right."*

Hope remained high in her mind throughout the day and into the evening when the nurse announced that "Your nice Mister Stone" would be coming to see her "at or about seven-thirty p.m."

"Glad it's not at or about seven-thirty a.m. ", rang through her mind as she started to rearrange the bed-clothes and asked for a hand-mirror and comb. Lipstick was considered but

considered too painful to worry about. If he were to see her, if not 'warts an' all' at least scars and all, then she need not concern herself with such cosmetics.

Half past seven on the dot saw the assistant commercial attaché from the British Embassy in Beirut entering the private hospital in Surrey with his usual reputation of stealth well in hand. With him were the customary offerings of flowers and sympathy, warm words and cold comfort, but nothing more. Nothing that could suggest advancement of their brief encounter into anything more than his official capacity would expect. Nothing to raise the temperature or raise her hopes.

The conversation soon passed the 'how are you' stage. The answer to that was displayed all too prominently in Helen's case. The cool impression that he had given in their first meeting returned to Helen when he started to ask questions concerning her assailant and the evidence given to him by the Red Cross officials at the scene of the crime.

It was almost as if he was more interested in the two unusual female refugees in Bekaa camp than he was in Helen. She tried to dismiss it from her mind but the impression remained stubbornly. When he mentioned Cocky Lloyd as well she thought at first that he was changing tack to more convivial and social subjects but then he returned to ask again about the refugees.

Over the course of nearly an hour of conversation, Helen only spent ten minutes or so talking about personal matters relating to herself. She hoped that he would reciprocate by divulging enough of his more personal feelings to pave a way to closer understanding. Eventually, as the acceptable period for hospital visits drew to a close, he did divulge some more personal information. But it was not the information that Helen expected or wanted to hear.

As he rose from the chair beside her bed he leaned forward. Helen thought for a moment that he was about to kiss her but instead a strong hand met her bandaged one in the lightest of grips to say goodbye. He did say, "I hope to see you fully recovered very soon," but he would say that, wouldn't he?

He also said something that removed any feelings of being lucky. It left her, to use one of Mary's expressions, 'gob-smacked and speechless, both at once.' With an almost apologetic tone as he looked at his watch he casually mentioned that he had to get back to central London to see his wife and daughter "before they took to their beds."

A completely deflated Helen had no option but to take to, or remain taken by, her own hospital bed. Her bandaged hand dropped from his to the bed-covers and she tried to nod and smile understanding without blanching in shock or bursting into tears. Her world seemed to be as empty as the rest of room following his departure at eight-thirty p.m. on the dot. But tears did run through her eyes again as self-recrimination ran through her mind.

"No use saying that I should have known he would be married. And have a child or children. Useless to say that I should have expected it, even though it was never mentioned before. I didn't know but I certainly know now." Another of Mary's expressions came to mind and from her sorely stretched lips.

"Bugger!"

Ch. 26. An unattached attaché.

Helen had felt very sorry for herself when she discovered that her hopes, for a long and loving voyage of friendship with the Beirut Embassy official, had been wrecked on the shore-line of matrimony. She might have felt less self-pity by considering the plight of his spouse and family in London. After his prompt departure from the Surrey hospital, Mr Elphinstone returned to London's suburbs to bid a less than fond farewell to Mrs Elphinstone, their daughter Sarah and son Freddy.

Since his career had taken him to various embassies in the Middle East it had followed a slightly different course from that of the standard diplomat. The usual round of receptions and dinners with businessmen and governments had been largely replaced by less respectable 'one-on-one' meetings with individuals without portfolio or visible official standing.

They had often involved some whose national allegiance might be to almost any country but the United Kingdom of Great Britain and Northern Ireland. People of either sex or sexual persuasion who might be described by many as 'shady', meeting in places of a similar description. These people were not likely to be seen at a Buckingham Palace garden party and equally unlikely to be seen at a party hosted by Mrs Juila Elphinstone.

After a traditional wedding in Belgravia, ten years of time and travel took their toll on an increasingly strained relationship that could not be held together by the arrival of daughter Sarah. A son was born two years later. Shortly following his birth, mother and children returned to London from their rented apartment in Istanbul and moved into a small detached house in Pinner.

By the time that Sarah had started secondary school Julia had started playing in a local bridge school near Hatch End.

Her husband had been transferred to an even more hostile environment in The Lebanon, where spades were more likely to be applied to hasty burials than hands of cards. By the time that he assumed his new role as the assistant commercial attaché at the British Embassy in Beirut an open mind to her marriage had been firmly closed.

His place in her affection was then occupied by charming but un-enterprising friends who considered the good life to consist of four no-trumps in their hand and two cars in their garage. Jock Elphinstone's slightly shady contacts in adventurous locations were downgraded to downright villainous characters whose negotiations were frequently applied with the aid of firearms or Semtex explosives.

In addition to the uncertainty and personal security fears suffered by Julia in Turkey and The Lebanon, suspicions of extra marital affairs were compounded by his failing sexual interest in her female charms. She was not even sure that he had an interest in sex with any female. Certainly he seemed to be more concerned with his male contacts although that might be due to the scarcity of female ones. Apart from the middle-aged receptionist and a committed Presbyterian secretary at the Embassy there was no obvious candidate for the role of 'the other woman.'

Julia was quite unaware of her husband's strong interest in one particular female, and it wasn't the recent victim of assault now lying in a hospital bed in Surrey. After a fast car journey across the Home Counties to Middlesex he completed his domestic duties and continued towards Heathrow airport's terminal five.

A room at the Hotel Sofitel had been reserved for him to rest before the next morning's flight to Beirut. Once checked in and refreshed with coffee and sandwiches he made a call from his cell-phone to the Beirut Embassy office to advise them of his position and be advised of developments. Most of the reports from his office were brief and routine. One unconfirmed report however was far from routine and deeply disturbing.

Before acting on any unconfirmed report he would do two things. Initially he would consider the source and who or what other persons or matters might be affected. Secondly, he would try to get confirmation or correction. Pending another report on the matter he thought of the 'who' and 'what.' Another phone call was initiated, this time to his friendly insurance investigator.

He didn't know where or what was occupying Cocky Lloyd but he wanted to know what or if he had discovered since their last discussion. The telephone call was answered but Lloyd's location was unknown to him. He guessed that Lloyd was answering from somewhere in the Middle East or the Balkans.

It was only slightly East of Elphinstone. In fact, it was from Chiswick. Cocky was also about to refresh himself – with a beer and a pork pie. He had returned from Kosovo three days earlier and from his office in Lime Street within the hour. After an exchange of locations and current state of health it was apparent that further conversation might be easier in a convenient venue between them.

It had taken Cocky nearly a week to search and locate the best oases within a short distance from his Chiswick flat. During his early years in London, Elphinstone had followed a similar search and rescue operation. The suggestion of meeting at 'The City Barge' pub beside the river near Kew was accepted by both without hesitation. Within twenty minutes from the phone conversation the two men were continuing their exchange in the company of each other and two pints of ale.

At a relatively quiet table ten feet away from the bar, Jock took his usual commanding stance in the conversation.

"What news do you have for me, Cocky? Have you found our little friend from Bekaa yet?"

Looking back on the discussion, Lloyd sometimes wished that he had simply answered "yes." A simple 'yes' would not be acceptable however, not enough to demonstrate that he had fulfilled his part of the bargain in tracking the elusive woman half-way across Europe. Apart from wishing to relate chapter and verse of the detective work involved he wanted to obtain a similar revelation concerning the missing yacht and its mysterious owners.

Over the next two hours and three pints Elphinstone listened intently to the story of the Alawite woman, the Kosovan men and the sinister Serbian, as described in detail by Lloyd. Only the occasional short question interrupted Lloyd's account of finding them, and meeting with 'those two imposters' of triumph and disaster in the company of his collaborator and guide Arian Bogdani.

In order to make the account more comprehensive Lloyd had related some of the history of past discoveries with Bogdani. He was still unsure of the Kosovan's continuing motivation or objective in helping to trace the refugee and her latest helpers. At some stage, he hoped, their objectives would harmonise.

His companion seemed to be quite impressed with the success achieved by Lloyd. He brushed aside suggestions of disaster. He was particularly interested in details of the Serb who had travelled to Kosovo without actually travelling on with the woman he was due to help.

"What, apart from money and possibly travel information, did he give to her? Any weapon or clothing... anything?"

Lloyd thought back to Aysil's meeting with Dragovic and Broz at the station in Pristina. She had only the clothes she stood in plus a small travel bag. Later, when she alighted from the Skoda car she had the same clothes and the same bag. There was no obvious exchange between either of the travellers. Not at the station anyway. Possibly at the house near the hotel but not before.

His mind travelled back to the hotel room when Aysil was there with him. The same clothes, the same bag, possibly with another smaller bag, an overnight purse with soap and toothbrush perhaps? He could not be sure because he had not been interested enough in her clothes, apart from removing them, or other effects.

"Of course," he added, "Broz, the driver, could have kept something else in the car to give to her. But I certainly didn't – couldn't see it – if there was anything." Elphinstone remained silent, pensive as ever.

Eventually the account was complete and Elphinstone appeared to be content, as much as he could be. At that stage Lloyd asked for his pound of flesh – a few ounces at least to put on the bone of his pursuit of the missing yacht. He was to be disappointed.

"I'm afraid I haven't much news to give you of your yacht, Cocky. The last we heard of it was when I told you that it was seen sailing – motoring – back from the Crimea. Probably heading south and west towards the Bosphorus and the Med. There are several ports and little places to hide down there but I suspect it'll probably stop for refuelling or re-crewing somewhere in or near the Ukraine or Bulgaria."

Lloyd was more than disappointed – almost deflated at the lack of news. Elphinstone's information of the yacht was his driving force – or excuse – for trying to trace Aysil. Without evidence of it somewhere his reputation as a tracker would suffer nearly as much as the huge insurance claim on his employers in The City.

Having tracked Elphinstone's quarry and given so much information to him about Aysil's progress and cohorts he fully expected to receive as much in return if not a putty medal. Had he been a civil servant his work and success would probably qualify him for an MBE or 'My Bloody Effort'. As it was, Elphinstone would probably get promoted and an OBE – 'Other Buggers' Efforts.'

The potential member of the Order of the British Empire fully appreciated Cocky's disappointment and hoped to provide more information and assistance than he could now.

"Sorry about that, Cocky. Really, I am sorry. But I'm confident we can get more news, perhaps even some evidence to save your boat and your bosses' money. Don't forget, it's in my interests too. But right now I have something rather more urgent to follow.

"You remember that guy Abdul-Nasir? The one you called Abdul the Bastard? I told you he was released after being accused of people-smuggling. Yes? Well, I'm still trying to find him too. I don't expect you've seen him in the Balkans but you might have heard something about him on your travels. Did you by any chance?"

It was Elphinstone's turn to register defeat. Disappointment returned to the pub table. The beer drinkers finished their last pints and conversation, accepting continued uncertainty in the searches for missing persons and the missing boat.

"I must get back to the Sofitel, Cocky. My flight leaves early tomorrow and I have some work to do before I go. I'll try to get some more sightings of our boat..." – *"No longer MY yacht then,"* thought Cocky. *"Must have gone down in the world. As long as it hasn't gone down in the Bosphorus."* – "... when I get back to the Embassy. We have some fairly powerful kit up in the sky that should be able to find it somewhere."

The tall man said he would hail a taxi rather than ask Cocky to drive him to the Sofitel. That was just as well as Lloyd had travelled to the pub in Strand-on-the-Green by time-honoured Shanks's pony. Hands were shaken as Jock said goodnight to Cocky and to the beer-drinking population of the bar.

Then he was gone – *' like another thief in the night'* – ran through Cocky's mind again. But that was too harsh, even if it were true. After all, there had been the vague promise of unofficial help from official resources. What was he talking about when he said *'some fairly powerful kit up in the sky?'* Had he been talking about aircraft with radar sensors? Or spy satellites?

"Could be an old woman in a basket, more likely on a broomstick." The City Barge's licensed drinking time was close to its moorings, as was Lloyd to his apartment.

He decided to have another pint of 'Pride' before walking back.

Someone else's life was also approaching its moorings.

Ch. 27. Abdul the Bastard.

In the opinion of most members of Her Majesty's Foreign and Commonwealth Office, unconfirmed reports are usually confirmed shortly before they are proclaimed official, or shortly after they have been published in the world's news media. Jock Elphinstone realised that he was dealing with an unconfirmed report and feared the worst.

The unconfirmed report told him that what he had suspected was almost certainly correct. A body had been washed up on the shore of a Greek island near to the Turkish coastline. That by itself was not at all uncommon. Bodies of the dispossessed were all too familiar a story – too familiar to warrant newspaper headlines or television news broadcasts.

Unless the body was either one who could stir the consciences of the world, or one who ranked as important to anyone other than nearest and dearest friends and relations, it would remain as 'just another body.' The unconfirmed report concerned one who was rather more important to Elphinstone. It was the body of an alleged people smuggler and all-round bad egg. The description matched that of one labelled by Cocky Lloyd as 'Abdul the Bastard.'

Little had been heard from or of Abdul Nasir since he had vacated his usual place in Bekaa camp. Most observers assumed that he had gone to extract more money from others who could afford to pay and not afford to stay. Despite a hard-earned reputation of exploitation and brutality amongst the huddled masses, the same masses continued to consider men like him as a last straw for a drowning man or woman to grasp.

What was unusual in the report of his assumed drowning was that no other bodies had been found at the same spot. If Abdul had been the conductor of several paying passengers and his vessel had floundered then up to fifty others would have shared his fate. The report mentioned only the one lone corpse on the water-line.

Of course, the telephoned report to the assistant commercial attaché had pointed out, he might have fallen overboard, or been pushed. But in that event the remaining passengers on a flimsy inflatable dinghy would be rudderless and probably helpless to fend for themselves in the rough seas. Pushing him overboard would be akin to the fabled scorpion stinging the frog who carried him over the river.

Other possibilities had been forwarded in the report. The corpse might not be that of the hated bastard Abdul. But if not, then who? Another refugee who happened to be a dead ringer for the well-known extortionist? Was he too wearing the flashy clothes and gold Rolex watch? That would be unlikely and remain unconfirmed for a long time.

Most of the theory of accidental death could be discounted. Another report, still unconfirmed, mentioned that the corpse appeared to have been stabbed through the heart and lungs before entering the water. The lungs contained more blood than sea water and the flashy clothes were now flashed with red stains. The back of the torso had been punctured between the left shoulder-blade and the spine with a thin bladed knife or similar weapon of some description.

Suicide was not considered to be likely.

Few would mourn such a man, a ruthless agent of illegal entry to the promised land. For some reason Elphinstone appeared to be one of the few, possibly the only one. His firm upper lip became firmer and his eyes became sadder as the hours passed without any denial of the unconfirmed report.

By the time that he arrived to board his flight at Terminal five of Heathrow Airport he knew that the report would eventually be confirmed. He also knew that he would have to consider more carefully and more urgently the 'who' or 'what' other persons or matters might be affected. In doing so he turned to the questions surrounding Abdul's last known location and possible fellow travellers between The Lebanon and Greece.

On the flight back to Beirut he pondered on the likely perpetrators of the crime, for he could now be sure that criminal action had ended the life of the smuggler. Once he could narrow down his list of likely candidates he would then ponder on the motive or motives. He had a host of ideas but this was a matter for a trained detective to analyse, and he had one detective in mind.

He might even have to tell him the truth, the whole truth or something like the truth. In exchange he would expect complete confidentiality and continued reports on his other moving targets in Europe. Possibly including Aysil's strange girlfriend, Leila the psychotic drug smuggler and grievous bodily harmer.

The impassive Elphinstone face was for once subject to mild emotion. He had rarely been too friendly with the characters involved in his vocation; they were either working colleagues or targeted opponents. Only occasionally would they include individuals for whom he had a closer relationship and more intense concern.

His current concerns had been the location and activity of the Alawite refugee girl and the hated people smuggler, and now one of them had ceased all activity to become a wet and bloody corpse. This was not in the plan and definitely not in the national interest. His attention would have to refocus on the assassin and his or her motive.

That took his mind back to his initial conclusion. It would be a matter for a trained detective. Even before his aircraft landed in Beirut, he had realised that he was not in a position to act as a professional detective, but he knew a man who could.

He had just left the company of such a person. Back in the Thames-side pub in Kew.

Ch. 28. Something like the truth.

The flight from London to Beirut landed without incident at Rafic Hariri International airport. A car was waiting for him near the 'arrivals' exit with attendant chauffeur 'en guarde.' Elphinstone hoped that the driver would guard his passenger as well as he protected the black Mercedes E350 saloon but he realised that the motor probably meant more to the chauffeur than any official from the Embassy.

Once safely, or as safely as might be possible in Beirut, strapped in to one of the rear seats, he inspected his cell-phone to ensure that it was more private than the Mercedes was. He would not risk a call whilst in the car. That would be inviting a breach of security as big as the breach in the Burj al-Barajneh building after the latest bomb outrage, and he was aware of certain 'leaks' of information from his organisation.

Telephones in the Embassy offices were as secure as could be expected of a diplomatic citadel. Security was never one hundred percent anywhere. Not in such a volatile city. Once restored to his own office desk and chair, after greeting and declining involvement in the other matters delivered by his secretary, he paused to consider what he could ask of Cocky without divulging a word more than absolutely necessary.

It took him just thirty seconds to arrive at the conclusion that there was little that he could withhold unless he was prepared to lose Lloyd's confidence and probably lose most of the details discovered in his report. It would have to be the naked truth, or something dressed up like it.

"Hello, Cocky, old chap. Yes, back in my office, thank you. Just phoning to thank you for the pint, or pints, at that nice old pub by the river last evening. What's that? Yes. I got back to the Sofitel all right. No problems. You too? Well, not to the Sofitel, I understand that. Where is it? In Chiswick. Very nice. Home from home, then." He forced a chuckle that he hoped would soften any anxiety in his voice. But he was definitely anxious. Time was passing. Time to cut to the chase, as the Ambassador was wont to say.

"I can't give you all the details just now but, could you possibly get back here asap? I know, it IS very short notice but very important. We'll cover all your costs and book your flight for tomorrow morning if you can do it."

The request sounded so urgent that Lloyd agreed immediately. It might concern the yacht – it probably did concern Aysil. He boarded yet another aircraft and was met by the same Mercedes with the same chauffeur. When securely behind the Embassy's closed doors, Elphinstone released more of his secrets and fears.

"Look, Cocky. I've had some disturbing news. No, not about your... the yacht. It's about, well, one of our less distinguished characters who's been fished out of the water – or his body has. And I need some expert help to try to find out 'who dunnit' and why.

"The deceased appears to be our old friend Abdul-Nasir. Yes, I know. Abdul-the-Bastard. It hasn't been confirmed yet but I know it will be soon. He might have drowned eventually but, with stab wounds in his back and through his heart and lungs it doesn't look as though it was a drowning accident. I expect you've seen lots of similar cases before, in your police days.

"Now, I know you think – or thought – of him as an absolute villain and I would agree with you under normal circumstances. I hate those people-smuggling bastards as much or more than any man. But this one's a bit different. He was probably – possibly – involved in shipping a bunch of refugees including a close pal of Aysil – yes Aysil our... uh... lovely friend – over the water from Turkey to Greece.

"The close pal of Aysil that I'm talking of has what you call 'previous' in the stabbing business. And I also have reason to believe that Aysil would say that she hated Abdul even more than you do... did. I'll explain all that later but for now my priority is to get more up-to-date information on her whereabouts and what she's up to, including any other contacts."

From the chair at the other end of the desk came a long silence followed by an even longer exhalation of breath. Elphinstone waited until he could tell whether Lloyd would say anything. Then the former detective's breath turned to speech. He spoke slowly and carefully to make certain of his questions being clear and understood.

"I can understand why you might want to find the girl with the knife or broken bottle, Jock. And what she might have had to do with the murder – I presume we're treating it as murder aren't we? Yes? Right then. But why involve Aysil? Just because she's friendly with the crazy girl doesn't mean that she had anything to do with a death on a dinghy in the Med. Does it? She's been miles away, in the Balkans."

Elphinstone remained silent. He wondered if Lloyd's infatuation with Aysil would cloud his professional judgement, ruin any objective analysis. But Cocky hadn't finished.

"And another thing. Apart from your interest in international justice... what's it got to do with us? He wasn't British was he?"

There would be no avenue for obfuscation now. No way to hide the salient facts of the relationships.

"No Cocky. He wasn't British. I'm not sure what he was really. But he was important to me. As is Aysil, but not for precisely the same reason. And I understand your concern for her too. We're all human... even Abdul is... was."

Lloyd could hardly believe that this touching little eulogy was coming from the mouth of British hard-nosed and euphemistically named 'commercial' interests. Elphinstone on the other hand was keen to secure the full co-operation of his captive audience and would assume the mantle of a saint to do so if necessary. The words of Alexander Pope ran through his thoughts. 'To err is human, to forgive divine.' And there were a lot of errors to forgive.

"Let me fill you in on some of the background to all this sordid business. You remember the vague theories I put to you concerning this region's tectonic plates and the flow of refugees, and others, along the geological fault lines? Well we all know that a large portion of the so-called refugees are not just seeking a quiet working life in Germany or Sweden, or Britain.

"There are some travelling along the fault lines to Northern Europe who intend to visit real violence on many of us. They might be crooks looking for easy pickings from wealthy foreigners or fundamental – with the emphasis on 'mental' – religious fanatics looking for terror and mass murder worse than any volcanic action."

Lloyd interrupted the long drawn-out details of human earthquakes and terror with a mild protest.

"Aysil's not a religious jihadist. She hardly goes to church – mosque – regularly. I know. I've had some deep conversations with her. Very deep... "

His voice trailed off as he thought of the last passionate murmurings with her in Pristina. Elphinstone brought the conversation to the point of revealing all, or most, to Lloyd.

"No. I know she's not a jihadist. At least I don't think she is. But I do need to know where and what she's up to. Believe me Cocky. It's very important. And if that mad girl with the knife is with her by now, I may have to do something about both of them. That's all I can say about her at this stage.

"As for poor old Abdul, I have other reasons to get hold of his killer and find out why he was murdered. It might have something to do with Aysil. It might even have something to do with you... the yacht."

Lloyd was losing the thread. Almost losing the plot.

"What on earth can the Bastard's death have to do with the yacht in the Black Sea? This is getting ridiculous."

"I know it sounds a bit far-fetched, Cocky. But believe me there is a connection somewhere. Why do you think I have been helping to trace it? It isn't only to help you or in payment for tracking Aysil, although that is a very important reason for me to help you. Let's ignore the yacht for the moment and concentrate on Abdul and Aysil.

"Can you – will you – help me to track her down again, please? I'll tell you now why Abdul's death is important but I can't know if there's anything in it connected to the rest of the problem unless someone like you can conduct a little professional investigation.

"Abdul was not the bastard that you and others think he is... was. Yes, he said he was involved with moving refugees across the water at some stage but he wasn't a real people-smuggler. That was just a front. He posed as a smuggler to stay close to the people and keep tabs on any undesirables moving into Europe without a just cause i.e. fleeing from war.

"The undesirables include jihadists in ISIL or any other terror group. They also include well-trained agents of countries like Iran and other Russian or Chechen affiliates. Hezbollah... Al Q'aeda... KGB... you name 'em. Abdul was my agent, keeping close tabs on their agents. And he was my friend. Got it?" His voice rose with even a hint of emotion.

Lloyd was not sure if he had 'got it.' Did Jock Elphinstone mean that he had what is commonly called 'a meaningful relationship' with the sweaty dark Abdul-Nasir? Was that a critical factor in the separation from Mrs Elphinstone, now back in cosy suburban Pinner? Or was it just an ex-army thing? An unspoken bond between a band of brothers?

"Whatever it was," he thought, *"it's serious enough not to argue with."* He would 'get it' and get on with the new task of tracing Aysil again. That would not be unwelcome work. He would be less enthusiastic about facing a crazy Hazzara girl with a knife and a protective passion. From his experience in the Hong Kong, and South Wales police forces, he knew too well that any form of 'meaningful relationship' carrying a

knife and fuelled by passion could be a murderous combination.

He was to discover some much more murderous ingredients in such affairs. But first he had to discover the whereabouts and activities of Aysil, with or without the cutting edge of Leila.

Ch.29. A port in a storm.

After he and Andrew Tulloch had discussed their proposed joint venture in the IBIS hotel in Geneva, Vasil Antonov prepared to return to his home and office in Astana, the former Akmola – or 'white grave' – that had been renamed with even less inspiring simplicity with the Kazak word for 'capital.' The capital city of Kazakhstan.

In his student days while becoming comfortably fluent in English and less so in Kazak, Vasil had been puzzled by the English term 'capital punishment.' His first few months in Astana seemed to confirm 'capital' as an alternative to 'white grave' and descriptive of his new home. His first few months there felt a like spell in the condemned cell and his contractual term of three years' employment sounded like a life sentence.

Putting, as he himself put it, 'the wheel to my shoulder' at his work place during those initial months had avoided boredom and soon reaped dividends for shareholders and employees. Improved extraction techniques at the company mine plus a dynamic marketing plan by his new Russian colleague Georgi Petrov had reduced costs and increased output.

But Vasil missed his old chums from university and home comforts in Sofia. Apart from avoiding all but the most essential studies and consuming the maximum volume of red wine, Vasil and friends had pictured themselves as Olympic sailors. One of their first journeys at the end of term at St Kliment Ohridski, also known as Sofia University, would be to the Black Sea port of Varna.

Without the finance to buy their own racing dinghies or a suitable training vessel, the undergraduates would befriend the harbour-master. This allowed them to beg, borrow or hope for a benevolent owner to let them sail in the quieter waters beyond the main shipping lanes. By the time that he had graduated with honours in natural sciences, Vasil had become a master in scrounging other people's boats, with honours in applied persuasion.

Leaving Andrew in the hotel with Mary and taxiing to Geneva airport, Vasil thought he should treat himself to a day in Sofia and possibly another to return to his student vacation days in Varna. His airline tickets could easily be adapted to permit a break in Sofia. Then a short trip to Varna and its harbour would be justified as giving mental refreshment after intense planning and negotiation. That was his opinion anyway, and there was nobody handy to challenge it.

There was nobody waiting to greet him either. Not at Sofia-Vrazhdebna Airport, Bulgaria's main airport located ten km east of Sofia. He didn't expect either of his parents to drive there just to see him arrive and then depart for Varna but he was slightly disappointed – no, very disappointed – that the former girlfriend who had begged him ten months ago to return to her charms had been too busy to meet him there.

A short phone call to her apartment told him why. The telephone was answered by a male voice, instantly recognised by Vasil as one of his former collegiates at St Kliment Ohridski University. After an exchange of short and slightly surprised greetings the men concluded that there was no point in challenging the situation. The girl had grown tired of waiting for her man to return from Kazakhstan and had succumbed to his old friend's new advances and nearly new BMW 525.

Vasil Antonov was a man of decision. He had already decided to travel on to Varna. He couldn't beat them so he decided to ask the man in his girlfriend's apartment if he would like to join him. A moment's brief pause was followed by enthusiastic acceptance and Stephan Borisov asked his new-found lady-love to wait for his return in two days time. He also asked Vasil to wait for him for an hour at the airport.

The journey to Varna by road would take nearly five hours and by air only three-quarters of an hour. It was, what he thought he had heard Andrew Tulloch call, a 'slow-brainer.' In the hour's wait for Stephan, Vasil acquired two return tickets at his company's expense and joined a short queue at the check-in desk. By the time that he had reached the front of the queue Stephan had joined him. Two hours later they were both entering a small hotel near the waterfront's array of big ships and yachts of various shapes and sizes in Varna's harbour.

The Hotel Ventura on the South side of the entrance to Varna's east and west harbours provided the two sailing enthusiasts with comfortable beds and was close to a vantage point where they could view vessels plying their ways in and out of port. After dropping their luggage in a double room and confirming to the curious porter that they were just good friends, a short walk before dinner took them to the side of the canal between the harbours.

Most of the vessels moving quietly upstream to the east harbour were large commercial ships carrying large commercial cargoes. Most of those slipping less quietly into the sailing club moorings were small yachts with no cargo but enough alcohol to pickle the crew for a year or two. One or two very large yachts provided accommodation more luxurious than any hotel in Varna.

One such floating vodka-palace appeared to be in need of an admiral and half the Bulgarian navy to obtain access without resistance. It sat serenely moored two hundred metres outside the main harbour entrance and carried a crew of hard-faced and heavily armed men. More than one of the men had shaven heads and with the aid of borrowed binoculars Vasil could just discern a tattoo like a spider's web on one of the tough scalps.

Focusing the binoculars on the stern of the yacht behind the stern crewmen, he could just read the vessel's unusual name. It looked for all the world to be similar to the strange name that he had explained to Tulloch and Lloyd as Cyrillic script. It was the unpleasant arachnid adopted as a badge of honour by former members of Russian special forces in Chechnya.

"Why would anyone with such a beautiful – or at least very expensive – yacht like this, give it such a nasty name as that?" he asked no one in particular. Stephan Borisov was near enough to hear him...

Stephan was not really interested in the name. He was still drooling over the lines of the graceful mini-liner and the thought of what it might contain. His imagination pictured himself at the wheel, if there was a wheel, commanding a smartly clad crew. The stewards on board would be jumping to his command, delivering cold vodka-martinis to one of his hands while the other hand was snaking round the waist and posterior of a beautiful blond girl. He would be Bulgaria's own Dmitri Bond.

His imagination had not worked out who was to steer the boat while both of his hands were otherwise engaged. He would have a man to do that, he supposed, or another blond beauty. His actual vision had been hindered by an oil smudge on his binoculars so he could not really see the name on the boat's stern. Day-dreaming was rudely interrupted by Antonov's scornful question. He blinked and turned his head.

"What name? What's nasty about it anyway?"

Vasil cleaned the binoculars for his companion and pointed to the yacht's stern.

"That name, of course. 'Skorpion.' What fat oligarth prat would buy a billionaire's yacht and call it a scorpion? Serve him right if he was stung by it."

Stephan was not interested. He returned to his dreams of luxury aboard it with the retinue of men and girls crawling to his every wish and whim. Vasilov was still puzzled and annoyed at the flagrant abuse of wealth and bad taste. He was also unsettled at the coincidence of the name and the translation of the mistaken code queried by Andrew Tulloch's friend 'Cockeye', as he called him.

Perhaps the owners were Arabs, he pondered. He had heard someone say that one visit to Dubai had convinced him that 'they had broken the poverty barrier but not the taste barrier.' Mind you, he reminded himself, that could apply to plenty of people in Moscow and other places too. Maybe even some in his current abode, in Astana.

By the time that the two would-be Olympians had worked up a thirst and were ready to slake it they had reached the end of the jetty. A white painted outbuilding proudly proclaimed that it housed the harbour-master's office – or one of them. Their old contact there had been promoted and they would have to explain some reason or excuse to pry into Varna's marine affairs.

That wouldn't deter Vasil Antonov. He walked straight into the compact office and asked politely if his former contact was available, even though he knew that the man had been transferred for nearly a year. The name-dropping was sufficient to allow for further enquiries if not for an offer of refreshment – not yet anyway.

"I was just wondering if he could help me further with some enquiries I was making with him last year. But if he's been moved to another post, then perhaps you could help us." At the mention of 'us' Stephan looked around to see who else was involved. He realised that 'us' included himself and nodded in silent agreement. The new assistant harbour-master looked faintly bored but felt that he had to show some level of public spirited interest.

"How can I help you then? Are you moored here or planning to be sailing here soon?"

"No. Not this week. It depends on... uh... various matters. But we saw a big warm-water boat, a vodka and whisky palace, in the harbour and wondered who owned it. It looks very much like one that we had an... uh... interest in and may have to contact the owner. It's that huge motor yacht with a name like a 'Skorpion' and a crew who look as though they're related to one."

Vasil laughed. He hoped that a show of humour might ease the way to extract more information. Like the name-dropping, it worked. Boredom left the official's face and was replaced by a laugh.

"Oh, that one. Yes. It is a daft thing to spread all over the blunt end of a multi-million dollars' worth of boat. The short answer is that I don't know. It only arrived here yesterday and demanded – not asked, you understand – demanded to bunker-up with enough fuel to drive a cruise liner. I suppose the daft buggers didn't tank up with enough when they left port. I think they came here directly from Sebastopol. That's not too far to run a full tank dry in one of those monsters."

This time it was the harbour official's turn to generate some levity into the conversation. Vasil and Stephan both returned his humour with their own laughter.

"Maybe they forgot that their engines don't run on fresh air and seawater. Or maybe they thought it had a nuclear powered engine. Those Russians on board don't look like scientists but you never know."

The mention of the dreaded word 'nuclear' brought the humour to an abrupt end. The memories of Chernobyl in nearby Ukraine and the disaster that followed was enough to kill any levity. The harbour official was very suspicious of anything resembling radioactivity, particularly if it came from Russia.

"Why do you say 'those Russians?' on board. Have you been talking to them as well? I don't like Russians, or anything nuclear. We don't want any of that here."

Antonov adopted a defensive stance. He wanted to get more answers to assuage his nagging curiosity but didn't want to spoil his two day break on the Black Sea coast.

"Oh, I don't know. The crew, with the shaven hair styles, looked like Russians – sailors or even soldiers. With those tattooed heads they could be androids for all I know. What did they say they had on board apart from a thousand litres of vodka and dry fuel tanks?"

Harbour-master's mate clamped his lips together. This conversation was getting less than jolly. It was adopting overtones of toxicity. Rather than continue in the unusual conversation and conjecture, he decided that it was time to establish the 'who's and 'what's of the vessel and these two nosey parkers.

"Perhaps you should just leave your names and business details with me and leave me to establish the facts of the vessel, if you think there's something fishy about it."

The Antonov defence turned to retreat.

"Yes. OK. No problem. Of course we can leave our contact details if you think there's something to investigate. You can reach us at the Hotel Ventura. Talking of which, we need to get back if we're going to get any food this evening. Thanks for your help and good luck with your enquiry. Hope it turns out well for you."

With that, and the assistant harbour-master's perplexed look, the two men extracted themselves from the small building and strode briskly back to the Ventura. Toxic or not, Antonov's curiosity had become contagious. By now the assistant harbour-master felt obliged to satisfy himself and any others who might ask questions of the unusually named luxury vessel outside his harbour.

He established the state of readiness of the yacht by telephoning the manager of the fuel supplier. The fuel supplier confirmed that it would be several hours before the vessel could leave port with full tanks and completed documents. That gave a signal for the assistant harbour-master to make another call. This time to the port customs office to whom he suggested that a quick inspection of the vessel and its contents would be in the national interest.

Within the next three hours a squad of armed customs officers had boarded the 'Skorpion' and interrogated the surly and aggressive master and crew. The message from the harbour-master's office had included the sinister word 'nuclear' which had prompted the customs office to add a military arm to its body of searchers.

Their combined search for anything untoward, from illicit vodka to a hydrogen bomb, was largely unrewarded and entirely unwelcomed by the crew. However, the military presence included a small Geiger-Mueller radiation measuring instrument. That had the irritating habit of emitting a series of buzzes and clicks whenever it passed near the engine compartment.

"Perhaps," one young customs official asked the military presence, "it does have nuclear powered engines after all." He laughed nervously but nobody else did. They were 'slightly scared shitless' as one observed later.

Nuclear or diesel powered, it continued to trigger off the little hand-held Geiger-Mueller instrument. After one of the shaven-headed deck-hands tried to produce a Makarov pistol from the back pocket of his jeans they all realised that heavier weaponry was required. Three of the combined customs and military investigators bundled the struggling gunman onto a bench and another telephone call to the local army barracks produced a fully armed squad of soldiers within a half hour.

In addition to some very heavy artillery, the soldiers brought some modern metal-cutting tools and an old-fashioned crow-bar. The combined efforts of soldiers, sailors and crow-bars eventually exposed a compartment beneath the engines where a small crated container was housed. As the man wielding the Geiger-counter approached the crate his instrument increased its emissions to near fever-pitch.

More urgent telephoning brought a new and powerful contingent of local politicians and – most powerful of all – newspaper and television media reporters. That evening's television news included a report of weapons grade uranium smugglers being arrested in Varna harbour and a stolen luxury yacht being impounded by police and army officers.

The harbour-master's officers, customs officer and every other office's officers vied for credit before the cameras. In the Hotel Ventura bar two puzzled guests still wondered who had mentioned 'nuclear' and why such a lovely boat would have such an ugly name.

Ch. 30. A Tartar by the tail.

After the excitement of sighting the vessel and its subsequent boarding and arrests, Vasil Antonov and Stephan Borisov endured a feeling of anti-climax. This was soon erased with the aid of some excellent Cabernet wine from the Terra Tangra vineyards and hot Meshana Skar mixed grill. That was followed by some more Cabernet and a good night's sleep after a good day's snooping.

Neither of the two former undergraduates realised the full implications resulting from the discoveries on the YS 'Skorpion', now safely impounded in Varna harbour with a skeleton crew from the Bulgarian Navy. Neither of them knew the true identities of the yacht or its owners. They returned to Sofia on the following morning's flight where Vasil said goodbye to his friend Stephan and boarded another flight to Astana.

Despite the reputed poor record of border control in the Black Sea ports, an incident that involved radioactive material and the attempted use of a hand gun against the customs officers was extremely rare in Bulgaria. It produced some fairly extensive news reports in local and national media.

Being the subject of a marine vessel search, the news was also reported immediately to Lloyds of London to appear in their account of marine movements – the famous 'Lloyds list.' Unlike the more sensation-seeking tabloids it would take some time to be published there because there was no official record of a super-yacht registered in Cambodia and called the 'Skorpion.'

Messages and questions flew between the Lloyd's building in Lime Street and the port authorities in Varna. Each was trying to establish the true identity of the floating nuclear arsenal. It remained radioactive but marine inactive. Having been impounded by the Bulgarian army, much to the disappointment of the Bulgarian navy, little or no information was released by either of its military guardians for nearly a week.

One of the first steps towards health and safety measures was to subject the hull to extensive cleaning in order to reduce radioactive residue to a minimum. This exercise was delicately performed with the brutal use of high pressure hoses and heavy-duty wire brushes. After the hold and engine compartments were declared safe – or safer than before – the crew's quarters were scrubbed and treated to a purgative dose of disinfectant. Then the H & S armed squad turned their attention to the exterior of the hull.

Work on the surfaces of the 'Skorpion' was slow and ponderous. The cleaning officers and men wore thick rubber gloves and protective clothing including face-masks and helmets. During the sloth-like progress with brushes and hose-pipes there were several collisions between the men due to detergent on the decks and dirty spray on their goggles.

To the army's squad of cleaners the disinfection process was like a long haul home after a stormy voyage in filthy weather. Then at last the exterior began to appear clean and safe. Working carefully from bow to stern, the yacht started to look more like the oligarth's luxury toy again as the white surface gleamed in the sunlight.

Finally, brushes and hoses were applied to the blunt surface of the stern, bearing the 'ugly name' on the lovely boat. As the high pressure jets of water forced the weed and algea from the glassy surfaces, it revealed some traces of older paintwork. Beneath the 'ugly name' was a much prettier and romantic name – 'Anna ' –in cyrillic script, followed by small patches of black paint that could have once been a Cyrillic letter or a number.

Eventually the puzzled army sergeant reported his findings to his superior officer who returned to the harbour master for guidance. As the harbour master was unaware of the ownership of the 'Skorpion' he was equally ignorant of whoever owned the 'Anna... (whatever.)'

Once again the messages and questions sped along telephone lines between Varna and London, until a clerk in Cocky Lloyd's office referred to his 'minefield of information' file. It suggested that the vessel in Bulgarian custody might well be the good ship 'Anna K.' That yacht was currently posted as missing, believed stolen or sunk, with a multi-million dollar insurance claim on its mast-head. It seemed that the Lutine Bell would remain silent as far as the 'Anna K' was concerned.

Being the registered proprietors of the 'Anna K', the strange RKM Group and its even stranger Russian Tartar chairman Mr. Bekir Kazakov, whose daughter was also named 'Anna', were swiftly delivered of the good news – and the bad news.

First, the good news. Your yacht has been found and is safely in custody.

Now, the not-so-good news. Your claim for many millions of dollars is extremely unlikely to be accepted, let alone paid. To add to the bad news, there may be international criminal charges against the acting master of the yacht and all who sail with her or him. These charges, which could include smuggling illegal weapons or proscribed material; piracy and/or fraudulent insurance claim, may be extended to the owners if any evidence of collusion or instruction is revealed.

Pending clarification and evidence, the vessel would remain in custody, leaving the owners without recovery or reimbursement but with the smell of scandal and possible arrest hanging over their heads.

As the news appeared loudly in broadcasts and publications, so the Chairman of the RKM Group disappeared quietly from public view. A brief statement announced the withdrawal of the proposed takeover bid for Vasil Antonov's mining company in Kazakhstan.

Relief and astonishment joined forces in the Antonov camp in Astana. Vasil was bemused by the unusual combination of arms smuggling and insurance fraud. Being primarily an honest engineer he was unfamiliar with such illegal affairs. His first step was to telephone to the other half of the joint venture agreement that he had recently signed.

"How", he asked Tulloch, "were these things involved with their takeover plan?"

Tulloch had been equally astonished at the news. He understood much more of the motives and modus operandi from his investigation of the RKM Group's previous acquisitions. Two days later he returned the call and offered an explanation. It was an old tale of complicated actions camouflaging simple theft in order to confuse the innocent.

"Hello Vasil. Yes I'm fine, much finer that we were last month in Geneva, although I enjoyed that too. Listen Vasil. I've been doing some detective work on the Tartar – yes, 'Ivan' as we called him – and his group. It seems that all of his companies spend more than they earn but keep going and keep taking over others. And each new takeover is bigger than the last one, like a chain letter scam or pyramid selling.

"As far as I can see, when they have spent all the money they had borrowed in their old companies, they take over a new one and use the money in each new company to repay the borrowings in the old ones. We call that 'robbing Peter to pay Paul.' In the meantime, they have been buying assets in the West with money borrowed or stolen in the East.

They have been spending some on foreign property and luxury boats but, there must be something else. What drove them to claim millions of dollars from insurance claims and presumably get more from smuggling nuclear fuel? Do you have any ideas? I don't think now that it's just a straightforward case of money laundering.

"Perhaps the insurance money from the yacht claim plus whatever they got for the uranium or plutonium would buy enough of your company's shares to get a controlling interest.

Then they could take it over completely without opposition. After that they would have grabbed whatever you owned and used that money to pay off their old borrowings. Çlassic asset stripping.

"But I'm still unclear as to what they needed your entire company's asset value for. Whatever it is – or was – it must be something very big and probably dangerous. Hard to tell with some of these outfits in the old Soviet bloc. Sorry Vasil, I don't mean you or your company. Something else... "

Vasil assured Andrew that he was not offended. Like many honest people faced with complicated fraud he was not at all clear about the financial jiggery-pokery. He was just relieved and glad that his company appeared to be safe for now and that he had someone to work with who seemed to understand these strange events. More was to follow that would also not be clear to him.

Another telephone call brought more mystery than explanation. Tulloch had been studying the markets in commodities trading.

"Hi Vasil. It's me again. Yes. We're all fine. Who? Oh, by 'all' I mean Mary and me. Sorry. I should have said that. Why? Well... because we are well and we are going to get engaged. Yes, engaged to be married. Thank you. I'll send an invitation as soon as it's official and I get my orders from my new boss. No. Not the company boss. Yes. That's still me. I was joking. I meant... oh, never mind." He paused for breath and returned to the subject of the call.

"I think I may have stumbled on – uh, I mean found out – another reason for Ivan's attempt to steal so much money from us and the insurance market. You know that we make a lot of our business dealing in futures – options – for various commodities like metals and other minerals. Yes, I thought you would be familiar with all that.

"Well, we know that the RKM Group has a huge exposure, a commitment, to buy billions of dollars worth of oil - at fairly high prices by today's standards. I can't see those prices being as high as that for ages yet and their option contracts close in a few weeks time. Unless the selling price goes up very quickly, they will owe someone up to half a billion dollars. It should be one of the biggest company crashes since.... since... the last one!"

They both laughed. It was driven by a mixture of schadenfreud and revenge – poetic justice. News had also been broadcast of a warrant issued by legal authorities in Bulgaria for the arrest of the RKM Group chairman Mr. Bekir Kazakov. Mr.Kazakov was – the news article explained – still unavailable following the impounding of his company's yacht and its lethal cargo.

The Tartar had disappeared with his tail between his legs.

Ch.31. Troubled oil on troubled waters.

As Andrew Tulloch and Vasil Antonov were digesting the events in Bulgaria leading to the Tartar's exposure and their companies' release from danger, Cocky Lloyd was trying to make sense of the latest developments. As had so often happened, his first port of call was telephonic – to the British Embassy in Beirut.

He had received the news of the yacht being identified and impounded through his own syndicate at the same time as Tulloch had told him of Vasil's adventurous trip to Varna. His friend had also tried to explain the apparent motives of the RKM group and its enormous liability in the commodities markets but that had been too much for 'a simple copper' to understand completely. All he knew was that the yacht owners would owe someone an absolute fortune unless matters changed dramatically.

Lloyd was well aware of the effects on world economies by movements in materials' prices. He could see as well as the rest of the workers in the City that the world of oil production and supply was undergoing a tumultuous upheaval. How that had driven the Russian Tartar and his company to try smuggling dangerous materials such as uranium was just too much to grasp, even with the aid of Tulloch's specialist knowledge. *"Perhaps"*, he thought *"I should ask a man who could."*

When the usual frustrating enquiries about the nature of his call had been resolved he heard the familiar measured tones of the assistant commercial attaché.

"Morning, Cocky. I trust you're well and happy to hear the news of our... " (*"No longer 'Your' I note"*, thought Lloyd,)... "our yacht. Collared in Bulgaria, eh? That makes a change. In the bad old days Bulgaria was an outpost of Moscow. They did as the Kremlin would bid them and that included a lot of the comrades' dirty work. Now it seems that the Comintern worm has turned into an EU good guy."

Elphinstone emitted a rare chuckle. A degree of satisfaction worked its way out of his standard non-committal voice. "Well, I did promise to help tracking it and I hope you've received due satisfaction from the insurance market for our combined efforts."

The loss adjustor from Lloyds of London confirmed happily that he had received not only verbal satisfaction, but also the promise of a 'more than expected' cash bonus at the end of his syndicate's financial year. Irrespective of who or what had traced the insured vessel and scuppered its nefarious activities, the potential loss to them had been adjusted down to a bare minimum.

Elphinstone then turned to the subject of his own targets. "Now that you're happy and revelling in glory and cash, how about my missing persons bureau? Have you any news of the errant refugees from Bekaa? Or have the ladies vanished again?"

Lloyd's euphoria dissolved in a wave of embarrassment. He recognised that he had failed to maintain contact or even a sighting of Aysil or any of her companions since leaving Arian Bogdani in Kosovo.

"I'm sorry, Jock. I must admit that I've not had sight or sound of her since she left Pristina with the taxi-driver chap we – Bogdani and I – met there. I know she was reported to be heading for either Slovenia or Italy or Austria and then possibly going on to Germany or Sweden."

"Oh great. That really narrows it down then. What about the other twenty-odd countries in the EU? Can't you do better than that? I really need to find her again – and very soon."

"OK Jock. I'll talk to Bogdani again now, or as soon as I can find him, and then get back to you." He put the office phone down and then picked up his cell-phone to call to the Kosovan capital and his friend Arian. "*By now*", he calculated,

"Josip Broz should have got back to Pristina and Bogdani can get some news from him."

He calculated correctly. Bogdani was sure that he had seen Broz in the town and would get the latest news from him. Within the hour Lloyd received a return call from Pristina.

"Hello, Cocky. Yes, it's me, Arian. I have just met Broz at his house, you remember? Near the hotel? Yes? Well, Josip took your girlfriend"... (*'I wish - if only'*, thought Lloyd,)... "to Sarajevo and then she was expected to go over the border with Croatia and on to Ljubljana."

"Where? Lubli-what? Is that in Croatia? I thought it was a big prison in Moscow, isn't it?"

"No. That's the Lubyanka, the KGB headquarters. Ljubljana is the capital of Slovenia. I would have thought that you knew that."

"Yes. Of course, just kidding," lied Lloyd. It sounded genuine as long as he put a reassuring emphasis on it. "Where would she go after that? Oh. I nearly forgot. Was anyone else with her?"

"Where to? I can't say. But there is a good connection from there into Austria. Graz is only a few hours away from Ljubljana – about two hundred kilometres... "

"Graz," muttered Lloyd. "How far is that from Germany?"

"Germany? I don't know. Maybe another two or three hundred. Depends on where in Germany she wants to go. Vienna is quite near. That's about two hundred from Graz."

"Vienna? That's... uh... interesting. Thanks Arian." Lloyd stopped talking and pondered. While he was pondering, Bogdani was answering his forgotten question.

"She did meet someone who might have travelled on from Sarajevo with her. Another refugee girl. Another Muslim girl in a hijab and long dress. But as I said, definitely not her sister. She looked almost oriental – not Syrian in any case – Josip thinks."

"OK If the other girl's not Syrian, where d'you think she might come from? Oh. And if she's not Aysil's sister or whatever, how did they meet up? Just by chance? In Sarajevo? Sounds too much of a coincidence after she had mentioned something about meeting her sister."

Bogdani listened to the barrage of questions with fading patience. He didn't mind helping Lloyd after the co-operation they had shared a few years ago and this investigation might lead to other matters in which he had an interest. But Lloyd's questions were probing into detail that no one could expect to have unless they were party to the refugees' agenda.

"I can go back to ask Josip – you know, Broz – if he picked up any other talk of who or where she was likely to meet or where they planned to go. But I've already told you as much as he's told me so far."

Lloyd calmed down and backed down. He realised that he sounded like an interrogator in a police cell. He also reminded himself that without Arian, he would not have found Aysil at all after she left him in Athens.

"Sorry, Arian. I'm asking for the impossible, I suppose. Tell you what – I'll see if I can find out any more from my end... " (He meant *'I'll talk again to Elphinstone'*) – "and perhaps you can squeeze some more clues from your pal Josip. How does that sound? OK? Could you – no – could I phone you again this evening? Say around nine p.m. your time?"

Bogdani relaxed and confirmed that nine p.m. would be fine. By that time he could have had a drink with Broz and talked again about football and girls. The first would command Broz's undivided attention and interest. The second would lead naturally to more discussion and conjecture about the two girls that he had driven to Sarajevo in his makeshift taxi.

"That would do nicely, Cocky." He laughed at the imitation of the TV advertisements that he had seen. Lloyd picked up on it and returned a light reassuring laugh as well. Then, rather less assured, he put down the receiver and looked for the British Embassy telephone number in Beirut.

When the voice from the Embassy answered and was asked to connect him to Elphinstone, he noticed a marked improvement in tone and speed of connection. Almost as if they had been expecting him to call and were impatient to hear his news. That tone was reflected in the assistant commercial attache's voice too.

"Oh. Hi Cocky. Glad to hear from you so soon. What news?" Friendly, but still slightly curt. Lloyd maintained the friendly tone without being so short.

"Oh, thanks Jock. Not much news but what there is – well, it's quite interesting. Might be encouraging if I can get a bit more detail.

"It seems that our girl..." (*I'd rather say 'my girl' but... whatever...*) "she's gone to somewhere called Lubljana - sounds like the Kremlin prison, doesn't it, and possibly, fairly... uh... possibly going or gone on to Graz in Austria. Maybe going from there to either some German town or over to Vienna.

"Don't know much more, not yet anyhow but, might get more later this evening. Yes, I know. It's already this evening for you but I said I'd call back at nine p.m. local time in Pristina.

"And one other thing. She's met up with another girl, probably another refugee, who we... I think might not be Syrian – seems to look a bit more oriental. Sounds very like crazy Leila. Don't know who or what she is, really. She had said she was going to meet her sister in Sarajevo but this one doesn't sound like, or look like her sister, if she has one, that is. Does that make any sense to you, Jock?"

After a very short silence there followed a soft sigh from the Embassy telephone line.

"Yes. It might. At least it might fit into one of my possible scenarios. I won't go into that right now but if you could get more about any connection with Vienna and also any confirmation of who you think that other girl is, then I'll have more to go on. Then we'll see what we can do after that.

"You might also ask if there had been any mention of what she might have been looking for in Vienna, if she really has gone there. And, I know it may sound a bit far-fetched, let me know if there had been any mention of oil. Yes, oil. Just in case she or her friends have any connection with the Russians or others dabbling in oil trading."

Lloyd agreed at once. His curiosity whetted by the return of oil trading and Russians to the conversation. It sounded as though Elphinstone's commercial and security interests might be linked to his willingness to trace the missing yacht and its cargo.

Having spent a large part of the day talking on the telephone, his ears and mind were a little numb. A short break for a snack would refresh body and soul and allow his ears to recover. A few minutes later he was walking through Leadenhall Market to a popular house of refreshment. There he could find some casual beer-slurping acquaintances and something to slurp with them. A couple of cohorts and a couple of pints soon restored order to his body and his thoughts of Aysil and the other 'not her sister' companion.

Returning to his desk in Lime Street was something like the calm after a short storm. Most of the underwriters and clerks had either gone to talk to other syndicates or simply gone. The tension of the missing yacht and its owners' false claim had been forgotten as soon as the facts concerning its whereabouts and cargo had been exposed. By four p.m. the drink almost drove him to sleep, lightly dozing at his desk.

He woke with a start. Blinking and snorting more oxygen into nostrils and lungs, he realised that he should have returned to his telephone marathon. First to Pristina and Arian. The cell phone in the Kosovan's pocket was swiftly extracted and answered. He muttered excuses to his companion, who by now was certainly not Josip Broz. Lloyd could hear a female voice suddenly abandoned in the wilderness of their cafe. Then Arian confirmed that he had extracted as much information as Broz could remember from his journey to Bosnia.

"Yes, Cocky. I have some more things... uh... information from Josip. He says that she... " His voice lowered to a muffled shout against the background din in the cafe, "... you know who I mean, told him that she was to take her sister – we know she is not her sister, but anyway – to take her from Sarajevo someways to Vienna to get a job there.

"For some reason – she wouldn't say what – she seems to have some appointment with someone there. Something to do with people who need an interpreter. Seemed to be in a bit of hurry but didn't say how she got the job, or if, for that matter. As we thought before, they try to get there by way of Slovenia, Libljana or somewhere near there and on to Graz.

"Josip left her when she met the other girl, the so-called 'sister', then she had another car to drive to Graz. That's as much as we can get, probably more than I expected. Hope it helps you. Does it?"

"Yes. That's great... well, very helpful, Arian. Did Broz say anything about her meeting that other chap – the Serbian – in Pristina?"

"Only that he had something to do with the job arrangement and he'd given her some money to help her with travel. However... ", he added in a lower gravelled tone,"... I know he also gave her a small parcel of something other than money."

"Oh, really? What did Broz– Josip – what did he think that was then?"

"Well, he didn't know any more than I know. He said, that she said, she'd been given some toiletries to smarten herself up when she got to Vienna. I don't know why. She could get that in Vienna or Sarajevo. But that's what she told Josip and that's what he told me."

"Arian. That might be very helpful. Like you I just don't know yet but I'm very grateful for all the help you're giving... have given me. What are your plans now?"

"Now? I'm going to finish my drink with my friend here, if she hasn't left me and gone home already. I might be talking to our mutual – that's what you call it, isn't it? – our friend Petric. You remember, Dmitri Petric who worked for Klevic?

He's still down in the West near Djokavica or Bela Crkva but we might meet somewhere between there and here. Shall I give him your greetings?"

"Yes, Arian. Please do give him my... uh... my regards." Lloyd was still apprehensive about anyone who had been close to the late Patrick Klevic. He didn't know what or where Bogdani and Petric might be planning – he nearly thought 'plotting' – or meeting. Better not to ask.

"Thanks again, Arian. Don't forget to give me a call when you're... uh... back from wherever and let me know what you're doing. Anything I can help you with, just ask. Bye now... Bye."

He disconnected the call and immediately re-dialled to Beirut and Jock Elphinstone. This time he used Elphinstone's personal cell-phone, as his office should be unoccupied by now.

"Hello, Jock? Yes, Cocky. You – we – were right. She and the other girl are heading for Vienna and they're talking about some job or other as interpreters for someone. That's all I know about that but, I believe she was handed a small bag from the Serb – Dragovic – supposedly containing toiletries. Don't ask me what that was all about."

As usual, Elphinstone remained silent for a second. Lloyd thought he could hear his brain ticking over.

"Jock? Are you still there? Did you catch that – about the bag and Dragovic? Does that mean anything to you?"

"Er... no. Not much anyway. I need to think about that. But the bit about Vienna could be relevant. Very relevant indeed."

"OK Very relevant is it? It may be to you, but it certainly isn't to me."

"Sorry, Cocky. I know I haven't kept you entirely in the loop. Afraid that's part of my job – my modus operandi as they say. Before I can tell you any more, I need to know – did she say anything about oil?"

"No. You asked me that before but it's still 'no'. Nothing about oil or water or anything else that I can think of. Now, what were you going to tell me?"

"Well. The reason I asked about oil is, that there's a big OPEC conference coming up in Vienna soon. And a certain gentleman of our previous acquaintance is due to be there."

"OK. So he's going to be in Vienna and it looks like Aysil will be there too. What's that to do with our 'follow that girl' exercise? Tell me, is she another of your agents? I suppose you're worried that she will suffer the same end as old Abdul."

"No Cocky. She is not one of what you call 'my agents'. Far from it. I have reason to believe that she, and possibly the other one, may be working for someone. But they're not working for – well, not for 'us.' I have very good reason to believe that she is working for either Iran or an Iranian associate such as Hezbollah."

"Good Lord. Good Lord! I'm what you might call... well, stunned, Jock. I thought all along that she was one of yours. Mind you, I never thought that Abdul was one of yours so I shouldn't be surprised at being wrong again. So, what d'you think she's up to in Vienna with the OPECs?

"And", he added with genuine and sincere puzzlement, "what on earth is she doing, getting mixed up with that Serbian what's-his-face, Dragovic?"

Elphinstone remained silent once more. Then he spoke quietly and quickly.

"Can I phone you tomorrow, Cocky? On a secure line? You do have one in your office don't you? Those mobile toys are so easily hacked. I really don't want to go into detail over this line, and it's getting late here."

Lloyd understood only too well. Elphinstone needed one of two things right now. Time to get more details checked or time to go to the bathroom. It had probably been a long day at the Embassy office.

It certainly had been in his.

Ch. 32. Good-night Vienna.

The dawn in London was very similar to those earlier Eastern dawns in Vienna and in Beirut. Mildly warm without being hot. Mildly damp without being wet. By the time that Lloyd reached his desk in Lime Street, the humidity in Vienna had condensed into light rain and the temperature in Beirut had risen to lightly scorching.

Cocky wandered into The City at a very early hour. A much earlier hour than he was accustomed to wander unless there was a special reason such as a live TV broadcast of a rugby match from the Antipodes to be viewed in a friendly pub. This morning would include a special reason but unfortunately not related to rugby or anything as important as that. This morning would include an almost full and frank explanation of certain security matters that had crossed his path, or on Elphinstone's 'tectonic fault lines', during the last six weeks.

Only two hours separated London from Beirut but he was aware that the assistant commercial attache was wont to start his day at the office as early as seven a.m. That meant that Lloyd should be available to receive what he hoped would make him truly thankful at a similar hour in London.

As he crossed the threshold floor of the insurance market building he sensed that the telephone line was already burning. By the time that he reached his desk and a comfortable chair the answering machine was registering an incoming message. The message was almost superfluous. He played it anyway and winced at the thinly veiled sarcasm in the request to return the call *'if you are not too busy drinking coffee.'*

His return call to Beirut was answered immediately. That in itself suggested that Elphinstone needed to take some action that was dependent on their forthcoming conversation. *"He must need to know something from me. That will be his business",* thought Lloyd, *"but I need to know what it is in order to give the correct information. I can't turn my back on him now."*

Following the briefest exchange of polite – or almost polite – greetings, Elphinstone went straight to the point, and to his problem.

"You know that I've been almost fixated by any mention of oil in the reports of our lady friends in the Balkans, Cocky? Well you might also be aware that Iran has just received the all-clear from the UN, or in practice from the US, to start exporting oil again. Now that they have confirmed abandoning their nuclear weapons programme the old international sanctions have been lifted. You will also be well aware of the antipathy – that's a nice word for hatred – between the Iranians and the Saudis.

"None of that... uh... difference of opinion has been softened by the Saudi backing for anti-government forces in Syria. The Saudis have been trying to keep the world floating in surplus oil in order to drive competition out of business due to the price dropping through the floor. But now countries like Iran and Russia want to drive prices back up and keep in the game.

"There's another meeting of OPEC members due to take place this week in Vienna. One of the delegates is the chap I mentioned yesterday – the Arab from Dubai who's son was the hostage we recovered from those Palestinian kidnappers a few weeks ago. He apparently has two reasons for keeping production up and prices down.

"The first reason is that he wants to keep his job. He is naturally friendly with the Saudis and enjoys enormous side benefits from them. And secondly, he stands to make a lot of money from options that he took by short-selling oil at a much higher price. Those options were part of a private contract he took out ages ago. I understand that the RKM group also have contracts but probably with the opposite end result. Like the

Russians and Iranians, they need to be able to sell at higher prices.

"Unless the Saudis in OPEC agree to cut production the price of oil won't rise much and whoever holds contracts to sell at the higher price cleans up in the oil futures market. As the Arab is a representative at the OPEC conference, he can effectively block any vote to increase prices. And that means that the RKM man will lose his shirt, a king's ransom, you might say roughly equal to the Arab trader's profits.

"As matters stand, as far as OPEC is concerned, Mr Kazakov and his colleagues are financially as good as dead in the water.

"All those attempted scams; the kidnap of the Arab's son, the ransom money, the insurance claim on... uh... I nearly said *'on YOUR yacht'* ... and the dangerous plutonium, or whatever it was – smuggling expedition – they were all aimed at one thing. They were to drum up enough cash to shore up his losses from gambling on the price of oil.

"The whole affair – it was all about oil. Always oil."

Lloyd listened as carefully as the noise from other staff entering the insurance building would allow. He almost stopped breathing while he absorbed the string of scams and attempted crimes and tried to understand how they were linked. Insurance, takeovers, smuggling and oil. The common factor was obviously money. That was not at all unusual.

The link with Vasil Antonov's mining company in Kazakstan and his business with Andrew Tulloch, although slightly tenuous, was almost understandable to him now. That was just another attempted crime disguised as a corporate takeover. What was still completely mystifying was how the movement of a young Allawite woman in a flow of refugees from Syria and the Lebanon could have any bearing on either the Crimean Tartar, or the yacht, or the mining company. Or anything.

"What" he asked himself *"has that got to do with the price of fish?"* Then he remembered. It was not about the price of

fish. It was all about the price of oil. Aysil was travelling to Vienna. Vienna, where the OPEC delegates would be meeting any day soon. And Aysil was working for the Iranians or worse, for one of their Hezbollah or Russian allies' organisations.

Suddenly the other connections connected in his mind. Aysil had not been met by Allawites or other Muslims when she first arrived in Pristina. She had been escorted and supplied with money and – and toiletries? What was that about? But she had been supplied by a definitely non-Muslim Serbian, Vulkasin Dragovic. The Serbian friend of the late Patrick Klevic. Was he a friend of the Crimean Tartar as well?

"No use asking Elphinstone about any past connections between Dragovic and Klevic," thought Cocky, *"Jock probably knows less about that than Bogdani or I do. After all, he relied on us to get that sort of information. And if he did know anything then he wouldn't admit it, unless he had to in order to get more help from me. "*

Nevertheless Lloyd thought he had to extract more about any link between today's assumed bad guys, Bekir Kazakov and Dragovic. He put that as a direct question to the assistant aommercial attache, adding that it concerned the attempted insurance fraud.

Elphinstone was unusually open and informative. *"Told you so."* Thought Cocky *"He wants something else from me."*

He was right. Although the 'something else' he wanted was effectively 'more of the same.' More shadowing and tailing the same furtive refugees.

"All I know about the Serbian and the Tartar in days gone by," replied Elphinstone, "was that they were involved with arms smuggling from Chechnya to Kosovo during the then civil war. 'Civil' – that's not a very apt description, is it?" He gave something approaching a dry grunting laugh. "The Tartar was one of the Russian special forces who conspired with the Chechens to sell high-performance weapons to their Muslim comrades-in-arms fighting the Serbs in Kosovo.

"Your late boss Patrick Klevic was the quartermaster in Kosovo and sold the arms to the insurgents there, I understand. Dragovic made sure that the arms could pass through Serbia, but also made sure that the Serbs knew all about it and could take care of any opposition from the people buying the weapons. It was an object lesson in betrayal on all sides.

"If Dragovic is still involved with Kazakov then it'll be a simple commercial contract. 'Contract' probably being the effective word. What we still don't know is, how, where, or when the 'contract' will be executed. So, my old buddy, now I need you to find out what those two girls are up to in Vienna."

Lloyd was about to exude a groan when he remembered that he had a good excuse – no, a very good reason – to visit the Austrian capital. A long-standing invitation from a grateful client from a rescue party of two years ago. Not as dramatic or dangerous as the Arab's son in Beirut but nevertheless successful and demanding of the rescued party's gratitude. Time to call in his client's obligation and to accept his invitation.

To Lloyd's mild surprise the grateful client agreed immediately. He would probably be entertained in style by the client and might even try one more time to convert Aysil's relationship with him to one more sensual and caring. But before he could prepare for what he hoped to be a no-expense-spared – by the client – holiday, Elphinstone reminded him of the task in hand.

"If you can get to Vienna by this weekend, Cocky, I'd like you to pick up a message that I'll leave at the Hotel Stefanie in Leopoldstrasse. It should give you confirmation of where the Arab is staying. Might be the same hotel but I doubt it – not expensive enough. Try to get there by Saturday mid-day and ask for a message for 'Herr Schmit' – I could make it 'from Herr Stein' if that's not too corny."

"Would that be 'from Herr LFN Stein?'" Chuckled Lloyd.

"I suppose it is a bit too near the mark. OK, let's make it 'from Herr Larssen.' that should be easy for you to remember and neutral enough for the desk clerk to have forgotten if he's asked later."

School-day memories of English literature poetry readings flashed through Lloyd's memory cells. Of Horatius defending the Roman bridge against the Etruscan army of Lars Porsena. Sometimes he had felt as though he was standing like Horatius, with perhaps only Jock Elphinstone and Arian Bogdani, 'facing fearful odds' at his side - facing the enemies of Her Majesty's Foreign and Commonwealth Office and Lloyds of London insurance market.

"Larssen? Were you thinking of Lars Porsena in the poem, Jock?"

"Not really. Although one of my middle names is the same as his side-kick – Tarquin. Don't you dare tell anyone that though. Let's leave it at that for now. You get to Vienna and I'll get what I can from my... uh... correspondent in Ljubljana."

"I didn't know you had one in Ljubljana."

"Well, 'ye ken the noo,' as they say in Scottish jokes. Ljubljana is the capital of a Sovereign state, unlike Pristina in Kosovo so we... I have 'colleagues' or correspondents there. I'm hoping that they can tell me who crossed the border into Slovenia and who left it for Graz or Vienna."

"If you can find all that, why do you need me? Not that I'm refusing to go to Vienna."

"We don't know yet if either of the girls are in or near Vienna and I don't want to discuss such a... uh... delicate subject with our people in Slovenia. Not yet anyway. Is that all right with you now?"

Lloyd was unsure whether he was being asked for his approval or subject to a little mild sarcasm. He decided to accept the possible offer 'without sarcasm' and gave his approval. It was received with a contented sigh which he took as the nearest he would get to 'thank you.'

He was beginning to wonder if all or any of his numerous travel expenses would be recoverable from HM Foreign & Commonwealth Office or if he would have to rely on Lloyds of London to continue to subsidise the Treasury. For the time being, he resigned himself to buying yet another airline ticket and booking another hotel room at his employers' expense.

A quiet day in the office turned into a concerted rush to catch up with his administration, including his expenses account, and rushing back to his flat in Chiswick to pack yet another compact suitcase. No need to carry too much to Vienna. Just the bare essentials. Perhaps not too bare but only essential baggage.

For some reason, the words 'toothpaste and pyjamas' kept running through his head. 'Toothpaste and pyjamas', 'pyjamas and toothpaste'... 'and pyjamas',... 'and toothpaste.' A disposable razor and some change of clothing joined the small toilet bag in his case. Why did those little implements of the bathroom keep coming back to remind him?

Lloyd tried to wash them from his mind and move on to travel arrangements. London Transport, or, 'Transport for London' as they called it now, that would take him to Heathrow once more and British Airways business class would take him on to Vienna. Getting from Vienna's airport in Schwechat to the city centre at Wien Mitte took only about sixteen minutes on the City Airport train, from where a taxi whisked him to the Hotel Stefanie in Leopoldstrasse.

His first task after checking in and unpacking his small carry-on travel bag was to ask the desk clerk if there was a message to Herr Schmit from Herr Larssen. Silence at first was followed by "no message" from the clerk. Lloyd telephoned his friendly Austrian host who had received acceptance of his grateful offer of hospitality. The host quickly arranged to meet him for a tour of the night-life and a typical Austrian dinner, something between a slap-up and a knees-up.

Despite the warm welcome and even warmer Tafelspitz in the famed Plachutta Wohlzeille restaurant, Lloyd found it difficult to absorb the lively atmosphere. His host's interesting stories of Vienna during the immediate post war period were over-ridden in his mind by thoughts and questions about Aysil.

Where and when was she likely to appear? And what and how was she likely to do then?

At a suitable point in their conversation he tried to steer it to the subject of oil and OPEC. His companion confirmed that the representatives would meet soon in the offices in Helferstorferstrasse and also that the hotel widely regarded as the best in that area was the Palais Hansen Kempinski. Without even remembering the name of the Arab representative at the OPEC meeting, Lloyd realised that he would have to await the promised message from 'Herr Larssen.'

He resigned himself to waiting and to using the waiting time wisely, by enjoying the delicious beef Tafelspitz and plum-rich red Zweigelt wine from the vineyards around the Danube. A traditional strudel after the beef was dissolved in his mouth by two glasses of a golden late-harvested Trockenbeerenauslese, the German-speaking world's answer to Chateau d'Yquem.

Memories of 'The Third Man' film featuring Orson Welles as the notorious Harry Lime character and of chases through the Russian sector and Viennese sewers drifted through his thoughts. The cold war-torn rubble of 1946 Vienna contrasted starkly with their current warmth and elegant surroundings.

"Why?" his mind kept asking, "why would anyone but a fanatic want to pollute such a warm rich environment after all the horrors of the refugees' struggle in the Middle East?" That rich and warm environment brought his thoughts back to sleeping once more with Aysil. Surely she couldn't be a party to the sort of destruction hinted at by Elphinstone, could she? Would she?

Surely she was not a fanatic. Those soft whispers and touches. That far-away look, *'of love, or was it pity?'* he mused – there was nothing remotely destructive about that. But then he remembered that Aysil was not travelling alone. And he remembered that the vast majority of those desperate souls occupying the refugee camps were all fanatics of some sort. Most were fanatical survivors or fanatical travellers. Some were fanatical religious or political fundamentalists, others just fanatical fanatics.

His eyes glazed over and thoughts almost turned to day-dreams when his companion's simple but repeated question brought him back to Austrian ground with a sharp jolt. "Would you like some more coffee?" he was asked again. Blinking and looking around towards the sound of the enquiry, he appeared to be considering the proposal and then confused his host and the waiter by nodding acceptance and saying "nein danke" simultaneously.

The host considered the response and decided that it was time for his guest to return to his hotel and the refuge of a comfortable bed. Lloyd could only concur silently by continuing to nod his head which the waiter ascribed to the relaxing benefits of Trockenbeerenauslese. A steadying hand and strong arm from the waiter helped the confused guest to his feet and out of the restaurant to another mobile haven that drove him to the Hotel Stefanie in Leopoldstrasse.

Once more he asked the desk clerk for a message from Herr Larssen and once more he was informed that there was no message. Disappointed and uninformed, he retired to his room and allowed the golden Trockenbeerenauslese to assume control of his tired mind and body. Its analgesia delivered an early and deep sleep after which he awoke to a bright dawn and a more optimistic horizon.

Showering and shaving in the en-suite bathroom delivered a small boost to his appetite. That was soon filled by another strudel and hot coffee. He returned to the bathroom to clean his teeth with the toothbrush and paste that he had carried in his overnight bag. With a fresh mouth and warm feeling in his digestive tracts he was once more ready to face the day.

He was sure that he would find the promised message at the reception desk and his assurance was justified by a sealed envelope. It was addressed to 'Herr Schit', which Lloyd considered to be an appropriate epithet for his hangover state, and marked in pencil by the courier as sent by Herr Larssen.

The sealing tape was rapidly cut and an A4 page of script extracted from the envelope. The message was stark and coated with urgency.

"Cocky, our travellers appear to have separated.

"The first one is still in Graz or travelling on elsewhere. Her companion is somewhere in Vienna.

"The subject of our concern is Mr Hussein Ahmed bin Q'etta. He is a representative in OPEC of an important oil-producing operation in the UAE He is also the father of the young Arab lad we recovered from kidnap in Beirut. He may be staying at the Hotel Palais Coburg or Ritz Carlton or Imperial hotels. Sorry I can't pin it down but you can find out from your hotel management I'm sure.

"We believe that Bin Q'etta may be in serious danger. He is likely to veto any move in OPEC to constrain oil production. As discussed, that would result in an immediate increase in world market prices for oil products. That's the last thing he wants but it is also just what some others would like.

"It is possible that one or other of the travellers may attempt to prevent him from attending the conference and/or blocking any move to cut production and raise market prices. Please find out where he is staying and stay there to watch out for either or both of the travellers or anyone working with them.

"If you find anything suspicious please tell my colleague Brian Knight, not at our embassy there but by telephoning his private number (43) 1 8455 9121. Just say that you are Schmit and have a message for me (say 'Larssen').

"Good luck. Don't take any chances. Stay out of trouble. Jock."

Lloyd closed the envelope and stuffed it into his inside jacket pocket. "Stay out of trouble?' That's rich, coming from him. If it were not for him dragging me into all this, I wouldn't have been in trouble in the first place."

The vague information concerning the OPEC representative's location could be resolved with the help of the hotel staff. The suspected female agent and her follower were another matter. How could he possibly find either of them without more specific details? It took only ten seconds for his down-to-earth approach to decide on the obvious practical plan.

"If those girls are trying to get at the Arab, the first thing to do is to find him before they do. QED" He was not sure of the exact meaning of QED but it usually completed a simple assumption of logic, even if the assumption was completely wrong. He made his way back to the reception desk and asked for help.

Requests for assistance are not always answered completely but, the mention of OPEC brought an air of importance and official international celebrity to his question.

"I wonder if you could help me?" That challenged the desk clerk to deny, if he dared to, that he could and would. Nodding and smiling knowingly, the clerk assured him that it would be most unlikely for him to fail, even if he didn't know what he was about to be asked to do.

"I need to contact an official" – *"that would sound good,"* he thought – "representative at the meeting this week of OPEC. You know what that is, do you?" Once again the clerk offered a withering smile and a wave of the hand to reassure the customer of his vast knowledge of everything that went on in the Austrian capital.

"Can you find out where Mr. 'Herr?' Hussein Bin Q'etta is staying and telephone him for me please? He is, as you probably know, the representative for... uh... well, you know..."

At this stage, the clerk was about to say 'of course, Mein Herr,' but he paused with a slightly quizzical frown, to remind the stupid customer that he could not just dial an as-yet unknown telephone number unless there was a message to deliver.

"And what should I say when I telephone Herr...uh... you know? After I find where he is and what number to dial?" The clerk's command of English was demonstrated to show that it exceeded the customer's intelligence quota by about three hundred percent.

"Mr Bin Q'etta. Anyway, that's all right. Just give me the name of the hotel – better give me the address too – with the telephone number and I'll phone him from my room."

The clerk smiled that withering smile again, but this time it was less patronising and more sympathetic. The time was only just nine-thirty a.m. but the customer had obviously had a long day. With another soft wave of the hand, he dialled a number that was quite familiar to him and jabbered quickly to the answering party.

After a few more jabbers and a pause to get his breath back and for the other party to examine his or her records, the information was, as Elphinstone had predicted, 'soon found out.' A hastily scribbled note on a pad with the hotel's letterhead was handed to Lloyd with a modest 'I told you so' smirk and a final wave of the hand.

Profuse thanks from Lloyd, who could hardly believe his luck - followed and were reciprocated by the weary 'no problem' nod of the clerk's head. Lloyd returned to his room and looked at a map of the city centre, Wien Mitte. To his slight surprise, the hotel was not the grand Palais Hansen Kempinski but a smaller exclusive hotel nearby within a short drive, or even a walk if one was feeling energetic and completely secure, from the OPEC venue.

A quick call to the telephone number on the clerk's note confirmed that the hotel would not disclose any information concerning its guest or guests but could take a message. The message given by Lloyd was simply to say that he had been involved with helping the Arab's son in Beirut and would like to meet him whilst he was in Vienna on insurance business. He left a note of his own name and hotel telephone number.

Lloyd was sure that he would not receive an answer at all but if he did receive one, it would be to say that Bin Q'etta could not see him. He was amazed when his room telephone rang and a vaguely familiar voice asked if he would like to meet at the nearby Cafe Central in Herrengasse. Within ten minutes, Lloyd was greeted, not by the OPEC delegate but by the young man who had been rescued from Palestinian kidnappers in Beirut. Soon they were shaking hands and drinking coffee.

Considering the near-death experience and trauma of his adventures in Beirut, the young Arab was composed to the point of being laid-back and almost blasé on being reunited with one of his rescuers. The rough handling and death threats appeared to have had little or no adverse effect on his confidence. Lloyd wondered if he might be resigned to his fate as, in the words of the old Arabian cliché, 'it is written.' Although in his position he would be unsure of the writer's identity - assistant or assassin.

Coffee and traditional Viennese sweet strudels decorated the table of friends reunited while they talked lightly of the comparative delights of elegant Vienna and explosive Beirut. After a few minutes of saying nothing in particular the young Arab explained his position, his visit, and his father's business. It was emphasised that his father would effectively hand over the latter to the son, together with his powerful position as representative to the OPEC council.

"My father is getting, not old but ready for a more comfortable life," he explained. "This week should be his last one in the OPEC discussions and then he should be able to enjoy the... uh... results of his valuable work."

Cocky eyed the young man quizzically. Was his father really so confident of his DNA passing to the young man that he would allow such an influential position to pass into the hands and mouth of one so immature and naive? One who had been duped into becoming a hostage to desperate terrorists and almost ended his own line of DNA for the promise of a night of hedonism?

The young Bin Q'etta continued unabashed. "My father has a very valuable business, dealing with the international oil

237

markets as well as OPEC negotiations. He will continue to sit on the controlling board of the business but I shall be in charge. And," he added modestly, "I shall represent him and our family in OPEC matters. This week will be his last."

Those words were to be horribly prescient. As the coffee drinkers continued their conversation, the senior Bin Q'etta was preparing himself for his short journey to meet another member of the OPEC council. He had got as far as leaving the bathroom of his hotel suite when he was overtaken by a violent pain in his chest. Unbeknown to either his family or other OPEC committee members, his breathing diminished to a few gasps as he collapsed onto his bed and tried to telephone for help.

A few minutes later his room was entered by one of the hotel staff with a message to tell him that the meeting had been delayed. Seeing the prone body of an overweight Arab guest in a state of undress, he excused himself and retreated, leaving the envelope with the message on a bed-side table. Some forty minutes later he returned and knocked softly on the door of the suite. Without any response or a sight of the OPEC representative leaving the hotel, the hotel sub-manager retreated once more and reported his concerns to the hotel's senior manager.

More time passed before the senior manager suggested that the room be opened and examined for either the guest or an opportunity to clear the half-empty bottles of champagne and other evidence of excessive consumption and untidy debris from the suite. On entering the room, he saw the prone Arab still on the bed and gasping for breath.

He immediately gave orders for the room to be cleared – cleared of the residue of the previous night's activities and of the occupant's sick or dying body. A stretcher was procured and Bin Q'etta was unceremoniously but discreetly carried out before the message could be read by its addressee.

Apparently unaware of the drama in the nearby hotel, the two cafe customers continued their conversation. A second round of coffee and strudel had been ordered by Bin Q'etta junior for himself and Lloyd but, it was to be abandoned before it reached their mouths.

The junior Bin Q'etta's telephone sounded the knell of passing father as an urgent message was conveyed from the distraught hotel manager's office. His valued guest, Mr Bin Q'etta senior, had been rushed to hospital. After a cursory examination the patient was discharged into the care of the UAE embassy, from where he was despatched by private jet to Dubai for emergency treatment.

Despite the urgent attention of skilled paramedics in the hotel bedroom, the former valued guest was now subject to extreme devaluation. He had been assumed to be beyond recovery before he could leave the relaxed luxury of his suite for the tension of a hospital operating theatre. The cause of such a sudden collapse could not be diagnosed before either a possible recovery or a more probable autopsy.

It appeared to be due to cardiac arrest or stomach ulceration associated with rich food and excessive body weight, coupled with excessive body coupling. More than one of the staff voiced rumours of liaisons with regular female, or irregular male, visitors. One recent account concerned a young temporary employee, a chambermaid of Middle-Eastern or Asian origin. But she had left the hotel's service several days ago and had not been seen since.

"Such things are not unknown in the hotel and restaurant industry," explained the anguished hotelier, adding that a full enquiry would of course be undertaken in order to investigate the tragedy. He would guarantee that the enquiry would absolve all members of the family from any possible scandal. By which he meant that he would make sure it would be published to absolve the hotel owners and staff from any responsibility.

In Dubai, a medical examination was about to create a more dramatic investigation.

Ch.33. Deadly activity.

The sanguine acceptance by Bin Q'etta junior of his father's sudden removal from his hotel, and probable removal from life, continued to puzzle Lloyd. He had seen dependants shrug off the loss of a family member before but with such a prominent and wealthy figure as Bin Q'etta involved, at least some display of weeping, albeit with crocodile tears, was to be expected from his son. So far it appeared that only the hotel manager could express a suitable measure of grief for the departed guest and his departed expensive hotel bill.

Not unexpectedly, the death in Dubai of Bin Q'etta senior and the succession of Bin Q'etta junior as head of the family and the family business was reported some fourteen days later. What was completely unexpected was the result of the autopsy. Far from being a simple case of cardiac failure or stomach ulcer due to bad diet, over-exertion or hypertension, the primary cause of death was a very rare form of poisoning; one known to international security organisations and sensationalist reporters as having traces of a radioactive element.

Polonium had been identified by the legendary chemist Marie Curie, who had named it after her original home of Poland. Some radioactive elements are often applied to help otherwise terminal illness in patients, such as prostate cancer. Bin Q'etta senior had no record of cancer of the prostate gland nor any other gland. Indeed, his prostate gland had been overworked by countless calls to duty in hotel and other bedrooms and had no time to contract cancer.

A much more sinister application of Polonium had been claimed in two high-profile reports of poisoning. The death of Alexander Litvinenko, the Russian KGB agent who defected to the British MI6 intelligence agency, was widely attributed to Polonium poisoning. The widow of Yasser Arafat had also claimed that her husband had been poisoned with Polonium. In both cases, the backgrounds of the deceased were deeply involved with politics and violence.

However, the late Bin Q'etta senior had no history of espionage or political violence. Nor had he any link with organisations involved with radioactive elements. His political activities were confined to the world market in petroleum products and its control by the OPEC cartel. The only remote connection with any source of nuclear products was his relationship with oil producers and dealers in the Russian Republic and its allies.

An OPEC delegate's personal business with international traders in oil and its future market prices was questionable. The Bin Q'etta family business had generated vast profits by trading in a market over which they could have a large influence. Insider trading is a criminal offence in many countries but trading before the market is effected by independent actions is considered speculative rather than fraudulent. Conflicts of interest would nevertheless be subject to accusation if not evidence.

The Bin Q'etta organisation had been selling vast amounts of options in future oil values, safe in the knowledge of the OPEC cartel's control over production and market prices. That was partially secured by his position as a representative of one of the largest producers. Although Bin Q'etta senior could not set the world prices he could influence them and possibly veto any motion that might not be in his interest. His reputation as an obdurate defender of uncontrolled production and low prices made him less than popular with those demanding tighter controls.

In the same way as Isaac Newton's third law states that "for every action, there is an equal and opposite reaction" so every profit generated by trading has an equal and opposite loss somewhere. In Bin Q'etta's case, his potential profit from selling Brent Crude and West Texas Intermediate oil at high prices on New York Mercantile Exchange was a potential loss for the buyers of those options.

The identity of one probable loser was painfully simple to establish. Several massive buying options at high prices had been placed by one company. That was a commodities trader called 'RKM Group.' The RKM Group was based in Ukraine but the location of its chairman Mr Bekir Kazakov was unknown. All that was known about him now was that a warrant for his arrest had been issued in Bulgaria, where a large yacht carrying radioactive material had been impounded by the authorities.

In Vienna, police received a request to examine the last known places where the late Mr.Bin Q'etta had been active – "possibly radioactive" said one unsympathetic officer. Of those places, the hotel suite from where the terminally ill man had been rushed to hospital was the top priority. As some form of poisoning involving Polonium was possible, the Viennese police inspection team copied the customs officers in Varna and armed themselves with portable Geiger counters.

Finding minute traces of radioactivity was not difficult but finding anything that resembled a significant risk to human health was less simple. The hotel suite bore such traces but not in anything connected with food or drink. The table which usually bore the trays of champagne and cognac was relatively clean. The only strong readings on the Geiger-counters were emitted in the bathroom.

A verbal report on the initial investigation was telephoned to medical administrators in Dubai. The chief officer for health there was as puzzled as the police in Vienna. "Why," they asked, "would anyone wish to eat or drink anything in a hotel bathroom when they could enjoy a banquet in the comfort of the dining room or sitting room, or even the bedroom, of their luxury suite?" The Viennese police were requested to return to the search.

In the puzzling circumstances confronting them, the police were quite agreeable to continue their searches. Geiger counters in hand, they combed corridors and elevators without success. They then turned their attention to the public rooms – reception rooms and kitchens – pantries and garbage areas. Only in the yard where rubbish was removed did they find any significant readings.

That led them to visit the public land-fill and recycling depots that had received the rubbish from the hotel. After two weeks of searching through masses of filth and disposed articles from the hotel the Geiger counters started to register a significant number of ionising particles. The high readings centred around a black sack containing used toiletries from guests' bathrooms.

The mention of 'bathrooms' set the investigators' juices flowing. It appeared that they had cornered their prey, even if they did not know what it was. All of the disposed articles seemed to be infected with radioactivity and there was no clue to any material that might have been ingested by the deceased Arab.

Only one very young and very inexperienced constable would raise the question that warranted further examination.

"Why is this posh hotel providing the guests' bathrooms with Colgate toothpaste packed in old fashioned lead tubes? Do they think that those are more up-market than modern plastic tubes?"

If the mention of 'bathrooms' had started the policemen's juices flowing, the mention of 'lead' turned the flow into a torrent. Nobody had seen Colgate toothpaste in lead tubes for years but they all knew that lead was one of the strongest protective materials to shield from radioactivity.

A call to the Austrian office of Colgate-Palmolive Gmbh in nearby Wagramer Strasse soon confirmed their suspicions. No lead tube of Colgate toothpaste had been produced since God was a boy and the rivers started to run. Somebody had deliberately taken an old lead tube, inserted toothpaste into it and painted a replica Colgate logo on the outside of tube.

That somebody had also inserted a small particle of polonium into the toothpaste. Using that lethal mixture, the user's teeth would not only gleam – they would probably glow in the dark.

Ch. 34. The fountain pen of youth.

While the Bin Q'etta family suffered the loss of its father figure and the Bin Q'etta business appointed his son to succeed him, Lloyd and his Foreign Office friend had been attempting once more to trace the two refugees from the Bekaa camp. Having tracked Aysil as far as the Slovenian capital and into Austria, further reports had dried up. After she arrived in Graz her companion Leila had apparently moved to and from Vienna but no further trace of either remained.

An increasingly emotional young Afghan girl had moved rapidly after her brief employment as a chambermaid in the exclusive hotel near the Palais Hansen Kempinski. The employment agency had accepted her resignation and the reason for it. She had explained that she was desperate to reach her relations in Germany. They were aware that many people in Austria were equally desperate to see the refugees moving on to another country.

In the British Embassy in Beirut, a pensive assistant commercial attaché discussed recent developments with Lloyd. Elphinstone was fairly certain that Aysil was now in Germany and in contact with members of the Iranian legation or Hezbollah. His interest in her travelling companion was almost non-existent other than the possibility of Leila leading the searchers to Aysil.

In a long and relaxed conversation with Lloyd, he explained his prognosis regarding the two girls' activities.

"I'm afraid we have failed, Cocky."

"Oh WE have failed, have we?" thought Lloyd. *"What did I do, or not do, to rank as a failure?"* He tried to sound calm and matter-of-fact whilst extracting further explanation from the diplomat at the other end of the phone.

245

"Oh, I don't think it was a complete disaster, was it, Jock? We tracked them as far as Austria and you seem to know where they are now."

"Well, we're fairly sure of their whereabouts now but it doesn't alter the fact that Mr Bin Q'etta has effectively been murdered and the killer or killers are still at large. The only slight consolation seems to be that his absence from the OPEC meeting has had sod-all effect on their decision, or non-decision." He paused for a brief intake of breath.

"The only outcome of the last OPEC meeting, apart from rejecting Bin Q'etta junior as a delegate, has been a statement to say that they will consider some restrictions on oil output 'IF the international situation deteriorates,' whatever that means."

Lloyd smiled to himself. "The international situation, as they call it, can't deteriorate much more anyway can it? Some people think that the third world war has already started."

"Umm... maybe it has. But we don't want it to get any worse than it is now, do we? The Iranians are determined to pump out more oil as soon as their sanctions have been lifted but they still want prices to go back up. The price of oil will only go up if and when the Arabs like Bin Q'etta's friends agree to restrict output and REDUCE production.

"Meanwhile, the Russians also want prices up but they'll support Iran's increased output to strengthen their influence in Iran and Syria. They probably thought that killing Bin Q'etta would make OPEC change their position and restrict output from Saudi and Qatar. What an eff-ing mess!"

Cocky was slightly shocked. "You don't think that the Russians murdered Bin Q'etta, do you? That WOULD start a war!"

A soft and slightly cynical chuckle answered his question. "No, Cocky. They may be murdering bastards in some circumstances but, not in such a delicate arena as this one. This was not entirely of their doing. It was a renegade operation, perhaps using some of the old Russian military camp but not any official action.

"We know now the modus operandi but not where it came from. 'The Polonium poison in the toothpaste tube?' That's so bizarre, like an Agatha Christie plot or, something in a 'Cluedo' game – 'killed by Colonel Mustard or Tommy Toothpaste'. It's almost unreal. However, it obviously worked. The tongue could absorb enough poison to kill a rhino after a couple of brushes.

"I don't suppose that whoever put that stuff into Bin Q'etta's bathroom knew what was in it or what it might do. They probably didn't even know whether he cleaned his teeth, or had any teeth! It wouldn't do its work so drastically if he had dentures."

The mention of toothpaste and poison brought the answer that Cocky was looking for.

"Of course. The 'toiletries' bag handed to Aysil in Pristina by the Serbian. She must have given it to Leila and told her to go to Vienna and leave the toothpaste tube in the Arab's hotel bathroom. Leila's head-over-heels in love with Aysil and would walk on hot coals for her."

"Mind you," he thought *"I would walk on a few myself if I thought it would do me any good with her."* He fell silent, wondering whether Aysil returned young Leila's passion. Whether she was a card-carrying lesbian or just a little ac/dc and manipulating her as a pawn in her 'great game.'

His mind then turned to another great game – the billions of dollars speculated in future oil prices by enterprises dependent on supplies of petroleum products. Airlines and shipping companies, fleet vehicle operators and others throughout the world: they all had to try to fix the best prices for fuel in order to maintain their businesses.

Lloyd and Elphinstone now knew that RKM Group's chairman Bekir Kazakov was disastrously exposed to low oil prices. He was the main party to the false yacht insurance claim while it was actually smuggling radioactive material.

247

The attempted fraud, and the bid to get control of Vasil Antonov's mining company in Kazakstan, were to cushion the losses that his toxic oil contracts would bring. The only complete reprieve for the RKM Group would have come from a change of policy on oil production by the OPEC cartel, and that had been blocked by Bin Q'etta senior.

. However, Bin Q'etta's assassination had not had the effect that the 'Skorpions' had hoped. The representatives of Arab oil producers actually hardened their stance and resolved to continue high volume production indefinitely, which caused the market price of oil to fall further. Bin Q'etta junior had replaced his late father as chairman of their trading business but not as he had hoped as representative to the OPEC cartel. He would no longer be of value as a hostage.

While Lloyd and Elphinstone pondered on the whereabouts of Aysil and Leila, an unexpected call from the new head of Bin Q'etta Trading Group brought a gleam of light on the mystery and a small beam to Lloyd. Bin Q'etta junior explained that he was about to visit a business associate in London and would like to renew acquaintance with his former rescuers.

Lloyd assumed correctly that the 'business associates' were probably a prostitute in the West End and an unscrupulous banker to supply the means of paying her. He resolved to avoid association with either but agreed to meet the young Arab for afternoon tea in The Savoy Hotel in the Strand. He would have preferred to meet in his favourite pub in Strand on the Green but assumed that its treasury of draught beers and lack of brothels would not appeal to the visitor. Afternoon tea, probably followed by 'afternoon delight' for the Arab – and a quiet walk home for him would have to do for now.

Tea and cakes in the comfortable home of Gilbert & Sullivan operettas was a pleasant change from the violence and misery of the Middle Eastern refugee camps and Viennese murder scenes. Lloyd harboured a faint hope that his visitor would extend the invitation to include dinner in the Savoy Grill after a couple of hours in the American Bar. However, he realised that other earthly pleasures were probably powdering their bodies and boudoirs for the Arab stallion and would not wait until dinner-time for their generous payments.

They would not have to wait for long. Armed with a fat wad of £50 notes from his Mayfair cash laundry and refreshed by two cups of Earl Grey tea, into which the waiter had discreetly injected a large measure of gin, the new head of Bin Q'etta Trading Group expressed his thanks to Lloyd again for the rescue from Palestinian kidnappers in Beirut.

With a cynical smile, he referred to it as "a saving of one life but a loss of another." By 'another' Lloyd assumed that he meant the life of one or other of the kidnappers. Still smirking, Bin Q'etta continued to talk of the loss. A loss, he explained, which he wished to recover for Lloyd. Cocky appreciated the mention of 'loss' and 'recover' as he was at a total loss to understand what the blazes Bin Q'etta was talking about. Perhaps the gin-flavoured tea had overwhelmed his feeble mind.

Taking another sip of the Earl Grey gin in his porcelain cup, Bin Q'etta suddenly inserted his free hand into a fine leather handbag. The hand returned from its short journey, holding a fine leather presentation case containing a very expensive fountain pen which was placed in the hand of his rescuer.

"To replace that which you sacrificed in my defence," he said, with as much pomposity as he could manage without laughing out loud.

Lloyd appreciated the joke, and he appreciated the new pen. He just hoped the wealthy Arab would not expect him to use it to sign the bill. His hopes were not in vain, as a couple of bright new £50 notes were extracted from their fine leather home and tossed onto the silver tray proffered by the expressionless waiter.

Then with no more than an "I hope we can meet again soon," the young and foolish Arab and the older and wiser Welshman took their leave and walked into the courtyard leading to the Strand. One to a waiting Rolls Royce and the other to the pavement and Charing Cross station.

Only when he returned to his office and a telephone call from Elphinstone did his amusement fade and then disappear completely.

Ch. 35. Petric and the Wolf.

Most of the news from Elphinstone was already known to each of them. Latest sightings of Aysil and Leila were vague and based on assumptions of travel to Germany. The two young femmes fatale were possibly hidden amongst thousands of refugees and could be anywhere between Nuremburg and Hamburg. No mention had been made of further contact with either Bekir Kazakov nor the Serb, Vulkasim Dragovic. They both appeared to be maintaining very low profiles.

The mastermind behind the insurance fraud and nuclear fuel smuggling had failed to master either of those scams. He had also failed to master the bid to take over Antonov's mining company. Elphinstone said that he was probably behind the kidnapping of Bin Q'etta junior in Beirut. That had failed as well.

But despite his many failings, Kazakov had succeeded with one major coup; he had achieved the murder of the man who was thwarting his attempts to manipulate the price of oil. It was a pyrrhic victory as the OPEC cartel had continued to maintain production even after the representative from Qatar had been eliminated. The Bin Q'etta Group continued to make millions while the RKM Group lost a similar fortune.

Even this coup had not come easily to Kazakov, and not without a great deal of help from others with similar objectives. Aysil had been employed by those acting for Iranian and Russian interests whilst her Afghan assistant Leila was acting only in her own interests, mainly her interest in Aysil.

Aysil had also not acted alone. Apart from promotion from her masters in Iran and their associates in Syria and Russia, she had collected help from others ad hoc as she went along on her murder mission. Assistance from her unbalanced lover, her accomplice in Austria, had resulted from a chance meeting in the Lebanese refugee camp, as had the unexpected support given by Lloyd.

Neither of her two admirers had any benefit to gain from Bin Q'etta's death and neither had received any reward or complete fulfilment of their hopes. They remained relegated to the rank of minor pawns in Aysil's great game – to be discarded if her progress was checked.

In Lloyd's eyes the true villains of the piece were Bekir Kazakov and Vulkasim Dragovic. The lethal material for the murder had been supplied by Kazakov 'the Skorpion' and delivered to her by Dragovic 'the Wolf.' Not the nicest beasts to encounter at any time and quite the nastiest animals in their zoo of espionage and civil wars.

If anyone deserved retribution – their 'come-uppance' – in their latest violence it should surely be the two principal perpetrators. And a strange incident in a region near to the border of Kosovo and Serbia came up with evidence of what many assumed was the deserved delivery of it.

News of this was announced to Lloyd a month after the death of Bin Q'etta. It came from Lloyd's old friend in the Kosovan capital. An unexpected call from Arian Bogdani in Pristina reminded Lloyd that he still owed him at least the favour of more regular contact and any business leads that he could offer.

"Hello, my old friend Cocky. How are you? How's business in the insurance world? Any business you can put my way?"

Lloyd deftly side-stepped the request, pretending to treat it as a friendly joke.

"Oh, hi, Arian. What a nice surprise. Hearing from you after all this time. Yes, business is... well, busy. You know how it goes."

Bogdani of course did not know how it was going at all, which was why he had enquired.

"No. Not really, Cocky. But I'm sure you won't forget to let me have any that comes this way. I'm working with Josip

Broz now and get around lots of places between Macedonia and Serbia and... lots of other places... "

His voice trailed off as he turned to the real reason for his call to London.

"Josip and I... we started to operate a fleet – well a couple – of taxis here and I came across our old friend Petric a week or so ago when I was in a place near Bela Crkva. You probably remember that name from the – uh – fighting there." Bogdani held back from calling it 'massacre.' He continued as Lloyd remained silent, wondering what was coming next.

"Well, I had thought that Petric – Dmitri – was still living in Albania but... he was arrested there after your boss Klevic's grave had been damaged. There's still a bit of mystery about that as the grave seems to have been empty, apart from some stones, but who knows what happened to the body.

"Anyway, Dmitri was released and came back here. Well... not right here in Pristina but over near the border with Serbia. That's where I bumped into him. No – not with my taxi – just in a cafe. While we were having a drink and talking, someone came over and patted him on the back and said something like 'well done.' So, I asked him what had he done?

"He said it was nothing. Nothing to do with him. The man had been mistaken."

Lloyd was now somewhere between bored and frustrated. Curiosity had overcome the ache in his ear from holding the telephone too hard against it. He interjected with the natural response to Bogdani's unfinished symphony.

"OK. What was it? What was 'nothing to do with him' if it was enough for someone to congratulate him with it, whatever it was?"

Bogdani smiled at the other end of the line. He had achieved the interest he wanted to generate.

"A couple of bodies were found in a ditch near the border. Both fairly well filled with gunshot. Everyone thinks they were filled by Petric."

"Well, Arian. That's very interesting. But apart from knowing something about Petric, who never actually met me, what's it got to do with me, or you, for that matter?"

"The bodies, Cocky. The bodies. That's what it has to do with us. One of them was the Serb who met up with your sweetheart when she passed through here and pissed off sudden with Josip to get to Croatia and other places. I know the Serb pissed off too but he went back before she left in Josip's taxi.

"The other dead one, I don't know. But I heard that he was working with the Serb. Probably worked with him when Klevic was alive, assuming he's dead now, who knows?"

From his office in Lime Street, Lloyd could not see Bogdani in Pristina but he could almost feel Bogdani shrugging his shoulders as he spoke. Lloyd sensed that he wanted to be asked for more.

"So, Arian. Tell me. What do you know about the late Mr Dragovic and his fellow corpse? Sounds like a revenge hit from someone who was – uh – disappointed with past activities. The supply or non-supply of weapons during the fighting near Bela Crkva, perhaps?"

Bogdani was less certain. There was less excitement in his voice.

"All I know is that Dragovic WAS involved with Klevic's cheating. And the FARK fighters who were supposed to get their weapons from Chechnya, at least those who survived, were sure to want to kill any involved with that double cross.

"The other thing I heard, but it was only gossip, you understand, was that the second body was a Chechen or someone from that part of the world. Whoever he was, he got the same treatment as Dragovic. Whoever killed them either knew that he was in the double cross long ago or some other business with Dragovic. Not likely to be honest business, that's for sure."

Another brief moment of silent contemplation interrupted the conversation. Lloyd knew that he could guess the identity of the second body even if his informant could not.

"Yes. That's for sure, Arian. That's certainly for sure." His tone adopted a more grim level. Terminal acceptance of the unlawful justice that appeared to have been administered to the two gun-runners. The identities of the two corpses and evidence of their past crimes might have been uncertain but their endings were quite sure.

"What do you think, Arian? Did Petric do it? Do you think he knew that they were involved in cheating FARK and the other Chechens? And in the massacres? He seems to know now that Klevic was behind it and he had been associated with these two, or at least one of them.

What do the police think? Have they charged Petric, or anyone?"

"No, Cocky. No one's been charged. I'm sure they think they know who's responsible but, like the man in the cafe, they would rather give him a pat on the back than a noose round the neck. No one will be charged.

"Now. When are you coming back to Pristina? And when are you going to give me some business? I can't live like – how do you say it – 'in the manner I'm a-customer to?' Not by working a couple of taxis in Kosovo."

Lloyd chuckled and tried to assure Bogdani that he would find some business soon to help the Kosovan's personal economy. They both knew that it wouldn't happen. Not soon anyway. The favour would be returned at some time but not now. For the moment it would just be added to a long list of favours. And Lloyd's list was getting longer by the week.

As they each said their goodbyes and ended the telephone connection, Lloyd's thoughts turned again to his former contacts in the Lebanon. Aysil would probably be on a hit list of either the Arab oil traders or the Austrian police, or both. If she ever returned to the Balkans she might well be added to the list of unsolved killings that people there resolved to their own satisfaction.

He had not spoken to anyone in the British Embassy in Beirut since receiving the new fountain pen from Bin Q'etta junior in The Savoy. As usual, the initial attempt to telephone Elphinstone was intercepted and obstructed by both the receptionist and the secretary, who cheerlessly intimated that she would not transfer the call to her superior but would take a message. True to her word she refused immediate contact but restored it within the hour when Elphinstone returned Lloyd's call.

He too had some interesting news; personal news which he wished to share.

Ch. 36. Home thoughts from abroad.

Before Mr JST Elphinstone could divulge his news, Lloyd told him of the deaths in Kosovo. Cocky waited for the sound of a shock wave hitting the diplomatic mind but the report of corpses in Kosovo was either too common or too late for Jock to register surprise.

"Well, we might have expected that, don't you think, Cocky? Are you sure they were who you think they were? 'Mister Big-zakov and Mister Nasty-vic?' It wouldn't be the first time that bodies had been dumped in order to hide someone else's disappearance."

Lloyd's mind momentarily swept back to Bogdani's mention of the grave in Albania filled with stones. Could Klevic still be alive and hiding in the Balkans or in Russia?

"Your guess is as good as mine, probably better, Jock. But my contact in Kosovo seems to be sure who the corpses belong to. It looks fairly certain that one of them was, or had been, Dragovic. My man probably got the inside information from one of his old gang in the area of Bela Crkva.

"That was where there was some awful mass killings and Klevic's old crew were implicated in double-crossing the local fighters. Petric would be careful to avoid any finger-pointing at himself and one of the best ways to do that would be to knock off the Serbian who had cheated them.

"The other body seems to be unknown to the locals but Bogdani did say that the skull had a tattoo of a scorpion in a rifle-sight on it. That's a badge of Russian special forces veterans from the Chechen wars. And that was where the arms for the Kosovans were supposed to be supplied from.

"I don't know why someone like Kazakov would risk being caught in Kosovo. My guess is that he and Dragovic were hiding in Serbia but Petric and others crossed the border and snatched them. If they were brought back to Bela Crkva, they wouldn't have lived for long."

From the Beirut Embassy telephone, there came another long silence. The Elphinstone brain was quietly whirring through the combinations of possible and probable explanations. He had many other reports of significance. Confirmation of the Lloyd and Bogdani reports might be only a formality.

"Well. That's all very interesting, Cocky. Very interesting. I'll just check a few items; information that's come in recently and get back to you on that. Now, any more news of Mata Hari and her little helper?"

Lloyd had almost forgotten that Aysil and Leila were still assumed to be somewhere in the EU. Footloose and fanatical. Possibly involved in further lethal missions on behalf of Iran or Hezbollah.

"Sorry, Jock. Can't help you. I lost track of Aysil after she was spotted entering Austria, and Leila had left Vienna before Bin Q'etta was poisoned. As far as I know, they might be in Germany as you said but I have no more than that to go on."

Elphinstone appeared to be satisfied with Lloyd's admission of ignorance, or possibly apathy.

"Don't worry. I expect I'll hear some more soon, from our people in... uh... other places. We'll find them and deal with them – in due course." The words 'in due course' were often his cover for 'don't know.'

"In the meantime I can let you into my own news. I'm leaving Beirut soon. Not leaving the service but going to another... uh... office. In London but not sure exactly where. I'll keep in touch and maybe we can meet up for another chat, maybe another meal, when I get my feet under the desk there."

True to his word as always, or nearly always, a call to Lloyd's mobile phone from somewhere in London announced the arrival of the newly appointed C4 grade second secretary for Foreign Affairs (Commercial). Jock Elphinstone had returned in modest triumph from the violence and danger of the Middle East to the greater violence and danger of the Civil Service in Whitehall.

Two weeks later an appointment for lunch was freely offered and freely accepted. The venue was the dining room in what Elphinstone referred to as "my monastery"; The Naval & Military Club in St James's Square, the famous 'In and Out'.

Lloyd walked to Monument underground station and took a Circle Line train to St James's Park. From there he walked across the park and up the steps to Pall Mall. Then onward and upward to St James's Square and the reception area of number four.

St James's Square was described by the Victorian writer Max Beerbohm as, 'quite the finest in London.' Although the hoary old wit had dismissed its quality as having vanished with the passing years and property developers, it had retained much of its dignity and reassuring presence. With the afternoon sunlight bouncing off the trees and over the roof of the East India Club on the opposite corner of the square, it reminded Lloyd of a slightly faded mature beauty of the Old Queen's reign.

A quick greeting from Elphinstone was followed by refreshment in the Goat bar. That increased the feeling of being in a time-warp of a century before. Cool Belgian beer dispelled the body heat generated by the walk. That was soon replaced by a measure of cranial heat from their conversation over lunch in the 'The Coffee Room', washed down by cold water and followed by hot coffee.

There was a mutual understanding of each man's need for discretion. No mention was made by either of the recent violence in the Balkans and in Vienna, other than a quiet promise from the host member to deliver a fuller explanation later to his guest. As far as the other members of the club and the staff were concerned, they were just a civil servant lunching with an insurance executive.

Elphinstone was quite open with his domestic affairs though. It was as if he wanted to share his personal problems and his hopes for an early solution.

"I don't know whether I mentioned it before, Cocky but, my wife and I have not been living together for some time. Nothing acrimonious, just the old story of separate homes and separate lives. I've been posted here and there and she has been stuck back here for some time... uh... looking after the children, and probably looking after her lifestyle. She may have another man in her life but that's not a major problem for me. Anyway, we're going to divorce, as quickly and as smoothly as the lawyers will allow."

Lloyd wondered why he was being presented with the details of the other person's misfortune when they were hardly the closest of friends or confidantes. Perhaps it was a result of the bond established between two people who had shared danger; the 'band of brothers' syndrome. Or, perhaps there was another, a more straightforward motive behind the recently promoted diplomat's diplomatic approach.

Jock continued his frank disclosure. Although he appeared to be relaxed, his situation smacked of domestic distress.

"As far as I know, my wife just wants to stay here, or rather in Pinner with her bridge parties and tennis club friends. The children are happy, as happy as children can be with only one parent at home and without many friends at school. So we can each pursue our own paths, so to speak. I'll get a flat when the FO stops accommodating me here. And I'll go wherever they put me as soon as I get used to living back in Britain."

When Lloyd heard the words 'pursue our own paths' he felt a sense of déjà vu. He had experienced a similar situation when he had been ejected from the South Wales Police and abandoned by his girlfriend Gladys Watkins – 'Glamorous Gladys' – in Swansea. Jock Elphinstone was about to become an eligible bachelor again and was seeking a fast track to the society he had left years earlier.

In particular, Lloyd imagined, he probably wished to extend the hand of friendship, or other parts of the body, to one or more eligible or ineligible ladies. What one of Lloyd's cruder colleagues had called 'enlarging the circles of his acquaintances'. *"Well, there's no such thing as a free lunch,"* he thought. *"What can I offer to help him with and what can I charge for the service? What will it cost him?"*

"I think I know... uh... how you feel, Jock. I've been somewhere near there before. In my case it was the other way round. I was pushed out of my comfort zone in Wales and moved to what was sometimes a very uncomfortable zone in Hong Kong. But I must admit, after a few months it became a lot more... uh... comfortable. Especially when I got into..." He was about to say *'got into bed'*... "the local scene and had a great relationship with a lady out there."

Elphinstone tried to appear politely disinterested. The politeness was achieved but not the disinterest. That disappeared quickly, as did his diplomacy.

"Oh. I didn't know you were involved with a girl out there. Is she still on the map? Still in touch?"

Lloyd's face told him in stony silence that his diplomacy had failed to turn up.

"No, Jock. She's not... uh... on the map at all. As a matter of fact, she's not anywhere. She died after being kidnapped and drugged by... well it doesn't matter. I managed to get her back from the crooks but she never really recovered from the drugs they pumped into her. She never even recognised me, even after two years."

The silence returned and remained at the table while the two diners sipped their coffee and Elphinstone tried to think of a way to escape from his faux pas. He knew that there was only one way out.

"Sorry, Cocky. What a stupid prat I am. Forgive me and my big mouth."

"No. That's not a problem, Jock. It was, as they say, a long time ago. Well, not very long but completely 'ago' now. You weren't to know anyway and being a copper I just had to accept it as an occupational hazard. Now then. Why don't we have a drink with some friends soon and in the meantime you can fill me in with what information, or disinformation, you're allowed to let me have."

Elphinstone looked very relieved and immediately accepted the invitation, reciprocating with one of his own.

"I don't think I could tell you much here. Oh, the staff are quite discreet but I haven't been back long enough to know just who's listening in and who might tell tales out of the service." He didn't expand on his definition of 'the service.' Was it the civil service in general or his more secret variety?

"If you have half a morning to spare, come to my new office. I'll give you my card to guide you through the corridors of power, and we can compare notes, so to speak. Oh, and when would you suggest meeting to air our more social graces?"

Lloyd didn't know any girl called Grace but, he did know who might help. Even if he was working in Switzerland, Andrew Tulloch would be calling in to see his London office soon and that would be the cue for a social gathering, graceful or disgraceful, of old pals and pal-esses.

Sure enough, Tulloch flew to London within a fortnight and Lloyd was there to 'meet, greet and eat' as he put it, in the restaurant that lay between their respective London offices. Tulloch's news of his business activities in Switzerland and Kazakhstan was encouraging – almost an anti-climax after the drama in Vienna and Kosovo.

No further attempt had been made to take over Anatol Vasilov's mining company and no news had been forthcoming from RKM Group or their lawyers. As far as Tulloch could establish, all threats were off. Lloyd remained silent, not knowing whether to relate all the details of the violence and deaths of Bin Q'etta and Dragovic. For the moment at least he would let dying dogs sleep.

Before Lloyd could broach the subject of more enjoyable social affairs, Tulloch delivered the news he had been holding under wraps.

"If I ask you to guess what I'm about to do, Cocky, what would you say?"

"I really don't know what you're talking about so, I can't possibly guess. Unless you're going to get married."

Tulloch's face subsided to a pale blankness. "How did you know that? We finally agreed to do it yesterday, just before I told her I was coming here." He stopped to gather his wits and breath, now raising a low smile to himself. "She said that if I wanted to see her over here then I had better bring an engagement ring with me and get a wedding ring as well. Sort of bulk purchase. Hope I get a discount." Lloyd's face warmed.

"I didn't know at all. Just sounded like the sort of thing people ask others to guess. I thought that you and Mary had an understanding – staying together but apart – sort of thing. Oh... uh... I presume – no – I shouldn't presume anything I suppose. But it is – will be – Mary, will it? Or is there something else I have to guess?"

Tulloch's smile strengthened and joined a wry chuckle at the thought of Mary's demeanour if she had been told of a replacement. Vasilov's deepest mineshaft in Kazakhstan might not be deep enough to hide in if his newly-appointed fiancé were to be given such a slap in the face. Unrequited love was one thing but unrequited marriage might trigger off another war.

"Don't worry. It's Mary all right. She knew that I would chase her until she caught me. Or maybe it was the other way around; she was chasing me until I caught her. Anyway, I – or we – are going to do the decent thing by each other. With a bit of luck she'll let me do the indecent thing as well."

They chuckled again. Lloyd thought of introducing the subject of a party to include Jock Elphinstone, and perhaps Mary's beautiful friend Helen. Introduction to 'La Belle

Helene' would be a perfect offer to persuade the half-secret civil servant to explain all.

"No, there's no such thing" thought Cocky. *"It's either secret or not. There's no halfway house with secrets."* But Jock could surely release the missing facts behind the Arab's murder and the Crimean's crimes. He raised his glass – a small dry Albarino to join gastric forces with his grilled sea bream.

"Well. Who would have thought it?"

"You obviously did, didn't you?"

"Yes but, I didn't really expect it. However, the deed's done now, or will be by this afternoon I think. Now, how about a little party? I'd like you to meet a... uh... friend who has been a great help to both of us although you possibly don't know it. I have mentioned him before, when I was working in the Lebanon. Jock Elphinstone. He's just been posted, sent back to London and I said I'd introduce him to you and some others. D'you think Mary would persuade Helen to come?"

"Still fancy Helen then, do you? How does she feel though?" There was no sneer in Tulloch's voice or in his mind. Everyone admired Helen, even after her enforced facial surgery. But did Helen fancy Cocky? That was another question. A silent shrug and nod from Lloyd answered the first question. No one but Helen could answer the second.

"Right then. I have to get to the jewellers. Ratners still open, are they? I might spend five bob on a ring. I know. It's a lot but, if you want the best, you have to pay for it." They both laughed at Tulloch's old joke although spending money was not always a joking matter for him. "I'll phone you tonight to confirm after I've spoken to Mary. She'll tell me where we're going to meet and who and what to wear. I'm only obeying orders from now."

Andrew Tulloch always liked to display the manner of a latter-day Scrooge but in fact he was almost blissfully content at his forthcoming change of lifestyle. Mary was a perfect choice of managing partner and he knew that he should just let matters take their course. Whether Cocky would follow suit -

that was his affair. His and perhaps Helen's. *"Who knows,"* he thought. They were both free agents.

The term 'free agent' was one that seemed to fit Cocky's position in many ways. Free to get hitched or stay single. Free to take another job if the life he led was no longer to his liking and, as an assistant to Elphinstone's plans and plots, his unpaid help was indeed free, or it had been so far.

When the two men had parted from their lunchtime retreat, Lloyd returned to his office to check the progress of his latest insured loss-saving task. It was to find and return a young girl who had been abducted by her professed lover who now demanded a large ransom. The insured girl was the daughter of a wealthy Central American sugar mill owner and the false lover was a former French nightclub 'bouncer.'

Lloyd had traced them both to an address in Nantes and requested help from his contacts in the French police and Interpol. The gendarmerie were only too pleased to help as they had previously tried to charge the man with drug offences but had insufficient evidence. The opportunity to arrest him for kidnap and extortion was too good to miss.

After a short message to his police contact in Paris and an agreed plan of action, wheels of justice were set in motion. Falling to a mixture of promises and threats from the French special psychologist in crimes of that nature, the perpetrator surrendered and the victim was soon recovered without Lloyd's presence being necessary in Paris or Nantes.

The local police in Nantes were happy to make the arrest and hand the kidnapper to their Parisian colleagues while the unharmed but embarrassed girl was held for medical examination and a tearful reunion with her parents a few days later. A grateful mill owner accepted his daughter without undue cost to either himself or the insurance underwriters.

"Sweet as a nut" was Lloyd's verdict on the outcome. The sugar mill magnate was puzzled by the reference to nuts but accepted it just an example of "the English madness." When he suggested that, Lloyd adopted a pretence of insult.

"I'm Welsh actually, Senor. It was WELSH madness." The rescued girl's father simply smiled and said nothing. The 'Welsh' label meant nothing to him. It was yet another example of English madness.

While Lloyd was earning his keep with one of the more straightforward cases of his career in the great insurance market, a phone message was recorded on his answering machine. It was from Tulloch and gave details of a smart restaurant with which he had warm economic relations as a corporate client. His engagement party would take place there in ten days time and his Bulgarian associate Vasil would be there, as well as Mary of course.

Tulloch had also invited Lloyd to offer similar invitations to *'one or two friends including the chap you mentioned at our last lunchtime chat.'* He added a cautionary note to Lloyd to let him know that Mary's friend Helen would be there so there was no need for Lloyd to invite her.

Thoughts of Helen's presence at an exclusive social gathering were certainly stimulating for Cocky. He wondered if she might be more receptive to his attempted advances this time. Having experienced more disaster than triumph recently in the field of romance, he decided to construct a 'Plan B' by inviting a lady friend of his own. The trouble was, as he complained to a sympathetic colleague, he didn't have one on him at the moment.

'Plan B' tended to dominate his thoughts for a few days, during which he tried to engage some of the girls in his office with talk of parties and weddings without suggesting anything which might either be miss-construed or absorbed as a mild proposal. He also tried to contact Elphinstone to add his name to the invitees and claim more information as a quid pro quo.

Another telephone message told him that the new C4 grade second secretary would like to see him in his – 'the office.' THE Foreign Office in Whitehall – foreign although in the heart of London. A short return call to the impressive Victorian palace that had once controlled the lives of half of the world's population soon had an appointment appointed.

On entering the former corridors of the British Empire's power, Lloyd was almost disappointed. He had expected to be met by grim liveried flunkeys with their noses rising as they ascended the Grand Staircase. Instead, a pleasant young lady conducted him to an ordinary office in George Gilbert Scott's masterpiece. Elphinstone was there to greet him with coffee and biscuits in close attendance.

"Good morning, Cocky." The greeting brought a smile and raised eyebrow on the young lady's face but she withdrew quietly before she could laugh. "Thanks for coming over and thanks for the invitation, which I readily accept. Any particular dress code? Black tie or what?"

"Anything you like Jock. You don't have to wear a dress but that would certainly bring a smile to everyone's faces. I'm just going to wear a reasonably smart jacket and tie but nowadays even the tie part is considered to be old hat." Elphinstone wondered how a smart tie could be considered to be an old hat but kept the thought to himself.

"That's good enough for me, Cocky. I may treat myself to trousers and socks as well but I'll decide on the finer points later. Now, I suppose you would like to hear what I can tell you about our exercise in the Levant and your experiences in the Balkans. Most of it you will either know already or have guessed but there are some things that might need clarifying."

Lloyd nodded and grunted his agreement. He also suggested that they consume some of the coffee before it cooled to freezing point. The coffee was duly poured and six chocolate digestive biscuits on a china plate placed on the desk. Lloyd's coffee cup was gently pushed towards him with an invitation to help himself to a biscuit or two.

He listened carefully as Elphinstone began to unravel some of the tangled details of his current affair.

Ch. 37. What makes the World go round.

"You may recall my saying that the turmoil in the Middle East is driven by the great powers of the day, plus some not-so-great powers. The big dogs and big fleas, and their quest for more influence. As we all know, their influence is obtained by offering something that other states need or want. In most of these cases it is simply the supply of oil.

"This whole affair was about oil. It was always all about oil. Until a few years ago the income from oil was just a matter of selling to whoever was prepared to buy it but then - when religion became more important than money - various states entered long periods of self-destruction. The Iran/Iraq war killed millions and started to produce more suicide bombers than oil drillers.

"To add more destruction, the invasions of Iraq and other places killed off much of the sources of supply and the world price of oil went through the roof. Nice work if you were sitting on an undisturbed oilfield and were friendly with everyone in sight. But as the governments got greedy for power and started to spend the revenue faster than they could sell their oil, instability - as we saw in the so-called 'Arab spring', made the situation even worse and the biggest customers took action.

"In some countries that meant investing money in renewable energy - pretending that it was to save the planet from contamination. But the biggest customer of all, our American cousins across the pond, found new sources of oil and started to go from being a buyer to being a seller. Shale oil and fracking is already making the US almost free of supply from places like Saudi and Venezuela."

Lloyd's mind flashed back to Maracaibo and the disintegrating economy he witnessed there some years ago.

That situation could only have got worse as oil prices sank faster than the drills on the off-shore rigs. Elphinstone continued with his lecture on economics.

"The result is obvious to all. The price has dropped enormously and those countries dependent on selling at high prices are desperate to restrict production by their competitors. The OPEC cartel is still refusing to cut back, hoping to break the banks of the others. Russia, Venezuela and the others will do almost anything to make them change their mind.

"There is one paradoxical exception. Iran has wheedled a cut in the embargoes on exports just as the price went down. They can now sell it abroad but only at a low price like the others. Their allies will agree to let Iran produce and sell as much as it likes if OPEC agrees to cut back and allow the prices go back up.

"If that happens, then Russia is on a promise to get controlling influence in Iran and Syria. That will give them clear access to the Persian gulf from the Caspian Sea. At the same time they will control Syria's Mediterranean ports. Our major NATO ally Turkey will be squeezed between a wealthy and grateful Iran and the ruins of Syria and Iraq.

"Now perhaps you can see why I referred to the fault lines of the tectonic plates: Arabian and Asian. There could be much worse than earthquakes in Turkey and Southern Europe if or when that happens."

Lloyd felt like regurgitating his biscuits and coffee. It sounded as though the Russians were about to reverse the fall of the Soviet Empire and stamp an iron shackle on Western nations.

"Well thanks for all that happy news and the lecture on oil economics, Jock. That makes me feel much better I must say." The irony in his voice was not unexpected. Nor was his next question.

"So, tell me. What has this to do with Aysil and the refugees, or with what you kept calling 'my yacht' and the pirates who took it? Were they all Iranian too?" Elphinstone cleared his throat before responding.

"There was one common link, Cocky. Before I get back to that I must ask you a question of my own. While we have been useful allies in the hunt for 'your yacht' in the Black Sea and 'my Danger-woman' in the Balkans, what would you say to some form of alliance continuing? Quite unofficial, of course but more concrete than being on a promise. Nothing on paper. Only secured by a handshake and returned favours."

Before Lloyd could ask the obvious, a sketchy outline of the proposed 'alliance' was delivered.

"It wouldn't be too time-consuming. Not formal in any way except for our agreement to supply perfectly legal services – mutual benefits. I can't define them but you can imagine that our help for your investigations would be supplied willingly, and your information supplied to me – us – equally willingly."

Lloyd summed it up in simpler terms. "You mean you scratch my back and I'll scratch yours."

"Exactly. Do you have any problem with that? It's been beneficial, up to a point, for both of us so far. Why not extend it?

"OK Jock. Why not?" The motto of the City traders, 'my word is my bond' came back to him. He held out an open hand which was grasped very firmly and shaken briefly to avoid any misunderstanding or change of mind. "Now, what can you... uh... fill me in on?" He thought 'fill me in' was probably not the best slang expression for the grandiose location and his host's new office but it would have to do for now. His host started filling.

"As usual it's a bit complicated but you know most of it already so I'll whiz through the main points and answer any others as we go.

"Firstly, as we know, the late Mr.Bin Q'etta was a sharp trader as well as a representative in OPEC. He had put a massive bet on the futures markets for oil prices to go down and stay down and intended to ensure that OPEC would keep production levels up. Basically he had sold oil options at high prices and was determined to buy them at low ones.

"Secondly, we also know that Mr. Kazakov was another sharp trader – too sharp for his own good. But he placed his bets on prices going back up. He was not involved in OPEC so had to resort to other means.

"His first move was to bribe those wretched Palestinians in Beirut to kidnap Bin Q'etta's son and force his dad to persuade OPEC to restrict production. That's where you and I became involved directly. We removed that threat but Kazakov tried other methods.

"He then offered to smuggle radio-active material to Iranian agents or Hezbollah in Syria using his company's yacht, which he claimed as being hijacked. As well as a large payment, he persuaded his old friends in Russian intelligence to supply his agent in Serbia with the means of murdering Bin Q'etta. That was his only hope of getting the price of oil back up.

"His main cash reward would be for smuggling the radioactive stuff to Syria. The insurance claim at Lloyds for the yacht was a cover but it would fetch several millions and that would be enough to pay his gang and the ex-Russian special forces.

"At the same time he tried to take over a valuable company – in this case your friend's mining business in Kazakhstan. The mining company would be milked of cash to pay for his losses on the oil futures markets. Unfortunately for him, the insurance scam was exposed which prevented him getting approval for the Kazak company takeover.

"The polonium supplied by the rogue Russians, assuming they're not all of that ilk, was smuggled to our 'danger-woman' who was and as far as I know still is, not just a Syrian Allawite refugee but also an Iranian agent and now roaming free somewhere in Europe.

"The good news appears to be that Kazakov and his Serbian cohort may have fallen foul of someone with a serious grudge against them and are now lying in a ditch or shallow grave in Kosovo. I simply don't know if their assailant was a former Kosovan survivor of the massacres there. You seem to know something that I don't about that.

"It might of course have been someone working for the Chechens or Russian ex-servicemen who hadn't been paid, or one of the former gun-runners in the Kosovo wars. Some of those Russians do have a Scorpion in a rifle sight tattooed on their scalps. It's supposed to be a badge of honour or dishonour. They are all fairly nasty specimens of humanity as I'm sure you also know."

Of all the violent and ruthless characters discussed in the Foreign Office room, only one was of personal concern to Lloyd. He still could not accept that the girl who had shared his bed and his body so passionately in Pristina could be the same 'danger-woman' and murderer. She who had portrayed her feelings and a kindred spirit with – he nearly said *'look of love'* to himself but dismissed it as immature – she couldn't be such a monster.

As if to demonstrate the hand-shaken bond between them, Elphinstone seemed to read his mind. "Our vanishing lady will probably turn up somewhere in Northern Europe – Germany or Sweden most likely – and she might well be a target herself now. The Sunni Arabs won't have taken kindly to one of their own being treated in that way and may well have put a Fatwah on her and her girlfriend. That's their problem now, not ours.

"Our problem is to get any information available to block further action that would prejudice our countries, and or allies too if absolutely necessary, by infiltrating our political or economic organisations. Especially if that increases Russian or Iranian influence. She doesn't have to do that personally. She just has to get some sympathetic no-hoper to do it for her and sit back to enjoy the view, as she appears to have done in Vienna."

Lloyd gulped. The hot coffee in his mouth drifted down his throat and he had to emit a gentle cough. "Well I don't see how I can keep tabs on her and do my day-job. I'd be sacked if I tried to arrange my work to fit any 'cherchez la femme' game. "

"You don't have to. We'll do all that. All I ask is that you try to follow up any information you get from me and use your contacts to get some more from a different source. You have lots of contacts in various countries and can travel to meet them while conducting business at the same time. You never know, you might even drum up more business that way. Is that too much to ask?"

The words 'free lunch' and 'flying pigs' seemed to collide in Lloyd's mind. He decided to change the subject quickly before he agreed to something he might later regret.

"It might be possible. Let me think about it, will you? In the meantime, my friend from Switzerland – he's British but managing a business over there – is here for a few days and is holding the party I mentioned this weekend. It's to celebrate or mourn his escape from bachelor-hood. In other words it's his engagement party.

"If your diary's still clear, let me know and I'll confirm it to him and his wife-to-be. She's a nice girl, Mary something or other, and a friend of a friend that you know."

"Oh, really? Who's that?" Elphinstone's face relaxed. It took on a brighter, lighter demeanour.

"Helen Tiarks. We met her in Beirut when she was helping with one of the refugee camp's charities."

The brighter, lighter expression became tighter. Elphinstone remembered only too well that she had been all but disfigured in that dismal place and he also remembered the look of disappointment when she realised that he was married. But that, as the Beatles had said, that was yesterday.

"I can tell you now, Cocky. I'm still free for the entire weekend and would be delighted to join you and your friends.

It'll make a good change from sulking around here or the FO. Remind me, is it black tie?"

"Just a big smile as usual, Jock. If anyone's wearing a black tie, it'll be Andrew. He was convinced that he could stay free all his life."

Ch. 38. Wedding belles.

Despite Andrew Tulloch's insistence that he had an understanding of unmarried bliss with Mary, he made no secret of his pleasure in obtaining such a great companion for life and limb. The engagement party was set fair to be loud and enjoyable if not riotous. Tulloch's contentment was matched by the happy look on the faces of Mary and her closer friends.

Of all of those close friends, none was closer than the still beautiful if slightly scarred Helen. The wounds and surgery had certainly left their marks but had not eliminated her classic features and cool smile. Awareness of the cosmetic damage had even developed a resigned and more sympathetic aura that radiated gently to any in her company. Even to the tall man who had disappointed her in her hour of need.

All Lloyd's remaining thoughts of Aysil as a lover were now in tatters. Realistically, any hopes of rekindled friendship, let alone sex, with a refugee-come-assassin were as dead as the late Arab trader. He still nurtured a faint hope of a chance affair with Helen and made little secret of it. But hope was getting fainter and fainter.

If he had tried to disguise his polite attempts at seduction when in the company of the engaged couple then he had been as successful as a burglar with a striped vest and a bag with 'swag' writ large upon it. Helen was aware of the prospective divorce in the Elphinstone marriage. Although as charming to all as she was attractive her charm was inevitably focussed on the tall man on whose shoulder she had hoped to lean or cry as the situation required.

Lloyd was left with what he realised was a cooler, if not completely cold, shoulder. He also realised that he should not waste time in anything resembling dead horses and flogging. It was time to reconfigure – where he was going and what he was doing. Visions and voices from the past entered his thoughts and exited with the sound of his present company...

The thoughts were already rather hazy and slightly confused by a combination of dry champagne and wet mouth. They were stirred by the sound and scent of some very attractive girls chattering and giggling within an arm's length. He was tempted to reach out and grasp one of those soft arms or a firm waist to call his own for the evening and perhaps beyond but that might embarrass the host or his fiancée.

Eventually as the party's temperature rose to simmering-point he followed the wise words of Oscar Wilde boasting that he 'could resist anything but temptation.' Llewellyn Lloyd became Cocky again and returned to being a mellow extrovert with a girl on his knee and a smile on his face. The smile was returned with interest and a succession of smiles and banter exchanged until more primeval instincts rose. Irresistible temptation overtook all thoughts of resistance by either party.

By the time that the parties to the party were beginning to flag and the witching hour had long passed, Cocky and a warm body on his knee agreed that it was also time to go to bed. The only question remaining was "your bed or mine?" That was answered by the young lady's suggestion to take the nearest, in her bed-sit in Fulham.

Goodbye kisses for the hosts and their guests quickly followed as old friends and happy strangers faced the morrow morn. Not sadder and wiser after the event, but happier and sillier than before the party started. Mary hugged Cocky for almost a minute and warmed his face with multiple wet kisses. She then turned to his new-found friend and repeated the performance with squeals of laughter and knowing winks.

"What was that all about?" gasped Lloyd when they had both disentangled themselves from the gushing hostess. "She seemed to be very happy, which I can understand as Andrew's paying, and she obviously likes you. How do you know her? Work, or the Mary Deans sewing circle?"

The question was answered with a smile of amazement at Cocky's question. "How do I know her? Well, I know her as – as well as anyone should know her sister."

He was still smiling and chuckling from Mary's embraces when he realised that it might be time to utter an admission of identity ignorance. "Sorry... uh... I know this is the oldest cliché of this sort of situation but, I really don't know your name. Or maybe I did get it but lost it in the wine lake. By the way," he tried to add lamely, "mine's... "

"I know yours of course, silly. I'm Mary's sister Susan, her younger sister, and Mary's told me all about you. How did you get the name 'Cocky'? Is it a Welsh name or what?"

Despite having faced the same inquisition many time before without embarrassment, Cocky almost blushed. The wine within managed to act as a barrier to deference. "No,it's not Welsh or any other thing. Just a nick-name from schooldays, from playing rugby football and, well, from boasting a bit, I suppose."

"Boasting? About what?"

Another smile enveloped Lloyd's features. "We did say 'your bed or mine' didn't we? And we did agree on yours. How soon can we get there, so you can find out."

That brought more peals of laughter from the belle of the ball and a loud cry of "taxi!" at the door of the restaurant. The taxi journey was short enough to prevent serious sexual contact but long enough to confirm that it was only a temporary postponement. By the time that the hot-breathed couple had mounted the stairs and tumbled into Susan's bedsit near Earl's Court station, which she preferred to describe as South-West Kensington, any thoughts of sitting had been abandoned in favour of bedding.

The punishment meted out to the mattress by two very active lovers was also inflicted on the sweaty bodies. After a long evening of food, drink and seduction their stamina began to fade in the small hours. Having completed two hours of active physical engagement, described by Lloyd as 'the horizontal gavotte', they remained horizontal but dormant.

Dawn brought a semblance of recovery and sheepish concerns of possible remorse or recrimination. One quick look into each other's bleary questioning eyes answered the unasked question. The silent voice in their pillowed heads sang 'Non. Je ne regrete rien', in rough and croaky harmony. No regrets lingered in the bed with either one. A happy win-win situation.

Susan moved first. She brought her mouth to Lloyd's and his hands to her nipples. Clichés were replaced by clinches and more punishment for the long-suffering mattress. Another clinch, another hour of Saturday morning toil and sweat. Then they drifted off into a short doze and forty or fifty winks before a shared shower to seal their fresh contract.

If anyone had suffered the pangs of remorse it was not Susan. The annoying prospect of her sister beating her to the wedding register had stimulated her towards nailing down a satisfying relationship. She was ambivalent of the formalities as long as she could satisfy herself spiritually and physically. Her new-found bed-mate fitted the part ideally.

The professed star of rugby field and bed was perhaps not so free from doubt. The evening's party, with seduction added to the bacchanalian ambiance, had been all that he could have desired in his present circumstances. The ensuing night and morning of white-hot passion and electrifying orgasms had fulfilled the promise of the previous evening for both but Lloyd's mind was not completely bathed in sunshine.

The shadow of Aysil's un-given smile still lurked in the background. His mind kept wandering back to the Aegean ferry trip and to the night with her in Pristina. Where now? His memory could not quite escape from the prospect of reunion with her. For all he knew now, she might be dead or plotting someone else's death. The expression 'smiling assassin' might be a journalistic eye-catcher but in her case it might be a very apt description.

Meanwhile, the weak-kneed remains of the engagement party had also drifted back to their various abodes. Host and hostess to Mary's apartment in Belsize Park and Elphinstone to his retreat in St James's. Before directing the taxi to the Naval and Military Club, he had personally ensured that Miss Tiarks, the Hellenic beauty, had been delivered safely to her own apartment near Covent Garden.

He had also ensured that she was told to expect a call to arms, hopefully his arms, within the next twelve hours. As a 'belt and braces' precaution he had slipped his calling card into her evening purse so that she would have his phone number. Unusually for one trained and practiced in precise security measures, the champagne and he had forgotten to keep a note of hers.

By the following afternoon, Helen was beginning to fear the worst. Either her admirer had suffered alcoholic amnesia or worse still, he had not forgotten but had not intended to pay more than lip service to further contact with her. Having discovered his card in her evening purse and toyed with it for an hour, she threw it into the waste paper basket in her bedroom. She was certainly NOT about to call him. Then the telephone rang.

Jumping across the bed to the cordless phone beside it, she knocked the receiver from its base and expressed a rare expletive as it struck the carpet. Scrambling for it under the bed and muttering curses on modern technology, she took a few precious seconds to place it against her left ear and utter a breathless 'hello.' An echoing 'hello' returned her greeting, followed by a puzzled query.

"Hello, is that Helen? It's Jock – Elphinstone – from last evening at the party. Sorry to be a bit late but, I had to... uh... had to take a call from your friend Mary, our hostess." His voice tailed off as he wondered whether his white lie would be exposed as soon as the two girls met and gossiped, as they surely would.

He had consumed most of the morning trying to contact the bed-ridden Lloyd as he had failed to find Helen's unlisted phone number and had not remembered anyone else's surname at the party. Eventually Lloyd had heard his own cell-phone, chiming frantically in the trousers heaped on Susan's bedroom floor.

Lloyd didn't have Helen's number or address but he knew that Mary would. Mild amusement at the similarity of the two men's weekend activities provided a rare softening of their attitudes to each other as he passed Mary's telephone details to the man in St James's. As soon as their conversation ended, another started. Jock called Mary and sheepishly admitted that he had mislaid Helen's number after promising to phone her so soon.

The gold-medallist match-maker in Mary Deans was surprised and delighted to learn of Elphinstone's renewed interest in her friend Helen. Despite her natural attraction, Helen had been reserved to the point of shyness since her facial re-arrangement. Self confidence had all but collapsed.

Mary assumed that this had been caused by her earlier disappointment on hearing that there was a Mrs Elphinstone. However, that situation had changed. With a broad mind and a good friend such as Miss Deans, a rekindled romance for Helen would put the proverbial icing on the Tulloch wedding cake. With the additional possibility of her sister Susan becoming interested in Cocky Lloyd... well, anything was possible.

Could this, Mary wondered, be the start of something big in the wedding stakes? A frantic shout from her fiancée in the next room soon brought her romantic mind back from Barbara Cartland mode to grim reality with a bump.

"Mary! Where are my underpants? I'm sure I had them on when we got back from the party. Ooh! My head's still a bit fragile. Do we have any aspirin? It must have been the prawns."

The future Mrs Tulloch began to realise that there were still a few rough edges to file away before the wedding bells could ring with a completely smooth tone. And there were several expensive details, boring to her lover but exciting to her and the other girls, awaiting completion. Church or Register Office, reception, guests, food and drink – *"HE can organise that, and don't be stingy"* – flowers, bridesmaids or whatever they were nowadays, speeches, honeymoon travel and hotel, the list seemed endless but very exciting.

While Mary daydreamed of multiple weddings and endless encircling married companions, Elphinstone tried to compensate for his omission. Dinner at a quiet restaurant in King Street would allow him to be within walking distance of Helen's flat. It would therefore allow both of them to relax and not be concerned about transport back to her home. Now, all he had to worry about was booking a table on a busy Saturday evening.

Cocky Lloyd had more to worry about. He had always tried to believe in the philosophy of Confucius: "Not to worry but, if to worry then not to worry unduly." With mind and body trying to focus on relationships with women past and present the worry was hard to keep from entering the 'unduly' area.

His immediate worry was how to maintain a warm, preferably hot, relationship with Susan without committing either of them to a state of attachment that they might regret sooner or later. All he had to go on was a marriage made in bed; one night's passion with Mary's sibling. Neither of them knew much about the other's real life and where it might lead them.

As the wedding day of Andrew Tulloch and Mary Deans approached, invitations were issued to Lloyd, to Vasil Antonov and to Jock Elphinstone. Mary's sister would be a matron of honour; "too old to be a bridesmaid," she had protested, so wouldn't need to be invited. Helen Tiarks was also expected to be a senior member of the official wedding party.

Unable to throw off the mantle of a volunteer dating agency, Mary carefully mapped out seating arrangements to ensure that the eligible males were close to her female friends throughout the reception. However, with her sister and her best friend at a so-called 'top table' it would be difficult to place their current male companions close enough for knee stroking or polite groping.

"Round table!" Mary cried out aloud as the inspiration entered her temporarily vacant head. Tulloch was puzzled. He had only just arrived from Zurich and was looking for a newspaper to get some quality time with the sports pages.

"Do you mean I... uh... we... should invite people from the local business club? Perhaps you mean 'Rotary' or 'The Lions', do you? I'm not a member of any of them anyway."

"What on earth are you on about? I'm talking about the dinner tables for our reception."

"Oh that? What about it... uh... them?"

"We have to get the men as close as would be decent to the... uh... girls. I don't want Helen or Susan isolated on a long straight table while Cocky and his friend Jock what's-his-name are miles away from them. We must have a big round table for us and the main party with enough room for those two at least to sit with us."

"All right. What's the problem then? Oh, can you make room for my mate Vasil from Kazakhstan? He'll be coming. Don't know about a wife or girlfriend. Maybe both. Who knows?" He shrugged and resumed reading the sports pages of the previous day's newspaper. Since the problem of the attempted takeover of Antonov's company seemed to have died, Tulloch's life had returned to as near to normal as the markets would allow.

Life for Cocky Lloyd had also returned to what passed for quiet in the murky world of kidnap and ransom surrounding his occupation. Contacts with Susan were more frequent and more relaxing than those with the Foreign Office. Contact with his parents and his old friends in Port Talbot had been conspicuous by their absence and that had to be restored before anything more dramatic could enter his present or future.

As so often happens it was something from his past that returned to surprise him.

Ch.39. The prodigal son.

The wedding of Andrew and Mary Tulloch was as smooth and enjoyable as Mary could have planned and plotted. Her sister and her best friend were both seated at the circular nuptial trough and both received due attention from Mary's matches. Neither Helen nor Elphinstone were familiar enough to start groping but a well-anaesthetised Miss Tiarks did let her guard slip far enough to allow her hand to drop onto Jock's thigh for a moment.

By contrast, Lloyd was quite uninhibited with his application of free-roving hands and mind when close enough to touch Susan's. She was of a similar roving mind and hands even before the Champagne had worked its way into her affections. Only after their second cups of coffee did second thoughts challenge them. Susan's thoughts drifted to open questions about her recent inamoratas and Cocky's to his erotic former ones.

Still trying to put Aysil out of mind but wondering where and how she might be in sight, his mind and hands oscillated between Aysil's journeys and Susan's bottom. As his hands and legs closed in on the shapely figure so close to his, he couldn't avoid comparison with others; those he called his 'paramours of the past.' He considered what other options he could keep open.

His lovely flat-mate and partner in Hong Kong would never return. She was completely irreplaceable but another, much nearer to home, might still be contactable. Somewhere in South Wales was a slightly myopic but very attractive lady, 'Glamorous Gladys' Watkins. Her reluctance to wearing spectacles had been overcome by wearing contact lenses.

"Shame", thought Cocky, *"she probably preferred to look at me when she couldn't see properly."* He had no qualms

about seeing her though, clothed or not, and his eyesight was in perfect working order. All too soon the wedding party and close contact with a now-wobbly Susan were over.

Bride and groom repaired to a hotel room and a change of clothing interrupted only by twenty minutes of emphatic consummation and a last glass of champagne. Meanwhile the guests congregated around a limousine taking the married couple to Heathrow and flights to the West Indies. A well filled Vasil Antonov and a lady companion followed them as far as the airport and their own flight back to Astana.

The hardcore remains of the reception party returned to clear the bar and cement friendships old and new. In a lull between drinks and fondles, Lloyd decided to tell his parents to prepare for a rare if brief return of their prodigal. He would only stay in Port Talbot for the following weekend and would be travelling alone. Susan's passion and Elphinstone's inquisition would have to wait. Being unable to get an answer from his parents' telephone, his message to them would also have to wait.

Sunday after the wedding was wet and quiet. Elphinstone took the Metropolitan railway to Pinner and his wife Julia. The children were at boarding school and the damp day was a good time to discuss a well mannered and civilised divorce that would minimise disruption to their lives.

Separated but not completely estranged, the two adults agreed to minimise costs with an uncontested action that would be as quiet as it would be quick. Access to the children would be as free as possible and finances would remain in place until alternative partnerships materialised. Until then any adultery would be accepted or ignored.

Julia Elphinstone's personal finances were fairly comfortable and her main passions, outside the care of her children, were to Waitrose and her bridge and tennis clubs' companionship. She agreed to almost everything that her husband proposed. Although weary of his devotion to duty in Foreign Office affairs she trusted him, almost completely, to provide for their children's well-being. Any other affairs would be kept out of sight and out of mind.

Having made what he considered to be the best of a bad job, Jock Elphinstone thought it best not to rush back to see Helen but to return to St James's. He would send his thanks in words of platonic love to the wife he had just left. He had always considered Julia's conduct to be exemplary and was determined that acrimony could be avoided.

He realised that she must be feeling somewhat empty and almost abandoned when he left the house and wanted to reassure her of his enduring care, if not his enduring affection. But before he could call her again, his telephone announced that a contact in a foreign place, not in Whitehall, had news of possible 'unhelpful activity' involving a female posing as a Syrian refugee.

The call came from an office in Hamburg. The caller had seen Aysil and Leila in the city and tracked them to the home of 'a well-known Syrian agent in Germany' who worked as a Turkish shipping clerk. Turkish or Syrian, it made little difference. The important matter was that two targets of both British Intelligence and Arab revenge seekers were on the move again.

'Our man in Hamburg' had an associate of Turkish extraction who had obtained information considered to be more than fifty percent reliable. His informant advised him that the two Middle-eastern ladies were "likely to be heading back to Greece and from there to either Turkey, Syria or... uh... or somewhere else."

'More than fifty percent reliable' was almost gold-standard on intelligence gathering scales. Elphinstone's call to his 'lonely hearts' home in Pinner was placed on hold while he tried to contact Lloyd. Annoyingly, Lloyd's own phone was engaged and he had to leave a message requesting – almost ordering – an urgent return call.

The return call followed within the half hour but if the intelligence officer from the Foreign Office expected the loss adjuster from Lloyds to drop everything in order to fly towards where he might expect to find Aysil and Leila, then he was to be disappointed. Before he could do that, the officer had to use his own intelligence to calculate how far and in which direction his two birds of prey had flown.

Lloyd was unsure of exactly what task he was expected to fulfil. Pending clarification he informed his caller of his forthcoming trip, not to Eastern Europe but to Western Wales. It had been many months since he had seen his parents in Port Talbot and many years since he had seen some of his old friends and former colleagues in Swansea and Mumbles. Too much water had flowed under the Severn bridge.

With so much of his work beyond the confines of the insurance market building or justifying the cost of garaging a rarely used car, Lloyd was happy to use the rail network. Following a productive Monday morning's appearance at his office, the Circle Line from Monument station to Paddington saw him comfortably seated on a fast train to Port Talbot Parkway by mid-afternoon.

Warming the GWR train's comfortable seat with the aid of afternoon tea and a glass of Scotch, Lloyd thought of his parents and the smoky town that he used to call home. Then he suddenly remembered that nobody there had been informed of his sudden dash to reunite with them. Another call to whichever of his parents might be at home was urgently demanded.

The response from his mother was almost embarrassment. She was taken by surprise at such a sudden unexpected return of the prodigal son. There was a distinct lack of fatted calf in the Lloyd household pantry but no shortage of sausages, potatoes, and baked beans by the tin-full. The combination of those three ingredients would ensure a warm meal and even warmer vote of thanks.

By seven p.m. on a wet Monday evening the taxi from Parkway station had deposited Lloyd at his old front doorstep and reunion with a proud mother and relieved father. The

Cocky Lloyd career path had taken their son to some places from where one was not always guaranteed to return. Far, far away from what the minister at the Cwrt Sart Bethesda Chapel in Briton Ferry would call 'the paths of righteousness.' Sausage and mash with baked beans and hot tea, followed by a long chat and his own warm bed would be safely reassuring for all of them. A real family homecoming.

Tuesday morning greeted Cocky with more showers and a slate-grey sky. Mr Lloyd senior still had and occasionally drove a Ford Mondeo that had rarely seen active service between Sunday's church and Friday's shopping. Gently removing the empty plastic bag bearing Tesco's logo, from the driver's seat to the floor behind it, the former police detective drove along the Swansea sea front by Saint Helens and on to Mumbles.

There were pubs aplenty in Mumbles though he preferred not to try turning the clock too far back with a visit to Langland Bay. Eventually nostalgia and curiosity overcame the fear of disappointment. A shiny new Brasserie overlooking the sullen sea looked appealing enough to a hungry traveller or optimistic seducer. Having eaten a breakfast worthy of a condemned man only an hour earlier, Lloyd passed it by.

Then he thought he must have forgotten to return to earth from his bedtime dreams. A fair-haired girl, perhaps a young housewife, wearing a light raincoat and forlorn face was crossing the road towards his car. He braked as gently as a split second's pressure on the pedal would permit and looked again. The woman had gone. Probably walked round a corner or into the Brasserie across the road.

Lloyd blinked a couple of times than acted decisively. He got as far as unbuckling his seat belt and then buckled it up again. The chances of Gladys being so near to his thoughts and his vehicle at the same time? Remote to say the least. Improbable... but not impossible. He unbuckled again and this time opened the door of the Mondeo and strode quickly to the door of the Brasserie.

His hand touched the door but before he could open it he stopped again. If the girl was indeed his old flame and if, but only if, she had entered the restaurant then he would still have to hunt around the room to find her. And if she was a complete stranger then he would have to take a seat at another table and order something. He could have egg on a plate or have it on his face.

"Fortune favours the brave," he said to himself. He stepped bravely into the restaurant foyer. As a waiter approached he suddenly saw her again. Not within the shiny walls of the restaurant but walking back on the other side of the road, near his car. This time he was more certain. The girl may be a little older than the Gladys of his memory, but so was he.

After adjusting the image for the years that had passed since they parted he had no doubt. Gladys Watkins was within a few yards of him. The waiter was still waiting. He would have to wait elsewhere. Turning and uttering a grunted apology Lloyd stepped back into the present day to greet his partner of the past.

Gladys stopped and blinked. She too was taken aback at her former boyfriend suddenly appearing out of the morning grey rather than out of the blue. Her blinking dispelled any lingering doubt from Lloyd's mind. He could almost see her removing the spectacles in order to squint at him. But now he thought that he could see the glint of contact lenses on her attractive human ones. Through them she saw a possible answer to her predicament.

For two seconds neither uttered a word. Then they both spoke at once. Gasping greetings. Names that they could never forget were questioned and answered to confirm identities. The tones of the greetings and answering nods and glances also spoke to each of them. There was a hint of hope and relief in each. No question of indifference or embarrassment. They were both pleased, and hopeful, to see each other again .

"Glad to see you, Glad," joked Cocky gently.

"Yes? Yes, so am I, to see you again. I didn't expect you to be wandering around Mumbles any more. Any particular reason... uh... back on leave from Hong Kong, is it?"

"Not from Hong Kong. I left there a few years ago – five or six years I think. It's always longer than you think, isn't it?"

"What about you? Still living in Swansea – with Peter – isn't it?"

Gladys looked down at the wet pavement. Not blushing but reluctant to show her embarrassment at letting her former boyfriend down. Her present predicament could offer Cocky an opportunity to say 'I told you so.'

"Yes and no." Before Cocky could ask, she continued. "Yes, in Swansea but no, not with Peter. We separated eighteen months ago and the divorce goes through next month. It's a bit of a long story. Do you have time to – to talk?" There was only one answer to that in Lloyd's mind, and the Brasserie across the road was waiting to hear it.

Once the two ex-lovers were safely cosseted at a small table by the window, they were facing each other. Below the window, only thousands of miles of sky and Atlantic ocean lay between them and the Falkland Islands. Gladys ordered "coffee and sticky buns for two, please Dai." She seemed to be familiar with the establishment and its staff.

"I get over here about once or twice a month. The owners are clients of my accounting bureau. I do the books for the month, and the payroll. It seems to be quite successful." She wanted to get that explanation out of the way, away from her story of marital collapse. Perhaps she could squeeze a trickle of sympathy from Lloyd to wash some of the guilt she felt at abandoning her promise to wait for him.

"I did wait. I waited for months to hear when you were either coming home or sending for me. When I heard nothing, nothing concrete, for nearly six months then I thought you must have found someone else... " Her voice tailed off as she realised she was repeating a well-worn cliché that wouldn't convince a worldly-wise Lloyd or a naive choirboy.

"Anyroad, when Peter told me that he had just been made manager of his firm in Swansea, well, I knew why he was telling me and I thought, as you were stayin' in Hong Kong and I was stayin' here – well Peter an' me – might be all right..." The voice lost its way again. "Sorry, Cocky... Sorry."

Her face rose to look him in the eye for signs of forgiveness and redemption when she admitted her fault, perhaps even hope of reunion. In the weeks before her marriage would be finally dissolved she had become almost frantic at the prospect of enforced independence. It worried her more and more.

Fate had dropped an opportunity onto the pavement beneath her feet. She only had to grasp it in order to land on them. In the meantime she grasped his left hand. The right hand was holding a cup of very hot coffee, some of which spilled onto his trousers. Verbal evidence of lightly-scalded testicles was suppressed with a wince and acceptance of another, very genuine, apology from Gladys.

Cocky listened and weighed up the possibilities before him. Of the recent runners and riders in his love-life, Aysil was now a non-starter; Susan was possibly a full-time flirt who might fly away tomorrow; and Helen was now fairly close to serving his Foreign Office friend. Gladys might not be the only glad one in Mumbles.

"So, Glad. What happened to Peter? Did you have a lot of rows? Was he violent, or what?"

"No. Not violent. Unreliable perhaps. No, that's not true. He was absolutely reliable. He would always let me down!" She didn't laugh but hoped that Cocky would. "I know he had some other silly affairs. Girls from his office for one or two one-night stands. That's all. But he was almost jailed for selling dodgy PPI policies, not even authorised by his firm.

"And there was talk of him pocketing the premiums to pay for his gambling and girls. That was what caused him to be sacked and charged with embezzlement. The charges were dropped but still... you know what it's like, don't you?" She looked up again to see assent in his eyes and a tightly closed mouth. His left hand was still held in hers, now squeezed and held more tightly than before.

All semblance of reserve was abandoned. "Why don't we start again, Cocky? Unless you…" She realised that she had not even asked about his marital or similar status. "Sorry. I should have realised that you wouldn't still be free, would you?" By now, her expression was almost pleading for rescue. Lloyd just shrugged and offered a miniscule shake of the head.

"No, Glad. I'm not … uh… attached as such. I've got some good, close friends. But that's all. Nothing more serious. I'll be honest…" She gave a tiny shudder at the word 'honest.' Lloyd caught the startle in her expression. *"Unlike your ex husband,"* he thought. "I hoped that I might see you and… well… yes. I'd like to see you again if you really want to – to try it with me."

The tight grip on his hand was released and substituted by a soft fondling motion along his wrist. She would have extended that to his coffee-heated trousers if they had not been so visible to the other couple of customers and her friend Dai-the-waiter. Gratitude or love's labour regained, it mattered not. As far as Gladys was concerned they would be Cocky Lloyd and Glamorous Gladys again and she would no longer be an unattached woman.

Cocky could feel her emotion washing over him like a warm wave. For a moment he wondered if Gladys would express her joy by removing all inhibitions and her clothes right there and then. Jokes concerning women recounting their husbands' reaction to medical treatment, usually ending with 'we don't eat at that cafe now', came to mind but remained unspoken.

It was no joking matter for Lloyd. Gladys was there for the taking. As for the former Miss Watkins the title of 'Mrs Lloyd' might be there for the taking too. And she was hell bent on taking it.

Ch. 40. Holidays with pay.

The sudden development in Lloyd's social life left him suspended between breathless and mindless. Only a few days had passed since his bachelor friend Tulloch had become a married man and Lloyd had become a willing victim of the bridesmaid's passion. Now he was facing a metamorphosis approaching Andrew Tulloch's change of lifestyle.

His intentions towards the glamorous old flame in South Wales were as honourable as might be expected in the circumstances. Less honourable intentions awaited his pleasure in South Kensington. Not experienced in double-dealing but not averse to playing the traditional role of the sailor, Cocky thought that his best strategy was to keep his options open and his mouth closed.

The remainder of the return match with his parents passed quietly. His mother maintained a constant supply of tea and questions about his life in London. When in Cocky's company Mr Lloyd senior also kept an open mind and a closed mouth. The evening before Cocky returned to Paddington saw the exception.

"Going back tomorrow, aren't you?" There was no secret in Cocky's planned return trip but Mrs Lloyd had mentioned that her son's collar appeared to be perfumed and pinkish. On hearing that his wife had smelled perfume, Mr Lloyd senior smelled a whiff of suspicion. His son was a big boy in every way and his frequent absence from his old home was to be expected if he was to catch up with old colleagues and club-mates.

Dismissing the possibility of a bi-sexual rugby player having embraced his son, and in the tradition of maintaining a respectable distance from the affairs of off-spring, Lloyd the father decided to approach Lloyd the son. He would offer any advice after poking his nose in as far as he dared. He broached the delicate subject of Cocky's past love-life.

"Seen your old girlfriend Gladys, 'ave you then?" *"Nothing better than a direct approach",* he decided. "You goin' to take up with 'er, now that she's gettin' a divorce from that plonker she married?" *"In for a penny so far, now to get a pound's worth."* "She couldn't do worse than bein' married to 'im but I don't know if you couldn't do better than gettin' hitched up to 'er again."

Cocky was taken aback for a second. His initial reaction was a sarcastic, *"Go on, dad. Why don't you speak your mind?"* Then he realised that the straight talking parent had actually expressed more paternal concern in ten seconds than he had in the last ten years. A softened smile and warm feeling took charge of his emotions.

"Don't worry, dad. I'm not goin' to jump in at the deep end, not now anyway." He took his father's hand and shook it gently. "Thanks for... well... thanks. You know what I mean. And don't worry, right?" He smiled again and nodded. *"I might jump in at Gladys's shallow end though, before I go back."* He returned to assure his parents, as Mrs. Lloyd joined them.

"I have seen Gladys. And I'll probably see her again fairly soon. But that's as far as it goes for now so, don't think I'm goin' to get caught out again. We'll just take it easy and see how it goes." Mrs Lloyd looked at her husband and smiled with relief.

"Oh, we're not worried, are we Jim?" Another statement dressed as a question and accepted as such.

James Lloyd shook his head in agreement and returned the smile of relief. He had some emotional baggage of his own to discard. For nearly a year he had continued to pretend to his neighbours that he was still employed as shift manager at the huge steel works. A near collapse in the industry had enforced redundancies and his position had been one of the first to be vacated. Each workday had seen him dress and leave his house as if setting out for his usual employment at Margam.

Eventually he realised that the respect and friendship that he had earned over the last thirty years was not going to be terminated along with his job. Others had suffered more and received less in compensation. Mrs Lloyd and a former colleague convinced him that there was no shame in misfortune and he had fronted up to his fate with the same dignity that he had shown throughout his employment. In a few sentences, James Lloyd explained his situation to his son and acceptance of it to all.

Lloyd junior was impressed at his dad's honesty and courage in what must have been a shattering blow to his self-esteem. The short trip to Port Talbot had produced some eventful adjustments to his closest relationships. He faced both of his parents.

"Well, if you're not worried, why should I be then?" Cocky smiled and waited.

Mr Lloyd senior knew how to close the subject.

"Worried? What's there to worry about? Anyone fancy a small scotch and water?" If no one else fancied it, he certainly did. Father, mother and son sat down to two glasses of whisky and three cups of tea.

After a short and passionate farewell to Gladys at Port Talbot Parkway station, Lloyd boarded the express to Paddington. From there he went straight onto a Circle Line underground train and in to the Lime Street ant-hill that houses the insurance market-place. Throughout the journey he smiled to himself at the closer bonds between his parents and himself, forged in such a short visit. Closer relationships turned his thoughts to the undoubted attractions of his old female partner and those of his new bed-mate in London.

"Least said to either of them, soonest mended," ran through his thoughts. *"And the least said to anyone else the better."* Gladys had already invited – almost instructed – Lloyd to live with her in Swansea. There was no chance of

relocation to Wales for Lloyd and she insisted that she had to remain in or near the client-base of her accounting bureau. *"EC3 is East and West Glamorgan isn't,"* he mused.

Once back at his desk and ploughing through a field of letters in the so-called paperless office, his eyes focussed on a request to phone a number that smacked of somewhere in or near Whitehall. His guess was correct. A lady's voice confirmed that the other end of the line was in a section of the Foreign and Commonwealth Office. A message was taken inviting Mr Elphinstone to call Mr Lloyd.

Later that afternoon the invitation was accepted as the little device in Lloyd's jacket pocket sounded the return call from the new C4 grade second secretary. Unlike the pleasant female voice from his office, Jock Elphinstone's voice was gruff and almost aggressive. Cocky was on the point of reminding him that he was not addressing one of his junior staff when the C4 grade officer remembered that Lloyd was an A1 civilian.

"Listen, Cocky. And listen very carefully."

"Don't tell me, Jock. You're only going to say it once. Is that it?"

"What? I don't know what you're talking about. But what I'm talking about is extremely important and urgent. You'll have to act immediately."

"Have to? Have to what? I don't work for your Whitehall circus, you know. I've got my own very important work to do before running errands for the FO"

"Ah. Sorry. Of course. This is... oh... look, I have a once-in-a-job-time chance to do something very... well... very important to us – me – and a very little time to do it. That's why I'm being a bit... well, a bit boorish. It'll involve a quick trip abroad again. Do you think you could help right away? Perhaps it could fit in with one of your investigations. If you use a little... imaginative... flexibility, let's say."

"Can you tell me exactly what you expect me to do that's so important?"

"Err... uh... no. Not on the 'phone. Walls have ears and so do mobile networks. I should know. We have thousands of 'em down in Cheltenham. Almost certainly listening as we speak. That's not a problem but someone else listening might be. Can you pop over to St James's Park underground station in Broadway? I'll meet you at the entrance there and explain.

"Bring your overnight travel bag and passport. I'll supply the rest."

Within the hour and after the briefest note to his colleagues to tell them of his sudden priority to investigate an emergency overseas, Lloyd completed his second Circle Line train journey of the afternoon.

Under normal circumstances he would have waved a mental 'hello and goodbye' to the home of London Underground in Broadway when plodding his homeward weary way to Chiswick. Today would be different. The only underground that he expected to enter would be Elphinstone's misty network of foreign agents.

So far he had acted as an unpaid assistant to the network's ringmaster on a mutual co-operation basis. As far as he knew there was no current insurance investigation requiring help from the Foreign Office. Whatever work he was asked to do for them this time would involve his employment and tax-payers' money.

A sudden braking and halt of the train applied the brakes to any thoughts of recompense. Stepping briskly from the carriage to the escalators and the portals of the station on Broadway, he saw a tall figure standing on a narrow strip of the pavement. He greeted the man with an over-familiar pat on the rear of its trousers and a jocular cry of "Gotch-ya!"

The figure turned. It was not Elphinstone but someone very like him. Before Lloyd could mutter an apology to the startled stranger, a firm hand took his elbow and a familiar voice issued the explanation to both of them.

"Don't worry, Caruthers. Your secret is safe with me. He usually reserves that sort of greeting for young men in

Leicester Square but must have found you irresistible." The stranger frowned at Elphinstone but offered an understanding grin to Lloyd.

"Bugger off, Jock."

"Precisely, old man." Then, turning to Lloyd. "Come on... uh... " He was about to say 'Cocky' but decided not to exacerbate the innuendo. "... uh... we're just a few yards away from... where we're going." Then added to the other man, "G'night, Charles. Probably see you tomorrow."

Charles Caruthers smiled and waved a friendly "good evening," adding, "don't take any notice of him – he had a bad upbringing."

They walked in silence for about fifty yards along Broadway towards Victoria Street. After crossing the road they turned abruptly into a building with the name of one of Britain's last remaining crown dependencies. Through the ground floor reception area and up two flights of stairs, a Yale key turned in the lock on a nondescript brown door revealing another door with a digital security lock on its panel.

Four buttons were tapped and a soft click told Lloyd that the secure area beyond the second door was open for business. Elphinstone sat on a leather chair and beckoned Lloyd to take another.

"Now Cocky..." He issued a firm smile as he spoke. Still recalling his Foreign Office colleague's face when greeted from behind by Lloyd. "Oh, don't worry about Caruthers. He's getting de-mob happy and can take a joke. You were joking when you patted his rear end, weren't you?" They both chuckled. Then he got down to the business of the day.

We... all right, 'I'... I hope 'we' have about forty-eight hours to try to secure – gain – a rather important advantage for our country. I know that sounds melodramatic but I really think this opportunity is just that. Your former target in Greece and the Balkans is on the move again but, this time she's running from the West, trying to get home safe and sound before something awful happens to her in Europe."

He paused as if for effect. It certainly had an effect on Lloyd who was not sure whether to believe him or just take it all as a fantasy to generate a sense of importance.

"What sort of 'something awful' are we talking about, then?"

"I don't have the details. They're usually only revealed when the remains of the victim are unearthed or washed up on a remote beach somewhere."

"Like your pal Abdul?"

"Yes. Probably just like poor old Abdul. Our information – we think reliable – suggests that the same or a similar group to that who probably put paid to him plan to do the same for Danger-woman and her accomplice. We're not quite sure who's behind it but it could be someone in the pay of revengeful Sunnis or even the Russian or Crimean desperados who haven't been rewarded by her pay-masters.

She may not realise it but it's more likely to be her own pay-masters who want her out of the way because she could be an embarrassment to them. It may be that they are getting information from someone... perhaps I'm getting paranoid about it.

Whoever they are, we believe that they probably want to eliminate the two ladies. And we also think we might be able to change the girls' allegiance completely if we can convince her – Aysil – that she would be safer and better off working for us instead of the Iranians. But we have very little time to get in touch with her and persuade her. That's where you come in."

"Oh. Do I indeed? Aren't you forgetting that I have my own work to do? And what's more, how am I supposed to get her to believe me when I don't even have any official position in your establishment?"

"I'll take care of the second part and I'm sure that you can deal with the first. Tell your masters that you have to investigate some claim or something in Greece. That's where Aysil will be by the time you get there. We'll give you some money – that's always a good sign of our sincerity – and papers to guarantee her safety here and asylum if required. She can soon see the difference between safety with us and danger with the others. And there are probably an awful lot of others," he added grimly.

"One of our chaps will fly to an island near the Turkish coast tonight where we think she... they... are. You should join him asap and try to find Aysil and talk to her. I'll give you a script with details of the bait... the offer from us. All you have to do is to turn on the charm again and ensure that our offer is one that... I won't say 'offer she can't refuse' but that's effectively what it will be. Live with us or die with them."

Lloyd pondered the melodramatic plan for a moment before spotting the missing question.

"Why can't your man do all that instead of me?" Elphinstone looked down at his size fourteen black Oxfords.

"He's a Kurd. If she was seen talking to him she would be disowned by the... uh... the others. But he does have a lot of her background and should be able to find her and give you a head start."

Lloyd voiced more objections.

"I still think she's unlikely to take the risk of even talking to me. She must know now that I was helping you before. And as you say, if she sees your Kurdish chap, she'll probably not go near us. He'll be treated like old Abdul, a pariah."

"Old Abdul, as you call him, wasn't a pariah. He was a good man. And she didn't really believe that he was her enemy even though the Russians clearly did. In fact that's one of the main reasons why she'll want to disown them."

"What do you mean? She hated him. Tried to get him arrested."

"No. That was also a front. To throw the scent off him – and her. She really loved him but couldn't show it."

"Loved him? Why would she 'love him', as you say?"

"Abdul was her father. That's why."

Lloyd started to speak but the words dried in his mouth. The mention of 'love' and 'father' struck a recently forged chord. Elphinstone continued his revelations.

"He agreed to keep close to her as long as we didn't try to harm her. We kept our side of the bargain but the people working for the Crimean – the so-called 'Skorpions' – must have got wind of his work and tried to liquidate him. She knows that now and that could be the reason why she might agree to work for us. Apart from your charm of course."

Lloyd's mouth became drier as he tried to speak and think at the same time. Not being accustomed to multi-tasking he settled for speaking.

"What... how do you want me to approach... uh... to say to her?" That was all he could say. All he could think of saying.

"Your usual way. Just go up to her and tell her that you love her. That should be a good start."

"Very funny. It's a good way to end the conversation before it's really started. She must know by now that I was stalking her, even though we both developed some level of unspoken relationship. What am I supposed to offer her from either of us to make her change horses?"

"As I said before, you can offer her a chance to stay alive for longer than she would at the hands of the Ayatollahs or the Skorpions. They all know by now that Abdul was her dad and that he was working for us. Abdul today, Aysil tomorrow. And," he added more cheerfully, "we will give her an escape route, a safety valve, in case she thinks she's recognised and in real danger. That'll probably happen very soon, so she really has to make her mind up quickly."

Lloyd's mind and imagination were working overtime. Visions of British agents' betrayals, both real and fictional, flashed before him. The fifty or more sent to their deaths as a result of George Blake's treachery and the exposures of MI5 and MI6 by Kim Philby and his Cambridge spy ring. In his mind they developed into the cruel final scene in a film he had seen, aptly titled 'The Spy Who Came in from the Cold.' But that was fictional, wasn't it? Or was it?

One motive ensured that he would accept the brief – and it wasn't money. His mind and part of his body still rippled when he thought of Aysil and his last night with her in Pristina. He could not believe that she was really infatuated with the crazed Afghan girl who would kill or maim if asked to do so. Nor could he believe that she would be so cynically cold-blooded to abandon her unbalanced accomplice.

That meant that both of the girls would have to come in from the cold of Iranian and Russian or Syrian intelligence forces. Perhaps he could persuade each of the girls to accept whatever he could offer in order to protect the other. But first, he had to decide whether to accept Elphinstone's offer for himself.

It was an easy decision to make. Protecting the female of the species was an old-fashioned idea but one that was embedded in his old-fashioned gut. All that was required now was to receive the details of the escape route and timing and the wherewithall to put it into effect. Travel documents, contacts and money. He knew that Elphinstone would have it all assembled and ready for action – and he was correct.

Within twenty minutes he had possession of boarding passes and newly issued EU passports for the two lady assassins. How the Foreign Office would justify them if they became subject of public exposure was their affair. Then Elphinstone delivered some more bait to add to the hook. A wallet containing ten thousand Euros and another with ten thousand pounds sterling were handed to Lloyd with the vague promise of more to come if required.

"Here you are, Cocky. This is only to be used to offer an initial incentive – a 'starter for ten' as Paxman says – and of course only to be handed to Aysil if and when they accept and they get on that plane to London." He chuckled as he pointed to the recently printed boarding passes.

"Your reward will be two-fold. One in reasonable remuneration and the other in knowing that you are serving your country." The last bit was delivered with a completely straight face. No suggestion of sarcasm or cynicism. Lloyd realised that his friend Jock really meant it. He was a true Brit of the old order.

"You mean I'll be serving Wales, do you? I'm sure Owen Glendower would be proud of me."

The joke was met with a completely blank stare from Elphinstone.

"Owen who? One of our men in Cardiff is he? Or one of your relations?"

Lloyd was about to say that the only relations he wanted to be involved were sexual but he restrained himself and adhered to the job in hand.

"I'll need a few hours to get my things together. And a cover for my bosses. If you can add a couple more boarding passes in the name of Gladys Watkins, I'll have all the cover I need."

"Who the blazes is Gladys Watkins? Another relation of Owen Glen-what's-it?"

"No. Gladys will be my girlfriend, my partner. We'll be on a short holiday in Greece. That's all. I'll meet up with your Kurdish gent when we get there and he can point me to where Aysil should be. Gladys can go shopping or testing the local hairdressers' salons while I find Aysil and make my pitch. Provided of course that I can find her quickly."

"Fine. Go to it. My Kurdish gentleman as you call him, is called Egid; it means 'brave' as I understand. Hope it's true. Anyway, she would recognise the name as Kurdish rather than Iranian Farsi or Alawite, so don't mention it to her. He'll contact you when you arrive in Lesvos and tell you what he knows. Between you, you should find Aysil either on Lesvos or somewhere very near there by now.

Meet me outside St James's Park station again as soon as you can get organised, preferably tonight, and I'll give you the extra boarding passes to and from Lesvos. Better still, get yourself and your girlfriend to Heathrow and pick them up from the Aegean Airways desk. I'll make the arrangements with them."

Elphinstone rose abruptly from his chair and beckoned Lloyd to follow suit. At the door to the street he patted Lloyd on the behind and offered a rare joke. "Watch out for Caruthers now. He'll probably think he's made a conquest."

But Lloyd had another conquest in mind.

Ch. 41. In from the cold.

Gladys could hardly believe her change of fortune. The phone call from Cocky offered her an instant change of scenery, from a cold Swansea to the warmth of Lesvos. More importantly it had the prospect of a complete change of lifestyle from lonely divorcee to happy partner, possibly future wife, of her recovered man-friend. The summons to London airport was accepted and 'action this day' was implemented.

The express train to Paddington took her to the waiting Lloyd. From there the apparently happy couple took their scant luggage by Heathrow Express into the airport terminal. Excited at shedding worries and frustrations, her grasp alternated from Lloyd's arm to his hand and back again.

Gladys trembled as they walked. Not having encountered anything resembling serious passion for several months she was looking forward to welcoming some heated advances from Lloyd. She expected they would follow as soon as they were in a suitable environment. As far as she was concerned, the railway carriage could serve the purpose provided that the inspector limited his attentions to their tickets.

As the train rumbled and gently rocked along its tracks, she moved her hands along the inside of Lloyd's trouser legs in a motion synchronising with the wheels crossing the gaps in the rails. No resistance was offered by Cocky who was enjoying the ride and reflecting that even the most onerous task had its compensations.

He wondered who would weaken first and whether the airport had a secluded lounge to contain the volcanic pressure before it erupted. One small fumarole had already dampened his underpants and the muffled gasps from his travelling companion suggested that her own under-garments were in danger of needing replacing or dry-cleaning.

Unfortunately for their erotic aspirations, the airport offered only hard seats at a cafe table and the prospect of slightly softer arrangement on an Airbus A320 of Aegean Airways. On the first leg of the flight, stopping in Athens, Lloyd's thoughts of ever-closer union with Gladys gradually cooled.

He realised that they were flying over a path taken by Aysil to get to her Arab victim in Austria and escape to Germany. Thirty thousand feet below his aircraft seat were the tectonic trails through the Balkans that had seen her collecting the radioactive poison from Dragovic. Now he was to try to recruit her to deliver her services to his own country.

"Do we really want to employ an accomplished killer? Surely she's literally a poisoned chalice?" he wondered. *"Who or what would she dispatch next?"* He would have to handle her with the metaphorical kid gloves. Perhaps some lead-lined claws might be safer. His eyes turned to the still heated form beside him. Gladys may not be quite so intriguing but she would offer a better chance of survival.

After a three hour stop-over in Athens to take the second leg of the flight to Mytilene the hot-blooded passengers resumed their seats on the Airbus. Gladys was not excessively tall but her cramped buttocks were beginning to tingle. It was restricted circulation rather than unrestricted pleasure. Cocky was able to realign his frame without disturbing Gladys or the pins and needles in her bottom.

The rush of hot air onto their faces when they left the aircraft and walked across the tarmac apron to Mytilene's terminal was a welcome change from the previous combination of cramp and cold air-conditioning. Within a few yards from the Airbus and a further five minutes' walk to collect baggage and present passports they had recovered their warm feelings towards each other and their destination.

Holding Lloyd's arm tightly to her ribs, Gladys murmured sweet nothing except for a plea to find the toilets. His bladder would have to wait its turn until he had collected the luggage and she had relieved herself. Once safely refreshed she kept watch on the suitcases while he followed her example.

As he emerged from the men's toilet he was slightly surprised to see a man approaching Gladys and their suitcases. A furtive whisper in her ear resulted in her looking round to find Lloyd and gesture to him. The stranger moved away from her side and stood three feet from the luggage with his back to Gladys. Lloyd held out a hand to reassure her and then stepped up to face the stranger.

"Mr Egid?" The stranger shook his head. Lloyd asked again. Again the stranger shook his head but spoke softly and quickly.

"Egid told me to... uh... to tell you... if you are Mr L Stone, that is." It was Lloyd's turn to shake his head. The stranger ignored the head-shaking and continued. "I am taxi driver. Do you want taxi to hotel, Mr Stone?" Lloyd was beginning to understand.

"I'm not Mr.... uh...Mr Stone but, I would like a taxi. Yes – Theofilos hotel. Take these cases please."

Once in the taxi they sat back and relaxed as much as they could. Gladys was still disturbed by the approach from the driver and Lloyd preferring to stay silent. The taxi stopped at the door of the exotically named Theofilos Paradise Boutique Hotel and the driver took the cases into the foyer. As he turned to leave, Lloyd offered a few euros to him and spoke quietly.

"Tell Mr.Egid to meet me here in the bar at seven this evening. Do you understand?" The driver understood very well and nodded briskly.

"Seven hours this evening in hotel bar," he replied. They both nodded to confirm 'over and out,' and the driver walked away without thanking Lloyd for the money. Gladys was out of earshot and ready for a shower and closer encounters of the passionate kind. Cocky threw an assuring smile and they took the elevator to their second-floor suite with more telling exchanges of smiles.

The next two hours saw their combined use of the shower for fifteen minutes followed by the use of the large bed by two naked bodies for the remaining hour and three-quarters. Another half hour witnessed a short sleep and the second use of the shower. Far from dampening her desires, Gladys increased her appetite for eroticism and more ideas to fulfil her fantasies.

Cocky was happy to wait until he could meet Egid and sketch out a rough plan of action for the next days' hunting. His imagination had been stimulated by Gladys's writhing body and sporadic cries of mildly pornographic demands. She would have to ration Lloyd to more regular bedtime hours. His appointment with Egid would take priority.

"Cometh the hour, cometh the Kurd," he thought. A stocky figure walked uncertainly into the hotel foyer at precisely seven p.m. and asked where the bar was located. As the figure walked past the armchair in which he had parked, Lloyd looked over the top of the magazine that he pretended to read and asked softly if Mr Egid was in the hotel.

Egid walked away from the chair and into the bar, followed after twenty seconds by Lloyd. At the bar, Egid ordered a beer and Lloyd did the same. In true Hollywood fashion, the two men faced away from each other whilst talking in low tones and short sentences. The barman looked on in carefully uninterested curiosity and then shrugged at what he assumed were two rather sad men trying to arrange a gay tryst.

The conclusion of their staccato exchanges was that they were to meet again the next morning at eight-thirty. The meeting point would be a roadside cafe near the coastal road. Lloyd wondered what excuse he would have to give to Gladys for his planned absence. In the event, after much of the night quenching her thirst for attention and genital welding - she was happy enough to return to the bathroom and her cosmetics while he exercised his shoes and lungs in the sunshine.

Fifteen minutes of brisk walking brought a spray of perspiration to Lloyd's brow and a second sighting of the Kurdish agent who came straight to the point of their meeting.

"I know exactly where she might be now," he started to say. How he could 'know exactly' where someone 'might be' eluded Lloyd's grasp of English grammar but he decided not to quibble.

"OK Mr...."

"Just 'Egid'... just 'Egid' will do Mr Loyal." 'Mr Loyal' was amused by the affirmation of his loyalty but decided again not pursue further pedantry.

"OK Egid. Just tell me exactly where and how to get there - I'll try to see her as soon as I can."

"OK Mr Loyal but you must see her now. Later will be too late." Lloyd accepted the circumstantial logic. Besides which, he wanted to try to get the task completed in the shortest time possible and get back to Gladys and to London. Egid continued almost frantically.

"She and the other girl – watch out for her, she is crazy bad – they are staying only today in a house in... " He stopped and grabbed a grubby piece of notepaper from his pocket... "in here." He pointed to the address of a house in the area near to the ferry port.

Egid looked very worried. He was very worried, and understandably so. If the limited opportunity to persuade Aysil to turn her loyalties were lost, then his own position would be exposed to retribution. That might be anything from revenge-seeking dissidents in Europe to a very sticky-ending Fatwah from Iranian or Syrian Ayatollahs.

The opportunity was now beyond him and in the hands of the amateur agent from London. The grubby paper was thrust into Lloyd's hands and a grubby Kurdish finger prodded the address. The moving finger poked again in the direction of the ferry port. Lloyd took the hint and the paper together.

A hired car was waiting to take him post-haste to the address but he would have to drive it himself. Egid could not take any further risk or any further part in the immediate proceedings. Opening the passenger's door Lloyd stopped, remembering once more that the steering wheel was in the usual place for driving on the right hand side of the road. He skipped around the car's bonnet to take control of it.

Fifteen minutes later he was parked in a side street near to the given address and walking to the house near the ferry port. With no sign of a door bell he slapped a hard fist on the wooden panel and heard some commotion on the other side of it. A defiant Afghan face appeared between the door-frame and the lock, staring rolling-eyed and trying to hide the fear she had for her lover and herself.

Whatever Leila wanted to say to the intruder would not, could not be said. Her lips parted but the bone-dry inside of her mouth grabbed any words before they could pass her tongue. Only a faint gargled moan came out. Lloyd pushed the door open and her aside. Once in a position to discern what was or was not going on behind it he grabbed Leila's arm and growled a very simple order.

"Aysil! Get her – now!" Leila's reaction was to shake her head and arm violently as she tried to stab Lloyd's hand and arm with the kitchen knife that she had slipped into her sleeve before opening the door. Her reputation had overcome her efforts. Lloyd was expecting nothing less from a psychotic girl, even one so sad and helpless. His grasp of her arm quickly twisted Leila until she fell and nearly stabbed her own leg.

Leila's screams and sobs were immediately stilled by a softer cry from the kitchen doorway beyond the entrance hall of the house. A very much calmer Aysil placed a hand over the one holding the knife and ordered the young Afghan to get herself to her room. After a whisper of assurance and a soft stroke of the frightened girl's hair, the trio was reduced to a duo and only the distant sobs from Leila interrupted the silence before Aysil spoke again...

"Hello Mr Lloyd. I was not expecting to see you here, now. Have you come here alone? Just to see me, us?" A silent nod from Lloyd and an attempt to penetrate Aysil's defensive stare gave her the answer. "Why? What do you want from ... me... from us? You are not a policeman, I think? Are you?"

This time the shaken head was supported by confirmation of his non-police role.

"No Aysil. No, I'm not involved with the police. But I am involved with trying to save you from extreme danger..." She smiled wistfully at the thought of this urbane 'English admirer' being able to defend her from dangers that she faced every day. Lloyd ignored the mocking expression.

"You must know that every police force in Europe might be trying to arrest you and there are all sorts of people wishing to eliminate, to liquidate you." He used the old term for violent death to direct her thoughts towards the ex- Soviet military who had conspired with her to kill the Arab magnate.

It had the desired effect. The sarcastic smile was washed from her face by a tiny involuntary shudder. Now it was his turn to apply irony to his appeal. To drive the hard unpleasant message home, he added,

"You have actually managed to create some very nasty enemies – amongst your colleagues and their own enemies at the same time. Congratulations Aysil. That's quite an achievement. Just in case you doubt my... uh... sincerity, you should remember what happened to your father."

The last part of Lloyd's message completely destroyed Aysil's stable appearance of control. She turned her head towards the window and then to the door as if looking for an explanation of the baffling suggestion. The half-smile tried to return to ward off such an unsupported hint.

"What are you talking about? My father is fine, in good health, back in Syria where he has always been. If you're trying to frighten me... well... you're wasting the time."

Lloyd realised that perhaps she knew less than she had thought about the fate of Abdul Nasir. He wondered how he could provide the truth without smashing the fragile truce between them.

"No, Aysil. I don't think so. Sorry but, well if you really don't know the truth, well, I'm sorry." He ended lamely. Not sure how to expose her to the unpalatable facts of death. "I know, and so do several others, that the Abdul Nasir that you pretended to hate was your father.

"And we know that he was not just a refugee trafficker but in reality he was helping you. What you might not have known was, that he was also working for my... uh... friends. Unfortunately for us and for him, YOUR so-called friends from the Crimea found out and... you can guess what they would do then..."

He broke off, letting Aysil's mind digest what he had revealed and condition her for the inevitable truth. She simply shook her head and looked around the room again. "I don't believe any of it, of your silly story. Abdul was, well you know what he was. Anyway, he was nothing to do with me."

Lloyd realised that he could not convince her that he was not bluffing. He also knew that time was running out and Aysil would do the same unless he could make her abandon her pretence and take his offer of escape seriously. Help came from an unexpected direction and flew down the stairs.

Leila was still sobbing but this time she was sobbing for her lover in her hour of awful distress. She flung her arms around Aysil's neck and cried tears of compassion for Abdul's daughter. Lloyd could not expect to understand the tear-washed words in a foreign language but he immediately saw the change in Aysil's attitude. She knew that her game of pretence was over and Lloyd knew that she knew it.

"Come on. We both know I'm telling you the truth. And we both know what your bosses – your masters in Tehran or Damascus or wherever will do when they find out. That can only be a matter of time – probably a very short time. Then you can add them to the Arabs and Crimeans after your blood.

"I'll tell you the truth about my position and what I can do to help you. To begin with, I admit, I was trailing you when you came over here on your way to Austria. I agreed to do that

312

in exchange for help in my own business and, well because I hoped that you and I might become close friends. I really thought we had done that when we met again in Kosovo."

Aysil simply stared at him and beyond while he tried to deliver his own form of compassion. Her expression remained unchanged and stony faced. Leila was still sobbing and trying to kiss her. Lloyd's confession took a slightly different direction. Time was getting shorter by the minute and so should his appeal.

"The people who helped me have offered a better deal for you." He hoped that 'you' would be taken to include Leila, if Aysil wanted it to. "They can protect you completely but only if you agree immediately to work with them, perhaps I should say 'us', to prevent disasters in Europe."

Once again he hoped that she would consider 'you' as singular or plural as preferred. But once again there was no sign of change in her facial expression. It was time to spread some details before her. The decision to perform such a radical U-turn would be momentous. But the alternative would be short and probably brutal for her and her follower.

"We" – *"no point in pretending that I'm not involved personally",* he thought – "we want you to come with us... me... to England where you will be given a completely new identity. A job and home in a safe place. You will help us to find out who and where any false refugees or other agents of your old employers, or others too, are plotting to harm us. You will be helping to save innocent lives." *"That should appeal to her,"* ran through his spinning mind.

"We all know that there are some who have either come over as refugees or even have been born in Europe but want to kill or damage people because of religious or political reasons." He hoped that she would understand what he was saying. It was hard enough for him to understand it, let alone a foreigner who was also in another country.

His hopes were realised. Aysil was extremely distressed at the shock of Lloyd's reports but she was also extremely intelligent and aware of the perils accompanying her work. Fleeing from Germany had been prompted by tip-offs concerning someone planning her disappearance and certain death. Her mind was still troubled but working at a furious pace. One quick glance at Leila told her what she had to do. Lloyd jumped into her mind while she was deciding.

"Come on. This place is dangerous. We don't have much time if you want to stay alive." Aysil nodded. Having decided on her only safe option for survival she was not going to allow procrastination to rob her of it. Lloyd released a tiny sigh as he continued to apply the pressure. "Get your things together," – *"would that include Leila?"* he wondered, – "and be ready to go in five minutes – no longer!"

Aysil snapped an order to Leila who continued to appear bewildered. She almost cried back to Aysil in Farsi, "Where are we going... doing now?" Aysil patted her hair again.

"We're going to the ferry – going somewhere safer – for both of us." The mention of 'both of us' seemed to calm Leila. She followed Aysil to their bedroom and Lloyd soon heard the sound of snapping catches and zip fasteners on their travel bags. In much less than the permitted five minutes they walked down the stairs to the front door, as if they would be glad to escape from it.

Each of the girls wore their usual hijab head-dress and Aysil had a saffron coloured silk scarf around her neck. Despite the extreme haste the pair were not unduly dishevelled; they could have been embarking on a shopping expedition. Lloyd took two papers from his wallet and some paper money. He handed them to Aysil.

"There are papers here for you both to fly from Mytilene to London. You'll have to change planes in Athens but there are passes for the second leg of the flights here too. You'll need some money, not much. One of my friends will meet you at London Airport when you get off. He or she will take care of you from there.

"First, walk from here to the ferry. Ask someone loudly which ferry goes to the nearest Turkish port but don't get on a boat. Just wait around for a minute or two and then get into a taxi, a black Mercedes, that will be waiting outside the ferry entrance. The driver will ask you if you want to go to Athens. Just get in and he will take you to Mytilene airport and help you to check-in for the flight. You know how to get on to an aircraft flight, don't you?" Aysil nodded to Lloyd and again to Leila, muttering something in her hijab-covered ear.

Leila nodded back, smiling for the first time since Lloyd had met them. She followed Aysil from the door and onto the pavement outside as they walked calmly towards the ferry terminal. Lloyd watched them go as far as the street corner where they turned to walk the final half kilometre to the terminal's entrance. When he was satisfied that they were really going to follow his instructions he also walked to the corner and watched as they complete the short journey.

A few passengers had gathered near the ferry entrance and he saw Aysil stop to say something to one of them. The passenger talked back and nodded before moving on. The two girls duly followed for twenty metres and stopped to open a handbag. As the other passengers continued forwards so the girls turned and walked away towards two or three black taxis.

Lloyd held his breath and started to sweat. They might get into the wrong car. No. A figure emerged from the second of the three taxis and beckoned Aysil to enter his car. Lloyd breathed again. The taxi driver was the man who he knew to be under orders from his Kurdish companion. Egid was nowhere to be seen but the man in the taxi seemed to be following orders to the letter.

The Mercedes drove away and Lloyd strode back to his hired car and tried to follow. The taxi with the girls was already well in front of him but he simply drove to the airport departure point where he knew it should be.

Sure enough, it went straight to the departure gate and the driver led the girls to a desk with their luggage and the papers from Lloyd. After a short discussion the desk attendant gave some more documents to Aysil and she gave the driver some money. It was all very ordinary, two girls being assisted to their flights by a helpful taxi driver. As they walked into what served as the departure lounge Lloyd walked to a cafe table where he extracted his cell-phone and called the authority in Whitehall. His call was accepted by a recorded answering service and he left a simple message.

"Please tell Mister Stone that the birds have flown." He knew that the message would be timed and that 'Mr Stone' would calculate the flights and their ETA in Heathrow. He would also be in contact with people in Athens to ensure that 'the birds' could fly to Heathrow on time. From now on, he decided, the recovery process was in the hands of Elphinstone, Caruthers and Co.

He could, and did, go back to his hotel and the waiting warmth of Gladys. Only a nagging doubt prevented complete relaxation.

He imagined that he had seen a familiar figure following the girls into the airport.

Ch.42. A game of singles.

Gladys was there in their room as he expected. She was also as warm or warmer than he expected.

"Oh, Cocky! This place is lovely, but it is bloomin' hot, innit?" There was no answer to that. Despite the hurried journeys and drama of the last two hours he was well aware of the temperature, and of a complete absence of clothing adorning his companion in the bedroom.

"Well," he thought, *"if you can't beat 'em..."* His lightweight jacket and trousers swiftly became lighter as they preceded his shoes, shirt and pants to the carpet. Soon only his socks remained attached to his body. Shortly after that there was only a small part of his body that was not attached to Gladys. But all was not accepted without protest.

"Ooh, Cocky. You're sweatin' like a... well, I won't say 'a pig' but you know what I mean. Don't you want a shower first?"

"Since you ask – no – I'll have one after, if it's all the same to you."

"All right. Anything you say," she giggled. "I'll have one after as well. Maybe we can do it together – the shower, I mean." She giggled again and snuggled her nose into his sweaty chest. "But you are a bit wet with it, aren't you?" He simply nodded and gave a muffled grunt. It had been a hot day's work and he wasn't going to argue about showering. The tension and pressure of the past couple of hours had left him ready for some rest and recuperation.

Gladys was willing and ready to help but she desperately wanted to be sure of her longer-term future. Not just a holiday romance. She was determined to have a stable relationship in their old stamping and loving ground, in Swansea. Her holiday companion just wanted to take his mind off the latest tense situation, that he hoped had ended successfully.

By the time that he had clambered aboard the bed and Gladys he realised that Aysil's removal from her Iranian employment, and sudden defection to a British one, would not remove her from his memory. He needed to 'warm down' as if he had played a full eighty minutes of energetic rugby. Gladys could sense the tension but not the reason for it.

"What's the matter, Cocky? Lost your sense of duty? Or don't you fancy me?" She knew that the last question was unlikely to be answered honestly even if it were true. "Why don't you have that shower first as I suggested then you'll feel more... uh... up for it." She forced a little giggle but was uneasy at the apparent change in Lloyd's priorities. He accepted the offer with an apology and a little white lie.

"Sorry, Glad. I'm still too hot outside and too cold inside I think. Tell you what, let's have that shower and then have... a cold drink." He tried to laugh but in fact a cold drink was suddenly more appealing than hot sex. "I think I have to cool down to warm up, if you get what I mean." A relieved Gladys smiled and tried to join in the humour by opening her legs and whistling softly.

"I'll have an iced lemon juice with a splash of brandy in it, my love." She hoped that would not sound too demanding or possessive. "And you can have... whatever you want... after we've had our drinks and showers. Is that OK?"

For Lloyd, that was absolutely OK. The combination of cool liquid and warm contact would, or should, enable his thoughts to focus on the present and relax over the immediate past. He returned the soft smile to Gladys and she received it with thanks. A life together in Swansea was still on the cards, perhaps.

Twenty minutes later they were both wrapped in towelling bathrobes and sipping their refreshments. Iced brandy and lemon for her, cold Heineken for him. As they reached the base of their glasses she put out a testing question. A verbal feeler. Probing gently and hoping that she had judged the mood without exceeding the limits of acceptable requests.

"That's better. How do you feel now then? Come on. The bed's waiting and I think you and I need a little slap and tickle, maybe a lot. I'll vote for that, won't you?" Her man moved to accept the motion and cast his vote with a strong grip on her bare legs and trunk. Her voice dropped to a bare whisper as hands and legs entwined. "Oh yes. That's better. Much, much better."

He could not argue with that. Almost all thoughts of foreign agents and foreign office activity were replaced by his current activity. Almost but not all. One little chink of darkness remained stubbornly in his mind. What if Aysil had not flown to London? Or worse still, what if she had gone there but was only pretending to work for Elphinstone while really still in Iranian employ?

He tried to obscure any further concerns by pushing harder onto the pulsating form of Gladys beneath him. A few months ago he would have offered his eye teeth for this opportunity and now it was being delivered on their bed if not on a plate. But now it was being delivered with contingent aspirations, if not deal-breaking conditions.

Sleep came in the form of a ten minute doze, still touching the body cuddling against him. It completed half an hour of honesty that they both exchanged with gratitude. The only words spoken were mumbled thanks with meaningful eye to eye contact. After another quarter of an hour they rose and spent a few minutes in the shower before drying and considering their next move.

The next move was to discuss a meal for two. Gladys was happy for the decision to be made by Lloyd. That would avoid the risk of dissent. Most of the available restaurants were offering similar menus anyway so why argue about it. She also wanted Lloyd to believe that he was in command of their situation so that she could lead him into making another decision, one that she had already made. A meaningful relationship would only be meaningful if he agreed, or preferably decided, to live with her in her home territory.

Although neither the venue nor the menu would be the subject of debate, it did not follow that re-camping would be taken for granted. In his fragile state of mental exhaustion from completing Elphinstone's task, Cocky was not so easily given to acquiescence when Gladys suggested that they should spend their remaining years in South Wales.

The nearest he could offer to even considering such a physical translation was a tired "I'll have to think about it."

In fact he was thinking only of eating, drinking and getting back to London, returning to resume his work in the insurance market and his cosy flat in Chiswick. Even the probable de-briefing by Elphinstone would take priority over a move back to his old homeland. The more he thought about it, the more appealing the status quo sounded.

Lime Street and Leadenhall market's bustle, Chiswick and Strand-on-the-Green's pubs, St James's Square and the In and Out, and... Susan. Susan? He had almost forgotten about Susan. How could he forget?

A rising volume of verbal elbow jogging from the opposite side of the Tropicana restaurant table brought his mind and Gladys's prospects of consensus back to earth. It was a very pleasant earth overlooking the Aegean Sea to North and Gladys's ample cleavage to East but the landing was close to being bumpy.

Cocky realised that Gladys would always occupy a special place in his pants but not necessarily the whole of his life. *"Not yet, anyhow,"* he told himself. The rest of the meal, a traditional mix of lamb with prunes and a bland local wine, was more relaxing. Sitting at an open table under the trees in the Molyvos village square almost took both of the diners back into the clouds. Aysil and Leila and flights from Eastern danger to Western security were put to the back of his mind.

Those concerning Swansea and co-habitation remained stubbornly in Gladys's mind but she contented herself to think that they had not been completely rejected. Driving back to Mytilene in contented silence a temporary truce broke out with resolve to enjoy the remains of the vacation. A soft bed and deep sleep welcomed them back.

Less welcoming was the shrill cry from Lloyd's mobile phone during a late breakfast. Inevitably, it brought worrying news from Whitehall. Breakfast was sidelined as he carried the instrument of torture to his room while Gladys continued '*pas seul*'. The voice from London waited patiently until the caller was assured of Lloyd's undivided attention.

"Hello, Cocky. Can you talk now? We seem to have a problem." This sounded as though he was signalling pending disaster from outer space to Huston. "Our Kurdish friend has just reported... uh... it seems that only one girl got on the flight to London. My man here went to Heathrow and confirms that he's collected her and taken her to a safe place but doesn't know what happened to the other one."

Lloyd gave an inward groan and asked the obvious. "Just a moment, Jock. Is he certain that one of them hasn't slipped away into London without him seeing her? I definitely saw both of them boarding the flight to Athens. Oh, and by the way, which one has he got with him?"

There was an embarrassed pause in Whitehall. "He's quite certain. Well, he's certain that only one girl was on the plane. He's checked with the airline. I... uh... haven't asked him to confirm her identity – the one he has with him." Another pause. "I'll call you back."

An hour later came the news they both feared; a report from Athens airport. The body of a young woman wearing a hijab and partug-style shirt and trousers had been discovered in the airport terminal lavatory. She appeared to have been strangled. A saffron coloured silk scarf was around her throat. The report had identified the corpse from a medical registration card in her purse as Aysil Husseini.

The initial report suggested that she was a refugee who had committed suicide. Athens airport could not add to the report. Elphinstone almost seemed to have accepted it as an occupational hazard. Lloyd was still reeling from shock and remorse at the news when he returned to the breakfast table. He knew it was of no use asking for more detail at this stage. Jock would no doubt gather whatever information he could get - or what was of use to him, soon enough.

Lloyd's thoughts turned to the sole survivor. What would happen to Leila in London? She would be of little use to the Foreign Office unless they could train her as an agent amongst the Afghan or Iraqi and Syrian refugees in Europe. She might present more of a hazard than an asset, unless they wanted to adopt assassins or suicide bombers as agents. They would be far better off without her.

Later that day the two Welsh holiday-makers completed their brief vacation in Lesvos. Each had reason to be pensive. She for her receding hopes for life in South Wales with Lloyd and he for his failed mission. He was absolutely bewildered by the death of his beautiful defector. He drove to Mytilene airport without discussing it and flew in comparative silence to Athens and on the connecting flight to London.

The two acting honeymooners parted at Paddington station. The words of Robert Burns: *'Aye fond kiss, our paths to sever,'* almost dripped from his lips as he embraced Gladys and walked back towards the train to the City. Before boarding it he wondered if he should reverse his intended route and travel to Fulham to restore his connection with Susan.

Evening rush hour traffic was already building up on road and rail routes. It would be nearly six p.m. before he could open the backlog of mail and recorded messages on his office desk. The District Line to Fulham Broadway beckoned and he obeyed. By five forty-five p.m. he was at the entrance to Susan's apartment and ringing the doorbell.

Despite three attempts to elicit a response the apartment remained silent. *"Too early,"* he thought. *"She must still be working or on her way home."* But rather than abandoning his plan to allow Susan to clear his mind he returned to the pavement and a nearby Victorian building in which a pub was conveniently situated.

Only one pint of Fuller Smith & Turner's 'London Pride' found its way down his throat before he adopted the old 'if at first you don't succeed' approach. He left the warm saloon bar and walked back to Susan's apartment. The evening shadows were now firmly established outside the apartment block as his finger pressed on the doorbell.

His efforts were rewarded with the sound of slight commotion from within. Not one female voice but two voices, one of which was decidedly male. When the door was finally opened by about fifteen degrees he could see a dishevelled Susan wearing only an overcoat and a shocked look of surprise. More sounds – a man's feet moving rapidly towards the kitchen door – thumped along the bare floor of the corridor behind her.

"Oh God, Cocky! I wasn't expecting to see you!"

"What, never? Or just not this evening?"

"Oh, this evening. Although it might be either or both I suppose. Where have you been for the last three weeks?"

The speed of her returning composure impressed Lloyd but he could not disguise his own surprise and disappointment. Before adopting the look of a cuckolded lover he had to remind himself that he had only parted from a very steamy physical relationship some two hours previously. Gladys Watkins would not even have arrived at her own apartment in Swansea by now.

He tried to look hurt and the attempt had a limited success. Susan dropped her defences and nearly dropped her coat but clung on half-heartedly to both. The feet in the kitchen were ordered to start marching as a partly clothed man emerged with his shirt, jacket and tie wrapped loosely over a muscular torso. He gave a sheepish grin and a wave of the only free hand before calling "have a good evening" as he shuffled from the doorway.

"That was Winston. He works with the firm that services my boiler," explained Susan. She waved Lloyd towards her bedroom and followed him into it. Closing front and bedroom doors, she abandoned all hope of cover for either her situation or her body and surrendered to what chastisement Lloyd cared to issue.

As he had been absent from the doorbell for less than an hour, Lloyd calculated that Winston would not have had time to service either the boiler or its owner before he had surprised them.

"Is this a regular form of service call? Or was it only an introductory free offer? More importantly, what the hell are you doing behind my back? And when?" Susan was a shameless woman, he told himself. But then he remembered again that he was just as shameless, or more. He had not even hinted to Susan of his contact with Gladys before he embarked on the latest mission.

Every setback provides an opportunity. His only sensible course would be to feign divine forgiveness for Susan's misdemeanours and keep quiet about his own. That should earn enough brownie points to keep him in Susan's affections for as long as he could prevent her finding out about Gladys. After all, if it came to a showdown he could enlist someone's testimony to say that he had been engaged in essential work for the three weeks since they last met.

Susan started to shiver. It was partly due to her nudity and partly in nervous anticipation of a spanking on her bare bottom. In the circumstances she almost hoped for the latter. It would clear the air and show Lloyd that she accepted guilt. He had never been interested in physical violence to women of any description though and the pint of London Pride in the pub had made him rather peckish.

"Get dressed then. We're going out for a bite to eat. You can decide after that whether you want to be with me or another boilermaker."

Susan sighed with gratitude and wondered again if she would have preferred to submit to the corporal punishment or to continued humiliation. In the event she had no choice but to submit to the meal at Lloyd's expense and to continue in his moral debt as far as she understood it. One thing was certain. If she wished to resume as Lloyd's very close friend or lover she would have to start demonstrating her affection very soon.

"Thank you Cocky. I don't know what came over me..." She stopped before digging herself in deeper. Lloyd looked askance as she donned some crumpled underwear beneath a light dress and cashmere sweater. She continued with the hint of a giggle but suppressed it in case he thought she was not serious enough. "I've never done that before, with a tradesman like that - or anyone else," she added quickly.

"No? Well... don't worry. Nor have I." That brought a laugh and air-freshening relief to both of them as they stepped from the flat. They walked along the pavements of Fulham to the cafe only two doors from the pub of Cocky's recent acquaintance. Seven o'clock shadows of twilight had brought the air temperature down to cuddling level and she pressed her arm and shoulder against Lloyd's until they reached the cafe and a small table for two.

Susan was aware that she had been closer to seduction than she cared to admit. No point in going over it again, she thought. Glancing at his set face and look of apparent satisfaction she was relieved at her narrow escape from potential fury. *"If he only knew..."* she thought.

Lloyd was still thinking over the events of the last three weeks since they met. Most of those had been in close contact with Aysil or even closer contact with Gladys. Still, he didn't have to offer further explanation or excuses. He glanced across the table to Susan scouring the menu for something satisfying but pretending to be healthy. *"If she only knew..."* he thought.

Morning in Fulham saw them smooching and warm in Susan's bed. Lloyd was beginning to consider staying there for the rest of the day but once again his thoughts were dashed by the shrill siren in his phone. Excusing himself to a sleepy eyed Susan, he took it to her kitchen and listened like the little dog to His Master's Voice.

Elphinstone was already well into his day at the office and had some more news to pass and some more questions to ask. Lloyd's own office would have to wait until they had exchanged information and the small office near St James's Park station was the designated venue for the exchange.

"Please be there before ten o'clock," said the voice in the cell-phone. "I don't want to start coffee without you." Nor did a thirsty and slightly jet-lagged – or that would be his excuse – and fuzzy-headed Lloyd. At just after nine fifteen a.m. he stepped warily out of St James's Park station onto a blindingly bright pavement. The silhouette of a very attractive woman walking towards him nearly caused a collision but he had the presence of mind to side-step her and she to stop before him.

"Good morning, Cocky." The familiarity of the voice caused him to blink in the sunlight and peer at the shadowy figure. Before he could discern just who had issued the greeting he instinctively returned it.

"Oh, hi. Good morning. I wasn't expecting to see you here." In truth he wasn't able to see her clearly at all but the riposte provided a second or two to think. He took a step to one side and out of the direct light. Another dazzling sight emerged. It was Helen. Helen of Troy or Helen of the Red Cross legal department and Bekaa refugee camp, it was one and the same.

Helen's face was still beautiful despite the cruel cuts and stitches after Leila's assault. Her face had also been rinsed with a few tears recently. Carefully wiped away but leaving telling traces. By now Lloyd was becoming familiar with the traces of tears on women's faces. Unlike Gladys or Susan, Helen's tears had no direct connection with his activities, as far as he was aware. He waited for the next reply.

"No. I don't suppose you were. I was almost expecting to bump into you though. I knew you were coming here sometime this morning. Jock told me – told me he was expecting you – for coffee."

"And you? Are you..." He broke off. Not knowing how to ask further or just mind his own business.

"Having coffee? Not yet. Perhaps you would care to have one with me? I could do with a coffee." She offered a sad smile that only emphasised the tear-tracts. "There's a Costa cafe just across the way there."

Lloyd tried to restrain the impulse to look at his watch. *"Sod it. Jock can just wait. I could do with some coffee before I see him, anyway,"* he grumbled to himself. He put on his most caring smile to offer a shoulder for Helen to have another cry if she wanted one.

"Come on then. Let's go for it, and hang the expense."

That was meant to comfort her. The mention of 'hang' however, did nothing to cheer him when he remembered the strangled young woman in Athens airport. They skipped over the kerb and into the cafe with its aroma of freshly ground and roasted refreshment. Helen came straight to the point of unburdening herself from her second tranche of disappointment.

"You know that Jock and I have been seeing quite a lot of each other recently. Oh, by the way, are you still seeing Susan? I haven't heard from her for a while." An answering nod while hiding behind a steaming coffee cup allowed her to continue with her thread.

"Well when he told me that he had a proposition to put to me – and I knew that he was planning to divorce – I put two and two together but, I'm afraid I just made it twenty-two. It seems that he and his wife have decided to keep the family and children together and he – they – are going to settle somewhere outside London. I don't know where." She paused to look down and take a sip of her own coffee before continuing. It was either that or dropping her guard and leaking more tears.

"Whilst I thought - well you know what girls like to think – but what he wanted to see me about was –" she gulped with rising indignation, "to ask me to work for him. Not even a proper job. he probably knew that he couldn't match anything

I can expect to get in the City, but just to be on call to do some translating of something he couldn't even talk about – some secret in that civil service den of his." The word 'couldn't' was beginning to sound repetitive, as if Elphinstone's shortcomings were getting longer.

Lloyd was dumbstruck. Not due to the *alter face* in Elphinstone's domestic life but to the thought of Helen becoming entangled in the spooky world of Foreign Office intrigue. That had been Lloyd's bailiwick, or at least he had thought it to be. Did Elphinstone really think that Helen could be a substitute for the late Aysil? The two women were equally clever but in completely different disciplines.

The horrified look on his face must have struck a chord of sympathy with Helen. She shrugged as she gave him a silent look of thanks for his condolences. He expressed it with telling honesty.

"I just don't know what to say. That's astonishing. What was he thinking of?" His mind stated to spin again. *"Come to think of it - well - what should I think of it?"* Thinking was not an option. His mind was as blank as his facial expression. Helen perked up and finished her coffee.

"I don't know, Cocky. He's a funny man. Not very funny for me right now but I'll just have to grin and bear it, I suppose. Come on. You'd better finish your coffee too or you'll be late. You don't want to get a bad mark in your next report do you?" A resigned grimace followed by a smile told them both that she felt lighter and better for the confession.

As they said goodbye and shook hands, Helen moved forward and sealed her vote of thanks with a kiss that brushed between his cheek and his lips. Light enough to be unemotional but close enough to offer closer friendship. His thanks and hopes to see her again soon were entirely sincere.

Back across the road, and around the corner in the discrete office on the second floor of the Elphinstone outpost, saw a more composed Lloyd entering and helping himself to a chair in front of the incumbent's desk. He was a few minutes later than agreed but that was of no consequence to either of them.

What they both sought was as much information as they could extract from each other. Before Elphinstone could start the proceedings in his own office Lloyd fired the first salvo.

"Well Jock. It looks as though your plans have taken a bit of a hammering. All that effort, mainly by me, and no result. What the blazes has happened? Surely someone could have protected her from who or what killed her. I saw her, in fact both of them, right onto the plane at Mytilene."

To his astonishment and extreme anger after hearing of his attitude to Helen, Elphinstone accepted the outburst with calm, almost indifference. He very nearly shrugged his shoulders and glanced away from direct eye contact.

"I don't know exactly how it happened or why we couldn't prevent it, Cocky. And don't think we're not grateful to you for trying..." Lloyd interrupted.

"Trying? I was doing more than trying. I was succeeding. Had her all but home and dry for you. What more did you expect? And what's happened to the other one? Has she been killed too? Or have you got her in a safe house somewhere? I don't know what you expect to get from her. A bullet or a knife in the back most likely."

"Don't worry. We'll take care of her, including medical attention if necessary. She might be of very good use – service to us. So your efforts won't be for nothing. Speaking of which, I owe you some money, and a good lunch, I think."

"Well as you seem to be keen to employ a new assassin and I agree that you owe me something, I accept both offers. Now. What happened to the girl? Who killed her?"

"We do have some information concerning the cause of death. She was strangled from behind with the scarf and dragged into the ladies toilet before they could go into the boarding area. Could have been one of several with a grudge. The Iranians might have found out that Aysil was defecting. Or the Crimean 'skorpions' – yes, we all know about them –

329

or even a Sunni Arab who knew about her deal to eliminate Bin Q'etta.

"Any of them could have been involved. Fortunately for the diplomatic service, we're convinced that it wouldn't have involved the Russians officially. They don't need any more bad press in the international world than they already have. Those ex-Chechen military might have been working for them at some stage but they just don't want to know them now.

"My hunch is that it was someone close to her and connected with the Iranians. Could even have been a 'Reading gaol' sort of thing. Anyway it's done now. Always sad when something like this happens but that's how it is. Now Cocky. I have to ask you for something else. I know you can't be expected to leave your day-job and work for us full-time. As I said, all I ask is that you make yourself available as and when I – we need someone outside our organisation to go somewhere on his own business and contact whoever we have in mind.

"We can't offer a lot of money but whatever it is will be on top of that from your own employment. And we'll make sure that someone in the insurance business will be primed to protect that. What d'you think?"

"I think it sounds outrageous. Expecting me to want to do more errands for you after what's just happened. But, I'll give it – uh – due consideration. That's all. Now what about what you owe me?"

Elphinstone smiled. "That's excellent, old chap. I won't ask you to sign anything with that new pen our young Arab friend gave you and I won't ask you to do anything you really don't agree to do."

"How the hell did he know about the pen?" Lloyd pondered. *"Was he one of the waiters in Vienna, or in the Savoy, working in disguise? Incredible. I'd better accept but I'll get a damn good lunch and more from him first."*

Elphinstone paused as they stood by the door of the office. "I've booked a table at The Savoy Grill. Very public and quite expensive but good value considering the quality. So many shady people showing off there they won't notice two more." He chuckled and waited for Lloyd to laugh. He was still waiting when they reached the taxi in Tothill Street.

Over a long and well wined lunch, Elphinstone mellowed and exposed his domestic struggle, much of which was by now old news to Lloyd.

"I – or my wife and I – have decided to stay together for the children, and for our own benefit in the long term I hope. A divorce would cost a fortune even if we didn't contest it, and our son's hoping to get a place at Harrow."

Lloyd stayed silent. He didn't want to discuss his earlier meeting with Helen. Jock continued, unemotional and unaware of Helen's tearful disappointment. No remorse. No regrets.

"I'm looking to sell the house in Pinner. Probably move further out. Perhaps near Great Missenden – that's quite near Chequers by the way – and I can get into town easily or stay at the club if I'm working odd hours. When I'm settled out there, you might like to come out for dinner, or for the weekend if it suits you. Bring your girlfriend if you like."

"Which one? And why is he telling me all this?" Thought Lloyd. *"Is it something to do with Helen? Or is he just lonely for male company? Perhaps he's just trying to impress me."* He might have been talking out loud. Elphinstone seemed to read his thoughts and lowered his tone.

"You remember your friend Helen, the girl we met in Beirut? Oh, and at your pal's wedding party." As so often the recollection was a statement rather than a question. "She's a very bright lady. Speaks several languages including some that I don't, and don't know many who do. I spoke to her recently and asked her if she could help me – us – with some of the information we might be able to get... "

His voice broke off as he realised that he was approaching a misty area that he might not be able to navigate. Any further detail could qualify as either 'unknown-unknowns' or security breaches. He looked at his watch again and returned to the subject of food and drink.

"How's your halibut? As good as they said it would be? I love the Lebanese food when I'm there but you can't get this sort of fish so easily. Is this Sancerre all right for you?"

Lloyd was inclined to agree with everything about the meal that Elphinstone said or offered. He did like the lunch and the surroundings and said so. But he also wanted to get as much background information as possible. He knew by now that he would only be fed with as much as the Foreign Office wanted him to eat or hear of their plans. To develop his own plans he would have to piece together some of the scraps from the master's table.

The usual delivery from Elphinstone would be presented in straight lines; explanation and instruction. Some of the fragments now dropped at the table were irrelevant and some were not. Lloyd determined to assimilate as much as he could from listening between the lines. There was obviously something very relevant to his position that concerned Helen and her linguistic skills.

Lunch concluded with coffee and a single glass of port. The bill was served to the host with space for a gratuity. Elphinstone scribbled on it and complimented the waiter on the meal. The white jacketed waiter was more skilled in cooking the accounts than meals but returned the compliment with thanks and hopes for an early return of the guests.

Another staff member made an offer to retrieve any coats or hats. That fell clearly into the 'irrelevant' category. The man smiled and thanked them again as the two well fed customers took their leave from the hotel and each other; Elphinstone to Whitehall and Lloyd to Lime Street.

So much had happened in the last three weeks to change his perceived relationships. Gladys had unwillingly left him again, back to her life in South Wales; Susan was still in Fulham but possibly with any number of other men; and Aysil, he could only imagine her lying on a mortuary slab in Athens.

As he stepped out once more from the home and ghosts of Gilbert & Sullivan to Embankment station he found himself humming a tune from a similarly named entertainer.

It was Gilbert O'Sullivan's song, 'Alone again, naturally.'

Ch. 43. The Scorpions' sting.

After the rushed journeys, the suspense and disappointment of the previous weeks, the following month was relatively relaxing. Routine work in the insurance market and research into two new cases of kidnap and blackmail requiring relief or damage limitation, they occupied most of his days.

One of the new claims involved a visit to Hamburg to discuss the problem with a German insurance broker and his client. From their office by the river Elbe he telephoned one of Elphinstone's contacts to enquire of his Kurdish agent 'Egid the Brave,' only to be told "never heard of him." This was related to Jock who simply said "That's good. That's what he's supposed to say. "

After explaining that the contact in Hamburg was new to the role of British security agent and had assumed that Lloyd's phone call to him was simply a test, he asked Lloyd to visit his office again. Another short trip was required of him. This time only as far as Gloucestershire. One contact there would be very well known to both of them.

A second name was also supplied to Lloyd together with a phone number. Charles Caruthers, the tall figure whom Lloyd had mistaken for Elphinstone outside St James's Park station, would conduct Lloyd on a short tour of the Government's huge listening post and communications centre. The tour would be limited due to obvious security precautions on a 'need to know', or not know, basis.

The 'well known' contact would also be 'just visiting' rather than a permanent employee. Only a few hours would be spent at the GCHQ building and any further time would be at the visitors' discretion and expense. After Lloyd's protest at the 'expense' part of the briefing, Elphinstone relaxed the official civil service rule and agreed to cover all out-of-pocket costs as well as the usual travel expenses. Caruthers, he said, would deal with that side of things.

Two days later, on the pretext to his colleagues of visiting his parents Lloyd borrowed a car from his employers' pool of executive saloons and drove Westwards on the A40 to Oxford and on through Whitney and the Cotswold hills. Someone had told him that Cleeve Hill above Cheltenham's National Hunt racecourse was the highest point of the Cotswolds and boasted a splendid old coaching inn. A single room at The Rising Sun was booked for the Friday night following the GCHQ visit.

Driving past so many historic places of interest would have been of greater interest if he had time to stop and admire the view. But time as usual was of the essence in the busy world he had joined. Viewing was limited to the road ahead and stopping was not an option. An easy drive taking less than three hours saw his car entering Cheltenham and winding its way through to Churchdown.

Not familiar with the immediate area, he followed advice from Caruthers to park in Hatherly Lane car park and walk to the security station on the periphery of 'The Doughnut' building. From there he was directed to a door where his guide was waiting to conduct him on a brief tour. Most of the work within the building was completely classified and he had to admit that he wouldn't or couldn't understand it even if he had been offered a closer inspection.

Caruthers explained that much of the intelligence gathering involved analysing massive computer systems' output to detect cyber crime or attempted hacking: breaking and entering into national control systems for services such as electricity supply and government communications. In addition to attacks though the internet there was a constant stream of other electronic signals under constant scrutiny.

How so many signals were received and interpreted was a complete mystery to the bewildered Lloyd but he could understand the need to translate messages that had been intercepted by the secret listeners. Most of those had been transmitted by a standard cell-phone like the mobile device in his pocket. Many of them were innocuous calls from targeted foreign agents or activists arranging their dinner or calling their friends for social activities, but not all.

Included in the myriad of signals through the ether were more sinister or significant messages that were monitored day and night. These had to be translated into standard English and transferred to intelligence analysts for consideration and possible action. One area of the electronic fishing net was devoted to signals originating from what Elphinstone had called his 'cross-roads of tectonic plates' between Asia, Arabia, Africa and Europe.

Relatively small in continental terms, the volume of violence and warfare in Arabia belied its modest geographic area. It included vicious civil wars in several Arab countries and the mass migration of refugees and dissatisfied civilians into Southern Europe. It also included the traffic in arms and military personnel from former Soviet Union countries into the conflict zones.

A multitude of conflicts between different cultures and languages was under close observation by a host of intelligence gatherers and translators. And amongst those translators were a young woman from the Middle East and another from a large firm of lawyers in London. The latter was introduced as Lloyd's second and 'well known' contact of the day. It was Helen.

"Hello again, Cocky. I was expecting you to be sent down here while I was visiting Jock's empire. Hope you're impressed by all this magic."

Lloyd was indeed impressed. He was probably depressed at being unable to take it all in but his spirits were stimulated at the sight of a friendly face.

"Yes, very... uh... impressive. And I'm not completely surprised to see you here after what you told me last month."

Charles Caruthers was taken aback at the familiarity and the mention of 'what you told me.' He had not been told

336

anything, apart from brief résumés of the visitors' backgrounds.

"You know each other then? Excellent. Been working... I should say 'helping' Jock for long?"

Helen looked as though she would have preferred to have kept her pretty mouth firmly shut. She had assumed that Elphinstone would have told his colleague at least that the two visitors were familiar with his work and each other. Then she remembered that he was not in the habit of passing any information unless it was on a 'really needs to know' basis.

Lloyd saved her blushes by simply acknowledging the precautions taken by Elphinstone and apologising for not divulging more to Caruthers.

"Sorry Charles. I should have realised that Jock wouldn't tell his own mother anything unless he had to. Helen and I have known each other about the same time as we've known Jock. We all met up when we were in the Lebanon on our own businesses." He hoped that his explanation was vague enough to be discreet but specific enough to reassure Caruthers.

He added a smile and a friendly pat on his guide's arm to signify that there was nothing more to it than that. It seemed to do the trick. Charles Caruthers smiled back at both of his guests and suggested moving on. Lloyd confessed his lack of comprehension.

"As I said Charles, it's very impressive but I have to admit it's too much for a simple chap like me to take it all in."

"Don't worry, Mr.... uh... Cocky. Nobody's supposed to be able to take it all in. If it was as easy as that then we really would have a major problem."

Lloyd accepted the assurance as a message of comfort. After another bewildering half hour of peering through glass panels and muttering platitudes he was relieved to hear the news he had hoped for.

"Right then. That's about as much as I can tell you... for now anyway. Except that... it's about time for a spot of lunch. Jock HAS told me that you should be able to digest that

337

without a problem. I must say, I can too!" He laughed and wondered what else he should add. Then remembered that he had not booked a table anywhere. Being resourceful he tried to cover the omission with a question.

"I didn't book anywhere yet, as I... uh... thought I should ask you if you preferred any particular food. Or", he added quickly, "if you had anywhere special in mind for lunch?"

This was Cocky's big chance to impress his host and hopefully impress Helen at the same time.

"The Queen's, in town, is good but If it's all right with you", looking at each in turn, "I'd like to go out to the hill just past the racecourse and have a bit to eat at the old pub... the hotel up there. It's only about ten or fifteen minutes drive from here."

In truth he didn't have a clue as far as distance or driving time was concerned. Fortunately his guide did.

"Great Idea, Cocky. The Rising Sun on Cleeve Hill. Is that the one you mean? I love it up there. Should be fairly quiet – there's no racing this week. I'll phone them to reserve a table with a view over the valley while you get your car. Meet you at the front gate in a few minutes."

In this instance Charles Caruthers was the clueless one as he didn't really know whether Lloyd's car was parked in Churchdown or the South Downs. Nevertheless the trio met as suggested although nearly twenty minutes had passed. Charles led the way through the outskirts of Cheltenham and out past Prestbury to the crest of Cleeve Hill and the welcoming small hotel by the main road to Winchcombe.

Lloyd had not told either of the others of his room reservation there. He needed the overnight rest and recovery after the dazzling citadel of intelligence communications. The sight and appetising aroma of food and the adjacent bar told him not to worry about that. He would leave his overnight luggage in the boot of his car until well after the meal. *"I wonder where Helen's staying"* he thought. *"Or if she's going back to London tonight. Just a thought, that's all."*

Once safely installed at a table looking over the racecourse and the entire Severn Valley, Caruthers took charge. He recommended the food, the wine and the best place to place bets during the Festival and Gold Cup days. It took them all back to a time before mobile phones interrupted pleasant meals and spies spied on people rather than computers. Charles Caruthers was definitely one of the old spy school.

"I'm getting a bit long in the tooth for this modern way of conducting business. I can't tell you much, or anything really, about what I was involved with in days gone past. But it was much more... uh... more human. I must say it's nice to be able to just sit here and enjoy good food and good company. The manager told me once that this was Cary Grant's favourite watering hole when he came back to visit his old haunts."

Caruthers then went into some detail of the film star's origins in Bristol.

"Archie Leach, you know. Trapeze artist from Bristol. Remember that old film with Ingrid Bergman in Rio where the uranium ore was hidden in wine bottles? Reminded me of something similar about a boat in the Black Sea, eh, Cocky?" He laughed and Lloyd joined in agreement. Helen didn't know what they were talking about but smiled and put a delicate smidgeon of meat in her mouth.

His two guests looked at each other and mumbled satisfaction through roast pheasant and game chips. A second bottle of a light red Bulgarian wine was extracted from the cellar and carefully uncorked and served by the young waitress. Considering the quality and price of the food, Lloyd was puzzled at Caruthers' selection of a lesser-known wine from Eastern Europe.

"Is this what you ordered, sir? Is it all right?" The waitress stood patiently beside the table, still holding the bottle. She took it to a sideboard to be uncorked and returned to their table for three.

Caruthers nodded gravely and sipped a small tasting after swirling the wine round his glass and his throat. "Yes. That's fine, thank you." The waitress smiled back and left the bottle after dispensing a carefully measured one and a half inches into each of the diners' glasses. As she withdrew Caruthers turned quietly to comment on the wine.

"Got a taste for this when I was on duty during the sixties. Not much going for anyone in Bulgaria then unless they were involved with the Russians or with wine. I became involved with both. Preferred the wine naturally but, business is business." He looked wistfully into his glass and poured some more for his guests and himself. "Good fun at times, awful at others." He paused, looking down sadly as distressing memories flowed back.

"Incidentally, now that you're more of an official part of our team, you might like to understand a bit more of the background regarding that business in Varna. I'm talking about the radioactive cargo in your clients' yacht, Cocky. The owner of the boat made an agreement with the Iranians. He was desperate to cut his losses on oil contracts and they were equally keen to cut OPEC's oil production. Stop me if you've heard this before."

Lloyd didn't try to interrupt his host or say that he was aware that 'it was all about oil' in Jock's words. Charles Caruthers continued to expand on the background of the 'Black Sea Skorpion's' voyage. It was old news to Lloyd but a complete revelation to Helen. She listened with open ears and widening eyes.

"The deal was to get rid of the Arab on OPEC's committee in the hope that it would remove the main barrier to imposing production limits. In exchange they would supply some waste from their nuclear research plant that could be used by the Syrians to threaten their rebels – dirty bombs.

"Completely illegal of course and would scupper any chance of continued sanction-lifting but, if he would arrange it, they would be in the clear. Like the Russians with the MH-17 aircraft killings in the Ukraine, they would simply blame it on the opposition and hope that the West would blame dissident terrorists at worst.

"As part of the deal he would smuggle the Polonium poison through the Balkans using his old contacts in the Kosovo arms smuggling game and they would provide one of their agents posing as a refugee to use it. We know now how she managed to get it into the Arab in Vienna while she was already in or on her way to Germany. That was very clever, using a genuine refugee to do her dirty work. Very clever and absolutely ruthless, pretending to have a girly-crush on the poor little bitch."

Helen shuddered at the thought of 'the poor little bitch' who had tried to maim her in Bekka camp. The broken bottle that had disfigured her face paled into insignificance beside the Polonium poison that had destroyed the body of the Arab in Vienna. What a deadly mixture of love and hate must be encased in the Afghan girl's mind.

A dirty bomb in a dirty business. And – where was she now?

Ch. 44. The road to Reading Gaol.

After another cup of coffee to complete a most pleasant two hours lunch Caruthers wiped his mouth with his starched linen napkin and announced his departure to unfinished business elsewhere.

"I've had enough of this game now. It's not all beyond me but it is time to put it behind me. I have to get back to the office." He didn't say which one. "If you want a nice quiet drive back to London you can go on to Winchcombe and across the Cotswolds to Oxford via Stow-on-the-Wold. It's a nice drive if you have time to look at the scenery. I must go. I've taken care of the bill so, pleasant journey to both of you."

With that he shook hands and strode from the restaurant to his car and back down to Cheltenham. He felt out of touch with his modern 'Spooks' organisation and looked forward to retirement with his long-term male partner. The past had been exciting but the present, apart from interludes like today's lunch, was depressing. A better future with a good pension and the good life awaited both of them.

Helen looked at Lloyd. "I suppose I should be going back too. Could you give me a lift to the station, please Cocky?" That was her way of inviting him to invite her, to a lift in his car to London and home. He had a small confession and an alternative to offer.

"I'm not going back, not to London, immediately..." He paused as Helen looked quizzically over her unfinished wine.

"Oh. Are you going back to see your friends – your parents and... in Wales?"

"No. My 'friends', or rather my old girlfriend at least, she's back there in Swansea. But I've told her I'm not going to live there while I'm still working in London. We haven't argued or anything like that but, we haven't agreed to anything more permanent either. You understand, don't you?"

Having poured out her heart to Lloyd when Elphinstone broke a little part of it with his non-marital news, she understood all too well. Lloyd continued to advance.

"I've booked a room here for the night. Can't sensibly drive back after all this wine and I just want to have a quiet night here and drive back gently tomorrow morning. That's all. Don't think I'm trying anything funny but, why don't you do the same. Promise I won't do anything you don't want. Why not?"

Helen was not worried about unwanted approaches from him. She had always liked Cocky and was independent to the verge of loneliness since Elphinstone's apparent change of mind about divorce. A good heart-to-heart chat and a comfortable drive back would suit her down to the ground.

"All right old chap". She tried to sound like their recently departed host. "Why not indeed?" To show good faith Lloyd talked to the hotel manager and arranged a second room for Helen. She could always join him in his room if she was still feeling lonely. Each took their small cases from Lloyd's car, his from the locked boot and hers from the rear seats, and left them in their separate but adjacent rooms.

Back in the bar but not ready for another meal, Helen ordered a pot of tea and two cups. She poured the tea while she broke the silence concerning their respective roles in Elphinstone's organisation.

"I told you that Jock offered me a part-time job, didn't I Cocky? I suppose it's an alternative to being a part-time wife but I felt I had to agree, in the National Interest as they say. It seems that they have plenty of interpreters for intercepted messages in Pashtu and Farsi but not many in Hazaragi. For some reason I studied that when I was learning Farsi so I can help them to understand anything in either and perhaps explain any slightly unusual discussions in other Dari dialects."

An open-mouthed Lloyd just gaped but tried to restrict mouth movement to sips of hot tea. "Sounds great, Helen honestly. You don't expect me to know what you're talking about though, do you?" She sighed gently but persevered.

"I'm sure you understand much more than you admit, but perhaps it is a little unusual. Pashtu and Farsi are the main languages in Afghanistan and in Iran. But many – about twenty percent of Afghans are Hazarras – so they talk in Hazaragi. It's a little like Farsi but like all languages it's different in just the places that you want to know about. Because of the traditional links with what was once Persia it's possible that some Hazarras have more sympathy with Iran than the Pashtus who are closer to the Pathans in Pakistan. Does that sound reasonable?"

Lloyd shook his head slowly as he swallowed his tea. It seemed unfair to ninety-nine percent of the world that someone in the other one percent should be attractive and clever at the same time. Something in Helen's short lecture still didn't quite add up though. But like Caruthers, he tried to apply what was left of his own intelligence when unsure of the situation. He changed the subject to something more basic.

"Sounds amazing. Wish I could speak, or understand, more languages. A bit of Cantonese and a few words of Mandarin – from my days in Hong Kong – plus a little bit of Welsh, even a bit of English. Afraid that's all I can offer." He looked down at his cup and waited for Helen's contradiction. *"All things come to he who waits,"* he hoped. Surely enough, Helen's protest arrived as he swallowed his last gulp.

"Well, Chinese and Welsh. That's more than I can speak. I suppose we're all linguists in our own way. And the important thing is, that we speak the truth and talk sense. Now, talking of telling the truth, I need to go to my room. So why don't we refresh, as they say, and meet back here in an hour. We can have a drink and order dinner, and continue our intellectual discussion, in Welsh or Farsi as you prefer."

Despite the heavy meal and tea she felt lighter after talking to him. Her relaxed mood reflected in the mild sarcasm concerning dialects and intellects. After an hour alternating between bathroom and bedroom she felt lighter still. Tripping down the old oak staircase to the bar she very nearly tripped over Lloyd's feet, waiting with the rest of him by the bottom step.

He put his hands out to prevent her falling into anything other than his arms and was rewarded with a thankful little cuddle as she regained her balance. "If I'm like this now," she gasped," what chance have I of staying upright after a drink?"

"And what chance have I of her not staying upright later," he mused. But then he remembered his assurance of decorum.

"Don't worry. I'll catch you." Then he added quickly as she glanced at his eyes, "but I have promises to keep..." Helen caught the line of the famous poem.

"And we 'have miles to go', tomorrow. But at least it's not 'before I sleep.' I didn't know you liked poetry, Cocky." The admiration was quite genuine. Perhaps the joking reference to intellect had not been so sarcastic after all.

"I didn't know it was poetry," lied Lloyd. "Just a quotation I read on the page of a calendar. Don't remember who said it originally but I keep hoping it impresses the girls."

Helen laughed. "Well it impresses me. Robert Frost is a favourite of mine. I suspect you already knew that. 'The road not taken.' 'The woods are lovely dark and deep,' etc. I'm sure you knew that too. Come on, what shall we have to drink? Jock can pay for it when we claim our expenses from Charles."

The thought of a 'happy hour' drink with a blithe spirit such as Helen, at Elphinstone's departmental expense, raised his own spirits by several degrees. Helen ordered 'a G & T'. The supplementary 'ice and a slice' was plopped into her glass with the tonic. It splashed a thin spread of its contents on the bar and a thin smirk from Lloyd at the barman's discomfort. A large scotch with a more circumspect and carefully splashed drop of soda water wound its way into Lloyd's hand and from there to his lips.

"Well, cheers. Happy days, Helen. Hope we'll be working together again from time to time." That was delivered with complete sincerity and he hoped without any sexual innuendo. *"Not much, anyway,"* he added to himself.

"Yes. So do I. I'm sure we will at some stage. It's inevitable if Jock's controlling it."She thought again of Elphinstone exercising more control over their lives, little by little. At least his department in the Foreign Office, or MI5 or MI6 or MI-whatever, was now paying for that part of their lives. 'Salami slicing', they called it. And she was determined not to become a sliced salami.

Having consumed a substantial quantity of good food at lunchtime, dinner was a relatively light affair. The Table-d'hôte set menu was composed largely of reconstituted surplus ingredients from the previous day's A-la-carte. "The remains of the day," Helen joked. There was many a truth in her jest and many a terrine made from yesterday's meats, in today's 'house specials.'

They selected the lightest items from the main menu and limited themselves to two courses, until Helen spotted crème caramel being toasted by a portable torch, deftly welded by the waiter serving the adjoining table. Lloyd stuck gamely to coffee and a large glass of water, diluted with more Scottish elixir. Throughout the meal flowed a gentle stream of confessed information – scraps of little secrets.

All feelings or thoughts of being alone had completely disappeared. Just for the moment they were together. As together as gin and tonic, as scotch and water. Kindred spirits in a foreign land, or to be more accurate, in the service of the Foreign Office. That was more foreign to both of them than Elphinstone's tectonic plates.

At the top of the stairs leading to their bedrooms they paused and looked at each other. A few yards along the corridor lay their rooms. Another pause as they stopped at the architraves surrounding the doors. Not a word was said as they shook hands half-heartedly and Helen planted a soft kiss on her escort's cheek. It stiffened Lloyd's resolve to keep his promise but strayed dangerously close to his lips as one of her scars brushed against them. He knew instinctively that they would both appreciate the evening's closing friendship by leaving it unopened.

Whether it was the effects of a long day's journey into the strange world of cyber spooking and information jigsaw puzzles or just the quality of the meals and company, neither of the two part-time agents of the State could say. What they could say with certainty was that they both woke up feeling more relaxed than they had been for some time and wishing to continue with their association, whatever that was to be.

Charles Caruthers' advice on the route back to London was accepted. Unlike the subject of Robert Frost's poem it became the road taken. It took them through the ancient Mercian town of Winchcombe and past Katherine Parr's former residence at Sudley Castle. It took them along tight winding roads and through villages with strange names. Villages such as Upper and Lower Slaughter to Stow-on-the-Wold.

There they stopped for a morning coffee and a brief stroll round the old market town on the even older Roman Road between Lincoln and Exeter, The Fosse Way. Then past Chipping Norton close to the Hook Norton brewery. That brought an "I could get hooked on that" from Lloyd and a frown from Helen.

Eventually the car found its way onto the main road to Oxford and the A40 to London and their respective flats. Parting was again relaxed and platonic but each understood how dangerously close they were to something more sensual. Each hoped that the present soft relationship would develop soon enough without repercussions or complications to their already complex lives. 'Just good friends' would describe it for now. Everyone would understand.

Nothing of note came to Lloyd from the Foreign Office or from Helen during the month that followed. One short message from Caruthers told him that his 'new recruit from Greece' was settling into some sort of routine without major problems. Lloyd not sure what he meant but said he was relieved to hear it. If Caruthers was referring to Leila then he might change his opinion fairly soon.

Sooner or later the temperamental Afghan would become more mental than temperate, especially without her Alawite lady-love. That could suddenly flare up to explosive levels, and in a sensitive area such as 'the Doughnut' building it could have disastrous consequences. A call from Elphinstone heralded his concern.

"Hello Cocky. Sorry to have been quiet for so long, although you're probably not at all sorry. I've got a little task "– he never called them 'jobs' – "for you to do if you can take the time off your current work for a couple of days. I need you to go down to Churchdown again with Charles to sort out some problem he has with someone down there. "

The request was cryptic but Lloyd was sure that he knew what Elphinstone meant. There was no need to ask for further details. That would have meant meeting somewhere quiet for a discreet talk and he could only manage to take one day off from his latest insurance investigation. He confirmed that he would meet Caruthers the following morning.

Elphinstone was very pleased at Lloyd's immediate agreement. He called Caruthers and Caruthers called Lloyd to arrange to meet outside the car park in Hatherly Road at ten thirty a.m. The two men walked cheerfully to the government building. Lloyd was still puzzled at Caruthers' light-hearted approach. It didn't seem to be the attitude of one with a psychopath on his hands.

Entering the building and clearing the security post, he suddenly saw Helen standing near an office door some ten yards away. She was talking to a woman wearing a hijab and Western women's trousers and blouse. The hijab prevented him from seeing her face but there was something familiar about her figure.

The two women stopped talking and Helen turned to greet the two men as her companion returned to the office behind her. Charles Caruthers then conducted Lloyd to another office and closed the door behind them. He explained the 'little problem' to him although Cocky could not imagine any problem concerning a homicidal maniac such as Leila to be 'little.'

"This is something I wouldn't normally ask you to do, Cocky," started Caruthers. "I would usually try to do it myself but, with your... uh... close experience and success in the... uh...persuasion department, well... Helen and I thought that you and she could convince our new recruit to accept a short assignment overseas. It will be well rewarded and as safe as we can make it."

He paused for a moment as a knock on the door announced the arrival of two cups of coffee and a glass of water. He thanked the woman carrying the tray and passed the water to Helen. As the door closed again Caruthers continued quietly.

"We would like her to spend a few months backing up Egid in Hamburg. He's very competent but his personal knowledge of Farsi and Alawite dialect is thin to say the least and we are concerned at the recent increase in Alawites and Iranians in Northern Germany. So are the Germans.

"Unfortunately, the lady doesn't exactly like the Kurds, and certainly doesn't like Egid. Helen has talked to her and assured her of our support but we need a second opinion to sort of... make her see sense. She has spent some time in Hamburg and doesn't have a problem living there. It's just Egid that she has a problem with. You do see, don't you?"

Lloyd decided to voice his concern. Something was still not quite right.

"Why do you think that I can persuade her, Charles? I hardly know her apart from knowing that she might blow up at any moment, which I don't fancy getting in the way of, and she's a complete head-case. Just ask Helen. That girl nearly killed her in Bekka.

"And another thing. Why do you need an Afghan woman to keep tabs on Persians and Syrians in Germany? She doesn't speak German as far as I know and I thought that you needed

349

her here because you're short of people who speak fluent Hazari or whatever it's called."

"The people are called Hazarras and they talk in Hazaragi," interrupted Helen quietly. "They – Charles and his colleagues – are short of fluent Hazaragi speakers. That's why they asked me to help them. I told you that last month."

"Yes, you did. And that didn't add up either," spluttered Lloyd. "You've got a native Hazara or whatever right here now already and you want me to tell her to move to Germany? What's that all about? Why on earth do you want crazy Leila in Hamburg? Have you got another assassination in mind? Archduke Ferdinand's already been shot dead once you know."

In the stunned silence that followed Lloyd looked at Caruthers and then at Helen as they both looked blankly at each other. Then the penny dropped for Helen leaving Charles feeling as if he were in mid-air.

"They don't have Crazy Leila, as you call her, here or anywhere else. Leila's dead. She was strangled in Athens airport terminal lavatory. The poor girl. I don't know who or why but she never got onto the flight to Heathrow. Perhaps you know more, do you Charles?"

Caruthers suddenly came back to earth. The scale of Lloyd's misapprehension was not absolutely staggering but he was certainly put off balance by it.

"Oh I see, I see what you mean, or what you thought, Cocky. Sorry old chap. Surely Jock told you before you flew back from Greece. Did you think she made it after all? No. I'm afraid the reports were correct except that they got the I/D wrong. They found an old medical registration card – Aysil's – in her purse and assumed it was hers.

"Aysil arrived in Heathrow and just said that 'the other girl had got herself lost in Athens airport' but nobody told us what had happened to her until much later. By then the report from Athens with the wrong name had been circulated."

Helen came back to the main point of the meeting. "We're obviously not talking about the dead girl going to Hamburg, Cocky. Wait a minute. I'll bring her here. Is that all right, Charles?"

Caruthers was still a little dizzy. "Yes. Of course. Bring her in by all means. We have to bring her in sometime soon anyway."

Helen stood and walked quickly from the room. They could hear her footsteps in the corridor. Soon they heard them again but, she was still alone. She re-entered the room, flushed from walking so fast.

"Sorry Charles. I missed her. She's gone out somewhere - probably to the loo or another office. I'll catch her at the lunch-hour break and try to persuade her to talk to Cocky then. It's only half an hour away."

Caruthers breathed again. "Look. I have to talk to a man about a dog for a few minutes. Why don't we re-convene here at twelve-thirty and start again, with or without her, well, hopefully with?"

As he left the room Lloyd looked at Helen and Helen looked at Lloyd. They had not seen or spoken to each other since their return journey from The Rising Sun and neither was sure of what to say. Lloyd broke the brief silence to take the opportunity to ask about the death in Athens.

"Has Jock or Charles told you anything else about Leila's death? I suppose it has to be murder; she wouldn't strangle herself. She was mad enough to do that I suppose."

Helen looked vacantly at the wall. "No. Neither of them has told me much more than they told you. Jock said it could have been the Iranian secret service. Or an Arab family hit-man. I don't know how they would be able to find her in Athens airport when she was only there for an hour or so. Or it might just have been a mugger trying to rob or rape, or both. That's probably the most likely."

She shook her head sadly. "I know she was unbalanced and tried to kill me but... but... "

Lloyd put his hand on Helen's shoulder. "I know. You still have to feel sorry for her. So near to finding a safe home with her... her... I don't know what you'd call it. Her big sister? I can't really see them as outright lesbian lovers, more like mother and daughter almost."

Helen stood up again and wiped one of her eyes. The tragedy was distressing for her as much as anyone. "You know that she had only just escaped from Afghanistan with her brother after a local gang leader tried to rape her? And on top of that..." she choked slightly, "on top of that she had to watch her brother and her friend being hanged in public in Iran?

"Those people really are bastards. Absolute bastards. I'm quite pleased to help our people to guard against them in any way I can. That's the real reason that I accepted Jock's offer – of this job," she added quickly.

She walked out from Lloyd and the room again. She was still close to tears as she called out, "just going to see if I can catch her again." Whoever 'her' was. Lloyd followed a few yards behind her. Walking slowly enough for Helen to keep a gap between him and whoever she was trying to 'catch.' There was really no need for secrecy any more. He knew who the catch would be.

After looking into two offices and calling in Farsi to the occupant of the third one Helen entered it. Lloyd could hear the conversation but couldn't understand it. Three minutes passed and the conversation level increased and then softened. Helen emerged from the office followed by the girl wearing the hijab that Lloyd had glimpsed from a distance earlier.

As the two women turned towards Lloyd his suspicions were confirmed. The hijab covered much of the girl's head but her uncovered face was revealed with brown eyes open and downward. Then she raised her head slightly and once again he saw 'that look' from her eyes directly into his. This time the look seemed to bear a mixture of defiance and apology.

He couldn't work out which one to believe but he didn't need to work out who was the subject of the proposed assignment. It was Aysil all right. Who else could it be? She had obviously left her demented passionate admirer in the Athens airport lavatory and boarded the aircraft alone. Presumably she was fully aware of Leila's death, whether suicide or murder, but more concerned for her own safety.

Helen broke the awkward silence to state what was by now quite obvious. "You know Aysil, don't you Cocky? She is very... uh... reluctant to go to Hamburg because she feels more secure here. Perhaps you could reassure her. I can't because... well because I can't. I don't know the full details - or for that matter, any details. "

Lloyd didn't know the full details either but he understood why Elphinstone and Caruthers needed someone like Aysil to watch over the stream of refugees and asylum seekers pouring into Germany from the Middle East. He summed his feelings with a statement that was not completely false - it was just 'economical with the truth.'

"I understand." That was all he said. But whilst saying it he was returning the open-eyed look into Aysil's, staring squarely and coldly into the wide brown globes that were beginning to moisten. *"Could she be human after all?"* he asked himself. Then the visual stand-off was broken sharply. Aysil's stony gaze wilted and the eyes returned to stare at the corridor carpet.

The hijab-covered head turned to Helen and muttered something in Farsi before turning again to the office. Within a few seconds the conversation ended. Helen shrugged and turned to Lloyd as Aysil disappeared behind a closed door.

"Well, that was short and sweet. She's agreed to go. You must either have a hold over her or scared her witless. Hardly a long drawn-out negotiation but very successful I suppose, from Jock's point of view. He should be delighted. I'm just pleased that we can go back now, unless you want to stay here for something."

"No. I'm ready to go too. I'll just say goodbye to Charles."
Helen nodded.

"Of course. I'll tell him the good news then we... you can drive us back if you don't mind."

Lloyd did not mind at all. Charles Caruthers was found and informed of Aysil's agreement and the negotiators' departure. He repeated Helen's conclusion.

"Jock'll be pleased. I hope he displays his pleasure in more than words," he joked. Long experience had told him that it was not always a joking matter. Gratitude was not always a common currency in the Foreign Office or security services. Gratuitous currency even less so.

Helen walked on with him, back to his car in the Hatherly Road car park. He held the passenger's door open for her and made himself comfortable in the driver's seat. As he started the ignition he suggested an alternative route for the return journey.

"I'd like to get back into central London fairly soon if you don't mind. I still have some work to finish."

Helen signalled complete agreement without knowing what route would be taken as more economical with their time. Lloyd advised her of his plan without knowing if she would agree, or even care.

"If we get onto the motorway system – the M5's not far from here – we can then zip back on the M4 from outside Bristol to London fairly quickly. We'll miss the nice scenery but we'll miss the slow country roads as well. Is that OK with you?"

Helen laughed gently. She was completely in his hands, or in his car at least, and would have agreed to a route via the North Pole if he had said it would be their best choice. She was also relieved that their assignment appeared to have been successful so soon. There was something in Lloyd's voice that suggested that he had another agenda. She didn't know what it was but she might care about it when she did.

Nor did she know whether it would be pleasantly social – she hoped so – or less social and possibly less pleasant. As the car entered the motorway on its faster circuitous route she turned her head towards the driver. She prepared to be interrogated. After a few weeks helping Elphinstone in the suspicions business she had acquired some of its paranoia for herself.

Glancing to ensure that they were on a relatively clear stretch of road she put her suspicions to the test. "Did you want to tell me something, Cocky? Or ask me something perhaps? You can trust me. We're all alone here." *"That should be light-hearted enough to avoid any embarrassment or reticence,"* she argued.

Lloyd stayed silent for a few moments then revealed his hand.

"Yes. I would like to pick your brains, or ask your opinion about the other girl, Leila. Jock has told me who he thinks might have killed her but you know what he's like." Helen nodded without saying anything. She certainly knew what Elphinstone was like, as much as anyone did. Lloyd couldn't see her nodding but assumed that her silence could be taken as a 'yes.'

"I can't see how or why someone who was deliberately tracking her or just trying to kill her could have known that she was there, in transit for an hour or so. And I'm convinced that it wasn't suicide or an accident, unless it was a mugger who just wanted to pinch her scarf and accidentally pulled it round her throat."

The car continued for a few minutes before Helen answered with more than a few 'Mmm's and 'yes's. Soon they were on the M4 junction and speeding Eastwards. Past Swindon and still making good progress in travel if not in explanation or theory concerning Leila's death. Helen repeated some of the possibilities that had already been aired, adding some more of her own.

"I would think – these are only my own thoughts, mind you – that what you said about a mugger and accidentally pulling the scarf round her throat might be the most likely explanation. Maybe he – or she – tried to snatch it or pull it so that she would let go of her purse. And then maybe the mugger dragged her into the ladies loo but was frightened and ran away leaving her choked to death but with her baggage intact, such as it was."

Lloyd was not so sure. Too many 'maybe's to be sure of a clumsy mugger and accidental manslaughter, or woman-slaughter in this case.

"Hasn't Aysil said anything about it? She does know, doesn't she? She must. She must have asked everyone where Leila had got to when she boarded, and again when she was picked up at Heathrow."

More 'Mmm's and a solitary "yes" came from Helen. The car continued to make speedy progress, Lloyd looking in his mirrors for traffic police as they exceeded the speed limit by fifteen miles an hour or more. Helen offered an alternative theory.

"Aysil hasn't spoken much about it. She must be very upset and frightened by it all, obviously. The only thing I did get from her was that 'it was Allah's will.' That's not much help. I suspect that she thinks it might have been an Arab hit-man or woman or someone stalking her – one of the Iranian or Russian agents. More likely to have been a local thief or even another refugee, begging in the airport terminal and looking for an easy target."

They considered as many alternatives as reasonably possible without concluding that any one was more probable than the mugging theory. Suicide by self-strangulation using a scarf in a public lavatory was not impossible but completely unlikely. Leila had been on the verge of a safe passage to safety and comfort that she could only have dreamed about with the one she loved.

"She may have been crazy but she wasn't daft," was Lloyd's conclusion to that. The car sped on towards a sign announcing an exit to Reading. The town's name struck a tiny chord in Lloyd's mind. It was Elphinstone's mention of 'Reading' and a prison. He couldn't think of any reason for the old town's prison to enter into that conversation when it did. The strange reference reverberated in his mind for the rest of the journey.

Soon they were passing Maidenhead and the exit to Heathrow. As they were approaching Hammersmith Lloyd slowed down to the crawl-pace of the traffic. The car came to a temporary halt and Helen suggested that she should leave it to board a train at the next convenient stopping point.

"I won't say 'at your convenience'," she chuckled. "After what we've been debating it might sound rather tasteless. By the way, are you going to ask me out again soon?"

Lloyd looked around for a safe point for stopping and allowing her to get out without getting hit by another vehicle. "Yes, of course. In fact, yes please. I've got your phone number, haven't I? You haven't changed it in the last ten days have you?"

"No. It's the same old number, for the same old me." She bent down to kiss him through the open window at the same time as he tried to open the door to kiss her. Door metal and window glass collided with two human heads in the peck-on-the-cheeks position. He withdrew gracelessly as she recoiled to avoid more facial damage.

Lloyd suddenly recalled 'the curious incident of the prison' in Elphinstone's office.

"Incidentally, before you go," he looked around desperately in case an HGV might be bearing down on them, "does 'a jail in Reading' mean anything to you?"

"Never been there. Never been incarcerated in any other prison either. Why? Did you think I should be? Or have you got a girl into trouble?"

"No. Nothing really. Just something someone mentioned. I wondered what it might mean."

"Well the only thing I know about Reading and its prison is, that Oscar Wilde was banged up there – perhaps I shouldn't put it that way – for you-know-what with his boyfriend Lord Alfred Douglas. He wrote a famous poem about it afterwards.

It's too late for imprisoning crazy Leila. Anyway, as Ken Dodd always says, 'they can't touch you for it now' so you should be safe too."

"Very funny. Be careful crossing this road now. And I'll call you this week sometime, promise."

The words 'promises, promises,' ran through his mind as he completed the drive into the city and an underground car park reserved for his syndicate's senior staff. He had about three hours to clear the memos and e-mails received during the past thirty-six hours before handing car and keys to the attendant and travelling back to Chiswick and home.

After a long hot shower and a bite to eat with some expensive Cabernet-Shiraz from the local supermarket he returned to his lap-top computer and idly trawled the internet for the best offers in cheap wine. Google produced a host of websites and he felt spoiled for choice, resulting in his failure to select any.

Before logging off from Google he entered the words 'Reading' and 'Jail' on the search engine panel. "Do you mean Reading Gaol?" came the reply. At first he thought it said 'Reading goal' and was something to do with the football results but then he looked closer. It was definitely 'Reading Gaol' and several of the websites made mention of Oscar Wilde, just as Helen had said.

He clicked twice on a site that mentioned 'The Ballad of Reading Gaol' and was rewarded with a diatribe of references to Wilde's risqué lifestyle and... the long poem about a condemned man going to the gallows after murdering his lover. Lloyd's interest intensified as Wilde's poem poured out grief and remorse. Finally he arrived at the last verse, repeating one of the earlier moral judgements;

"Yet each man kills the thing he loves, by each let this be heard,

Some do it with a bitter look, Some with a flattering word,

The coward does it with a kiss, The brave man with a sword."

Elphinstone must have known or guessed the who and why of Leila's death. He also must know that nobody would be charged with killing the demented Afghan refugee. It would just have to remain a mystery, unless and until someone decided that the guilty party should also be discarded and abandoned to her fate.

As long as Aysil could inform the security watchdogs of suspicious characters amongst the refugees entering the area, she and her terrible secret would remain safe. A serious breach of duty or failure to act in her keepers' best interests could result in exposure to justice or worse. In financial employment it might be called 'golden handcuffs.' Here it was simple blackmail.

Leila had proved to be an unbalanced albatross around Aysil's neck. An impediment to their mutual security. She would also be a magnet for any potential revenge seekers. To a stalker or assassin, the safron coloured scarf was a beacon. To Aysil it had become a weapon. Aysil was ruthless but was undoubtedly a brave woman. Without the use of a sword she had used the weapon closest to hand. Some might consider the deed to be a form of euthanasia. Others might just say, "it was Allah's will." Most would shrug and write it off as just another dead sad refugee.

Lloyd closed the lap-top and finished the bottle of Cabernet-Shiraz. Tomorrow would be another day of insurance claims and kidnaps. Tomorrow would be a good day to telephone Helen.

Ch. 45. Release from ransom.

Only a few days of 'normal' work examining claims occupied Lloyd before he received the call to duty from an unlisted number in the Foreign Office. During those few days he had just enough time to establish that Helen was open to social offers and Susan was not. As Gladys was safely tucked up in her Swansea home he felt that life should be less complicated than it had been recently. That was before Elphinstone's message.

A pleasant lunch in St James's was always acceptable and time could be created to accommodate it. Rather than sitting in a dusty dry office they both agreed to test the culinary expertise of the 'In and Out' once more. Elphinstone was genuinely grateful for Lloyd and Helen's intervention and put the lunch bill on his personal account, carefully filing the receipt in his wallet for presentation to the FO accounts department.

Further reports of Aysil's translation, literal and physical, to Hamburg were limited to Elphinstone's tight-mouthed nods and grunts. Those were supposed to be taken as 'yes thank you' and 'it's going well' replies to questions about her activities and relationship with Egid in Germany.

Lloyd followed Elphinstone's example with digestive grunts when asked about Helen or Susan. The only suggestion of deeper interest in women came when the subject of the Elphinstone family was mentioned. That varied from a satisfactory situation, obviating interest in Helen, or suggestions of unrest, prompting interest in someone like Susan.

He was quite prepared to act as a contact between the unofficial Foreign Office officer and his overseas agents but he was not going to act as match-maker extraordinaire for his part-time controller. That would be too much like importuning and in any case could kill any chances of reuniting with Helen or Susan.

Another opportunity to disguise official business with unofficial pleasure came when Charles Caruthers phoned. He asked if Lloyd was familiar with any other part of the Greek archipelago. Yet another body had been washed up on the shore of a harbour near a smaller island called Lenios.

The washed up corpse 'might be that of an agent working in Syria who had failed to report to his local controller' for over a month. He didn't say whether the absentee agent could be Abdul or if they had written him out of their employment records long ago.

A short package holiday with a mini cruise for two was hastily booked and Helen invited to pack a swimsuit and very little more. After the usual crowded flight to Athens, two holidaymakers embarked on an old schooner from Piraeus harbour with a small crew and ten sun-seeking passengers. The itinerary included two days on the island near Lenios where Lloyd had originally met Cyrus Constantiou. He took the opportunity to ask Cyrus the chandler to meet him on his arrival.

As an exercise in espionage the visit to investigate the human flotsam was completely uneventful. "Just another wretched asylum seeker. Probably dumped from a leaking rubber dinghy when the people smugglers had taken all his money," was the ships chandler's verdict after talking to the local police and the examining doctor. It was probably not anybody's absentee agent and definitely not Abdul...

But as an alternative to investigating kidnap and ransom claims, and to a London office desk, the brief visit was as good as a rest. The report to Caruthers was short if not sweet and a returning call from Whitehall confirmed that the missing agent had re-appeared with the verbal form of a doctor's note to explain his absence and safety. "Took an Egyptian sickie," was

Caruthers' verdict, which Lloyd took to be his version of 'French leave.'

With no other requirement beyond relaxation and enjoyment the two temporary agents also took French, or Greek, leave, taking advantage of the island's facilities; a harbour and a noisy cafe. The harbour was almost as quiet as Lloyd remembered it from his last visit there and the cafe twice as noisy. The main source of the noise was also as Lloyd remembered and Cyrus condemned; a fat and smelly fisherman, still acting as the town gossip and consumer of raki.

Pathos Paramides, often rebranded as 'Pathos Paralytic', was no longer a member of the town council but remained a life member of the cafe's confirmed drunks and rumourmongers society. With a daily intake of raki exceeding the value and weight of his catch, the member's life was unlikely to exceed the shelf-life of his fish but that didn't prevent him from continuing to drink like one.

On the final evening of their brief sojourn Helen and Cocky were joined by Cyrus Constantiou and his wife for a delightful dinner in the town's sole restaurant of note. A simple meal was transformed into a banquet of moussaka, freshly caught seafood and clean white wine, completed with Metexa Amphora brandy to sweeten the strong coffee.

Four replete and contented diners walked slowly to the berthed schooner, along the narrow harbour-side road and past the roar of the raki-fuelled cafe society. Pausing for a while to listen to an old familiar voice, Cyrus translated it from Pathos gibberish to simple English. It appeared to Cyrus that Pathos had finally departed from whatever semblance of reason he had.

"He is saying," translated Cyrus, "that the dark island over there," – he waved across the bay to a misty shoreline some fifteen kilometres away, "where your... uh... friend was killed – it is still occupied sometimes by... what he says are Russians. No one believes him anyway so it doesn't matter. I don't know where he gets these stories from. Probably from the raki bottle.

"And he's saying now," Cyrus continued, listening more intently, "that they sometimes keep people... prisoner... until someone pays them for release or killing. Like I say, nobody believes him. Although," he added thoughtfully, "there was a body found last month in the water who might have been Russian. He had a shaven hair and picture on his head-skin, what you call 'tattoo', of rings with a stinging creature inside. So maybe Pathos is talking of that.

"But nobody believes him so it doesn't matter. Maybe the dead man escapes from being prisoner? Pathos even said he saw your dead friend Klevic over there when he was fishing near Lenios. Nobody believed that either."

At the jetty the two cruise passengers said goodbye and thanks to Mr and Mrs Constantiou. A dinghy took them and some other passengers to board the schooner which departed from the main island and sailed past the dark island of Lenios and on to visit two well-known island retreats the next morning. Neither Helen nor Lloyd discussed the affairs or rumours of the previous evening.

Nobody, as Cyrus had predicted, believed the rumours so, why should they?

Mary Tulloch - nee Deans - gave birth to twin boys and later continued to work as a solicitor on a part-time basis for the Zurich office of her husband's lawyer, Nigel Quickstick. She also continued to act as de facto match-maker for as many of her friends as possible.

Susan Deans - Mary's social and sexually pro-active sister - became pregnant and gave birth to a sallow-skinned girl. She moved from her flat in Fulham to a council apartment in Croydon where she lived with her daughter and occasional male partners. Susan met Lloyd at reunions with her sister and Andrew Tulloch but they did not continue their short relationship which she described as simply a 'Brief encounter - usually without the briefs.'

Andrew Tulloch - continued to run his commodities trading company in Zurich and also became a director of the mining company in Kazakstan when its president agreed the joint venture with Tulloch's company. The new joint venture company failed to make a profit in its first three years as commodity prices fell sharply but the Kazak government gave massive financial support, using funds that it received from Russia. Tulloch and his wife and twin sons continued to live in Switzerland but he returned every month to London for a serious lunch with Cocky Lloyd and others.

Bekir Kazakov aka Rustem Kazakov - disappeared from corporate and public life. His commodities trading company was declared bankrupt and unsecured creditors received nothing. Reports of his death in Serbia were denied by Serbian authorities. His company yacht 'Anna K', once renamed 'Skorpion', was impounded by Bulgarian customs and later occupied by Bulgarian government members for entertaining European Union trade officials in the Black Sea port of Varna.

Two years after the seizure of radioactive materials from the yacht 'Skorpion' in Varna, several members of the crew were released from prison and returned to the Crimea under Russian military protection. One was rumoured to have sailed through the Bosphorus and the Suez canal but kidnapped by pirates off Somalia. The ransom demanded is still unpaid.

Vasil Antonov - was promoted to president of the mining company in Kazakhstan and visited Zurich and London frequently to promote Anglo-Kazak trade and occasionally lunch with Tulloch and Lloyd. After three years in Astana he returned to Sofia to be appointed Bulgarian Trade Secretary to the European Union. He and Stephan Borisov bought a small sailing yacht on the Black Sea, berthed in the harbour at Varna.

Georgi Petrov - was promoted to the post of Marketing Director of the Kazakhstan mining company in Astana. He maintained contact with Vasil and also with Dimitri Levin and his friends from Russian military intelligence in Moscow.

Saadi Ali Bin Q'etta - was deposed from the board of his late father's trading company but re-applied to be an assistant representative to OPEC. He visited the OPEC conference in Vienna but would not stay in that city overnight, preferring to fly back to Qatar or to Monaco in his private jet. He did not visit the Lebanon either. Wherever he travels to he carries his own personal toothpaste.

Arian Bogdani - established a car-hire and insurance agency business in Pristina with his taxi-driver friend **Josip Broz.** They acted as agents for some of Lloyd's contacts in the insurance industry and retained occasional contact with Dmitri Petric in Kosovo but preferred to keep their business in areas further from the border with Serbia and nearer to Montenegro.

John Sinclair Tarquin Elphinstone - having received promotion as the new C4 grade second secretary for foreign affairs (commercial) was transferred officially to Military Intelligence and promoted by two grades. His current rank is classified information. He and his wife, Julia, were re-united and purchased a house in the Chiltern Hills near to Chequers. His son won a scholarship to Haileybury & Imperial Services College which saved his parents from paying a lot of fees to Harrow School.

Shortly after his return from Beirut, his former secretary left, to join her Iranian lover in Damascus. No further 'leaks' of information were evidenced.

Elphinstone and Lloyd continued to co-operate successfully on security matters. He received an OBE in the New Year's honours list. Lloyd received his gratitude.

Charles Caruthers - retired from the Foreign Office after more than forty years of valuable service. He received a comfortable pension and an MBE His former supervisor, who had nothing to do with the sometimes dangerous intelligence field work, was appointed as head of the department and knighted. Charles and his long-standing civil partner bought a cottage in Dorset and opened an antiques shop.

Helen Tiarks returned to London and her law practice. She continued to work pro bono for the International Red Cross and to advise GCHQ on translations from messages in Hazaragi and Farsi intercepted there. Her close friend Mrs Mary Tulloch asked her if she planned to marry. Helen answered, "I'm waiting for Mr Right."

She is still waiting.

LL 'Cocky' Lloyd - enjoyed a well-rewarded career at Lloyd's of London which he coupled with communications service for Elphinstone. His visited his former girlfriend Gladys whenever he returned to see his parents in Port Talbot. Like Helen Tiarks, Gladys is still waiting for 'Mister Right' if he returns to live in West Glamorgan again.

Lloyd's apartment in Chiswick is frequently visited by a very good-looking girl with almost indiscernible scarring on her face and hands. She also accompanies him on trips to Cheltenham and nearby Cleeve Hill. They sometimes travel abroad for vacations in Eastern Mediterranean islands.

Aysil Husseini - accepted employment with a travel agency in Hamburg, where she worked with a Kurdish man who answered to the name of 'Egid.' She and Egid advised their contact officers in London and Cheltenham of suspicious immigrants posing as refugees. Several suspected security breaches were recorded as being thwarted, partly due to information from Hamburg.

After two years in Hamburg she suddenly vanished from Germany. Nothing was seen or heard from or about her and it was rumoured that she had fled to Syria via Turkey.

Egid travelled to Anatolia and crossed the border into Kurdish Iraq. Two months later Egid reported to a communications officer and resumed service in Hamburg.

After another ten months in Hamburg Egid also disappeared.